BROKEN WINGS
A TRAIL OF CRUMBS

BROKEN WINGS
BOOK 1

BARRY N RAINSFORD

Copyright © 2025 by Barry N Rainsford

All rights reserved.

No part of this book may be reproduced in any form or by any electronic or mechanical means, including information storage and retrieval systems, without written permission from the author, except for the use of brief quotations in a book review.

Any connection of characters in this work of fiction to those living or dead is merely the result of superbly incisive and evocative writing.

❀ Formatted with Vellum

To my family - Jo, Nick, Phil, Al, Lawrence, and Will

To all those buying books and writing reviews with special thanks to those who have done so for my own! Also, Huw and all at the Elephant Rooms Writing Group who inspired the emergence of this series and whose fortnightly sessions keep me honest to myself and my voice. Also, to those at Reeth and Writing in Reeth who keep compiling ideas for locations for my books - especially the best places to hide bodies.

PROLOGUE
FLOWER MEADOW, MUKER

He'd lain there some time, the sodden ground turning blue jeans black, hoodie soaked through by the pounding rain. Lying there he's watched the flares of lightning sear the ink black sky, flashes of light illuminating the hunched outline of the old farm building; rolls of thunder like the stamping of Jurassic feet.

'*Gotcha, you bugger!*' he mutters as he rises from his vigil, the stirring of the shadows betraying the movement of his prey; Ayton rising close to the wall of the abandoned building to slip through the gap where a door once stood.

The storm had taken them by surprise, drenched from the first cloudburst, the three boys had quickly abandoned thoughts of a dash for home. Already wet, might as well wait it out with a game of hide and seek, Dales style - a good thumping handed out to the loser by the victors! Him and Ollie tracking Ayton.

Counting to a hundred, they'd split up - Ollie racing round the flower meadows and paddocks whilst Harry made for the derelict bothies, the old stone sanctuaries where shepherds sheltered from winter squalls. *Cow 'ouses,* his grannie calls them, now little more than ruins, haven for the odd wandering sheep, quad bikes replacing the shepherd's trudge from farmhouse to grazing.

He moves to the doorway; senses primed for the sound of Ayton's breathing or his boots slapping against the stone floor.

Inside, it's gloomier than he'd thought, the storm clouds shading the interior from the last of the fading light, but he knows the layout, they all do, they've been here before, him remembering the ghost stories they've sat and told each other. *Old Jed Arkwright; Long Tom; Kira Swanley - The Wensley Lizzie Borden.* He shivers, focuses on the lime-washed passage he knows leads off to one side, the doorways off it.

Hearing a footfall, he turns, relaxing as Ollie enters, his tall teenage frame silhouetted against what remains of the bruised outside light. Ollie nods he's seen Ayton enter. If they play this right they'll trap him in a pincer movement, give him a few jabs before sitting and waiting out the storm, the three of them eating the last of the damp chocolate stashed in the pocket of Harry's hoodie.

He points two fingers of one hand at his eyes and then towards the darkness, the way he's seen in films. They move off, each walking one side of the narrow passage, glancing into each room they pass, hearts racing.

In the last room, the largest space of the ground floor, they're aware of a sound like sobbing. Harry being the eldest steps forward, Ollie a pace or two behind. In the centre of the space Ayton stands staring at the far wall. He knows they're there but remains steadfast despite the promise of their punches. It's then that Harry realises Ayton is whimpering, a sound like his auntie Joan made at his mother's funeral. A cross between a sob and a groan. The sense of a pain so deep it can't find its way out.

They stand either side of him, look where he looks.

The last finger of light touches the wall, highlighting what appears to be a twisted line of a rope fixed there. It's plaited the way his sister does her hair, realising it reminds him of Moira because moving closer, touching it, he sees that it is hair, one end balled and twisted roughly around a hook. It's blonde and he's certain it's human. 'Cool,' he whispers.

1

It had rained for hours. A storm of biblical proportion says the constable holding up the Police tape. Omens, DS Lex Iverson thinks, ideas of *Scream* movies quickly added to his thinking whilst he shuffle-crouches his way under the tape, especially when his eyes catch the constable's silhouette, arm outstretched towards thundering heavens like an Old Testament Prophet.

Once clear, Iverson stands upright, nods his thanks and makes his way towards the shadowed outline of the barn, head down, chin pressed into chest. Only twenty paces from the car, he feels the icy water pooling in his shoes, something not helped by his right foot's successive immersion in two deep potholes. 'Jesus!' he exclaims to the retreating back of DI Zara Fisher on his second dunking. Fisher presses ahead, impervious to the weather or the grumblings of her Sergeant.

Inside, he shakes off the rain and dons the Tyvek overshoes, Fisher already having disappeared deeper into the building. He tugs on elasticated bootees, before cold hands fumble for the button of a flashlight. Taking a calming breath, he moves off, the shaft of torchlight piercing the darkness of the passage.

Even here rain has found its way in, a stone floor tormented by puddles as if oozing a tar-black bile. On either side doors droop open, slouched at angles that recall holiday club ushers offering up the gaudy attractions to be found inside. Even in torchlight, they appear hollowed out, joyless and unending.

Shivering, he fixes his attention to the end of the corridor, a doorway where two men in North Yorks Env Hlth stencilled jackets struggle with a partly erected tripod, an arc lamp at their feet. Ignoring a plea of "Gi' us a hand, mate" he steps past into the chamber.

Inside, illuminated by the reflected light of her phone's torch app, he sees Fisher staring at what appears to be a length of pale rope pinned to the wall.

'Is it what they thought?' he asks.

Without turning, she nods. 'Human hair,' she states, torch beam scouring the area.

'I don't understand…' he says.

'What's to understand?' she responds, returning the beam to the rope. 'Call it in,' she decides. 'You know the drill: *"what appears to be human hair plaited into rope found at site"*. We need the CSI lot to get off their fat arses to see if we have a crime scene or it's some fuck-wit's idea of a bit of fun, some idiot going all Halloween.'

He looks at her shadowed face. 'Then what, ma'am?'

She sniffs. 'Then?' She waves a hand, jiggling the beam of light. 'Unless you hadn't noticed, DS Iverson, it's pissing down of rain, and we're stood in a cold wreck of a barn waiting on those numpties from Environmental Health to set up some lighting so we can get more of an idea of just what we're looking at. There's been no report of missing persons, no report of blonde-haired waifs or strays being seen in the area – not even bald ones.' Her torch slips over the rope. 'Hair's too well looked after to be homeless. And as someone's seen fit to send Laurel and Hardy out there to check for "material hazardous to human health" rather than tasking CSI to investigate, then I have to assume we'll be standing in the cold a good while longer.'

Lex, certain the water in his shoe is becoming colder, looks around. After two days temporary assignment - him drawing the short straw in the CID lottery this week - he's been hoping for something a little more "*Hawaii Five-O* than *Our Yorkshire Farm*. 'Shouldn't we start to investigate?' he asks, the hope of prodding a reaction.

She turns her head. 'We have a kid and some mates sheltering from the rain reporting seeing a rope of what they think is human hair pinned to a wall. We have a constable – the big fella out there on the tape – coming out here and confirming it. We have the Environmental Health folk with a lamp and ladder who've been sent to remove anything deemed hazardous, or of any fly tipping posing a threat to the environment. And we have us, you and me DS Iverson, assessing whether what we have indicates a threat to life or if a crime's been committed at all. So, once you've kindly called it in, we'll have us awaiting instructions and you getting ready for a shit-ton of paperwork that'll go hand-in-hand with all this, whichever way it goes.'

Lex shines the beam of his torch on the rope. He stands, transfixed. 'I don't get it, Ma'am. Why not do something now? A search or something.'

'We are doing something. We're following procedure.'

Lex thinks he can feel his brow furrowing, deciding it's hard to tell with flesh that's been numbed Botox hard by the storm. But he does recognise a rising feeling of frustration, Fisher's response falling some way short of expectation, the sense of a juicy case being held at bay, the dangled possibility of something that might get his stuttering career off and running. Turning, he finds her expression remains shadowed, little more than an outline. 'But shouldn't we at least take a look around the rest of the building?' he suggests. 'The woods. The paddocks. Try to find her... the woman whose hair it is?'

She grunts. 'Blundering round in the dark and the rain? Messing up what might be a crime scene? And looking for what? Her? What's left of her?' She turns, holds up a hand to still his slow-moving response. 'And I know what you're thinking, DS Iverson. What is it this week? *Captain Birdseye? Elsa?*'

He says nothing, lips tightening, hoping his reaction is masked by the darkness.

She snorts. 'I know the names. You do this job long enough and you'll find it shaves even your tender edges, Iverson.' She turns her flashlight onto his face, a cruel action making him look away, hand held up against the sudden dazzle. 'Best save stuff like that for the doorstep knock, Sergeant. You know, the parents and loved ones. Them and the press conference. They expect stuff like that, pretty much a requirement. Concerned senior officer, best uniform...brass nicely polished, forest of microphones awaiting the soft words. The promise of early results. "No stone unturned" in the search for "our Mandy" or "lovely little Keith".' She moves the beam, returning her attention to the wall and its unnatural party streamer. 'It's the soundbite of empty promises. A last hurrah of hope.'

Iverson blinks. DI Zara Fisher. *Captain Birdseye.* He'd thought it a riff on her name, *Fisher.* Now he's thinking it's because anyone who's ever worked with her has at some point discovered the block of ice where her heart's supposed to be. *The Snow Queen. Elsa. Frozen.* And him, stuck as her temporary DS until her new Sergeant arrives, the bloke transferring from Birmingham.

Her looks don't help with the names – the high cheekbones, prominent and angular that add a chiseled haughtiness. The ice-cold blue of eyes that pierce and skewer rather than look. Her skin pale, almost snow white, something the lack of make-up on cheeks and lips heightens. The whole sitting under a shock of silver-white hair, bobbed and cut short. Somehow alien. Other.

When they'd met on her return to duty a few weeks ago, he'd found the phrase 'elfin' crossing his mind, like *Lord of the Rings.* Now, close-up, watching her going about her work, eyes screwing tighter, fine lines of concentration appearing around the edges as she focuses on the braid of hair, he's redefining that image. Too proud to wear glasses. Like his mom, probably ten years older than Fisher, but still making the effort - make-up, some lippy. Fisher seemingly takes little interest in any of it. Not that he thinks of her in that way. She's no-one's idea of a MILF... though she does have a way of looking at him that makes it appear as if she's seeing deep inside. Like an X-ray. It's intense. Unnerving. A hint of...something he can't quite fix a name to.

'Oh Christ!' Fisher exclaims.

'What is it, Ma'am?' he asks, pulling back from whatever strange thoughts he's spiralling towards, accompanied by the worrying sense she's been eavesdropping in on them.

'Give me your flashlight!' she snaps, hand outstretched, fingers clicking.

'What?' he asks, noticing she's moved closer to the rope.

'Your flashlight, Iverson. Give me your bloody torch. Now!'

Lex hands it over.

She levels it on the rope, at the same time grabbing his hand and pushing the torch back to him and folding his hand around it. 'Hold it steady,' she orders, her hand - soft and cold - clasped around his own. He takes a moment, hand wobbling before he holds it focused on the braided rope. Meanwhile, she's let go and leant closer to the wall, opening the camera app on her phone. She takes a moment, fiddling with the settings, pinching fingers together to zoom in on the braids. 'Keep it steady,' she commands before tapping the screen. She steps back, stands closer to him, gesturing he's to lean forward, her fingers sliding apart on the screen to narrow in on the plait of hair. 'Look. Do you see?'

'See what, Ma'am?'

'The hair. The texture. The colour. How it changes in shade from one plait to the other.'

He leans closer. 'Is it the light?'

'No. And it's not dyed or highlighted.'

'So?' He studies the hair, thinking maybe she's more interested in women's vanity than he thought.

She straightens her head, raising her eyes from the screen. 'It's the hair of more than one woman.'

'Really?' Lex feels his career nerve tingle.

'Really,' she repeats, scanning the image.

'How can you tell? I mean...don't they, I mean you...maybe extensions? Wigs?'

A bright light flares, filling the room like a lightbulb idea as the Environmental Health workers get their generator running. The erected lamps flood the space with pure white light. The taller of the two points at the rope. 'Fuck me!' he exclaims over the putter of the motor to his shorter colleague who stands propping up a bright yellow step ladder.

The light reveals the full height of the room, that the braid disappears through the broken rafters of the ceiling, of what they now see to be a two-storey void criss-crossed by blackened beams. 'Fucking Rapunzel!' he says, nudging the worker holding the ladder. 'Like them fairy stories,' he clarifies in response to the puzzled look on the man's face. 'Most likely nailed onto something,' he judges after a moment of more practical consideration. He wipes the rain from his hair, scratches his head, frowning. 'One thing's certain,' he concludes, pointing to the ladder, 'Won't get that up there. Never going to reach.'

He turns to Iverson, clearly judging an assessment of the problem to be a man thing. 'Strikes me we give it a yank. A bit of a tug. You know, bit of brute force,' he says, gesturing the motion with an arm and gripped fist. 'See if we can rip it down from whatever it's attached to. Either that or you're going to have to wait here whilst we go back to the depot and get a bigger ladder. With this storm, that could take a while.'

Lex turns to Fisher. 'What do you think, Ma'am?'

Fisher steps back from the wall where she's been staring up through the gap. She hands her phone to Lex. 'Call it in,' she instructs. 'It's not fly-tipping. Tell them it's a crime scene.' She turns to the two workmen. 'You two, out,' she orders. The two stand uncertain, the senior workman looking to Lex. 'Fuck off out!' she bawls.

Lex, puzzled, looks at the screen of Fisher's phone. Only then does he see the image she's captured: the uppermost length of the rope hanging over a roof beam of the space above. The rope ending in a noose, the woman's body, shaven headed, that dangles from it.

2

'Fucking shit show! Absolute fucking nightmare!' Gina Hargreaves moans, face contorting into a scowl. It is chalk to the cheese of the rictus smile used in her campaign literature, those flyers pinned to almost every lamppost and village noticeboard across the county. Standing opposite, Fisher holds fast whilst the North Yorkshire Police, Fire, and Crime Commissioner mumbles and blasphemes, the sound of a wheezy turbine shutting down. After a moment, the Commissioner looks up from angry contemplation of the mud in which her highly polished heels have become interred. 'Why now?' she asks of the room.

The simplicity of the question belies the swamp of problems that lurk beneath its surface. Fisher stands in silence, not even a shrug of the shoulders or sympathetic shake of the head. In contrast, Harvey Lawrence, standing next to the Commissioner, jerks like a marionette. 'I know, I know,' he repeats in a voice like polished glass. 'Don't worry. It's fine, Gina. It'll be okay. We downplay it. Low key.'

Gina Hargreaves fixes him with a Death Star glare. 'Low key? Are you fucking mental, Harvey? There's a woman's body strung from the rafters. She's not only dead, but her head's been shaved. On top of that, her hair's been made into a bloody lasso or something that's been used to hang her. How the fuck do we keep it low key?'

The Commissioner's PR guru shakes his head. 'I meant...I mean...' He fixes a smile in place, playing his templated Hugh Grant get out of jail free card, the one that comes with his foppish mop of hair, the thin lines of a lift evidence of work done on chin and cheekbones.

Hargreaves sighs. 'Look, if you sodding PR folk are stuck for words, then how the hell am I supposed to know how to play it? Isn't this what I pay you for?' she demands.

'Gina, I know you're upset,' he soothes.

'Am I Harvey? Am I upset?' she looks at her mired heels 'Or isn't it just possible that I'm pissed off traipsing out here in the middle of the night to find my election chances dangling from a rafter a couple of feet from where my highly lauded, highly paid PR guru stands telling me to "downplay" it.'

Fisher looks to the ground, wondering what vengeful fate decreed that Iverson's call to headquarters for CSI support should have coincided with one of Hargreaves' famed unannounced lightning visits. Her well-known insistence on once a month attending actual call-outs. Real policing ride-alongs.

It is, of course, election year, manifestos to make flesh, even if it's four years too late for her to be making a mad trolley dash for most of her pledges. Her term has been bland, unmemorable. Watching the PFCC stare horrified as Tyvek suited technicians shoot garishly glossy photographic crime scene images, Fisher surmises the Commissioner would have been only too willing for that state to have continued a little longer. At least the few weeks that remain until polling day.

She's pulled from her thoughts by the Commissioner turning to face her. 'So, what *do* we know, Inspector?' Hargreaves asks, lips pale and thin despite the lavishly applied blood red lipstick.

'Little or nothing,' Fisher states.

'Great!' The Commissioner tosses her head in judgement of

Fisher's less than hopeful summation. 'I gather from your answer you didn't have the chance to attend one of my courses on community relations, Inspector. Maybe the one on Public Facing Communication Skills?'

'No, Ma'am. Never had the pleasure. I'm sure it would have been as helpful and riveting as it sounds,' Fisher replies.

Hargreaves pauses, appraising Fisher's response. Deciding to let it pass, she shifts tack. 'Let's go with the *little* element of your response rather than the *nothing*, shall we…erhm…?'

'Fisher. DI Fisher, Ma'am. Northallerton.'

'Fisher,' Hargreaves repeats, an imperceptible nod setting Lawrence tapping it into his phone. Fisher waits for the moment of recall, the Commissioner's dawning of recognition, the sweary-scream of anguish - but nothing comes. She's surprised, shocked even, but once Lawrence has finished his note, Hargreaves simply continues her questioning. 'So, DI Fisher, just what *do* you have for us?' she asks.

Still non-plussed, Fisher decides to let it ride, instead flicking open her notebook. 'There was an emergency services call earlier this evening. Group of lads reported seeing a length of rope they thought to be human hair pinned to the wall over there.' She points at the far wall, Hargreaves and Lawrence's eyes following her arm even though the rope has been taken down and sealed long before their arrival. Fisher's hand and their gaze return to the notebook. 'Local station took the incident. A unit got here about thirty minutes after the initial call-out - a quiet night by all accounts, the weather and everything. The officer confirmed it wasn't a prank. Reported he'd found what appeared to be human hair fixed to the wall. He was told to follow procedure, which meant securing the site whilst CID were despatched along with Environmental Health. DS Iverson and I arrived soon after, along with the council workers. I think the Scouts might have once used it, or maybe outward bound or something. Seems they were sent to check for Environmental Health and Safety issues – the council workers, not the scouts. They'd been told to hygienically dispose of anything needing to be removed. Once we'd checked things out, they were supposed to seal the building. That's when we found the body and called it in.'

'What about the body? It is a suicide?'

'We're waiting on pathology for cause of death. Looks like suicide...though there are oddities,' Fisher offers.

'Oddities?' Hargreaves asks, fixing what could be taken for concern on her face.

'The choice of location. The fact the body's up there and there's no ladder. I mean, it's a bit of a scramble. You'd expect marks on her body and clothing. Needs a closer inspection than we can get from down here. The doc will sort that out once he arrives. Oh, and of course, there's the rope of human hair. Not your average suicide.'

'So, what do you think happened?' the Commissioner asks, hopes of a clear response fading.

Fisher blows out a noisy breath of contemplation. 'Female. No ID. No bag or anything. Whoever she is…Well, it's a long way out here. Not an easy place to get to. Could be homeless, but there's no evidence for that – no sleeping bag or blanket. Looks young, but not teenage young. Not like a runaway. Twenties, thirties. Like I said, hard to tell from down here. And then there's the whole shaven headed-ness.'

'Can't we do something about that?' Lawrence asks, pointing to the gap in the rafters. 'Get her down. Cover her, at least.' The humanity and compassion is immediately undermined by his seamless continuation that, 'All these mobile phones, it makes me nervous. Cameras. Leaks. The Commissioner being here. We have an election to think of.'

'Crime scene,' Fisher instructs. 'Nothing can be moved or touched until the doc's had chance to examine the body at the scene. Unexpected death. Standard practice.'

'Just our luck! Nothing bloody standard looking about any of this,' Lawrence opines. 'Supposed to have been a simple call-out according to Control. Couple of decent shots for social media and back home. Damned cold, too,' he adds, hands thrust deep in pockets, shoulders hunched up.

'Welcome to North Yorkshire,' Fisher mutters.

The silence pools around them. It's up to their knees before the Commissioner dives back in. 'Is this your first such suicide?' she enquires.

'I don't think anyone's had *such* a suicide, Ma'am,' Fisher responds. 'You know, body stuffed up there. Head shaved. The rope of human hair.' She allows a beat. 'That's of course assuming it is one. Suicide, I mean. Like I said, we can't really say for sure at present.'

'I suppose not,' Hargreaves says, pondering the possibilities.

'Even if she'd shaved herself and spun it into a rope, well, it takes a leap to see her stuffing herself up in those eaves,' Fisher observes, continuing her line of thinking. 'But then most suicides are by definition determined. Goes with the territory. Some want to leave a message, to have their death mean something. You know, a comment on the world they leave behind.'

'Let's pray it is a suicide. Bad luck if it turns out to be murder,' Harvey states. 'Violent killer running around. A creepy one, at that. It doesn't play well with our law-and-order theme.' He shakes his head; clear whose bad luck he's thinking about. Fisher bets good money it isn't the shaven-headed corpse hanging a few feet from where he stands waist deep in professional angst.

Hargreaves nods, the deft movement of her head setting soft designer curls bouncing. 'Well, let's be a little more present, shall we? As...Fisher here says, its most likely a suicide. And, if that's the case, we should remember that none of us are in any position to judge this poor woman or her actions,' she states, a noticeable rhythm appearing in her speech. 'Her quiet desperation finding its voice here in this...crumbling facade. Alone. Isolated. Shaving her head, defiling her own body. *Nolite iuicare* as my old Latin teacher would have said. *Who are we to judge?*'

'No, Ma'am. Expect not,' Fisher responds, nose wrinkling at a distinctive whiff of bullshit.

'Just run through that again, Gina,' Lawrence asks, fingers rapidly tapping at the Notes app on his phone. 'I didn't quite get it all. It's a fabulous idea. "*The quiet desperation of young women...*" Your compassion, you wanting to do something to help them. No, *determined* to help them, to bring change. We can work with that. Lose the Latin, of course...doesn't play well with voters after Boris. But the rest...it's gold, Gina, pure gold.' He scuttles back and forth around her, considering angles, taking a series of rapid shots with his iPhone. He looks at the results, frowning before putting the device away. 'The lighting's not great, but we can sort it out post-production. You know, this may work out fine after all.'

Shutting her notebook, Fisher turns from the scene. She senses closure, a chance to slip away before the Commissioner, now with nothing better to occupy her mind, recalls their previous meeting. It's at this point that the Commissioner sighs, reeling Fisher back in. 'Hmm...Tell me...Fisher. Given your experience, have you a gut feeling?' she asks.

'Nothing beyond desperate for coffee and a burger.'

Lawrence looks up from assessing the photographs. 'I thought that's what you lot ran on,' he puts in. 'Instinct, I mean. Not burgers,' he clarifies, putting his phone away and blowing on his fingers. He rubs them in front of his face, pausing to appraise just how pale they are.

'I think that's too much TV,' Fisher responds. 'You'll find we're not all *Poirot* or *Murder She Wrote* types. We're also not all drunks or burnt out fuck-ups. Most. Not all.'

'Let me be a little more considered in my question,' the Commissioner decides. 'Have you *much experience* of murder, Inspector?' she asks, this time taking a good run up at hitting her point with precision.

'A dozen or so.'

'Bloody hell!' Lawrence looking from frozen fingers exclaims. 'A dozen?'

Fisher shrugs. 'Most are nothing. Routine. Wife stabbing an abusive partner, drunks going too far in a brawl - you know, chucking out time. Pissed. Heads cracked on kerbs. The odd kebab-queue stabbing. None of them need a Holmes, most not even a Watson. In most the perp's standing around waiting for us to arrive. Often the weapons are still in their hands or dropped close-by.' She thinks of Kira Swanley. Her own father.

'Still, a dozen,' Lawrence says with something approaching awe, and if not awe then most certainly reversing his response into a parking space adjacent to it.

'You must excuse Harvey. He's always seeing the headline. The spin. It's like a sort of highly developed instinct. What is it you're calling it this week, Harvey?'

'The narrative.'

'Ah, yes. The narrative. The story. Five minutes and Harvey can have you the hero of the front page, can't you Harvey?'

'Attractive female officer? Dozen murders solved? Inspector, I could make you Joan of fucking Arc!'

3

Iverson sits back, exhaling loudly. Still soaked through from dashes through the storm, he contemplates the paperwork, the form-filling, the writing up of reports in the mind-numbing detail now mandatory for even the simplest of exchanges with Joe Public. The ever-present concern it turns out to be the one where everything goes tits up.

None of it is helped by a move to temporary accommodation whilst the decorators are in. ACC Musgrove's band of painting gnomes. Not that he's seen much of them. No-one has. They'd arrived one morning, covered everything with tarpaulins and then...nothing. They might as well be ghosts, mythical. Yeah, mythical is better, less of a worry sitting here in the early hours when he's pretty much alone in the building writing a report about ropes of human hair and a hanging shaven-headed woman.

He tries to push his mind to the mundane, the irritation that whatever else is happening with refurbishment, he's been stuck in this converted cupboard with Fisher and the rest for over a month. Files on every surface, keyboards buried. He'll be glad when they've finished and CID can get back to the old office.

He decides to look for some change for the snack machine, a

hot drink to thaw a chill that's both physical and a little bit mental too. He undertakes a fingertip search of the pushed together desks, in the process finding a sheaf of case files he now remembers are due at the Crown Prosecutors later in the week. He makes a mental note to slap a Post-It on them before they sink back into the swamp of paper strewn across the makeshift surface.

The Snow Queen is already pissed at the delay in sealing her crime scene, sending him back here to start the form-filling whilst she stays to vent her irritation in barking at the CSI team. It's clear there's been no 'cure', the idea rapidly taking hold that her return from a very public breakdown has only been welcomed by the hierarchy because it offers the chance to be rid of her for good. The 'give them enough rope' theory he'd overheard DCS Crosby muttering at news of her reappearance. The vitriol and unpleasantness that pre-dated her sick leave remains.

To some extent he knows why she's angry - her mundane assignments and late night shifts are slices of the vendetta DCS Crosby's been serving up to her since the last tribunal – but the consensus remains: good a detective as she once was, she's unfeeling, a woman whose icy blasts of anger and irritation pass for emotions.

He knows the story, they all do. Zara Fisher, daughter of a legendary DCS murdered Millennium Eve, his head blown off by a shotgun courtesy of the criminal gang who'd discovered where he lived, his body found in the converted stable office by a then teenage Fisher. With so many criminals carrying so many grudges there'd been an overload of suspects, but the perpetrators have never been found. Years later, Fisher joined the force, the idea taking hold that driven by the desire to find her father's killers she'd made an astonishingly rapid rise through the ranks. Every bit the maverick her father had been, medals and citations littered her path to DI and it appeared only a matter of time before she too made DCS. But then Kira

Swanley happened. The Swanley murders remain the most brutal and high-profile the region has ever seen. It had been Fisher who'd arrested the teenage Kira, Fisher who'd interviewed the *"Wensley Lizzie Borden"* as the press dubbed her. Her conviction had been routine, the evidence overwhelming despite the fact that Kira remained mute throughout, some sort of text-book psychological trauma according to the psychiatrists who'd assessed her suitability to stand trial. It had been over a year ago, a year in which Fisher had spiralled out of control. Aggressive, irritable, scathing and alienating of colleagues, she'd been the subject of way too many disciplinary boards and Professional Standards Panels for something not to be done. The assessment of stress prompting an emotional breakdown had meant six months of sick leave and therapy before they'd passed her fit to return to duty. Not that anything seems to have changed, Crosby already bringing charges of insubordination. The prevailing opinion is that she remains on active duty only through her father's ex-colleague's interventions on her behalf. The mood music now one that any remaining champions of her cause are finding it harder to excuse her behaviour.

Such things are thankfully not his problem. Not with the newbie DS arriving from Brum to be offered up as Fisher's latest Bobo doll, bashed first one way then the other. He's seen the man's file, came across it lying on The Ice Queen's desk a few days ago. And by that, he'd found it in the top drawer of her desk whilst looking for change for the snack machine.

It had made an interesting read during the time it took to wolf down a Mars bar and a packet of Cheese and Onion crisps. Not that long, really. Everything so much smaller now - bags of crisps more air than potato, Mars bars shrinking even faster. But it had been long enough to get the gist. DS Pan Demetriou is an officer transferring under a shadow.

Scribbling a Post-it and sticking it to the CP folders, he shifts the files littering the desk, certain he'd seen a pound coin lurking at the bottom of a pot of paperclips. He picks the container up, fingers broddling through the contents.

However long this Demetriou lasts before either the Ice Queen drives him to quit or take a swing at her – seemingly the option he chose with his last DI back in Brum - the break will be welcome. Iverson has been unlucky these past few days, drawing the short straw, the worry it might be him again next time.

He drags a finger up the side of the pot, plucking out the coin. Grinning, he raises it in front of his eyes, Arthur with a snack machine Excalibur.

It's surely a sign. An omen.

4

Paul Webb is on the up. Top of his game.

It hasn't always been this way. Twenty-five years ago the building supply business he'd inherited had been a mess, his dad's early heart attack leaving a rundown yard and a business owing money left right and centre.

Pauline had wanted to let go. "*Sell it*" had been his big sister's vote. "*The site, the building. Everything. It'll cover the debts. We might even get a bit of cash out of it, too. Kevin knows folk. Builders. He says they're looking for brown sites or something for houses. We can make a killing.*" Her heart was set on a holiday home in Spain, thoughts drifting to late summer sun, Magaluf, Autumn of her life consorts with tight-waisted barmen whilst a dutiful Kevin sweats life away in a planning office in Leeds. But Paul held firm. "*It's what dad would have wanted. Us to make a go of it.*"

She'd been incandescent, would have none of it, this "*madness, just like dad.*" He'd bought her out, she and Kevin settling for a two-week time share in Benidorm - her only complaint they don't do Midget Gems in Spain. He'd found the money through an off the books loan, shady Bulgarian financiers lending at eye-watering rates, much to his wife's anger.

His dad's dream of *Webb and Son* had cost him - his sister, his marriage to Sharon, his home. But it had worked, the gamble paying off. Ten years of fifteen-hour days, two years sleeping on a camp bed in the office - no contract too big, none too small. A chain of builders' yards across the county and expansion into construction. Thanks to the Bulgarians his family crest - *Webb & Son: Northallerton, Leeds, Barnsley* - sits in italic script on the cab of each of the fifty lorries in its fleet. Business is buoyant, contracts flowing. He has a mansion outside Harrogate and a new wife, Kendra - all *Yorkshire Life* and black-tie functions, fitting like the last piece in a jigsaw.

And now he has government, *Special Advisor to the Prime Minister*. A title fresh and shiny, untainted by spin or failure: *Minister of the North*, like some bureaucratic themed *Game of Thrones* spin-off. He's the construction industry James Bond, Licensed to Drill. A multi-billion-pound budget: levelling up the North. Road. Rail. Broadband. Contracts to give and contracts to deny. Contracts for business and contracts for construction.

It helps that he's one of the PM's constituents. Helps that it was his financial backing that secured the PM a safe North Yorkshire seat. Helps that he'd introduced the PM to his future wife and her billionaire family.

He's thinking this whilst standing at the foot of a flight of white concrete steps built by his own company, hand poised on the polished chrome safety rail they'd supplied and installed. All around him is a cheering crowd, state of the art PA speakers crackling into life across the arena.

'Laaaadies and gentlemen,' the announcer hails like a boxing ring Emcee, all long vowels and weird emphasis on syllables. 'Paul Webb will now declare Harrogate Water Park open by riding the Serpent's Tail.' The cheers of the crowd gathered around the Olympic sized pool rise at the announcement. 'The Serpent's Tail is the longest covered water flume in Europe.' More cheers. 'And it's North Yorkshire's Webb Construction who have built this landmark leisure park that will soon become our county's premier tourist attraction. Ladies and gentlemen, Paaaauuul Webb!' The applause hits crescendo.

Paul disrobes. A month with Kendra's personal trainer has done its work, he stands Instagram-ready, body buffed to perfection. As agreed, he poses for the cameras before beginning his ascent to the topmost platform.

Halfway there he catches sight of the PM at the side of the pool. Ever the politician, the local MP has his *man-of-the-people* smile fixed in place, the one he uses when cos-playing at serving in restaurants or pulling pints in locals he's never been inside before. It's as if this is somehow his achievement, his event, his money. Paul smiles. He'll allow him the moment, just as long as he remembers who it is got him here.

He watches him make his way to the bank of cushioned seats reserved for dignitaries. The plan had been for the PM to make this first ride, a chance for the party to lift the show-ground curse of Boris stuck on a zip wire, the then buffoonish PM dangling from the line like a baggy pair of pants in the wind. The idea had been abandoned only late the previous day, the news coming in a last-minute call. It seems that in the midst of the latest breaking government crisis, the PM's Chief Advisor had awoken from a fever dream. One where headlines of *'Going Down!'* or *'Drowning Not Waving!'* featured on the front page of every Sunday paper. Headlines accompanied by pictures of the PM shooting out of the flume's spout, his screaming face captured in all its glory. That the PM favoured budgie smugglers had already been the subject of heated debate. His advisor's dream was merely the final nail in the decision he be stood down from all water-based ribbon cutting duties.

It is Paul now taking the final step, raising arms aloft to bathe in the cheers of the crowd as he steps onto the platform. It's his dream. His risk. His money. His company that built it.

The platform is large, the base covered by a painting of a mythic Sea Serpent's tail, a photo-realistic 3-D image commissioned to give riders the illusion of the beast disappearing down the flume. It is the start of a 300 metres-journey inside a sky-blue tube dubbed *The Serpent's Tail*, a journey ending with the rider's emergence from a highly sculpted dragon mouth into the deep blue of the pool.

'Don't forget,' the announcer tells the crowd as they wait for Paul to pick up the ceremonial scissors. 'Everyone taking the ride has the chance to purchase a souvenir photograph of themselves emerging from the Serpent's mouth.' There's money to be made on everything in the Park, Disney has taught that lesson. Flume photos were just the start. Once the Park was fully open there would be food concessions, drinks, and merchandise – all of it *Serpent's Tail* branded.

Paul approaches the ribbon, cutting it with a simple snip, the strands floating to the side. Handing off the scissors, he steps into the mouth of the tube.

'Top of the world, Ma!' he shouts, hand punching the sky. It is a line from his dad's favourite film, Jimmy Cagney. *White Heat*. A film they'd always watched together. They are the last words he speaks as, with a final wave, his honed and toned frame disappears down the flume.

No-one knows what his next words would have been.

There was – so it was later rumoured – a speech. It was said they'd found a draft on a computer. Some said it was on his phone, left at the poolside ready for him to read after climbing triumphantly out of the water. Some said it was a speech praising the foresight of his close friend the PM, *"a leader without whom the North would continue to be ignored."* So they said.

It's a sentiment those who claimed to know him deemed too grandiose for a man with the common touch. For those who truly knew him, it rang false for a man obsessed with burnishing his own image rather than that of others. Especially so when the report was finally discovered as originating from Downing Street rather than Paul's wife or family.

In truth, no-one knows what words are in Paul's head when

it appears in the pool. Especially with it arriving some three seconds or so after his decapitated body.

Pandemonium is a word rarely used anymore, archaic, un-Instagram friendly, and way too tough to spell. Yet it's the word Chief Constable James Hyland finds himself groping towards as he surveys the scene at the foot of *the Serpent's Tail* ride.

The untimely demise of one of the county's most prominent sons happened almost five minutes ago. The first alert was of the PM's security staff hauling the PM out of the temporary bleachers. His journey – part dragged, part carried – down the pool-side was the least seemly of exits, propelled by his security team's concern that Webb's decapitation was the prelude to a full-blown terrorist attack.

It had taken less than two minutes for the PM to be bundled from comfy seat to the rear of a Range Rover tearing off through the car park, a period at the end of which Hyland's own officers began noticing something was probably amiss. The Olympic pool turning a nasty shade of crimson as Paul's body bobbed in it had been among the first clues they'd had. That and the soon after emergence of Webb's head.

Hyland is aghast. It has taken a moment for him to fully comprehend what he's seeing. A fact that won't prevent him from later launching a scathing attack on the officers on duty, even though their prime concern at the moment of the decapitation had been divided between drunks making good use of the beer tent and those political protestors that make up so much of the crowd wherever the PM appeared. Not to mention policing the queues at the concession stands.

It's whilst standing in line at a *Mr Smoothee* ice-cream van that ACC Neil Musgrove is first alerted to events. About to ask for the insertion of a second flake – the celebrated *Two Fingered*

Cone – the swell of movement of the crowd towards the pool almost knocks the waffle cone from his hand.

Caught between licking the ice cream dribbling down the sides and his intrigue at the crowd's sudden movement, Musgrove's initial view of events is an unusual one - head askew, ear almost touching a shoulder, the cone held high to form the most efficient licking angle - it's a speedy geometric calculation, Alan Turing-like in its swiftness, intricacy, and grace. A cone-tongue-elbow triangle to make Pythagoras proud.

Contents for the moment saved, he walks towards the gate that controls access to the Olympic-size pool and its giant flume. Getting closer, he is aware that for some reason a human blockage is forming. Unknown to him, it's the point where the piqued interest of those outside rushing to rubber-neck events inside the arena met the blind panic of those inside rushing to get away from the threat of further mayhem.

Whatever the cause, thoughts of football crowds race into his head. The lessons of Hillsborough reach deep into the psyche of any Yorkshire force. Tossing the cone aside, he begins running to the gate, eyes searching for uniforms, officers he might organise into some sort of chain to guide the crowd away from the crush of bodies threatening to overwhelm the flimsy fencing that funnels visitors along the pathways. He starts shouting instructions to those around him, his arms flailing in the air. He yells pleas for the crowd to stop pushing, to move away, all the time aware of the danger of someone falling that will have the mass of the crowd trampling over them. His progress is met with elbow jabs from those who think him a fellow queue jumper. The shouts of 'Oy!' and 'Watch it!' are only halted by the site of the shoulder epaulets and pips that Musgrove constantly taps as a means of easing his passage. The fact that in the end it is simply his sheer bulk that enables him to snowplough his way through the crowd is something he blocks from his thinking.

Arriving at the locus of the action - the swirling whirlpool of humanity where what had been incomers suddenly got the picture and turned to out-goers - he sets about organising the half a dozen officers he's found. A quick survey soon has them directing punters down a nearby slope, the crowd exiting the melee between the side of a hoop-la concession and the rapidly collapsing Yorkshire Air Ambulance tent.

After a few minutes the swell of bodies subsides, and he is able to appoint the sergeant he's found amongst the uniformed officers to take control whilst he himself goes in search of exactly what is going on. Anticipating some obvious possibility like the collapse of the sites' temporary seating gallery or some other structural disaster, he stands by the gateway scratching his head. The stands are empty. There is nothing to be seen other than a group of civilians gathered at the far end of the pool. A gathering interspersed with a handful of uniformed officers and two St. John's ambulance men carrying a stretcher.

Crossing to them, the event holding their attention is soon apparent. The water at the deep end of the pool is a dusky pink moving to deeper crimson at the centre of the flume's exit. Bobbling in the water is a human head. A kneeling St John's aide is playing what to all intent and purposes appears to be a macabre game of apple bobbing, attempting to use the pole from one of the stretchers to bring the head closer to the edge of the pool where he hopes his colleague can use the folded material of the stretcher to scoop it out. This attempt to instil some human decency into the scene by recovering the head succeeds only in making matters worse, the head merely dipping under at each attempt to ensnare it. Twice it bobs up between the legs of Webb's body, the final time becoming lodged immovably in its crotch.

Musgrove pushes to the centre of the assembly, ordering each officer he passes to move the remaining bystanders to the side. 'Unless you're direct family or material witnesses, I must ask you to leave the arena,' the ACC instructs. At the centre, stands a woman he instantly recognises as the much photographed and Instagrammed Kendra Webb, hands clutched to her mouth in the universal gesture of distress. He closes the distance, pushing aside groupings of men and women who stand staring at the sight.

'Mrs. Webb,' he begins, arriving beside the distressed Kendra. 'I think its best if you come with me. Perhaps we can find somewhere away from all this.'

She stands still. 'That's my husband,' she says, repeating the phrase over and over. At each cycle of the words, her voice becomes louder, soon reaching a crescendo approaching a primal scream. 'That's my husband!'

Seeking support, Musgrove performs a one-eighty-degree turn. 'Somebody do something!' he bellows, one arm locked around the distraught Kendra. The response is a herd shuffling of feet, heads looking to the floor with the odd furtive look back to the pool. No helping hands make themselves known despite the fact he's certain there must be some sort of retinue at these things. Family, PR people, friends, hangers-on, free-loaders and the like.

'For Christ's sake,' he mutters, aware of the tell-tale signs of a familiar red mist descending. It is then that the latent detective part of him makes itself known. The bit thinking, *this is a crime scene, it needs to be protected. That head mustn't be interfered with. Nothing should be moved before the pathologist gets here.* There is also the bit of him fascinated at watching a dead man's head bobbling up and down trapped in its own crotch, the whole edifice buffeted by the artificial waves that are a feature of the pool. There's also the bit of him aware of compassion, aware the man's wife stands at the side of the pool. Something had to be done. But what that something might be is lost in a red mist.

'You're just making it worse!' he barks to the St. John's men reduced to splashing their poles into the water, the idea they might propel the head to the side on the waves they're making. 'It'll be covered in bruises by the time you've finished. Stop messing around and get it out!' It had sounded more of a compromise as he'd formed the thought – one part police crime scene procedure: one part humanity. The words that emerge betray that intention, sound critical, passive aggressive. Okay, just aggressive.

The nearest of the St. John's men turns in his direction. 'What are you expecting? I ain't diving in there. In that,' the man says pointing to the gloopy blood-red scum forming in the precincts of Webb's head and accompanying body.

Kendra Webb stares at him, mouth flopping open and closed. No-one moves.

Musgrove, dropping his hands, pulls his trousers up by the belt, an indication he's taking command. 'Move!' he bellows. 'If you're not family fuck off! If you are family…Maybe you should turn your heads away. Go and stand over there.' His hands wave around reminding him of his Tai-Ji, *Parting the Wild Horses Mane*. He turns to a cluster of bystanders he's now clearly identified as neither officials nor family. 'What on earth is wrong with you? What are you expecting? I mean, he's hardly liable to pick his head up and step out, is he?'

Kendra faints. Three or four of the crowd immediately rush to her, crouch beside her. 'Oh, now you decide to do something useful!' he calls out as they tend to Kendra. The St. John's men drop their poles, abandoning all attempts at retrieving the head. A fainting woman is something they are trained for, especially one as wondrous as Kendra Webb. They race over, eager to administer all that pent up medical knowledge. Mouth to mouth.

Their movement reveals a young woman standing poolside taking selfies, Webb's floating head in the background. 'Oy! You! You stop! Stop right now!' Musgrove calls, advancing towards her. 'You, you bloody ghoul! You bugger off before I arrest you!' he shouts, arms shooing her away.

'What for?' the young woman asks, continuing her shoot. 'I'm not doing anything illegal. I'm an Influencer. This is for my podcast. I'm a citizen journalist. You can't interfere with freedom of the press, you bloody fascist!'

'Press? What press? Where's your accreditation?' he asks, advancing.

She flicks the screen of her phone, the lens capturing Musgrove, a shot requiring her to zoom out a little to encompass his full glory. 'This is Shivaughn Wingard-Thompson reporting from Harrogate Water Park where this afternoon millionaire businessman Paul Webb has been brutally murdered! His severed head is floating in the pool next to me, his headless body drifting on the water. The police have no idea who's responsible or what to do. They are clearly baffled by this gruesome crime.'

'Stop that! You can't say that. This is a crime scene! My crime scene! Who's saying it's a murder? We're having to wait for the pathologist for all that! You can't go saying things like that. We don't know what's happened.'

'His head's been chopped off! What are you saying? Suicide?' she flicks the screen back to herself. 'Dear viewers, the authorities are spreading fake news in an attempt to hide the truth from your reporter.'

'This is a restricted area. I'm designating it a crime scene. You have to leave.'

'And just who are you?' she asks flicking the screen back to him.

'I'm ACC Musgrove!'

'Who?'

'Musgrove. Assistant Chief Constable Musgrove.'

'Never heard of you. Are you even a proper policeman?'

'Of course I am!'

'Then what's that down your front?'

Looking down Musgrove sees chocolate flake smeared down his shirt surrounded by a Rorschach blot of raspberry sauce.

'Is that blood?' she shrieks. 'Is that the victim's blood? Oh god, it is! Dear followers,' she says, phone camera flipped back towards her, a close up of her face. 'I've stumbled into a conspiracy. It's clear that the police themselves may very well be involved in the murder of Paul Webb! No doubt as servants of the illuminati. The Lizard People.' She looks at Musgrove, her voice breathy with the horror of it all. 'Was Paul about to expose you and your Lizard overlords for what you are? Is that why you're covered in his blood?'

'It's fucking ice cream!' he shouts. 'It's fucking raspberry sauce! And fucking flake! *The Two-Finger*,' he states holding two fingers aloft at just the moment she turns the phone to him.

He is clearly not ready for his close-up.

5

Coverdale. It reminds Iverson of some misty reference to a band or singer his dad likes - old school, all big hair and loud guitars. He shakes his head. It would come.

He turns onto the narrow road that leads through the village and then down the other side of the Dale towards Skipton and from there to Harrogate, wipers slapping in the downpour.

It feels odd, three years in CID and finally he's part of a major enquiry. It's a step forward - and if not a step up, then at the very least it's a step in the right direction. A small one, but definitely a step, him interviewing the victim's grieving widow, Kendra Webb.

He slows the car, juddering over the grid designed to keep hill sheep on the tops of the dale. Scanning the track for stray sheep, he accelerates, thinking that though his trip is of the ticking a box variety, confirming that all procedures have been completed, there's good career mileage to be had. He's the *"no stone left unturned"* the Chief Constable spoke about at the media briefing. The same no stone stick Crosby beat him with at their own closed-door briefing.

The first briefing a few hours after Webb's murder had seen the enquiry divided into sub-teams – the uniforms processing witness statements with CID interviewing site staff, everyone from zero-hour parking supervisors through to senior management responsible for the opening ceremony. By evening they'd compiled lists of anyone who knew anything at all about security and access points.

By then the Spooks of Special Branch and MI5 had arrived, dark-suited men alighting two-by-two from four-by-fours to assess the situation. Before midnight Badgerman had arrived from London and taken control, the Commissioner, Chief Constable, and Crosby now support acts to his headline billing. Appointed by Whitehall and reporting directly to COBRA, Badgerman had overseen agents using customised web access to make background checks of anyone with the opportunity if not the motive to have made what he'd by then judged to be an attempt on the life of the PM.

Despite public statements of "no comment", the enquiry's assessment is that the target was the man originally scheduled to take that opening ride. That the time it would have taken to rig the wire decapitating Webb meant it had to have been in place long before any announcement that the PM would no longer do so. The killers had opted to leave it in place, letting their plan play out with the unfortunate Webb as victim, because to remove it without detection would have been impossible. Either that or they'd missed news of the change which, with the state of the phone cell signal in parts of the region, was entirely possible.

Terrorism is why Special Branch and Five have led the investigation in the thirty-six hours since the killing. The HQ coffee machine was the first casualty, dying early the previous day under the unexpected pressure of the demand for cortados and flat whites. Not that the London lot had been all that keen on the local facilities in the first place. They'd quickly sussed things out, leaving Northallerton to set up camp at the Harrogate Conference Centre. "Closer to the scene of the crime," one of them had said. Iverson wasn't so sure. The hotels in Harrogate were way nicer than *The Golden Lion* on the High Street. "Paddy"

Davies had made three trips to Harrogate the previous afternoon dropping off their baggage. He said he'd seen sack loads of coffee beans arriving. State of the art coffee machines too. Metropolitan elite slumming it.

For Whitehall, the situation is clear, laid out for anyone with half a brain to read. The terrorist cell responsible for the killing had made an error. They were lying low, shitting themselves at both their humiliating failure and the probability that the full might of Five and Special Branch would soon be rootling them out from whatever rock they were hiding under. Banging on doors, black uniformed men with cold eyes and hot machine pistols had already been smashing their way into high rise flats and inner-city tenements.

SAS teams were on standby across the county, every caravan site and holiday let scrutinised for suspicious groups checking in over the past few days. Special Branch in Leeds and the bigger towns of West Yorkshire had local agents with ears to the ground, leaning on every informant. They sought not only names but places where such terrorists might seek sanctuary, an operation requiring additional officers bussed in from surrounding forces. COBRA was in session because bungled or not, it was an attack on the state at its highest level, an attempt to quite literally chop off its head. In the day or so since the attack, the PM's home outside Richmond had been heavily fortified. As well as mobile patrols, roadblocks were in place around the town, much to the chagrin of local traders finding late autumn tourism reduced to a trickle as tourists are either diverted from the town and its castle or put off coming in the first place.

In the flurry of all this Kendra Webb and the Webb family are low on the list of operational priorities, their personal loss slipping further and further down whatever 'to do' lists the dark-suited agents of Five are adding to as quickly as their tablets let them.

With the focus on terrorists, Webb's death is seen as collateral damage just as much as if he'd been caught up in a bomb blast whilst out shopping. His killers would be found, but just not by what would usually have been a deep investigation of Webb's own life or any vendetta's against the man himself.

Iverson's brief from Crosby is clear. Interview the wife, get the basics. Make it look good, but whatever you do, don't go overboard. Keep to sympathies and understanding, bland statements of finding the killers and bringing them to justice. There could be no promises. 'Christ, you've been on the courses haven't you? Victim support?' Crosby had asked.

'RTA's really,' Iverson had replied. 'Traffic related, not murder. Not terrorism. I mean...It's the Yorkshire Dales, sir. No-one really thought that-'

'That's the fucking problem,' Crosby had responded. 'No fucker ever thinks!' He'd paced the room, angry. The corridor really, given that the decorators' stuff had taken over the briefing rooms. 'The good thing, DS Iverson,' Crosby had finally concluded, 'is that for this interview you don't need to think. You hold her hand. You listen. You nod. You get the fuck out. And for Christ's sake *low key*. Understood?'

He did, but it hadn't stopped him telling Carol. Carol is a fan, big time. Kendra Webb, ex-model, ex-WAG to at least three premier league footballers, is an Instagram queen. Women want to be her, at the very least to be her BFF. Men want to be with her, though possibly with different ideas - though these too most often involved the letters B and F.

So, he'd chosen carefully the words of a call home, his *"key role in the enquiry...The Webb estate...One to one with Kendra. Yes, Kendra...I know...I know...Yes, I know you follow her...A selfie?...May not be appropriate...Yes, I know...You'll what?...Okay...I'll try..."*

Career path aside, no matter how this day pans out, it promises a great night. A bottle of wine, an intimate dinner. Conversations trading on his interview with one of the most famous faces in the county with the woman who is her biggest fan. For Iverson, life looks better by the hour.

6

'What on earth did you think you were playing at?' tapping the pause button on the iPad, Hyland's question is rhetorical, requiring nothing other than complete submission. He taps the screen, rolling the video forward. Even with the sound muted, the torrent of expletives silenced, the image of Musgrove's face in extreme close-up - spittle at the side of his mouth, teeth bared - all too clearly conveys a man out of control.

'I...' Musgrove trails off.

'Over seven hundred thousand views. It's been on YouTube less than a day. What do you say to that?'

He knows a comment about the power of the internet is the last thing required but, truth be told, at this moment, standing in the Chief Constable's office, there's little else in his mind. His head is empty. A *Gone Fishing* sign, cartoon like, hangs there. A few buzzing flies.

'Maybe you think keeping silent gets you off?' Hyland asks.

Musgrove's pretty sure that too is rhetorical. It's Hyland's *modus operandi*. A series of questions that aren't really questions. At times, a conversation with the CC is like he's interviewing himself, cutting out the middleman. 'Pity you didn't think of doing that at the time. Would have saved us all a good deal of embarrassment, don't you think?' Hyland continues, a question offering further proof of Musgrove's understanding of the way the meeting is to be conducted. He has to admit it's efficient, an interview strategy leaving little room for misunderstanding or difference of opinion. 'Topping it off, Gina *bloody* Hargreaves has had to go on bloody national TV apologising for this bloody mess of yours!' Hyland exclaims. It's a statement, not a question. Not even a rhetorical one. It leaves Musgrove in a quandary as to what to do. Maybe now is the time to say something. But what? He wonders whether Commissioner Gina *bloody* Hargreaves is in fact all that upset about yet another TV call, even one featuring an apology. What was it they said about bad publicity? That it was good? No, that couldn't be right. Anyway, it's a spotlight, and everyone knows the woman craves illumination like a moth.

'What have you got to say for yourself?'

He leaves a beat to be sure a response is in order, obligatory in fact. 'I don't see that it is *my* mess, sir. I mean, there was a dead body. Headless. I didn't do any of that. I was just trying to impose some sort of…order. Following the book.'

'Just where in this book does it mention sticking your fingers up at a journalist and screaming your face off at her.'

'She isn't a journalist.'

'Wake up man. Everyone's a fucking journalist these days. Every busybody with a mobile phone and a social media account thinks that they're…I don't know. Some famous journalist. You know…like what's his name.'

The only journalist Musgrove can think of is Clark Kent, instinctively feeling it to be the wrong answer. Certainly not whoever it is that Hyland's grasping for.

'Pulitzer!' Hyland exclaims. 'They all think they're bloody Pulitzer. All "hold-the-front-page" and the like.'

Musgrove's sure Pulitzer is a *thing* rather than a *who* but lets it slide. 'It was a crime scene, sir. None of them had any business being there. I was following procedure. There was no one else. They all pissed off after the PM who'd hightailed it out of there as fast as his security team could carry him. You were nowhere to be seen sir. I had to do something. I mean…I'm an ACC.'

'Listen, Musgrove,' *never Neil*, 'I'd have thought you'd have understood the politics of it. Your role. You have to be flexible, especially where the media and politicians are concerned. Wear the public face, the concerned listener, the bobby on the beat. Accommodating. Accessible. Dixon of Dock Green. Not a chocolate and raspberry covered Rambo!"

'With respect,' never the best way to start a response, but the red mist is drifting in, an angry rolling crimson fog-bank. More specific is the sensation of a line of sweat building under his collar, a tingling behind the eyes. To top it, there's the familiar feeling of a balloon inflating inside his head. A balloon with no cut off valve filling his skull, pressing against the inside of his head, his temples. The sense it has to expand or explode. He tries counting to ten, sensing it's already too late for the breathing exercises he's worked on. He's being held accountable for things outside his control, a scapegoat. The Force's *Buckaroo* Donkey of responsibility, loaded with everyone's problems and ready to kick. 'It was a crime scene, sir!' he splutters. 'A man dead! Murdered! But right then, at the time, we knew nothing other than he'd been decapitated during a descent of the flume. His wife was there, surrounded by rubberneckers and Christ alone knows who else, with her husband's head bobbing in the water not five feet away. I *was* showing a compassionate public face! I *was* the caring bobby on the beat, caring for *her*. What I wasn't going to be was to be accommodating to any of the rest of them contaminating my crime scene.! All those ghouls, posting it on the internet for everyone and his mother to see. In the case of Webb, quite literally his mother!' That part was true. Daisy Webb, sitting in her expensive sheltered accommodation, had learned of her son's death through a shared Instagram post of his head bobbing in the water. That the post had accumulated over a hundred thousand likes hadn't helped. Some said it might have been what had brought on her second stroke.

'Musgrove, whatever you think it was you were doing, the footage doesn't lie.' Hyland taps the iPad. 'You were out of control.' He walks to his desk, sits fingers steepled. 'I've discussed it with Complaints and Professional Standards. They were, by the way, going to throw the book at you, IOPC, reduction in rank, the lot. However, the Commissioner, in her wisdom, has seen fit to step in with a solution. She's anxious to keep this as low key as she can. The thought of a full disciplinary hearing, a tribunal, well, she's deemed it too unsettling with these elections coming up. The public image of the force is bad enough without dragging this through the media for weeks and weeks. On the advice of her PR, she's persuaded Complaints to an alternative solution. One keeping it in-house.'

Musgrove stands awaiting his fate. Gina *"bloody"* Hargreaves coming to his rescue? He thinks not.

He was officially ACC, Assistant Chief Constable North Yorkshire Police. One of four ACCs, on paper the second most important police officers in the county. In reality he's *Constable Dogsbody. Officer Doolittle.* ACC Neil Musgrove, a re-decorating brief making him more like the cheerily gloomy bloke from *Grand Designs* or that show with Alan Carr and some woman from Brighton rather than a buster of crime.

The heady days of excitement at the Commissioner's decision of re-structuring had evaporated early in that particular Command Team meeting two years ago. The glossy folders had slid across the shining conference table - *"hand sawn swamp ash with inlayed blue resin"* a fact he knows from recent hand-to-hand skirmishes with the beatnik stylings of Hargreaves' imported metropolitan design team. Expecting *Tactical Firearms; Drug Squad; Anti-Terror* he'd got HR, *Refurbishment and Branding* making him officially some no-hoper sub-team manager off *The Apprentice.* Logistics, mood boards and colour swatches.

'So,' Hyland continues, 'there's to be an apology. A public apology. One to the widow and one to the influencer who filmed you.'

'But-'

Hyland holds up a hand. 'This is non-negotiable. It's this or full IOPC investigation.'

Musgrove deflates.

'In addition, she's offered the journalist you screamed at open access to the enquiry. The plan is to keep her on the inside, make her think she's onto a scoop. In reality, it's a couple of interviews. Access to a few briefings. An officer attached to keep an eye on her.'

'Not me!'

'No, not you. You'll be pleased to know that as a result of your little encounter at the pool it's been decided that some re-training in terms of self-awareness is in order. Your anger issues. You're to attend a new session Malcolm Pemberton's running.'

'Pemberton? The Psychologist?'

'The same.'

'He worked on those murders last year. The profiler.'

'That's the chap.'

'Begging your pardon, sir, but the man's useless. That profile he came up with fitted half the population of the county. And the fact that he left a hard copy in a taxi and the media got hold of it...Well, it was a disaster. A complete and utter disaster. We were inundated with calls. Thousands of them. Everybody was convinced it was their neighbour or a disliked colleague. It was like he'd taken the lid off a box, open season on *"dob in anyone you don't like"*.'

'But when we arrested him, it did fit the killer,' Hyland reminds him.

'It also fitted everyone else we arrested that year from shoplifters to drug dealers. We'd have been better off going on star signs. Chicken entrails.'

Hyland waves a dismissive hand. 'Be that as it may, he's running a new course. Anger Management. Hargreaves has persuaded Complaints that it's the ideal solution, the idea of her PR fella...Lawrence. Think of it as an emotional speeding awareness thing. Get through it without any more blemishes and there's no points on your license. From the look of this video you'll fit right in.'

What he actually thinks is from the look of this video, you're finally screwed.

7

Even in the early afternoon gloom of the rain, the Webb mansion is everything the word mansion implies. That is if the implication is that of one constructed as the realisation in white stone and glass of every romantic fiction reader's idea of such a property. And if that appears to be the case, it's because it has been. It is Kendra Webb's vision, the coming together of a series of Prosecco fuelled sketches scribbled on the back of restaurant napkins, sketches flowing from a *Twilight Saga* and *White Lotus* stuffed imagination. It was best summed up by a reader's letter responding to a feature article on the house in *Yorkshire Life*. The opinion of it being *"as if Barbie has been reborn as not only eccentric architect but also troubled teenage interior designer."*

At first, Kendra had been uncertain how to respond. There were things in that critique she felt drawn to, even to have kinship with. The pink kitchen for example with its glass floor looking down into an aquarium of tropical fish and baby sharks, was her interpretation of a Barbie dream home she'd built as a child. At other moments in the day - her Instagram famed *Prosecco o'clock* - her re-reading of the letter produced seething rage. She would look up the word "eccentric", finding it had interpretations that consoled her – *"character; original"* – others less so – *"bizarre; peculiar"*. She found she had no such problem understanding what "troubled" meant. In the end, a visit by one of Paul's many building trade associates delivering a good thumping to a critic who'd been foolish enough to have complied with the magazine's policy of *"name and address supplied"* had sufficed in resolving the matter to Kendra's satisfaction.

Iverson has no knowledge of this. Approaching, all he's seen is the immense sweep of the property, the Doric columns either side of a gold entrance doorway, and the gravity defying patio balcony above it. Now, sitting in the airy lounge, he ponders his chances of spilling the cup of Macchiato coffee the maid has just brought him onto the ivory rugs.

'*Faultless,*' Kendra repeats for a third time. 'I mean that's…no faults. It's…really good. Perfect.' The walk from front door to lounge had been accompanied by Kendra's quoting of the magazine's description of each section of the house they'd passed through. It was a one way conversation, part tour guide, part Right Move. There was, of course, no mention of the critical letter, its observations, or the subsequent punishment beating. It was in the past. Kendra's defining quality is that things in the past are no longer talked of unless they involve herself, a celebrity she's once met, or an exorbitantly expensive purchase. That Paul's death both directly affected her and had been witnessed by a myriad cast of B list celebs at the opening of the most expensive water park in the country, means there's hope of his securing the required statement without too much prompting to keep to the subject.

Having said that, official objective achieved, he knows that later tonight Carol will demand he recall every detail, every word Kendra bestows.

'Who would do such a thing?' Kendra opines sitting opposite. She wears what his mother would have termed "widow's weeds" except these are more in the vein of a little black number rather than sombre mourning. 'I mean, Paul was loved. We both were.

Really loved. Envied? Well, yes, of course, there's always haters aren't there? But we were really loved. We were *Yorkshire Life's Power Couple of the Year* two years running. Of course, that was until the PM and his wife came along and got themselves into Number Ten and took top slot. Not being bitchy, but that's all by default really, isn't it? Not really what he'd done himself. Not like Paul, building a business with his own hands. And anyway, there was no-one else left in the cabinet after all that stuff about Covid parties and expenses and the rest. And his wife, all that money from her father and mother. He hasn't earned it, not like me and Paul had.'

'No. Dreadful,' Lex responds, making a note of the moment. Carol loves the whiff of celebrity fall out, the juicy stuff that seeps into magazine columns and social media. She'd loved the Vardy/Rooney stuff, had even gone down to London for the trial on a couple of days hoping to pose outside the court for selfies with Rebecca or Colleen - she wasn't fussed which. But they'd just brushed past, shepherded by lawyers and minders. She'd had a whole day in bed when she got back recovering from the migraine caused by the upset. But this, this is first-hand, a front row seat, straight from what is the most expensively shaped and collagen plumped-lip horse's mouth he's ever seen. Kendra and the PM. Juicy.

'Mind,' Kendra says, kicking off her footwear and tucking a leg under her buttock to display even more of a deeply bronzed thigh. 'My Paul was a powerful man. Very powerful. You make enemies, you see, Lex. I can call you Lex can't I?' He nods. 'There are those that envy what we had, Lex.'

'Business rivals?' he asks, coffee cup shifting awkwardly in hand.

'Communists, Lex. Communists.'

'I...erhm.'

'Those that want to take everything from us. You know, scroungers. Them that can't be arsed to get out and earn for themselves. I mean, it's not as if we didn't do loads for charity.

We give to food banks and everything. But that's not enough for some. They'd take everything.'

Lex nods. He thinks letting her list a couple of possible enemies is sufficient for her to think it was all being taken seriously. *No stone unturned.* If later asked by the media Kendra could honestly say he'd listened, taken her and her ideas seriously.

'So, communists,' Lex repeats, other hand gripping the hand thrown saucer so tightly that it trembles as he looks for a coaster or something he can use to lay it safely onto on the glass topped coffee table.

'One of my friends knows people at *the Post*,' she continues. 'He told her MI5 and Special Branch are involved in the investigation. That's proof isn't it? Communists. You wouldn't have MI5 involved if it wasn't spies, would you?'

'No, that's true,' he offers in response to the wide blue eyes staring eagerly at him.

Kendra tucks her legs tighter under her, skirt hem riding higher, straining at the limit of its possible tensions. 'You're from Northallerton aren't you, Lex? You must have seen them over there. The Spooks.'

Coaster found, Lex stretches to slide it closer, lowering cup and saucer onto the table so he might drag his thoughts back to where they need to be. 'Well, there's a lot of coming and going. Busy. So…erhm…I suppose yes, there must be. There are. *Spooks*. Yes. *Spooks*.'

'I knew it! Wait till I get on *Insta*. I'll let my millions of followers know my Paul died a hero for his country.'

'Well…no. I mean. You can't.'

Kendra looks at Lex, struggling with a phrase she's clearly not had much experience of dealing with. 'What do you mean, *can't*? This is what they've been waiting for. They want to know. They need to know. My Paul was a patriot.'

'But it's all very…delicate. Yeah, it's delicate at the moment.

We don't want to alert anyone that we're onto them, do we? Give them the chance to escape justice?'

She slumps into the sofa. 'No, I suppose not. Hadn't thought about that. I can see why you're so high up in all this. I mean sending you here. You must be the heart of the investigation. My story. My evidence and insights. It could be a breakthrough for you.'

'Yes. It seems like it, doesn't it?'

'I've already had my agent on today. They want me to write a book, but he says they'll probably get in a secretary or something to write it down. Maybe a film.'

'Wow!'

'Who do you think they'd get to play me, Lex?'

'That's tough. I mean. Wow! So tough.'

'I said it should be me. I mean, I've done modelling and I did a couple of music videos. I had to convey all sorts of ideas and emotions without any words. You know, my expressions. That's acting. Proper acting.'

'Yes. Yes it is.'

'I wonder who they'd get to play you, Lex?'

'Me? Well...I couldn't...wouldn't. No idea.'

'I think Benedict Cumberbatch. Ooh no, he's a bit too old. Ooh I know! Michael Fassbender! Or that bloke from *Harry Potter*...not Daniel Radcliffe, you know, the spin off. The *Beasts* ones.'

'Eddie Redmayne?'

'Yes! Yes, he's the one. I bet we could get him. I'll tell my agent in the morning. He knows loads of people. He can get him, I'm sure.'

'I think maybe we're getting off the point a little, Mrs Webb.'

'Kendra. Call me Kendra, Lex. Mrs. Webb's Daisy, my mother-in-law.'

'Kendra,' he nods making mental note number two. First name terms, him and Kendra. 'The thing is...We're still in the early stages. We have a number of ideas, leads and such like that we have to follow up on before we can talk with any certainty of motives and the identity of potential suspects.'

'Oh I understand. Paul was big on his *CSI*. Loved a detective show did Paul. Watched them all. We joked that he was almost a detective himself. So, what next?'

'Well, this bit would be the police procedural. I get myself back to Northallerton and write up your statement. Then we piece what you've told me with all the other bits - the evidence, the witness statements. Then we speak to anyone with information that might help us identify the perpetrators and anyone who helped them. Then we set about catching them.'

'It all sounds so…exciting! Paul would have loved all this. If it hadn't been him being the one murdered and everything.'

Lex nods. He knew what she meant. Bit of a spoiler.

Interview finished, Kendra walks him to the front door. Barefoot, she is even shorter than her photographs. As he reaches for the door handle, she holds out a hand, stopping him. He gazes into the depths of her eyes, wide and round. 'Before you go,' she says, releasing him, reaching her other hand into the drawer of a console table. 'Take this.' She hands him a card. 'It's my mobile. You can get straight through. Anytime you want.'

Despite the rain, Lex stands on the driveway holding Kendra's card in his hand; pure white, embossed gold font in a modern script. A direct line. His head is spinning. Carol is going to die!

8

'What do you mean it's my case?' Fisher asks, wafting the folder DCS Crosby has slid across his desk, at each upswing knuckles rapping against its cover.

'What it says on the tin, Fisher. What else would you think?'

She thinks hard about what she thought. What she might say. She knows for sure what she *wants* to say. She also knows where it would get her: yet another interview with Professional Standards for abusing a superior. She's enough on her plate after the news of a therapy support group her tribunal mandated she has to attend. Her earlier thinking that with teeth gritted and head down she might get through it, now looks as gossamer thin as a call girl's stockings. Her satisfaction at letting Crosby know what she really thinks of him is thus carefully weighed, tipping the scales as *not worth it*. 'I thought you'd be putting the most experienced officers on the Webb case is all,' she says.

'What makes you think I'm not?'

'Because if that were true, I'd be on it. Not Iverson.'

'Iverson's not on referral to the police psychologist though, is he?' Crosby points out.

'There's many think he should be. Most of his attitudes are primeval. Those that aren't give primeval a bad name. He's a misogynist. He's no respect for women. On top of everything else, he's plodding and unimaginative.'

'This is based on what? His opinion of you?' He pauses. 'You do know, he's not the only one who takes issue with your manner, Fisher. Your...attitudes. There's many think he's dead right in that,' he smirks. It isn't a good look, though she's long thought nothing short of a paper bag over his head would do the job right. It isn't that he's physically unattractive - which he is, a face you know would look the same if turned upside down - it's his unctuous manner, the oily charm he believes brings every heterosexual woman entering its sphere under his spell.

'So, this is pay back. Sending me off to Mad Malcolm's not enough for you,' she judges.

'DI Fisher, I don't know what you're suggesting. I'm a DCS. I have priorities. My decisions are based on practical matters of getting the job done. The regulations are clear.' He looks at a sheet of paper on his desk. *"Anyone the subject of referral to psychiatric evaluation and support must be placed on restricted duties until cleared by the police psychologist".*' He looks back up. 'Until Pemberton says otherwise, that line is fixed. Immutable.' He smiles once more; this time she thinks it's his pleasure at finding a use for the word *"immutable"* rather than the *"because I say so"* he usually relies on. 'After your Professional Standards hearing, I'm not about to let you loose on a murder enquiry, let alone one with the profile of Webb's. It's restricted duties only. Right now, Missing Persons seems somehow appropriate.'

She resists the temptation to leap across the desk and pound his face into it. Instead, she shifts her weight from one leg to the other, flapping the folder up and down, a flightless bird, wings useless. 'This is revenge, it's dressed up in an Easter bonnet of regulations, but revenge all the same.'

He smiles, leans back in his chair. 'I'm seeing it more as a story of redemption, your chance to salvage a once promising career. Attend Pemberton's sessions, work on his recommendations, and you get to see your time out as a DI rather than shipped out early on the *sick.*' The word *sick* is accompanied by a twirl of a finger pointing at his temple, tongue rolled inside his bottom lip.

She breaths deep. 'Seeing my time out was never the most pressing of my ambitions. You must be thinking of yourself.'

'There you go. You can't hold back, can you?' he says, sitting forward and appraising her. It isn't a good feeling. 'Your problem, Fisher, is that where your career's concerned you've not much of a survival instinct. Oh, I know all about your illness, and all that residual sympathy from what happened to your father. But it's water under the bridge. We're a police force, not a self-help group.'

She's known for some time that Crosby saves these scathing homilies for when there's no-one around, no corroboration, her word against his. Her own outbursts are always provoked by him when they're in public, her angry eruptions lending weight to his accusations of her "irrational behaviour" when he discusses her with superiors. She's seen her record, her file. She has form. Previous.

'I'll take your silence as acceptance,' he says. He sits, pencil tapping on his teeth. 'Regulations state that whilst you're engaged with your rehabilitation - this Anger Support Group - you're to have restricted duties.' He nods at the folder she's holding. 'Despite a few oddities, this suicide you picked up looks straightforward. You get to work it because Hargreaves' office wants the Commissioner to be seen to be working with you, seems they think it plays well, what with you being a female officer. It'll remind you of the basics. Paperwork. Filling in forms. Seeing the job through. No short-cuts. No intuition. A bit of good old meat and potato and two veg police work. Keep you humble. Down in the trenches. Feet on the ground.' There are so many mixed metaphors she gives up trying to unpick them, him speaking like the love child of a Hallmark card and a Christmas Cracker motto factory. She settles for a shrug of the shoulders. Whatever she says, unless there's a kick in the gonads attached, he's the type who'll always see it as a woman saying *yes*.

'If you do that, do it to my...' she feels the smirk before its arrival, 'satisfaction, then we'll see it as part of your story. Your redemption. Pemberton clears you and, in a few months, maybe, just maybe, we'll find something a little more challenging for you. Baby steps, DI Fisher. Baby steps.'

The words *"yes sir"* or any other deviation from cursing would stick in her throat. Instead, she forms a guttural sound which Crosby takes for gratitude, a woman overcome with emotions that were always destined to get the better of her. He's a man of the mind-set that you can't outrun biology. Hormones.

'I've looked at the initial report - the shaven-head thing and rope of hair. Weird as some of it appears, it's clearly a suicide. Probably some protest against her situation - the patriarchy or whatever the bloody *Guardian* crowd are calling it this month. Pathology's delayed, they're somewhat pre-occupied with the Webb thing - but you can get on and tidy it up. Push it along, you know, smooth the edges,' he says waving a hand in the direction of folder and door. 'See what you can make of it.'

She already has a vision of what she could make of it; a rolled-up cylinder with a final resting place that Crosby – unless he is a contortionist of exceptional skill and flexibility - would find a great deal of difficulty in reading

---

It's a boomerang existence. Quite the metaphor, she thinks. Or is it? Maybe a simile? No, similes are when it's *like* something. Metaphors were definite. Definitive. Unlike herself who remains...ill-defined.

She's a boomerang, hurled with the certainty that no matter where she's thrown, she'll always come back. Undeterred. Unflinching. After all, no-one's concerned what might happen to a boomerang in flight, right? Out of sight, out of mind. It's wooden after all, inanimate, a tool, a thing without feeling.

Fisher shifts the elbow she's been resting on, a movement sending the papers piled high on her desk, cascading to the floor. Cursing, she bends, scooping up sheaths of them that slide in her hands as she slaps them loosely back onto the desk. *How the hell is she expected to work like this?*

Sitting up, she tosses the last of the papers onto the desk, at the same time muttering expletives at a space masquerading as office for herself and five other detectives, CID stuffed into what amounts to little more than a cupboard at the end of a long dark corridor whilst the decorators continue occupation of their old suite. She's looked in a few times - filing cabinets and potted plants draped with dust sheets, everything not screwed down dragged into storage to await a phoenix like rise. Part of the New Look Force, they said, the backwash from the Met and its institutional failings. The long overdue first step on the long promised fresh start, they said. A restructuring executed in *"a palette of subdued grey with overtones of charcoal"* so the memo from the useless lump ACC Musgrove promised. "Contemporary and Corporate", all couched in M&S advertising bollocks, management vows intent on papering over the cracks. In the case of the decorators, literally papering over the cracks.

Like the last initiative, and the one before that, it had juddered to a halt, a sudden stop catapulting its passengers into the windscreen. The most anyone has seen of this exciting contemporary corporate remodelling enterprise are the dust sheets and ladders spread randomly about the place. The signs blocking off offices and closing staircases, the now narrowed corridors that turn officers and staff alike into no-fault show-jumpers as they scoot over cans of paint and rolled up carpet. No sign of painters. Not a single paintbrush unsheathed in anger, and no opened tins of paint. Nothing more than a few patches of rubbed in filler, spattered like pale bruises along corridor walls and the odd stairwell and foyer. Maybe that's the puzzle they should fix on. *The Case of the Mysterious Vanishing Decorator. The Enigma of the Disappearing Painters.* Maybe she'd write them. A series. *The Strange Case of Cones on the Motorway. The Mysterious Shrinking Twix Bar Affair.*

She's about to contribute another title forming her *Detective Fisher Investigates Real Crimes* trilogy when a ringing phone breaks her train of thought. She sits forward, propelling yet more papers to fan out across the floor as a poorly dealt hand of cards. Maybe the landline is something they should have buried under their sodding dust-sheets, see how good the SOCOs are then at finding things. An entombed piece of ringing plastic ought to be within their capabilities. Make a change from them sitting on their fat hairy arses eating biscuits all day – something they appear to be doing whenever she ventures into the sub-basement labyrinth serving as their temporary base.

A search finds the phone under an upturned burger carton, compliments of the night shift.

'DI Fisher? Its Gina.' The voice has a rising cadence like actors off *Neighbours*. Every utterance is coddled as a question, a vocal affectation requiring some sort of sheep gate be installed in the recipient to sort actual questions from Aussie soap stylings. 'Gina Hargreaves? The Commissioner.? We met the other night? The body in the rafters?'

You had me at Gina, Fisher thinks, a response betrayed by hearing her voice say 'Commissioner. How can I help?'.

'I was rather hoping for an update, Inspector.'

'Update?' She wonders why the Commissioner is ringing her to ask for an update on the Webb enquiry, an operation she assumes Hargreaves to have her fangs deep in the neck of, draining it to a dry husk for all the publicity she can extract. Even if she's unaware that Fisher's being kept at arms length from the investigation, surely she's best placed to know stuff like that herself. Given their past history, she'd also assumed she'd not be hearing from the Commissioner again, unless it was to spit in her face. 'Maybe your office has the wrong number,' she suggests. 'I'm afraid I can't help with Webb.'

'Ah...No, it's not Webb. That whole investigation is covered elsewhere. It seems your boss, erhm...' The sound of floundering. A management mind, scouring memory slots in the attempt to recall a minion too low in the organisation to deserve permanent occupation of valuable mental real estate in the PFCC's brain.

'Detective Superintendent Crosby?' Fisher offers.

'Yes, Crosby. Pale faced man. Balding. Surprisingly slick hair. Somewhat oily skin. A little bit creepy and stalker*ish*.'

A somewhat over-egged if not entirely inaccurate picture of the oily, balding, creepy, stalker*ish* DCS Crosby. Fisher grunts recognition, some part of her deciding it politically inadvisable to voice wholehearted agreement that yes, that is unmistakably her boss, DCS Crosby, that the Commissioner has described. Nailed, in fact.

'Well, anyway, DCS Crosby agreed we liaise on the progress of our case.'

'Case? Which case?' *Our case*?

'The body in the rafters.'

'Liaise?'

'Liaise. You know. It means that we–'

'I understand what it means. I'm just...' Fisher stops. What was she *just*? It takes a second to recognise she doesn't know. Not in this moment anyway. Not a clue – which isn't a great endorsement of her current mental state – certainly not for an experienced DI with a putative crime trilogy to be written about motorway cones and Twix bars.

'It's Harvey's idea,' the Commissioner states, an unexpected sharing of her limelight.

'Harvey?' Ah, yes, the high cheek-boned PR guru tugging at her sleeve last night, all soft manicured hands and designer suits, the one who'd never lifted anything other than his face.

'Yes. Harvey has a gift for these things. You made quite the impression, DI Fisher. Quite the impression. Seems Harvey's quite taken with you. Your story, I mean, not in any...stalking cancel culture sort of way. We're not the Met after all,' she laughs.

Fisher laughs too, though not sure why. 'Of course,' she hears herself say, the traitorous part of her mind striking again. Weasel words and sycophancy. The part of her clinging to the distant possibility of a future promotion existing in whatever parallel multi-verse it inhabits. The eager to please little girl putting her hand up to be called on. The one living in a world where good police-work counts for more than whichever Mason's lodge you belong to.

'Harvey thinks that what with all the negative hoo-hah surrounding poor Paul Webb's murder, a closer involvement with your rather more politically relevant investigation will prove super for the local media in the run-up to polling day. A few shots of us together. You know, scrunched at a desk or something. In front of one of those glass whiteboard thingies... You know? As if we're consulting. Harvey feels it plays well with the female demographic...the optics. Shows my concern for all those young women whose desperate lives have led them to such an end. Maybe we might start a fund or something? I'll get Harvey to look into it - fun runs and tee-shirts. Chin-Chin!'

The line goes dead.

And there it is. Boomerang. She is about to be thrown again, poster girl for the good name of the North Yorkshire force, flung into the wind and all the time wondering just when Hargreaves will remember who she is.

She drops the phone back under the oily Styrofoam burger cover. *T' Big One!* so the labelling on the box proclaims. Yeah. She should be so lucky.

9

Fisher opens the door, Training Room Six hastily re-purposed for the occasion. Entering, her head fills with memories of the last time she'd been here: the Safeguarding Committee, the top team investigating the death of a young child abused by teenage parents. She'd been the rostered CID representative, a brief to take notes, report back. "Don't say anything leaving us open to work or responsibility for any fuck-ups," was Crosby's standing instruction to the team. If a conflict arose between taking more work or taking responsibility, the brief was simple: duck whichever seems the most worrying at the time. As far as Crosby is concerned its always responsibility, the garlic to his Dracula.

Fifteen minutes in and the speech by the smarmy Lead Social Worker had made it abundantly clear it was a meeting with no higher objective than that of covering arses. Fisher's observations to that effect going down like a sausage roll at a *bah-mitzvah*. There had been a lot of humming and *'I don't think that's quite fair…looking at the wider picture…the success we've had with…the statistics tell us…the job of this committee isn't to find blame…'* etcetera. She'd lasted less than an hour before finding an excuse to leave via a fake phone call. The soundtrack to her exit that of a group sighing in collective relief at her departure.

She makes her way to a conference table shoved to the side and adorned with paper cups, flasks of tea and coffee, and a plate of biscuits. The chairs are gathered in a circle, like wagon trains in the westerns.

The man sitting on one of them gets up and approaches, notepad clutched in one hand, the other outstretched in greeting. 'I'm Malcolm. Malcolm Pemberton. Call me Malcolm.'

Fisher looks him up and down, her hands clasped around a dull black flask that a Sharpie label states to be *coffee* though the stains on the peeling label are sufficient identification of that claim. Even the SOCOs would solve that one, eventually.

'I'm chairing our little gathering,' Malcolm clarifies.

'Hardly *our*...Erhm...*Malcolm*?' she replies, hand working the button on the flask. 'Nothing to do with me, more *your* little gathering. I'm what I think you'd describe as collateral damage.'

'I think you relieve the pressure first....' Malcolm offers. His arm remains extended, but now with fingers pointing down like a spider, wrist revolving backwards and forwards in the air. Marcel Marceau he isn't, but Fisher gets the picture.

She twists the lid, an action extracting a puff of air. Pushing the released button, the coffee flows pale and thin. 'Is that a Psychiatrist joke, Malcolm?' she asks, nose wrinkling at the colour of the liquid. 'You know, *relieving the pressure*. Because if it is, it's not half bad. You should do that at one of your conferences. Break the ice.'

'Joke? Erhm...No. Not really. It's just how the flask works. I was trying to help.'

'I'm sure you were, Malcolm,' her tone that of a pat on the head. She screws the lid tight. 'You cling to that idea, Malcolm. Might come in useful this afternoon.' She picks up a UHT carton, 'How are you with these bloody things? I haven't got the nails.'

He takes the proffered carton, gently peeling back a corner.

'Brilliant!' Fisher exclaims. 'I can see we're off to a flyer.'

'*Collateral damage*,' Malcolm swills the phrase, rinsing it round his mouth. 'Why do you say that?' he asks, passing her the opened capsule.

'It's a cliche. What people say.'

'Interesting that it's how you choose to characterise yourself. *Collateral*...unimportant or secondary, whilst *Damage* of course implies hurt, suggests broken.'

Fisher, finishing dribbling the milk into her coffee, pauses in her search for a repository for the spent carton. She looks directly at him, inclining her head to one side as if it's listing. 'Oh, have we started? I thought there'd be a bell or something. At least us getting in the circle first.'

'No, there's no bell. No whistle. Nothing like that.' He looks to the carpet, a movement flashing a balding crown where the mane of swept back hair - the *Charlton* as her dad used to call it - fails to reach. She thinks of *Wile E Coyote*, follicles falling short, like fingers clinging desperately to a cliff edge. It's a style in keeping with the rest of the man, as if when a boy he'd read every fifties and sixties *Junior Book of Scientists* he could get his hands on, took the pictures of pipe smoking intellectuals and froze them in time, fixed as his fashion template. He appears a man caught in amber; a 1960s Foster Bros mannequin layered in sports jacket, leather patches, checked shirt, and cords.

He looks up about to say something when the sound of the door opening, the groan of a spring stretching the limits of its automatic closer, is accompanied by the spluttering oath of 'Oh for Christs' sake!' that announces the arrival of ACC Neil Musgrove. He stands framed in the doorway, meaty hand enveloping the door-handle, the very picture of a Hokey-Cokey dancer uncertain if he's putting a left leg in or out, let alone the rest of his more than ample frame. As for shaking it all about... Fisher turns away feeling no great urge to picture it either in reality or her mind's eye.

'No. No, no, no, no, no! This can't be right,' Musgrove continues.

Pemberton steps forward, arm circling the air inclusively, a market trader encouraging a reluctant punter to come closer and take a look at his wares. 'Ah come in Neil – I hope I can call you Neil. Nothing to be concerned about. We're all friends here.'

'I'm not her friend. I'm her bloody commanding officer,' Musgrove says pointing at Fisher. 'How the hell am I supposed to maintain respect if she's here listening to every word I say.'

Fisher sips her coffee. 'This should be good,' she mutters to Pemberton. 'Talk about delusional. He thinks he's got anybody's respect around here he needs committing *tout suite.*'

Pemberton crosses, hand outstretched, palm down as if talking to a nervous pet or rabid dog. Fisher stands watching. The size of Musgrove means it's more of a bear, a very angry and grumpy one at that. One just up from hibernation and not best pleased at finding it still winter. 'It's a bit like the confessional, Neil,' Pemberton says, his voice a sleep tape of intonation. 'What happens here, stays in here. No-ones' judging you, Neil. It's about discovering yourself. Your journey, Neil. Yours.'

'Will you stop talking to me like I'm some ADHD toddler! And, while we're at it, you can stop calling me Neil. It's Assistant Chief Constable, thank you very much.'

'That's a bit of a mouthful. Might prove a barrier. Your rank.' Pemberton says, risking a smile. Maybe he's nervous, but, from where Fisher stands, the smile comes across as more of a leer. Stress does that, she thinks. Like *Pervy Pete* down the market, bloke never could judge it right when talking to women. Over the years it has got him into a deal of hot water. By the look of it, Pemberton isn't doing too well with it either. 'We need to get to the person,' Pemberton ventures. 'Under the stripes and pips, so to speak,' he adds, smiling, top lip sticking to teeth in an ever-widening rictus grin.

'That's your problem, mate. I've earned these,' Musgrove replies, patting his shoulder to indicate the pips on the Senior Officer tee shirt that pulls ever tighter across his chest at each movement.

'Oh dear. Not a great start,' Pemberton observes.

'You think?' Fisher mutters to her cup.

'Start and finish,' Musgrove declares, free hand tugging a sheet of paper from the folder he carries. He waves the paper in Pemberton's direction. 'Sign this chit saying I was here and that'll be the end of it. You lot can carry on with...whatever it is you're up to, and I'll get back to my office. Catching criminals. The bad guys!'.

Pemberton accepts the form before rooting in his pockets. 'I don't seem to have a pen.'

Musgrove rummages through his own pockets, fingers fumbling at the contents. Sighing, he moves to the conference table where he begins laying out what he finds there. Yorkie Bar. Twix. Boost. Bounty.

'Is that what you do?' Pemberton asks, suddenly next to him.

'What?' Musgrove asks, looking up.

'Catch criminals.'

'Of course!' he snorts. He stands upright, once more tapping his pips. 'Does this look like I'm a bloody traffic warden. A School Crossing Attendant?'

Pemberton lowers his voice to comforting monotone. 'Tell me, Assistant Chief Constable, just when did you last catch a criminal? A *bad* guy?'

Musgrove stops emptying his pockets, stands Lion Bar clasped in one hand. His mouth opens and closes but no sound comes out.

The door opens, dragging attention to the doorway.

The figure standing there is tall, around six feet, hair dark, thick and brushed back. The eyes are brown, the skin olive, Mediterranean Fisher thinks, either that or he's having a long running affair with a sun-bed. He looks at a piece of paper held in his hand and then round the room: Fisher standing, staring, cup in hand; Pemberton and Musgrove stood in front of a pile of chocolate bars; Musgrove's mouth flopping open like a landed fish. The man looks from them to the still open door, the broken sign sellotaped to it. 'Is this Meeting room six? The Support Group?' he asks of the room.

Pemberton is first to break. 'Yes. Yes, it is. Well, the Support Group anyway. I'm Malcolm Pemberton. I'm the facilitator.' Hand stretching out. 'And you are?'

He takes Pemberton's hand, returning it with what to Fisher looks a solid grip. 'Demetriou. Detective Sergeant Demetriou.'

'Jesus! You've got to be joking!' she breathes.

'First name?' Pemberton asks, pen and clipboard magically found, part distracted by Fisher's less than *sotto-voce* utterance.

'Pan. Pan Demetriou,' he says head craning to check the list. 'DS Pan Demetriou.'

'Pan. Well, welcome, Pan. Let me introduce you to everyone.'

Musgrove stuffs the chocolate bars into his pockets and moves to the ring of chairs. Pulling one from the grouping, he enters the circle, tugging it back in place behind him. He sits with a soft thump, at the same time peeling open the wrapper of the Lion Bar. He stares ahead in what appears deep thought but could just as easily pass for a trance. After a beat, he begins chomping his way through the chocolate treat, oblivious to the world.

Pemberton guides Pan to where Fisher stands. 'Pan, this is Zara. Zara Fisher.'

Pan reaches out a hand, a movement halting part-way as he realises two important things. The first is that she doesn't make a reciprocal move to meet it. It's not a twitch; it's a deliberate docking failure. He looks from hand to face before he gives voice to the second thing he's realised. 'Fisher? Not…'

'…The very same,' she smiles. 'Assuming you're thinking *DI Fisher*. Your boss.'

'…Yes…Yes, I was. I uhm…Well.'

'Succinctly put, DS Demetriou. My thoughts too,' she states. 'Quite the mind blower, don't you think?' She turns and makes her way to the circle of chairs, sits at a point directly opposite Musgrove. The 9 to his 3 on the clock face.

Pemberton checks his list. 'Well, we're almost all here. We'll give the last one another minute.'

At that moment, the door opens, and a young woman appears – oilskin roll-top cycle messenger bag on her back, deep blue cycle helmet in one hand. She tosses the helmet onto a chair at the side of the room, the backpack sliding off and following it. 'Sorry I'm late. Traffic.' The voice is matter of fact. The sentiment throwaway.

She slips out of her blue puffer jacket, loosening hair that tumbles to drape across her shoulders. It is dark, natural curls framing her face in a Pre-Raphaelite artist's dream. Her eyes are blue like her jacket, burrowed into deep sockets either side of a slightly too large nose that sits above a generous, wide mouth. She glides to the circle, slumping into one of the vacant seats. She sits 12 to Fisher's 9 on the dial.

Pemberton stands at the six. 'You must be...'

'Sophie. Sophie Doyle. IT Forensics Technician if the rank thing's necessary...I mean, not sure how it all works, these things. You know, today...*Hashtag-metoo* and everything. This meeting.' She waves an arm casually taking in the room. 'But, if you see it as necessary, you know the patriarchy...I'm *Computer Forensics and Social Media.*' She gazes around the room. Fisher, Musgrove, Pemberton, the still standing Demetriou staring back. She looks down, starts to fiddle with the roll-top of her bag. 'More the social stuff, to be honest. Not had much of a crack at the forensics just yet. Dunno why. I mean, state of everything. Just look at the Met. I mean, it's 2025, Fourth Wave feminism and we still have institutions concerned with macho notions of rank and protection of the old boys' network. I mean...what's got to happen for that to finally change?'

'Can we assume the reason you're here is for your fulsome and forthright expression of such thinking about the patriarchy to those in command?' Fisher asks.

Doyle takes a water bottle from her bag, flips the top. 'If you mean kneeing some wanky officer in the bollocks who thought he could keep hitting on the newbie woman in data support, stalking and annoying her when she rejects his advances, and then go around spreading rumours about her sexuality, then no.'

'Ah, sorry.'

Sophie sips the water and presses the top back into place. 'Why would I do that when I could just hack the creep's computer and forward his search history and dating site profile to his wife.'

'Ah! So, you think the pen is mightier than the sword.'

'Well, the keyboard. Plus, I did do the whole *knee him in the balls thing* when he came storming after me in the car park.' She rolls the top of her bag closed, the water bottle cradled tight. 'His best mate, is the Forensics Data Support Manager. Seems he decided that was a step too far. So, here I am.'

Pemberton looks at his clipboard, a big tick going somewhere on the topmost sheet. 'Well, uhh…great that you're here. You've not missed anything…Sophie. And it's first names here. No ranks. We're all PC PCs anyway. No *patriarchy*.' The word sounds jolly in his mouth, imbued with levity as if trying to take the sting out. He shuffles the papers. 'I think we're just about ready to start. In the blocks, so to speak.'

'Hope there's not going to be any starters pistol.' Fisher tosses in. 'The ACC here's looking a little peaky. Don't want a gunshot shocking him. Man in his condition.'

Musgrove rouses from his stupor. 'Condition? What condition? I'm not in any condition.'

Fisher offers an appraising glance. 'Beg your pardon. You're quite right, Neil. You're in no condition at all.'

Musgrove's eyes drift to the band of fat pushing at his waistline, the muffin top overlapping the efforts of his trouser belt to contain it. He harrumph's, hefty paw scrunching the Lion Bar wrapper. 'Well, we can all see why you're here, Fisher. Too much lip. Mouth too smart for your own good.'

'Well, there's a first! The ACC's cracked a case. Quite masterly, too. One deductive leap and you've solved the mystery of why I'm here. But then again, maybe I'm giving you too much credit. You no doubt having had something to do with me being here in the first place. Complaints and Standards is under your HR remit, isn't it?' Fisher asks.

'Really? Do you really think any of this is my idea? That I'd put myself in this...company? With you?'

'Neil, perhaps-' Pemberton steps forward hands raised, catching a runaway train with a butterfly net.

Musgrove rounds on him. 'I've already told you, DON'T Neil me. It's ACC! I have RANK!'

Fisher, ignoring both, bundles on. '...Of course you're the reason I'm here. The Complaints interview. Conduct. The Disciplinary Board.'

'Even you can't expect to get away with calling Detective Chief Superintendent Crosby – and I quote – "*an unimaginative wanker*" in front of the whole of CID,' Musgrove points out. 'Not satisfied with that, your follow up comment was that "*given the amount of porn that's stuffed in his filing cabinet and on his laptop, I'm actually surprised he's so unimaginative in his wanking.*" I mean!'

Fisher curls her top lip. 'It had been a bad day.'

'That's what your police union rep offered as mitigation,' Musgrove reminds her.

'And look where it got me! I thought we were supposed to be all over this stress and work-life balance stuff these days. Pressure of work. Long hours. Someone over in HR ought to resend *that* particular memo.'

'It's the only reason you're here and not on suspension. That and your...Your...' Musgrove rummages his mind, landing on the best noun he can find. '...situation.'

Fisher ignores the sentiment, if that's what it is. 'That and the fact I'd just got a confession from the rapist your Superintendent Crosby said was – and *I* quote – "*never him in a thousand years*".' The bunny ears are a fine touch, she thinks.

'DCS Crosby was pursuing what he thought to be other more

promising lines of enquiry. He had...instincts. The DNA from forensics getting mislaid didn't help,' Musgrove retorts.

'Oh, so the fact the perp was a member of Crosby's own golf club - on the Committee of it in fact - didn't impair these instincts at all? Had nothing to do with the pressure for me to skip checking the man's alibi because he was – and I quote – "*a decent sort and it would embarrass the family.*" Christ he bloody well vouched for the man! A violent, sadistic raping bastard. A monster who'd raped three women in the parkland out by the course. So yes, I called him out.' She turns to Pemberton. 'And I'd do it again in a heartbeat if you'd like to add that to your notes, Malcolm.'

A silence lies across the room. 'Well,' Pemberton ventures, studying his clipboard. 'Maybe we should skip Zara's introduction for now. And the ACC's. How about telling us something about yourself, Pan?'

Pan walks to the circle cradling a Styrofoam cup in his hands like a medieval chalice. He sits at 10 to Malcolm's 6, splitting the segment between Musgrove and Doyle. He places the cup on the floor to the side of his feet, taking a moment to align it just so. Sitting upright, he lowers his hands onto his lap. He takes deep breaths, reminding Fisher of a yoga technique from a previous attempt at finding her inner tranquil self, the self still posted as missing on her mind's mental milk cartons and synaptic lampposts.

'I'm Pan. Detective Sergeant Pan Demetriou.' Fisher notes the effort to please everyone in the circle. An appeaser, a resolver of conflicts. 'I've transferred from Birmingham. Today, in fact' he continues, shaking his head. 'Quite the start,' he says, eyes falling on Fisher who observes him like a laboratory specimen.

'Welcome to North Yorkshire,' she mumbles, sipping her coffee.

'It seems my...erhm...reputation preceded me. Being assigned to attend this...workshop on the first day. Not had the chance to get my feet under the table, meet my colleagues.' He nods at Fisher. 'My boss, even.'

'I'm afraid scheduling isn't within my purlieu, Pan,' Pemberton states in best oil on troubled water manner. 'Bad timing…or maybe it's good. Chance to get things off your chest from the get-go, eh?'

'Another bloody screw up,' Doyle murmurs, striking a match and tossing it into Pemberton's oily flammable slick. 'Sick and tired of it. One bloody fu-'

'Perhaps we can let Pan finish and then you can have your turn…erhm…Sophie.'

'Suit yourself,' she says, shrugging shoulders and sinking deeper into her already extreme concave body slouch.

'So…barely unpacked and I'm here. My first meeting with my DI.'

'And you're here because?' Pemberton prompts.

'My old force thought it better I transfer. Fresh start.'

'And that's because…?'

'I punched my Inspector.'

'With probable cause I shouldn't wonder,' Musgrove mutters glaring at Fisher who contents herself by returning a comedy fixed grin.

'Ah,' Pemberton says before scribbling a note. 'Anger issues, then.'

'Given this is the Anger Management counselling group, I'd say that's almost as good a deduction as the ACCs. Wouldn't you say so, Neil?' Fisher asks.

'I'm choosing to ignore any provocation, Fisher,' Musgrove growls, arms folded in best cartoon harumph manner.

'That's good. You're making inroads with Neil already, Malcolm,' Fisher judges, a comment accompanied by an appreciative whoop from Doyle whose slump now verges on the brink of defying the limits of human anatomy.

'To be accurate,' Pemberton states, 'It's not simply Anger Management. You're here to explore things *blocking* your anger as much as those *causing* your anger. Emotions you're each of you bottling up, barriers getting in the way of finding your true selves. Your true nature.'

'So, you're telling us that this meeting - you in fact - are some kind of...what, emotional laxative. Is that it?' Doyle ponders from her slump.

Pemberton. crossing his legs, sits forward, torso leaning towards the centre of the circle. He sits perched on the edge of his chair, a bird on a wire. 'That's an interesting observation, Sophie. Very interesting indeed. That you see these emotions as something to be...purged. Expurgated.'

'What?' Sophie asks.

'Expurgated. Got rid of.'

'I'm only repeating what you said. You know...blocking,' she replies. To Fisher's ears it's a tone somewhere between fight and flight, certainly not freeze, though her posture suggests teenage indifference with a touch of angsty denial.

'Yes. Yes, yes...I did. But I also said it was about *exploring* these emotions. You seem keen to simply discard them. Get them out.'

'Well, that's what you do with stuff that's...messing up your workings isn't it?' Doyle asks.

'Yes, you do. But sometimes there are things stopping us doing that. Things getting in the way that mean we bottle them up,' Pemberton explains. 'They fester, block the system. That's when we're liable to sudden explosions. All that pent up emotion pouring out in one go. Anger.'

'Like fat-balls in the sewers,' Sophie nods understanding. 'I saw about them on *YouTube*. They need blokes with giant hoses and everything to clear them.'

'Maybe if we could get away from this mental soil pipe idea,' Musgrove puts in.

'That's an interesting thought, Neil,' Pemberton says.

'Listen, I've said... oh, it doesn't matter.'

'But it does, Neil,' Pemberton assures. 'It all matters here.

This is where you get the chance to talk. Talk about anything. Everything. Maybe see how you can organise these feelings better. You know...weight them. See what's important. The things you need to deal with right away, the stuff that can't wait. The things we need to face about ourselves or about the world we operate in. The things we have to get out, even if at times it seems it can only be done through violence – be it verbal or physical. The things we might resolve before they overwhelm us.'

'Like a...League table?' Pan offers.

Pemberton turns to face him, tipping further forward on the chair's edge. 'Maybe. Maybe that's a way. A ranking. Ordering the feelings. Deal with them according to a set of priorities. Our own rules.' He scribbles on his pad, the only sound the scratch of pencil furrowing its way across the paper.

'Jesus! Sounds like an inter-office memo. Some sort of Haynes manual. You know, Mental Health for Dummies.' Fisher finds herself saying, at the same time wondering who it is who's suddenly doing the talking, the sense her speech centre has been hijacked by terrorists on a suicide mission. 'To be honest, Malcolm, I'm not sure you can get what I'm thinking into a PowerPoint or whatever. Not even one titled *What A Waste of Bloody Time and Effort When We Could Be Doing So Much More.*'

'So, what would you suggest, Zara? What might be a way forward for you?' Pemberton asks.

'What? Better than Sophie's blocked lavvy or Pan's Premier League?'

'If you will.'

'I thought that was your job. Your role. The Big Idea.' Her mind takes back the controls, bursting into the flight cabin, pulling up from the tailspin, mental hijackers nowhere to be seen.

'Far from it. I'm merely a facilitator. I book the room, the time, the participants. Beyond that...Well, the agenda's not mine to decide. It's for you.'

'So, you're a clerk. A receptionist,' Doyle observes.

Pemberton grunts, a half-smile appearing as he pursues Doyle's analogy. 'Possibly. Maybe a little more like, oh, I don't know…Maybe the concierge. You know. I check the rooms are ready, manage the bookings. But I also see to my guests' needs. Make sure their stay is a positive one. Fruitful. A voyage of discovery.'

'I'm getting dizzy with all these bloody analogies,' Musgrove puts in, arms flopping at his sides in exasperation. 'Now we're a hotel? Is this Anger Management or *Booking Dot Com*?'

The rest of the group nod. 'A hotel with blocked toilets,' Doyle suggests.

'Bag's I'm not on plunger duty,' Fisher ventures. 'I'm usually the one holding the shitty end of any sticks.'

'I'd better not be customer relations,' Demetriou states. 'Not too good with complaints,' he adds, miming delivering a punch to his jaw.

'Maybe Neil can be catering,' Doyle suggests provoking a smile from Fisher.

After a beat, Musgrove grunts. 'Suppose it could be worse,' he says, finishing the thought by popping the last of a Yorkie into his mouth.

'Seems we're a hotel,' Demetriou murmurs to Pemberton.

'No,' Pemberton states, sitting back. 'I think you're becoming a group.'

10

Demetriou flicks the paper-clip into the waste basket. Six out of ten. He's getting better.

Taking his feet off the desk, he gets up, surveying the field of twisted metal. He knows all about scenes of crimes, and after an hour the floor is a bonanza for anyone making a case for his wasting police time. Except he's the policeman wasting police time, the sole command of DI Fisher upon leaving the Support Group a snapped *'Wait in the office.'*

He thinks *office* overstates the case for a space spending its defining years believing itself a broom cupboard. It's now a room with dreams above its station; two desks shoved together surrounded by chairs of varying decrepitude. There are files, loose papers, and greasy food containers stacked on desks and floor. Somewhere in the midst, he'd glimpsed a landline, a cheap Bakelite phone with a screen of the sort used by Alan Sugar on *The Apprentice*.

He's found a monitor and keyboard and tried logging on, but he lacks a password and HQ accreditation. He's thought about ringing Sophie who'd said she was IT, *Digital Forensics*, but he hasn't worked out if that includes IT support. Her demeanour carried all the indication that if minor bureaucratic business like passwords isn't part of her brief that such an enquiry would soon discover why she's required to attend the group.

Group. It was weird. He's just met people with whom he's shared a good deal of the intimate details of his life yet still feels an outsider. He knows a lot of weird stuff about Musgrove, Doyle, and Fisher – maybe more than he wants to - yet has no knowledge of even the names of the other officers who make up CID. And he's no sense of what his partnering with Fisher will now shape itself around. It can hardly be the typical DS and DI, certainly no Morse and Lewis. They were in the same Anger Management Support Group, and that seems wrong, a cock-up. The coordinator, Pemberton, hardly fills him with confidence, but then he wouldn't be the one to have had any say over who attended. That was higher up the chain, the Detective Super, this Crosby. Maybe he should ask him about a change of assignment. From what he's learned of Fisher there's bad blood between the two, so he might be willing to agree if for no other reason than to piss her off. Wouldn't look good though, first day here and asking for a transfer - especially when as far as he knows, there aren't many other DIs for him to be re-allocated to. Better he sticks with Fisher, sucks it up for a few weeks. Unless of course she decides different. Maybe gives him a hard time, pushing him to ask for a transfer, setting him up as a quitter to piss off Crosby who'd assigned him. His first day and already he's up to his neck in office politics. He'd not expected Camelot, but this, this is a nightmare.

The door opens, Fisher shoving it against a mound of files that quickly re-purpose themselves as temporary doorstop, the top layers sliding off, skittering across the floor to come to rest against the waste bin. Eyeing the scatter of twisted paper clips, Fisher arches an eyebrow.

'I won't transfer. I won't ask for one no matter what shit you give me,' Demetriou shouts, standing feet planted firmly on the ground or at least the sticky carpet with stains of unknown origin that passes for it.

'Wow. Steady Tiger. Who's shoved that massive tent pole up your backside?' she asks, a shove of her shoulder fully opening the door.

'I'm sticking. Making a fist of it. You won't push me out.'

'Is this anything to do with the meeting, or do you just have a whole load of mommy issues that we didn't get round to talking about? If so, Malcolm's going to wet himself when he hears.'

He stares ahead, eyes narrowing. 'I'm not a quitter. You won't get rid of me without a fight.'

Fisher slumps into the chair nearest the filing cabinet, the one he'd noticed has the words '*Ice Queen*' written in sharpie across the back, the ink only visible against the dark grey background when the light hits it in a particular way. Given the narrow slit of a window at the top of one wall means there's little light brave enough to enter, he assumes the graffiti has passed her by.

'Listen, DS Demetriou, I have neither the time nor inclination to plot your early exit. Considering the time and arm twisting it took to replace your predecessor, DS Givens, it's not something I intend to go through again anytime soon. And I'm certainly not keen on being stuck with DS 'flakey' Iverson longer than necessary. So, we're stuck with each other. That being the case, you might want to remove that stick from up your bum and sit down.'

'I...I'm sorry, Ma'am. Getting off on the wrong foot and all. I mean-'

'Oh god, please don't tell me you're one of those needy emotional intelligence types? You shouted at me, I shouted at you, it's passed. Done.' She prods a pile of files on the desk that tumble to the floor, clearing space to plonk her feet. 'It's dusted, never to be spoken of. Water under the bridge.'

'I just-' He stops. 'Thank you, Ma'am. Understood.'

She tosses a file she's taken out of her bag across the desk. 'Have a look at that,' she says, taking off her shoes.

He picks it up. It's flimsy, seven sheets of typed A4. Three are the draft findings of the examination of a body discovered in an old farm building. White female, late twenties. The conclusion that whilst a final cause of death would be determined by autopsy, she'd almost certainly died from asphyxiation, hanging.

Fisher busies herself massaging her stockinged feet, whilst he scans the other pages: a description of the call out; the rope confirmed to be standard DIY builder's nylon but with lengths of human hair wound into it.

He closes the folder, Fisher watching him. 'Weird,' he judges.

'Hardly cutting-edge analysis, DS Demetriou. How about donning your best Poirot and elaborating a little?'

'Seems a strange thing to do. I mean, suicide by hanging is a little old hat. Plenty better options these days. Not the choice of women, either. Quite a masculine end, like jumping off rooftops or under a train. Women tend to more feminine, more...graceful endings. Pills. Alcohol. Wrists in the bath.' He pauses. 'I don't want to sound out of step – liable to cancellation - but when I started in CID back in Brum, this old school DI I was assigned to always held that his experience of women committing suicide was that they choose a means where they can better pose themselves. He said it's almost like they're more concerned how they'll look when they're found. Blokes tend to just want to get it done. Step in front of a bus or whatever, not bothered about the clear-up. Quite violent ends, on the whole.'

'Well, neither you nor your old DI would be all that popular on *Loose Women* saying stuff like that about Instagram-*able* suicides, but there's something to it. It's what the statistics concerning means tell us. And we know statistics - unlike our raggedy scrotum PR conscious top team - never lie. So, hanging is suspicious, especially with the whole *rope of human hair and shaved head thing*. It might be a statement – you know, a last word comment on the patriarchy and women's perception by society. She might have felt herself exploited or abused. But we'd have to know more about her to know for sure. Like if she was a *Guardian* reader.'

Demetriou frowns but decides to ignore her postscript. 'What my old team called *walking back the cat*. Starting from her death in that building, the one certainty we have, and then tracking her movements and life backwards from that point - at least until we find an answer as to *how* and *why*. More vitally, if there's a *who* involved other than the victim herself.'

'Congratulations, DS Demetriou. You've won first prize in this week's crime scene lottery. Your prize is you get to shuffle through *Missing Persons* finding us a match. Once we know who we're really dealing with, we can start to figure what it was drove her to become Jane Doe.'

The search of Missing Persons – *MisPers* as the gloriously reductive label had it – proved productive. A hit on two possibilities. Both in the right age bracket, both blonde, both with a history of mental health issues resulting in prior periods of absence. One of the two had several such absences lasting over a month. The other, Sofia Kovalenko, was an asylum seeker whose absence from a Leeds hostel had ended with her arrest during an anti-drugs operation. She'd been found on an isolated Dales farm whose residents brewed meth amphetamine crystals. The term 'operation' was something of a misnomer, the police in fact arresting the occupants of the farm after being called to Northallerton's Friarage Hospital where most of them were being treated for burns, several fire engines having been called to blazing farm outbuildings. It hadn't taken long for fire-crews to establish the fires had been the result of rustic efforts at cooking meth, one literally blowing up in their faces. *Breaking Bad* had a lot to answer for.

Given her drugs charge, rather than returning to Leeds, a condition of her release had been placement in a local half-way house. After a few nights there, her social worker reported she'd disappeared. That was almost two weeks ago.

In late Autumn the Dales has its own quite particular travel issues. Not just the ebb-tide of late season tourists flooding the roads, blocking narrow lanes and by-ways with caravans and motorhomes, but avid cyclists and bikers adding time and frustration in equal measure to any journey. At least the farmers understood, pulling aside to let you through. Not so tourists whose determination to keep chugging along whilst slowing to wave arms at the views reduced everything to inner city crawl. Maybe they missed the commuter drag so much they had to bring it with them. Grid lock, Dales style.

But you could beat that trap. It was just a matter of knowing the roads less travelled.

The real issue, though, is accommodation. The area is full. No Vacancy signs everywhere, the consequence of villages like Aysgarth and Hawes, West Witton and Bainbridge becoming the target of second-homers and holiday lets. Easy prey for property vultures whose post-Covid intention is profit not community, avariciously gobbling up locations in a National Park with the added attraction of being a fraction of the price of their Cornish equivalent at just the point where that southerly county was - along with its tin - mined out of easy profit purchases. Channel 5 reality shows hadn't helped. *Yorkshire Farms; Yorkshire Vets; Yorkshire Shepherdesses; Yorkshire Foodies;* even the bloody *Yorkshire Police* and *Educating Yorkshire.*

It's why Fisher and Demetriou find themselves at a hostel isolated from the reach of Ocado Home Shopping deliveries, decent Wi-Fi, or roads big enough for second-homer's 4x4s. The building is sat in a location with little attraction to anyone other than the Swaledale sheep that idly wander the moors and grassland around its crumbling dry-stone walls.

There is, of course, a famous TV shepherdess but a few miles away, her *Instagram* life still attracting the odd celebrity hunter - though even the most addicted of these find sitting in a cold lay-by in Dales storms less attractive than stalking cosmopolitan influencers in city streets with a nearby *Costa*.

Swaledale Lodge is a down market take on *Bleak House.* Even

Dickens would struggle to find suitably evocative descriptors for the wind blasted building that hunches its shoulders against the biting westerlies that sweep down the Swale. A few months ago, the crew filming yet another Bronte epic here had given up, this part of the Dales judged too harsh a location to serve as the blasted heath of *Wuthering Heights*. The Bel-Air Heathcliff and Cathy, horrified on first putting Hollywood toes outside their Winnebagos, had according to rumour upped to settings further south.

Arriving in the exposed carpark - blue-grey shale chippings; tufts of grasses clinging on in sheltered corners in the driving rain - Fisher quickly grasps its attraction as refugee hostel. Nobody else wants it.

Standing in the foyer, she understands why Sofia Kovalenko walked out never to return. The hall is grimy. The wood-chip wallpaper, despite a recent coat of emulsion, is dogeared and ragged; gloss paint splashed on skirting boards with little thought or pride. She rings a bell next to a hatch knocked through into what would once have been the front room. On sliding open, the glass partition separating clientele from management shudders, no doubt actively considering leaping from a runner whose rubber fixings are brittle and crumbling. The resulting screeching grates, a fingernail down blackboard moment that seemingly has little effect on the man opening it, a hand placed in support of the glass ensuring it doesn't make its threatened getaway.

'Now then,' the man states to Fisher and Demetriou in official North Yorkshire greeting.

'North Yorkshire CID,' Fisher states through the stain of oily flesh where the man's hand had been placed on the glass.

'Oh ay?'

'We're interested in talking to anyone who knows this woman.' At a nod, Demetriou produces a grainy immigration photograph. 'Sofia Kovalenko. She's booked in here. Hasn't been back for a week or more.'

'Ay. That's right. We reported her t' immigration. Said it weren't their concern. It were Social Welfare. Told them, and they said it were Health authority. Health lot said it were police matter. I'm not surprised it took you so long to get here. Don't you lot talk to each other?' he asks.

'That, Mr...'

'Ambrose. Graham Ambrose. Clerk and Chief Dogsbody. Title's Warden if you need it for t' report.'

'Mr. Ambrose. May we call you Graham?'

He nods, watching Demetriou tap it into his phone.

'Graham. Lovely. As I was saying, that whole communication thing, Graham, is a matter of ongoing discussion. Seems we haven't got databases that talk to each other. Bloody AI. Seems they want less to do with each other than the folk running them. A bit...tribal if you follow?'

Ambrose tuts. 'Don't have to tell me. Same here. Have 't fill out forms in triplicate to get owt done. Then all that happens is it goes to some bloody committee who sit on it for months. I mean, look 't state of this window. Bloody health hazard right there,' he says, rattling the glass to back up his point.

'I know. I get it,' she responds tutting sympathy. 'But it's Sofia we're here about. She's a matter of some concern so we're keen to find out all we can about her. Get to the bottom of things, so to speak.'

'Not sure I can help. Barely spoke three words to her. She arrived. Checked in. Attended the house meeting the second night. Never really saw her much after that. I mean, she went off only a day or two after getting here. Christ knows where she is now!'

'You've kept her room, though?' Demetriou asks.

'Oh ay. That we have. Policy. But if she's not back by end of t' month it gets let out again. Stuff gets put in storage. If she's not back within three months, it gets sent off for charity or sold for whatever we can get. Usually sod all. I mean, who staying here's got owt worth having?'

Fisher smiles understanding. 'We'll need to have a look at her room, Graham.'

'Oh?' he risks a hand on his chin. 'Suppose...'

'It's procedure' she puts in. 'Helps us see if we can find out where she might have gone. You know, a letter or a card or something. An address book.'

'I thought it was all phones and clouds these days,' Graham muses.

'Well, you never know, but as we're already all the way out here don't you think it seems a waste if we don't?' she prompts.

'Okay. I'll get t' key.' He slides the window back into place, hand propping it upright on its return journey, before shuffling out of sight to whatever cupboard or draw he keeps the keys in.

'Is this strictly legal?' Demetriou asks.

'*Strictly Legal*? What's that? A solicitor's dance team?'

'We don't have a warrant, Ma'am. It could be argued it's a compromised search. Anything we find-'

'...Is better than what we've got. Which is sod all.'

Demetriou sighs his concern then moves to the side, checking the noticeboard, scanning handwritten pleas for lifts into town, the bright *Word* Template flyers for fruit or vegetable picking illustrated with clip art of smiling strawberries and happy carrots. There's an advert for farm clearance work alongside mobile hairdressing services. 'Looks like a full social calendar,' he observes. 'Hardly the land of dreams, is it?'

'Sorry?' she asks.

'This,' he taps the board. 'They make long dangerous journeys here for what? Slaving for *Captain Birdseye* or whatever. How desperate must you be?'

Graham appears in the hall with the key. 'I blame TV. The films. They grow up watching that Hollywood shite - *Pretty Woman* and the rest. They think once they get here, they'll find true love. You know, *The Princess Bride*, the happy ever after. The traffickers, well... its bread and butter to them. The girls almost recruit themselves. I'm told the traffickers just stand by the ramps, tickets in hand like bloody Pied Pipers. Young girls swallowing the dream.'

'You're saying it's their fault?' Fisher asks.

Graham shakes his head. 'It's this bloody world. Messed up. Broken.' He points for them to follow him up the stairs. 'Me? I'm just tired of sweeping up the pieces.'

'It's hardly Leeds, is it, Ma'am? Birmingham. Streets of the Big City,' Demetriou mumbles to Fisher.

She stops, turning to face him. 'What, you think, that because there's sheep and fields it's the *Waltons*?' She shakes her head. 'You've a good deal to learn DS Demetriou. The question I'm asking myself right now is whether I've the time, energy, or inclination to bother teaching it you.'

11

The search of Sofia's room yielded little in the way of clues. Little in the way of anything. Her belongings were meagre: a hold-all with changes of underwear, a few tee-shirts, pair of jeans and the expected feminine collection of lipstick, tampons, and hairbrush.

On Fisher's instruction, they'd opted for a slower route back, a vertigo inducing road over Buttertubs that winds down into Wensleydale, where they've stopped at a local farm shop, the attached cafe serving a range of homemade meals along with coffee and cake. Time out. The chance to re-think ways of progressing their enquiries. Time to play a game of *Detour or Brick Wall*; temporary setback or dead-end.

Fisher sits at a farmhouse table updating ideas in her notebook. It isn't that she's analogue, but experience shows paper and pen to be a more reliable tool when at any second a digital connection is liable to drift away on the winds that swoop through the upper and middle Dales.

Demetriou arrives with flat whites and pastries. 'What's with the Llamas?' he asks, placing a coffee and a cake in front of her.

'Tourists.'

'Tourists?' He arches an eyebrow. 'Sheep I can understand. Never seen so many pictures of sheep,' he says indicating racks of souvenir postcards. 'And paintings. But it's the Dales, so only to be expected. Like pictures of the Tower in Blackpool or the Pride parade in Brighton. But llamas? Why are there llamas in the paddock?' He'd been unnerved at the discovery from the moment they'd turned into the farm shop car park and they'd popped their heads above the dry-stone walls that line the driveway.

'They're turning it into a nursery in the New Year,' she tells him. 'Tourism's drying up now folk can get abroad again. Llamas were an attraction, will be for the nursery kids. Wait till you stop at Mainsgill. They've got camels.'

Demetriou's frown suggests he's uncertain if it's a wind up.

'So,' she begins, 'back to the matter in hand. Sofia. Is she our Jane Doe? What would the Big Trouser Boys in Brum do next?'

Demetriou considers his coffee. He notes that Fisher, despite not taking sugar, is a stirrer, spoon blending milk and coffee into an off-white shade of what Jessica would know to be *Elephant's Ear* or *Mouse Back*. He thinks maybe he should call her, add another to the ten or so unanswered calls he'd made last night, the five unreturned voice mails he's sent that morning.

'So,' Fisher encourages, tapping her spoon against the rim of the cup. 'Is there an answer brewing, or is this you getting in touch with your inner *Peaky Blinders*?'

'Sorry, ma'am. Just…I don't know. Maybe back to *MisPers*.'

'Hmm. I was hoping for something a little more…insightful. I know it's only our first day, and I can hardly hope for Derren Brown, but I must admit my thoughts were set a bit higher than a *back to where we started* idea. Maybe you've got your *"walking the cat back"* wrong. Maybe your inner moggie's not what it was.'

'Sorry, ma'am. Just…I mean it's…different. Takes time to get used to. Here.'

'It's hardly *Escape to the Country*. I'm talking ideas not geography. Surely even the Peaky Blinders expected something more than repeating everything you'd just done.'

'Yes. Of course. Ideas, I mean. I had them…Have them, lots

of them. Good ones.' He frowns. 'What I said about getting used to things…I meant…Me. This change. Moving. The Support Group.'

'Pan, let's get off the *woe is me* theme park ride, shall we?' She sips her coffee. 'Anyway, if we're going to be comparing who's the most fucked up and fucked around in our little therapy venture, I can give you a head start. A good long one.'

'Can I speak freely, Ma'am?'

'You can speak even freer if you cut out all the Ma'am stuff when we're not in front of Joe and Jane Public or the other troops. I mean, Christ, it makes me sound like your mom or something.'

'What *do* I call you? I mean, I know your name's Zara, but that's for Support Group. I can't do that out here. Zara, I mean.'

'Well "boss" or "gaffer" or "guv" or any of those *Sweeney* things if it makes you feel better. Least they don't sound ageist or sexist, which is ironic when you think about it, given where they come from.'

'Okay. Guv it is.'

'Good. So, speak freely.'

'Truth is…' he stops. Shakes his head. 'It'll sound like a whinge – and I'm not a whinger.'

'Okay. You're not a whinger. But?'

He sits forward. 'Everything's mad. The whole incident with my DI back in Brum. My transfer was "take it or leave it". And it's not like I had the pick of posts. It was here and Pemberton's Support Group or out on my ear.'

'Well punching the lights out of your DI was never going to be a great career move,' she points out helpfully.

'It wasn't just the fact he was my DI. It was who my DI was.'

She leans in. 'So, he's what, the Chief Constable's son or something?'

'He was screwing my girlfriend.'

She sits back. 'So that's why you punched him. I mean, given that bit of insider knowledge, I can see your point. It hardly seems fair. You being the one having to transfer. Surely you told Complaints in Brum, and they understood the provocation. That it was…personal. That it wasn't about work. Why were you the one getting punished for what's to all intents and purposes a domestic?'

'Yeah except for the fact that it *was* about work. I punched him because he screwed over my best informant. He messed up, let slip my CI's identity to a bigger criminal fish he was trying to land. He got careless because his eyes were fixed on his next promotion. Result of his negligence is she was thrown off a tower block. She's in a wheelchair. I lost it.'

'Especially knowing what you knew about him and your girlfriend,' Fisher summarises.

Demetriou nods. 'No way I could work in the same force after that. The Chief Super was clear on that. He could live with the one dispute, he said, but not the other. So here I am.'

'And your girlfriend?'

'Jessica?' He looks to his coffee. 'She moved him in.'

'That's harsh,' she judges, lifting her cake.

'Worse. I'm still paying the mortgage.'

'For Christs' sake!' she guffaws, almost choking on her Danish. 'What're you thinking?'

'She's selling up. We're selling up. He's let his flat go whilst they sort out a place together. It's just…convenient.'

'I bet it is,' she states, after sipping her coffee.

'What can I do? She's just been made redundant. She can't pay her share of the mortgage, but her name's on the deeds, she owns half the place. I'm up here, so I can't live there, and I can't buy her out or pay all the mortgage what with having to rent somewhere here - and I don't want a re-possession on my credit score.'

'So, he's paying her share of the mortgage,' Fisher says.

'Sort of. He's paying her a rent.' He holds a hand up. 'I know, but I don't want anything official, him on the mortgage thinking he can have a say. Wouldn't be right.'

'But her being poked by him in your bed's okay?'

'I wouldn't put it like that.'

'Clearly.' She exhales. 'So, I'm stuck with Mr. Nice.'

'My membership of the Anger Management Group suggests otherwise.'

'But you've just told me that you're a fraud. You're not really Mr. Angry at all. You had a perfectly good justification for punching the bloke, DI or not.' She finishes her coffee. 'I know people who would have murdered him, come to think of it they'd have most likely murdered her too. Wait till Malcolm finds out; his head will spin like *the Exorcist.*'

'Don't say anything, please.'

'Why not? You don't belong there.' She shakes her head. 'Thought you'd be glad to get a free pass, an early release out of the sessions. You know, over the wire. Freedom and all that.'

'Maybe you could give it a few weeks before you say anything. You see...right now...Well, you're the only people I know here. The only thing I'm part of.'

'It's not a club, you know. It's not like we're a secret society. The Freemasons. The Famous Five or anything. We're dangerous people, Pan. Violent, angry people,' she says, clenching a fist and waving it in the air.

'The only thing getting damaged in that group is the ACC's chocolate bars. Maybe Malcolm's self-esteem,' Demetriou states.

'What? You're saying you don't see me as the violent kind?'

'After what I heard...That DCS you had a go at about impeding your investigation of that rape case? Then no, I don't see you as just angry.' He looks her in the eyes. 'I think you had every right to say what you did. I mean, I literally punched my boss, you just called yours a wanker. Unless there's' something I don't know, something I don't know about you that is, Guv.'

'DS Demetriou, there's a great deal you don't know about me. I'm a bit like the camels at Mainsgill - real and true yet completely unexpected and unimaginable.'

The city can be a cruel and demanding mistress. Like most women she promises everything, guarantees nothing. Fickle and coquettish, moods changing quicker than the lights on Hollywood and Vine, she teases only to pull you deeper in.

And this morning she'd woken playful. A lazy, languid cat like stretch of her limbs, warm and comforting. Today would be a good day, she seemed to say, maybe one of her better ones, she promised. Come on, she whispered. You might get lucky.

And like a fool I'd believed her.

A few days ago, Donna told me I was cynical. The work I do, the things I see, well, that's hardly surprising, it goes with the territory – but it rankled, and I was determined to show her she was wrong. Leaving my apartment this morning, the sun was shining, its bright rays touching the spires of the old church on Mulholland and Vine. The day was looking to be a good one. I was neat, clean shaved, and sober for the first time in a week. Powder-blue suit, dark blue shirt, deep blue tie with matching display handkerchief. Black brogues, black wool socks. At that moment, walking down that sun kissed street, it was already harder to recall just how bad things had hit on my last case, how bad Laura had hit my life.

It had taken the best part of a week to clear my head of Laura Carmichael. Today was going to be the first day that I could start to think of getting things back to normal, whatever normal means, all the time knowing it would take more than a week to shake something like Laura away. More than the seven days I'd just spent hiding in the bottom of a bottle.

But I had an appointment and a reputation to preserve. A reputation for professionalism was among the many names LA's finest in blue threw my way along with tough, stubborn, righteous, ruthless and hard boiled. I couldn't argue with any of them. The cops had seen all those sides of me, and now they were like a business card for those searching for someone with my specialist services. Services pulling them out of whatever hole they'd found themselves in.

Arriving in my office I right away began to understand that whatever I'd promised myself the day was about to blow up in my face...

The door had been open. It didn't shock me that much; Donna sometimes got in early. But a cold coffee pot told me it wasn't one of those mornings. That and the thin man sitting in my chair indicated something different was going on, as did the man standing to the side of him. Big and ugly, with the hands of a prize-fighter, huge paws at the end of thick arms. Here was a man built for effect, his build a warning. Do not mess with me.

'Good morning,' the man behind the desk said. It was more of a whisper. Breathy. Part way between a snake hiss and a lover's sigh. It drew my attention straight away as did the eyes. Dark, like the remains of a burnt-out fire. The sense there'd once been a spark in there, but it had been a flame maybe burning too bright and one long ago put out. The sense of defeat hung on him. It was in the shoulders that, despite the silver topped cane clasped in front of him as a sort of tripod fixing his body upright, still drooped. The hands clasped on the cane were liver-spotted and bony. It was a body on its way to dissolution - the grey flesh, the tight lips, the sagging jowls mottled with a yellow hue. He was a man not long for this world and so one deserving to be heard. That and the large, barrelled revolver gripped tight in one hand.

'Sit down, Mr. Mangrove. Don't worry about your secretary. She won't be interrupting us. Mr. Laskin here has seen to it that she's taking a little...break this morning.'

I fixed him with my best cold stare. 'If she's-'

He held up a hand. 'Have no fear, she's perfectly fine,' he whispered. 'And will remain so until we've completed our business here.'

I sat, settling into the visitor's chair. Now was not the time for heroics. These were men who knew what they were doing. I was intrigued as much as angered.

'I'm here because I have a job of work for you. Now listen carefully, Mr. Mangrove, I want you to-'

'Take out the bins! For Christ's sake, Neil! Why can't you just take out the bloody bins without me having to remind you!' The shout jolts Musgrove from his reverie. 'Can you hear me, Neil?' The pounding of Jean's feet on the stairs have him hitting the space bar, closing the Word window as she bursts in.

'How many times do I have to remind you - its Tuesdays!'

Neil swivels his chair to face her. 'What? he asks.

'Recycling. Garden waste. Tuesdays. Since the Bank holiday. They changed it.'

'Oh, yes. Yes, I know. I was going to do it. Next on the list. Before bed.'

'You said that last time, but I was the one ended up chasing the bloody bin van down the road pulling the damn thing after me. I looked right stupid. Christ knows what the neighbours thought of me as I walked back trundling the empty bin. Mrs. Franks was standing on her step. She pretended she hadn't been watching, but I know she had.'

'Sorry, love. I'll sort it right away,' he says rising.

'What are you up to anyway. You've been up here a couple of hours. Work?'

'Sort of. Yeah.'

'At least it's not that bloody stupid book idea. You and your pulp fiction. Writing a crime novel! I'd have thought you'd enough of that at work. Crime and criminals. Daft idea. Glad you've seen sense.'

'No dear. I mean, yes. It was...silly.'

She'd already turned away, leaving the converted bedroom, his study, Charlie's old room. 'I'm off to bed. See you in the morning. And don't forget the bins,' she calls.

He slumps back in the chair.

Last Easter. Good Friday to be precise. Her brother the *Moderately Successful Businessman Formerly Known as Wanker* had tugged Neil's dream from him. His ambition. Dragged it out from its hiding place, like Dumbledore teasing out a memory wrapped around a wand of ridicule. And they'd laughed, her brother and his wife. They'd all laughed. *Neil the form-filling policeman having an imagination!* They'd made comments about

Conan Doyle and Holmes - though clearly none of them knew which was which, or who was who. *Murder He Wrote* Clive had guffawed before almost choking on a Celebration toffee.

On the drive home Jean had been clear. *Stop all the stupidity. Get a proper hobby. Fishing. Golf. The Townshends have done so much better since Michael took up golf.* The clubbable-*ness* of it. The dances. The events. *Why was he writing stupid stories?* No one's going to read them.

He taps the space bar, stares at the screen. His words. His latest idea. He shakes his head at the stupidity of it, looks across at the image of Bogart, the *Maltese Falcon* poster he's framed and fixed to the wall: Bogart, gun in hand, upturned raincoat collar, hat tilted across one eye, sultry woman in red gazing adoringly up at him. 'Here's looking at you, Kid,' he whispers.

He looks at the monitor. Takes a beat before highlighting and deleting every word he's written. His once upon a time piece. His escape.

12

DS Lex Iverson scratches his head. It's a puzzle. A conundrum. The covered bloodstained mound on pristinely neat block paving has him stumped.

For the fifth or sixth time he steps a few paces away from the remains to look up to the edge of the roof, the spot from where the body has clearly fallen. A jumper or pushed? It's hard to tell.

The placement of the body offers indication as to the means by which it vacated the roof of the Harrogate Crowne Plaza Hotel. A straight down plummet would be typical of a suicide: decision made, don't look down and one quick step. But a splatter further out from the building suggests a fall impelled by propulsion, someone pushing the body out and away from the roof's edge. Unless, of course, the suicide was looking to go out via a spectacular run-up and cannonball dive.

Standing against the wall in shelter from the rain, he looks up the dozen or so levels to the roof's edge. All he discovers is that craning his neck like that hurts and the rain gets in your face. So, he stops.

He steps towards the corpse, considering the twelve storeys from a fresh angle. Hand to brow as shield from the downpour, he gazes up, trying out the maths of it in his head, the basics of half-forgotten trigonometry. He shakes his head in frustration. Hard to tell.

He drops his hand, squeezing his eyes open and shut to get some sense of vision back. The SOCOs would measure it out once they arrive, enter the data onto iPads, their algorithm software working out the probabilities. It was percentages. Solve the equation, get the mathematical probabilities of jump or shoved high enough and it would be good enough for the coroner, eradicating the *might haves* or any *could possibly bes* of it.

It was old law. Newton or whoever. Every action has a reaction, he thinks - something about equals and opposites in there too, but that was just colouring in. Showing off. The essential premise remained. If the coroner found grounds for doubt it would require police time and money chasing it down, and he knows from experience that Senior Coroner Phillip Waddingham is a bureaucrat with a bureaucrat's mind. His background is law, not medicine. Like every bureaucrat he's ever met, Waddingham hates uncertainty, craves clarity. Above all else Waddingham seeks plausible deniability should the world come crashing down on a verdict and threaten whatever honour it is he covets. He requires positions to take, something the SOCO's calculations provide and Waddingham invariably accepts.

The certainty is that it wasn't an accident. Even at this stage of the investigation there appears to be no compelling reason for the man to have been on the roof. The Crowne Plaza and all of its twelve floors have no known or obvious connection to events or people in the life of Harrison Wrigley, eminent solicitor of the Royal Borough of Harrogate.

There is no legal business pending, no personal association with the hotel or its staff. He may have been visiting a guest but there's no evidence of that being the case and no-one has as yet come forward to say different. The CCTV footage shows him walking into the hotel lobby and crossing to the lifts. Less than ten minutes later, the roof access alarm had tripped, and soon after that his body had hit the pavement. Who could he have met in so short a space of time? You don't have a five-minute legal conference or friendly chat and then jump off a roof.

The staff are unanimous, it takes ten minutes to get from reception to the roof, the last part of the journey involving a maintenance stairwell which means passing through doors alarmed at both ends of a flight of stairs. In short, you couldn't get there by accident.

For whatever reason, ten minutes after entering the hotel, Harrison Wrigley had made that climb. It left two questions. Why had he made the journey to the roof, and was he alone?

Iverson steps back for another look around.

The scene is busier. It's morning rush-hour, and even in a town like Harrogate in the rain, it means a significant increase in the number of pedestrians making their way to nearby offices. Pedestrians halting, staring, distracted by police tape and the gathering of emergency services. It means mobile phone cameras and social media. It means increasing the pace of his investigation, the actions of everyone here now awaiting his instruction. His.

The duty coroner has completed his business. The headline: Harrison Wrigley is dead. Surprise. Cause of death to be determined at the autopsy required whenever an unexplained or suspicious death occurs. Wrigley clearly fell into the latter. Literally. The cause isn't open to much doubt. It was a long way down, certainly a fall the human body is not designed to prevail in. Gravity One - Human body parts that can be broken or squished - nil. The coroner would fill in the relevant forensic details; was he high or drunk? Was he medicated for depression?

Having completed his initial assessment of *"he's dead"* - and paid by the event rather than the hour - the medical coroner has departed for pastures and claimable hours anew. The Book is clear. The body and the scene are Iverson's to do with as he must. It's now his decision. His pressure. His.

He looks down the ramp to the King's Road, the major

thoroughfare bounding one side of the pizza pie slice that makes up the Convention Centre site. The Crowne Plaza takes up most of the side facing Springfield road, the Premier Inn a chunk of the other.

The body lies towards a flight of steps serving as pedestrian access to one of the Centre's entrances. Wrigley has fallen onto a curved access ramp running between the two buildings, narrowly missing the suspended glass walkway linking hotel to halls. The Plaza is a plum site, the adjacent Conference Centre attracting political party gatherings and concerts as well as business and trade exhibitions. The last thing the town needs flooding social media are images of a dead body lying on the convention centre steps.

That one of the halls has been requisitioned as boots-on-the-ground command centre by the intelligence services for the Webb murder investigation is an additional consideration. The nearby entrance is about to see the arrival of scores of secret service operatives starting the fourth day of the hunt for terrorist attackers. The lack of progress in that matter is more than a little embarrassing for North Yorkshire Police in general and its Chief Constable and Crime Commissioner in particular. The idea of outside agencies being forced to shuffle past a dead body is no-one's idea of good inter-service PR. He's heard that Special Branch and Five are pushing to take over all aspects of the case, Spooks popping up here, there, and everywhere. But mainly and for Iverson more worryingly, here.

The most compelling yet unspoken question surrounding Webb's death is why there has been no claim of responsibility. It isn't that they can't come up with potential perpetrators, the numbers were lining up around the block. There are far-left protestors blaming the PM for all things Brexit and the consequences assailing the country let alone anti-war protestors, anti-immigration groups, far-right Neo-Fascists, and weird far-right Q-Anon-*ists*. Even the climate activists had legions of the violent minded, a military wing of their eco campaigning. And all before he even got to thinking about Islamic state, those still active members of the IRA, or the 'Lone wolves', the lunatics espousing every crackpot idea you could think of. Not to mention cold and bitter pensioners who'd shown the capacity to get nasty with anyone who threatened their triple lock pension or winter fuel allowance. There are rumours of a military wing among those too, though taking out the PM might be considered extreme, not to mention too demanding of their attention span. Whoever they might be, whatever their cause, there should have been a hand up by now, a claim of responsibility.

As for whatever is going on inside the hall - the Command Team strategising - he's stuck outside in the pouring rain with the blob that was Harrison Wrigley, frontline of a suicide becoming a PR disaster.

He's already received a string of messages from Crosby and Hyland to get things moving. *Why hasn't he got the body away? Why hasn't the scene been scrubbed of all trace of what happened?* Wrigley's death, whatever the cause, is an embarrassment to be shovelled aside as quickly as possible, like sweeping up litter.

Lost in pondering, his phone rings. Fumbling to answer, he notes the display *North'ton HQ*.

'Bugger!' he mutters, thumbing the respond tab. The Commissioner's Office has already been on, Harvey Lawrence indicating the PR nightmare of the delay, reminding Lex three times that it's "your decision." He could of course, save unnecessary time and trouble, not to mention manpower, by releasing the scene to the clean-up crew currently sat in a van at the bottom of the ramp eating bacon butties, but it was "your decision, Detective Sergeant." Hargreaves herself has been on, indirectly reminding him of the impact on CID's budget of every minute he holds the relevant crews up, along with the veiled comment that he should be sure to forget about "*the impact on hotel guests, tourists and commercial clients and the like. The good name of the town.*" No pressure.

'Iverson?' the unmistakable tone of DCS Crosby trills down

the line, if of course they still used lines, which Iverson is sure they don't. A call from Crosby is never good news. If the Four Horsemen ever found themselves with a vacancy, this was the man with the bedside manner, let alone CV for the post.

'Yes, sir. DS Iverson here.'

'As I rang your bloody phone I should fucking well hope it is and that you are.' There's a beat enabling Iverson, if he is in any doubt at all, to realise that Crosby has a 4G arse-kicking to be executed. 'What the fuck is going on?'

'Well, sir. At the present moment-'

'That was fucking rhetorical, you turd!' Crosby blasts. 'I know what's going on. I'm the fucking DCS. I know everything. What you had for breakfast. Your favourite colour. The fact that your arsing around is costing CID a shit load of money, not to mention holding up the work of those a damn sight more professionally useful to me "at the present moment". The road sweepers, the shit cleaners and the caterers to name but three.'

'Yes sir. Sorry sir. But I think-'

'There we go. There's the problem right there! God save me from Detective Sergeants who think they think!' Crosby snarls in full-on arse-chewing mode. 'I don't want to know what you think, Sergeant. I know what you think. In fact, I'll do you a favour and tell you what you think. You think it's suicide. You think it's some poor twat who couldn't sort out his sad lonely life. Someone whose mommy never loved him or whose boyfriend just left him. Some sad fucker whose Daddy never hugged him. And because you think that, you can now release the body so that the clean-up crew can get on with removing it. Then, Sergeant, your sole focus will be in getting the scene disinfected before the nine o' clock rush of Spooks and Metropolitan analyst wankers - no doubt currently finishing their crushed avocado on sourdough – make an appearance! Are we clear?'

'Yes sir. But I just-'

'What you *just* want is to sign this off and get back on the

Webb case, maybe following up on that Kendra Webb statement. Whatever it is, it's a case that will prove a damn sight more influential on your future than some lawyer's suicide.'

It didn't need interpretation. It was an order disguised as delegation. The fact that Crosby knows about crushed avocado or even sourdough is a thought for other, less stressful times.

'Tell you what, Detective Sergeant,' Crosby continues. 'If it makes your decision easier, I'm about to re-assign any follow up of what you've just declared to be a straightforward suicide to another officer. They'll be the ones accounting to Waddingham about the following of established crime scene procedure. That newbie. The Greek bloke. Pan *What-you-me-call-it*. The Brummie. He could do with familiarising himself with the ropes around here, see how things are done Yorkshire style, wouldn't you say?'

'Yes sir. Very much so,' Iverson responds, wondering if prayers really do get answered.

'That's settled. You sign things off there and I'll get the paperwork through.' He snorts. 'He's paired with Fisher, and both are in the Pemberton looney-tunes thing. Do her a bit of good. Feet on the ground, trim her wings. They're already dealing with one suicide so they might as well have another, an investigational BOGOF. Pair of broken wings, the two of them.'

'Yes sir. Very much so.' Iverson agrees.

The line went dead.

Iverson considers the call. The ups. The downs.

The up is obvious, his being in what passes for the good grace of DCS Crosby and not pissing off the Chief Constable or the Commissioner. On top of that, he's snaffled a spot on the Webb murder, the glamour of a major investigation. The CV of every detective involved is guaranteed to orbit higher in the CID firmament, a dusting of career glitter and sparkle.

The downs, too, are simple: he's taking a professional punt that Wrigley's death is suicide. It certainly has the look of one, and any later evidence to the contrary, any blow-back will now go the way of the officer left holding the case file, Demetriou. A case of professional SIO pass-the -parcel. It was shitty - all the paperwork along with the chance of public and professional rollicking's from Waddingham about due process etcetera. - but the new bloke is new. It isn't as if he's any brotherly sense towards him. He'd not even a nickname yet. He's just boring DS Pan Demetriou.

For the first time this morning, he smiles. What was it Crosby had called them? *Broken Wings.*

13

He's tired. Tired of the not sleeping and tired of carrying a head full of Jessica. Tired of the dreams that haunt his waking and tired of those that arrive when sleep does come. Right now, he's tired of being stuck in whatever emotional waiting room hell this is, not to mention being tired of police-work that's become a monotonous paper chase, no matter the rural beauty of the drives they'd made through the different dales whose names he'd been unable to keep up with. Most of all, he's tired of the chaos his move here has brought with it.

Could it have been a worse start? The meeting; Malcolm; the group of broken people? The sense he'd been marked out even before having the chance to show who he is, what he can do. The growing sense that the officers he'd met, the ones in the Therapy Group, confirm a suspicion he's had for some time now. That policing has become a profession so full of its own anger and guilt that it's better thought of as a poorly organised cult, one whose members have gathered together in the hope of finding answers to their own personal woes and travails rather than being thought of as a force for law and order or - God forbid – justice!

He looks at the read out on his phone. 7:00 am. Just time to shower and shave and find the last of the ironed shirts he's brought with him. The realisation he's a weekend of laundry to look forward to, along with grocery shopping. There's a *Tesco* somewhere out Catterick way, so he's been told, and according to *Google* a couple of grocers and delis scattered around smaller towns of Leyburn and Hawes. Maybe he'll shop there, support local businesses. All the things he and Jessica used to talk about - farmer's markets and craft fairs.

He checks his messages. Nothing. The double ticks indicate the ones he's sent have been delivered. Nine of them, like the lives of a cat, the feeling he's looking at what Fisher dubbed his inner dead moggie.

He gazes around the bathroom. From where he sits on the loo it looks okay. Floor to ceiling tiles, glossy and white. Behind him, the wall above the bath is painted dark green, a sash window letting in the autumn light. Jessica would love it. At least would have, the real Jessica, the one he'd known and loved for more than three years. He's no longer certain he can speak for the new Jessica, her changing taste in men the most obvious indication of the transformation she's made.

He makes a final flick through his news feed. Locally it's the Webb murder, the idea taking hold of a bungled attack on the PM rather than Webb as the target is getting out. He wonders how the dead man's family feel about that. Cause of death: bungling incompetence.

And here he is, hardly in the eye of the whirlwind, more *the Slough of Despond*. Chasing pointless answers to a suicide making him officially up to his ears in sad. Every detail about the woman's lonely, desperate suicide - the empty life it points to, - has been gifted to Fisher and himself to document. They're Keepers of Souls, crossing the *i*'s and dotting the *t*'s of despair and rejection.

The Slough of Despond. Where'd that come from? A-level English? Ironic, given that it was Bunyan's fictional bog into which man sank under the weight of his sins. He smiles at the irony - him here sat on a bog in North Yorkshire as the result of his own sins.

His email pings.

He opens it. *Crosby*. The Detective Chief Super. *What could he want at this hour?* Maybe he's reassigning him? Maybe everything Fisher said about working together is bullshit. *She's having him transferred.* He should have seen it, read it in her reactions over the past few days. He's heard of her reputation of being distant, being cold and unfeeling - the nicknames attached to her. And he's discovered for himself she can be hard work, something that till now he's put down to markers being laid out, roles defined. He even thinks he's seen chinks of a lighter tone in her manner towards him. She's been decent about Jessica. She clearly finds his actions around that whole relationship make him a bit of a wanker, but she's also shown understanding. "*Love makes us all wankers,*" she'd said at one point yesterday.

He opens the message. The assignment of a new case. Harrison Wrigley, a solicitor who's taken a short walk off a tall building in Harrogate. Brief and to the point, Crosby's logic is of Pan's involvement in the investigation of one suicide meaning he might as well have another. A BOGOF. A criminal TWOFER.

He scans the basic details Crosby has included, the rest to follow later, forwarded from the attending officer on the scene, DS Iverson.

Another bloody suicide! What is he? *Keeper of the Dead? Watchman of the Sad and Lonely? Duke of the Depressed?*

Is it part of his punishment? If so, it seems wrong that he's been assigned to Fisher, yet, at the same time, from the HR perspective, perversely right: a pairing keeping maverick officers with anger issues together and more easily contained. Where he goes, she goes and vice-versa, an arrangement keeping both from mainstream investigations. Sidelined. Damage limitation of damaged coppers, him thinking maybe there's a collective noun for it.

He puts the phone on the low dividing wall that runs by the

side of the toilet. It's the second time he's got Fisher wrong. She hasn't double-crossed him.

He's barely put the phone down when it rings. He picks it up. *Fisher.*

'Yes Guv?' he responds.

'What the fuck's going on?' she demands.

'Sorry, Guv. Not sure I understand.'

She pauses. '...Where are you?'

'Home.'

'...Where at home?'

'...Getting ready for work.'

'That echo, sounds like you're in the bathroom,' she tells him.

'Yes. I am.'

'Oh god! You're not answering this on the lavvy, are you?'

'...Just finishing shaving. Brushing my hair,' he lies.

'The thought of talking while you're on the loo is too much before breakfast. Especially on top of this Crosby thing.'

'The suicide?' he asks

'Yes, the suicide. Or should I say, second suicide so as not to confuse things. I've just had a text from our beloved DCS. Don't know how he does it, but even in a text he comes across as smug and gloating. He ought to have his own emoji.'

'I've just had the email. A lawyer in Harrogate,' he tells her.

'We've already got Kovalenko. Are you playing *Suicide Snap* or *Unhappy Families* with Crosby and the rest of CID and not telling me? You know, collect the set or whatever it is you boys do with your *Panini* stickers,' she wonders.

'I'm as much in the dark as you, Guv. In fact, I was hoping you could put me straight about what's happening. I mean, why me?' he asks.

'When you say, *why me*, you need to remember that whatever shit they shovel onto your plate, I get a serving too, she reminds him. 'We're both looking at the Kovalenko suicide. You being given this solicitor means I have to tag along to eat my share of it whilst you chomp down yours.'

'Didn't think about that,' he admits.

'Yes, well, whatever your other failings may be – your anger issues, your weird sex triangles – it appears this one's not your fault. Who took the call-out?'

'Iverson,' he says, hoping to end the conversation as soon as is practicable.

'Iverson!' She makes a plosive sound down the line. 'Pah! Might have known. Bloke's so far up the DCS's arse it'd take a search team to show him the way out. The smarmy little wanker's got himself on the Webb investigation. Bit of a cling-on by all accounts, him interviewing the grieving sexy widow and family. Shoving this investigation to you means Crosby's demonstrating to Hargreaves, and the Spooks that he's focusing his best efforts on Webb with all the routine stuff downgraded to us lesser mortals stuck on the CID naughty step. Plays better with Webb's investors, all of whom are no doubt members of Crosby's golf club, you know, Masons able to give him a leg-up. He'll tell them he's dropping everything to solve it. *Got my best chaps on it* and all that bollocks. Iverson gets to play Sherlock and we broddle around the morgue with Creepy Crawley's band of ghouls.'

'Creepy Crawley?' he asks.

'Ah, of course, you've not yet had the pleasure of the good doctor,' she recalls. 'Creepy is a bit of a legend. Hit on me during my first autopsy. Him standing there holding the guts and liver of some elderly hit and run victim in his sweaty palms, and he straight up asks me out.'

'Christ!' he exclaims.

'Yeah. Asked if I wanted to go for a drink. Maybe a meal. I mean, him stood there with an armful of gory and bloody inside bits dribbling over his apron didn't exactly have me in the mood for an Italian.' She sighs exaggeratedly. 'Ah, my girlish eyes still mist up at the romance of it! A young girl's dream is Creepy. At least his own very moist ones.'

'Surprised you didn't report him,' he says.

'Different times, Pan,' she replies 'You know...what is it they say? *You had to be there to understand.*'

'Even so...'

'Oh, don't you go getting jealous,' there's the sense of a smile emerging in her tone. 'You thinking you're going to be left out of Creepy's Autopsy Funhouse. Creepy swings both ways. You know, plays for both sides.'

'Ah,' he says, realisation falling like a penny being dropped.

'Yes,' she confirms. 'Seems he's got all modern in his old age. He's an equal opportunities pervert. More of a *hashtagyoutoo* sort of creep. I warn you, Pan, if you feel the sensation of a cold hand squeezing your groin at any point during an autopsy, the likelihood is you'll be right. It'll be Creepy's.'

Pan shudders.

'Anyway, at least we can save some time, get them booked as a two for one autopsy. You know like Avenger's films. *Suicide Solution: Part 1 and Part 2.* We'll check if there's any overnight's about Kovalenko then get across to Harrogate and see about this Wrigley fella.'

'Okay, Guv.'

'Ooh, pick up a coffee from *Café Nero* on the way. Maybe a muffin, too,' she tells him.

'Right you are.'

'Oh, and Pan.'

'Guv?'

'Don't forget to wash your hands.'

14

Late Autumn, the season when late morning sun washes the stone of Harrogate a buttery yellow, burnishes the copper-purple tones of the slates and shingle of Montpellier, the spires of the nearby Kursaal.

Today it has rained heavy and hard, the sun hesitant, tiptoeing to the edge of rooftops. There it remains, teetering and doubtful, unwilling to take the final step into the shadows of the streets and alleyways below, wary of what lurks there. Today, much like a predator that comes across prey intent on turning the tables, the sun seems to retreat, backs away puzzled and afraid.

For John Gill, looking out of his second-floor office window through the etched copper lettering of *Archibald Gill and Son Publishing*, such things are portents. He tries shrugging the thought away, busying himself sifting the morning post of a failing family business, an imprint of nursery rhymes and folk tales finding itself in dire need of a handful of magic beans, maybe a goose or two laying golden eggs.

Since the death of their flagship talent, Gillian Brightside – an illustrator once described by *Publishing Weekly* as '*the Picasso of Illustration*' – the business has spent the last ten years embattled by market forces, a decline that is the result of a dependency on the now tainted reputation of a woman who's catalogue old Archibald Gill had steadfastly refused to lose control over.

Tearing open a FINAL DEMAND, John Gill ruminates on the tricksy nature of words like dependable. Times change. Trends, whim, fancy – elements that have crashed wave-like on the shores of *Archibald Gill and Son* with its dogged reliance on the work of a single client.

A decade ago, Brightside's sales had slumped. *Gill and Son's* stock plummeting accordingly, a cautionary tale of the failure to diversify, of the perils of personal loyalty at the expense of good business.

She'd passed soon after the slump in her sales had begun, twilight years spiralling her into chemical addictions offering temporary escape from the advance of obscurity, her final years spent hermit-like amid rumours of drugs, alcohol, and depression that dragged her brand ever further down.

Unlike a dead painter or a drug addled pop star, Brightside's passing failed to spark renewed interest in her work. It hadn't helped that there'd been little in the way of obituaries. Her last ever interview in a *Sunday Supplement* a decade ago had seen to that. Her right of right views had always been tricky issues to circumvent at book launches, Gill himself spending such events plying reviewers with drink aplenty in the hope of averting attention from her Neo-fascist ramblings. Securing the magazine feature had been a coup, in truth, a final desperate fling, *Archibald Gill and Son's* last hope of re-igniting interest in Gillian Brightside, legendary folklorist and children's illustrator.

It had been a nightmare.

Her reliance on prescription painkillers, alcohol, and cocaine had conflated with her politics to create a PR disaster. The *Sunday Times* article had focused on her mental state rather than her work. Her vitriolic views on refugees, trans-issues, and the Labour Party had provoked widespread condemnation. It was the biggest PR *faux pas* since the reviewer on the maiden voyage of the Titanic telegraphed home a feature for *the Times* extolling its unsinkable-ness. Her death generated a short piece in *the Guardian*. As well as managing to get the name of her best seller wrong, its few hundred words focused renewed attention on the loathsome political views of her diminishing years.

Tugging his jacket tightly around him, the heating turned off some weeks ago, Gill returns to looking out of the window. The sun, trembling on the edge of the rooftop opposite, looks back. *You know why I'm afraid*, it says, hunkering away from the ledge. And he does.

A few months ago, Archibald's hallucinatory death bed confession had been a fantasy as dark and grotesque as any in Brightside's books - a tale John Gill dismissed as the fevered ramblings of a dying man. Now, he finds it an account he can no longer ignore, his father's story of terrible deeds, nor his warning of the dreadful fate awaiting sinners, of monsters demanding bloody payment.

A worrying call taken last night has stirred that discomfort. A friend of his father's begging to meet. A rambling call, the man's manner disjointed and anxious, a drunk telling the same tale as Archibald's dying confession. The claim of a dark secret, a terrible truth they must confront if they are to escape the monster he says is coming to claim them.

That he was once his father's business associate and one of his oldest friends, meant he'd listened patiently but with scepticism. Ending it by saying that although he was thankful for the call, tying up old Archibald's mess of an estate means he's far too busy to meet, that he's had more than enough of old men and their tall tales.

Now he finds himself forced to re-consider. This morning his car had been delayed, stuck in a traffic jam created by a crowd that had gathered at the bottom of the street. A terrible accident. The later discovery that his late-night caller has jumped from the roof of the Plaza Hotel.

'He's a big one.'
'Massive.'
'...I mean... must have hit with a hell of a...'
'...Splat?' Fisher offers.
Demetriou considers the idea. 'Makes him sound like a cartoon. You know. Bugs Bunny. Road Runner.'
'Except Wile E. Coyote always gets back up.'
'...Maybe he should have used an umbrella.'
'...Umbrella?'
'The cartoons. You know. He always hovers in mid-air for a second or two then produces an umbrella from somewhere - like it's a parachute or something. He looks at you, ...sort of helpless, then falls like a stone.'

The soft whump of the doors' rubber seal puts an end to whispered speculations that had begun as soon as they'd entered the autopsy room to be confronted by the mound of what they know to be Harrison Wrigley covered with a plastic sheet. Both had been astonished at the size of the man, Demetriou trying to work out whether the width is the result of the impact, a sort of pancake effect, like a burst balloon or a cow pat. Fisher for her part in awe at the mountain of flesh still seemingly intact. At least she hopes it is.

'Good morning, good morning, good morning!' Crawley greets, hand waved in the air, alternately flicking through sheets of paper attached to a clipboard. With slicked back oily hair and wolfish grin he's the model of a quiz show host, an image only partly undermined by the translucence of his skin rather than the expected spray-tanned glory of daytime TV celebrity. For Demetriou, the flash of an embroidered silk waistcoat under the lab coat adds to the idea of well-oiled confidence that verges towards arrogance and most likely pratt.

Crawley dispenses with the clipboard and dons his lab suit, a more permanent variation of the disposable Tyvek ones that are the current hot fashion choice demanded of the two detectives.

'Ah! Fisher! So lovely to have you once more,' Crawley leers.

'Can't help myself,' she responds. 'Must be the chemicals. Maybe I'm addicted.'

'Ah, my little place has that effect,' he agrees. 'It captivates!'

'Eau d' Autopsy. Bet there's a market,' Fisher considers. 'Sad little fuckers, all black Tee shirts and wanking in their mothers' basements - and I don't mean mother's basement as a euphemism. Probably need a sock for that.'

'You're teasing,' Crawley simpers.

'Best get a move on, Doc, before we all succumb to its charms.'

Crawley lowers his surgical mask; a curved sheet of plastic that's a riff on a welding visor. Demetriou, sure he sees a wink aimed in his own direction, hopes it's nothing other than an off-target twitch that has skimmed Fisher's ear. He raises his own fabric mask, covering his reaction, noting Fisher, already secreted behind hers, has a twinkle in her eyes.

'And you're the fresh meat,' Crawley grins snapping on surgical gloves.

'...Erhm...' is the best Demetriou comes up with, worryingly aware it comes over as provocatively coquettish, especially from behind a mask.

Crawley fixes him with a stare. 'Must get to know each other a little better afterwards, if you're free, Detective. Tell me all about yourself.'

'Can't say he's your sort, Doc,' Fisher says. 'He's a Brummie.'

Crawley turns to her. 'I forget you can be such a tease,' he smirks.

'You got me there, Doc. I'm having treatment for it, though.'

'Lights!' Crawley snaps and the medical lamps above the stainless-steel mortuary slab miraculously bloom. Impressive if not for the fact of Fisher nudging Demetriou's attention to the skinny lab assistant by the light switches. 'He's like Paul bloody

Daniels, isn't he?' she whispers. 'Debbie McGee goes crazy for shit like that. He's out to impress you!'

'Not a lot,' Demetriou responds, certain her eyes can't hide the smile that her eyes say she's now wearing behind her mask. Yeah, maybe a chink, he thinks. A melt.

'So,' Crawley begins, whipping the sheet aside in full Magic Circle mode. 'Behold, Harrison Wrigley!'

The sight is more extreme than Demetriou anticipated.

In life, Harrison Wrigley had been a large man. A very large man. He'd seen the file, the shots of Wrigley at a gala dinner of some sort provided to assist in identification. He reminds him of an actor from the old black and white films, the Thirties or Forties detective ones, him always the bad guy. He thinks *Maltese Falcon*, but then again whenever recalling old detective films he always thinks *Maltese Falcon*. But this time he's sure it is. *The Fat Man*. That was him. Massive body ill-concealed inside voluminous pin stripe suits, the impression of waves of flesh undulating beneath cloth as he moved. Except Harrison Wrigley is neither moving nor constrained by cloth. In truth, his immensity is no longer constrained even by skin. What appears to be an explosion of blood and gore emerges through parted flesh. Torn apart, a body resembling a human *piñata*, one that has taken a sound thrashing at a particularly wild children's party. A party unsupervised by any responsible adults.

'My God!' he can't help but exhale.

'Yes, he's a big one,' Crawley comments, the proud fisherman exhibiting his catch. 'Better get your reactions out of the way, I'm about to switch on the tape and video and I don't want any come-back from the PC Thought Police at a lack of ethical standards whilst I have a broddle around inside this big boy.' He looks at the figure on the table, then back to his audience. 'Though, between you and me, I think he's pretty much done the job for us. There's more of him on the outside than in.'

Demetriou nods. 'Bloody hell! How far did he fall to do that?'

'He could have just popped himself under a steam roller or something. Might have been a cleaner job,' Fisher offers.

'I'm just astonished the medics got all of him. I mean...how did they. ...You know.'

'Shovels,' Crawley confides. 'At least that's what they used in Belfast and a couple of the bad ones in Afghanistan. Only way. I mean, due deference and all...But sadly, shovels and bin liners are sometimes the only way.'

'Fuck,' Demetriou sighs. 'Fuck.'

'Now, shall we proceed? Eyes down as they say in the Bingo Halls.' And with that he starts recording his description of what was once Harrison Wrigley.

15

'How can you do that?' he asks.

'What?' Fisher asks, dabbing an unbleached paper napkin to the corner of her mouth.

'That,' Demetriou states, finger pointing in the direction of her plate.

She takes a moment to swallow the mouthful of food. 'This?' she asks, waving a hand over her plate. 'This is breakfast. Brunch really. And this, this is magnificent!' she judges, prodding a finger at the half-eaten French Toast Brioche with extra bacon and maple syrup that is the specialty of *Hoxton North*.

Plates on a window shelf serving as a bench table, they sit watching the autumn tourists and shoppers slide by outside. For Demetriou, the relief of a seating arrangement that has placed them side by side on barstools is that he doesn't have to watch whilst she eats. When he speaks, he does so through their reflections in the window, images blurred and slightly off focus that phases out her chewing.

'After Wrigley I haven't the stomach to think about eating.'

'Carry on like this and you'll be sugar deficient and no use at all.' She pauses in eating to look at his reflection. 'It wasn't your first, was it?'

'No. Far from it. Too many. It's just it wasn't that...sterile or clean.' He sips his coffee, relying on the caffeine to revive him.

Fisher, holding her cup in both hands, gazes across the road to the flower bed of the small roundabout opposite, mindful that despite the early frosts and cold rain the council's summer planting remains in full bloom. The sense that some things do last, break expectations, that even after the overnight rain there is a chance of it becoming a pleasant day, a good to be alive day. That hope is always there, if you have the mind to grasp it, her mind drifting to thoughts of futures shaped by pasts.

Wet cobbles...Cold rain...The old stable door.

'Not clean at all,' Demetriou repeats to the window.

Disguised by a nod, a shiver pushes Fisher back to the now. 'Yeah, have to admit old Creepy was struggling,' her reflection shrugs. 'At one point I swear he was sifting bits of gravel from it. The remains, I mean.'

And remains it was. Demetriou has a hard time thinking of it as a body. Maybe it's why the term is used. *Remains*. What's left. And what's left of Harrison Wrigley is a mess of a human. Hard to think of as a body, a vessel full of breath, full of life. And thinking of victims as they were in life is how Demetriou has imagined his way into the deaths he's dealt with. A photograph, a document, a membership card, maybe some holiday souvenir or memorabilia. Books, DVDs, CDs – things finding the victim in life, the sense of who they were, what had been taken. It helped when motivation lagged, when a case seemed never-ending, unresolvable. A conjuring of the living person re-awakening his desire to find the truth of their end, truths that do little for the dead but help those left behind gain closure. After all, remains is what's left when everything else has been taken away.

Those Harrison Wrigley left behind amount to a business partner, Jonathan Small, along with a secretary at their office in Northallerton and another in Harrogate. No siblings, no family, no lovers. No friends, other than legal colleagues he's known to have had the odd dinner with every month or so. In under an hour, they've covered the life of Harrison Wrigley.

'What now, Guv?'

'Another flat white for me. After that Northallerton and an interview with the partner in their legal firm, this bloke...'

'...Small,' Demetriou states. 'Jonathan Small.'

'...Small,' she repeats fixing the name in place.

'Did you know him?'

'They're civil, so not much chance of our paths crossing. You know, deeds, wills, and the like. The Northallerton office is near to HQ. Name always struck me more as a pet shop – *Small and Wrigley*. Apart from that, nothing.'

'I assume we're proceeding with it as suicide?'

She wrinkles her nose. 'It's unexplained, but there's nothing overtly suspect about it. You've read the notes, the witness statements. No sign of anyone up there with him when he dropped. So, on the surface...'

Demetriou senses a *but* which follows a beat of her patting a napkin to her lips. 'But...there's niggles, lumps in the carpet. The uniforms sent to his house didn't find a note which means we're short of a reason. It's odd, but not unusual. There's some deliberately leave an enigma behind for the rest of us to work out, all Dan Brown and cryptic.' She pushes her plate to the side, knife and fork at five to four, tossing the crumpled napkin on top. 'End of the day, a suicide's a suicide, no matter the reason, but Waddingham - the coroner – he likes a note. A tidy up. Having said that, it could just be something out of the blue, spur of the moment stuff, you know, something sudden and desperate, snapping and breaking.' She turns to face him. 'So, without a note we see if there's anything in the way of personal or business troubles. Maybe his partner, this Jonathan Small can answer that. At least he can talk to the business and finance side. As for the personal...who knows. He seems a bit of a loner, though not necessarily lonely. He might not have had that much of a social life, but there's things to be had for a price even up here.' She looks at him. 'Prossies, rent boys,' she clarifies.

'Yes. I get it.'

'And then there's the matter of why here, the Crowne Plaza, him apparently just walking up to the roof and jumping. We'll have to wait on Creepy for tox analysis to know if there's drink or drugs involved. Leaving three questions: Why suicide? Why here? Why now?'

'Maybe it's medical? Maybe he got bad news and wanted to dispense with all the slow dying. Get it over with. As for why here, why the hotel, I assume it's the tallest building around. He wanted to make sure he did it right.'

'What? *Properly* dead?'

'Sort of.'

'Less fuss than booking a flight to Switzerland I suppose.' She taps a finger on the rim of her cup. 'Well, it's one for you to follow up. Check with his GP, see what they know. Check the private hospitals too, the clinics. You never know. He appears to have been a private man, so maybe there's stuff he wanted to keep private.'

'Not a particularly private exit if that's the case,' Demetriou points out.

'True. Spectacular really.' She slaps the back of a hand into the palm of the other, the smack of flesh causing a few heads to turn. '*Kersplat!* Right in the middle of town. The Conference Centre. The Webb enquiry boys are camped out there, and he'd have known that. Hardly low key. He must have known he'd be setting up all sorts of public intrusion into his life. Us looking for answers. If he was trying to avoid something - something tarnishing his reputation - then he picked the surest way to see his life gets a good going over. That we'd find whatever it is.'

'Maybe that's why he did it now. You know, everyone busy with Webb so maybe he thought it would get brushed aside, a quick do over. Maybe it's something he just couldn't face up to if word got out, and maybe he'd found out it was going to,' he offers. 'Blackmail or something.' He pauses. 'Then again, maybe it's the opposite of that. That there's stuff he *wants* us to know, you know, really bad stuff, but he's too ashamed to tell us. Going out like that guarantees there'd be intrusion, an in-depth investigation, and he wanted that. He wants us to find his secret.'

'Sounds all a bit Miss Marple to me, you'll end up tying yourself in knots. Every suicide I've known has turned out to be a matter of people checking out early of what they can't face up to – despair, loneliness, shame, grief, pain.'

Demetriou pushes his cup and saucer to the side. 'No chance of anything suspicious?'

She wrinkles her nose. 'Given the cameras didn't pick up anyone else up there with him, then no. My worry is Iverson.'

'Iverson?'

'The fact that the *Good Soldier* Iverson signed it off as suicide is as good a reason as any for us to be looking a bit further. That and Crosby's hands being sticky with it.'

'Iverson's capable enough don't you think?'

'What I think is that DS Iverson's only too willing to oblige the wishes of a Chief Superintendent who himself is groveling in his efforts to please local politicians, the Commissioner, and the Chief Constable. And let's not forget his golf club chums, Uncle Tom Cobley and the rest. Like you said, maybe the idea is that things get skated over, you know, rubber stamped, and the caravan rolls on.' She pauses, looks out of the window watching a young designer mother push a pram over the zebra crossing. 'I think we can afford to keep an open mind. Have a bit of fun. Dig around. See what we can find.'

'Maybe not the wisest move, Guv, given we're both on Psych Evaluation. What I hear Crosby is calling our broken wings.'

She smiles, but it lacks humour. There's little trace of the softness he's sure he's started seeing there. 'Broken wings, eh?'

she snorts. 'In that case, what better time? If we do anything making discomforting waves, we've got the *'what do you expect, we're crazy' card* to play.' She smiles, and this time it makes it to her eyes. 'This is a *Get Out of Jail Free* card I intend to play as often as I can.'

16

Sophie wonders why her. The fact that most of her wonderings begin or end with this same thought has been remarked upon more than once by those who know her. Parents. Teachers. Boyfriends. Colleagues. Though she currently thinks colleagues a misnomer, *colleagues* implying something in common, shared values, shared ways of seeing the world - like reading the *Daily Mail* or *the Guardian*. Currently, she has *workplace people*, those who share the space where she works. It's as far as it went, more than that, it's as far as she wants it to go.

She doesn't want drinking buddies, after work get-togethers. No *Pizza Hut* Xmas meals, no hen nights, no baby showers, and certainly no inappropriate liaisons. She doesn't want to be part of sports teams or give to collections. Her desire is simple: arrive at work, do the job, get the fuck out.

Police computer forensics was not her choice. It was more an offer she couldn't refuse after she'd been caught bang to rights in a hack.

Technically, getting caught wasn't her fault. How could it have been? She'd done her usual first-rate intrusion, securing the relevant files on the corrupt misdeeds of an ex-boyfriend's employer. Her failure arose from breaking her golden rule: that it was personal not business. The email demand she'd sent the company had been too close to home, threatening as it did to release commercially sensitive material unless said ex-boyfriend denounced himself as the all-round shit and catfish she knew him to be. The second problem was that the company was and still is a major service provider for the Ministry of Defence and other darker areas of intelligence. The clincher that her ex, knowing her capabilities, had tipped off said employers that she was the probable source of the hack. That was when the fourth horseman of her apocalyptic downfall had made its appearance, her confirming the previous three clues with the digital tag she left at all her intrusions. Her calling card, her graffiti handle, or, as her dad would have had it, just like Zorro.

She'd been scooped up *tout-suite* by serious looking Men-in-Black-types. Her interrogation had been low-key, off the record, sensitive - the company aware that news of a hack would end fat government contracts, the digital equivalent of leaving a briefcase full of secrets in a taxi. So, a compromise had been reached: Mutually Assured Destruction. For them, Sophie inside the tent using the appropriate toilet facilities they would provide seen as a more desirable option than that of her being in prison, outside the tent so to speak, peeing in on them. For her, the deal's sole attraction - given her mother's progressively ill health - is no jail time.

Her assignment to Northallerton HQ had been secured through the said company's consultancy role with the Crime Commissioner's Office and came with an NDA attached. She has to remain clear of hacking for three years. After that time she is free to move wherever she chooses. If word of her intrusion gets out or should she fail to complete the three years, the Men-in-black types had made clear she'd disappear down a dark disciplinary hole, one with charges of terrorism spikes waiting at the bottom.

It hadn't started well. Not by a long shot.

There had been the 'exchange' with her colleague in CID that she'd talked about in the Group Meeting. Bad enough as that had been, it was nowhere near as much of a blight on her life as her referral to the therapy group itself, a group she's overheard referred to as *The Angry Brigade*.

She thinks the threats are likely a bluff. However, even with a good lawyer - let alone the second-rate civil liberties defence she might afford - she's looking at years of legal wrangling that ends with the probability of jail, the chance of her mother's health worsening whilst Sophie sits in prison.

She's stuck. Stuck here. Three years stuck with the *Angry Birds* - or whatever they're being called - for company.

She flicks at the keyboard hoping to lose herself in work. Fat chance when it amounts to nothing more than setting up user accounts, the occasional decryption of a drug dealer or people smuggler's phone thrown in. A waste of her talents. Like asking Michelangelo to paint the local church ceiling magnolia.

She blows out her cheeks, a gesture she hates. It's her father's tic, a mannerism he deploys when things got weird or when he's puzzled - like when he's short of ideas or playing for thinking time. When he doesn't know what to tell her about her mother's deteriorating health. She wonders what he'd say if he realised the situation she's got herself into. Part of him would be proud, after all, he was Chris Doyle, once *Demon Doyle*, *Commie Chris*, celebrity rebel rousing activist and Trade Union man, bane of the *Daily Mail* and *Yorkshire Post*. Scargill's slightly more affable twin.

She also knows that one part of him, the paternal part, would be sick with worry. Her mother too, Annie Doyle, campaigning peace-marcher, Greenham Common dweller, patroller of the barricades of fourth wave feminism, bed-ridden and battling a double whammy of cancer and Alzheimer's.

At present, lectures on the patriarchy from her mother or one on Marxist dialectic from her dad were unappealing rocks and hard places to find herself pinned between. So she keeps quiet. Her parents believing she's working for the Anonymous

Collective, fighting the digital good anti-capitalist fight rather than living deep in the Belly of the Beast.

She looks at her Apple watch, the one they'd given her, the Men-In-Black, the one tracking her every move. It will tick away her life for the next two years, ten months and eight days. Exercise. Emails. Surveillance. Her digital warder.

It flashes a programmed alert. Time for her meeting. *The Angry Brigade.*

She picks up her bag, the weather-proof roll-top that goes everywhere. She'll arrive early, find a space, and keep her head down, tight-lipped. If experience has taught her anything it's that revelation, opening up, has a cost. As far as Sophie Doyle is concerned, she's paid more than enough. Time for her to be making deposits at the bank of *who-gives-a-fuck-about-anyone-else*. Me time. Me, me, me, me, me.

17

Malcolm Pemberton sits clipboard on lap, hands clasped, brooding on the judgement delivered by Sophie Doyle. He thinks it harsh, prickly at best. As a man trained to expect the unexpected, fathom the unfathomable, he is supposed to be able to deal with things like this. Tutored to anticipate the slings and arrows of frustrated and angry clients shot his way, schooled to sense and respond to sea-changes of mood. It shouldn't throw him off balance. But it has.

Doyle had spat her observation before sinking back into her familiar pose of distant disinterest: legs tucked up under thighs, upper body half-turned away from the circle, blank expression on her face. She's sat like that in each session, body language screaming her unwillingness to involve herself in discussion. The rest of the group at least appear to take an interest in what each other say, even if he suspects that from Fisher's point of view her contributions are simply a way to make the hour pass more quickly. The social equivalent of chucking a hand grenade into a crowded room in order to watch the resultant scrabble for safety. Not quite amusement, but a diversion from the awful things he knows to be going on inside her head. He's read her previous psychological evaluations, her mind a messy, harsh environment, certainly not one for the fainthearted to venture into unarmed. *Like the Somme,* one report had attested. To live there 24/7 is something he can't imagine.

The effect of Doyle's outburst has swept the circle, a wave of shock and awe. And it isn't just him. He's seen the reactions of the rest of the group, each turning to her with looks approaching admiration. Demetriou has stopped alternating staring at the floor, then the clock, then back again – his head in perpetual motion like a human Newton's cradle. Even Musgrove has stopped fiddling with the bag of sweets Pemberton knows lurk deep in a trouser pocket.

Silence sits in the room, most likely cross-legged in the centre of the circle considering its next move. Expectant. Wondering who was going to break, it sits, stopwatch primed.

Pemberton is first. 'That's an interesting point of view, Sophie. Would you care to elaborate?' Silence puts the timer away. No record today. No *Guinness Book of Awkward Pause*s trophy clutched Oscar like in hands, a tearful listing of those to thank for getting it there.

Doyle barely moves her head. 'No. I wouldn't care. Don't care. It speaks for itself, doesn't it?' She pauses a beat. 'I mean... What is it with you, Malcolm? Do we have to elaborate every bloody thing we say? Can't we just leave it at that. *This is shit.* End of.'

'I've read the books. She's pretty much nailed a definition of therapy right there, Malcolm,' Fisher offers. 'I mean, we could dress it up a bit...you know, *impetuousness of youth* and all that. *Refreshingly direct* was how I think my last Review put it when I expressed a similar opinion of their assessment of my performance.'

Pemberton nods. It's as much as he can think to do.

'Disagree,' Musgrove states flatly.

Pemberton sits up. 'Because?' he prompts, intrigued that Musgrove of all people is volunteering a contribution.

Musgrove eyes the group. 'Because?' He shuffles a little more upright. 'Because it's hardly a useful contribution to the discussion, is it?'

'Isn't it?' Fisher asks.

'Of course it's not. It just shuts it down. It's like...I don't know...putting a lid on it. *Here you are. That's all. End of.* Frankly, it's juvenile.'

'Much as I'm sure she appreciates the effort at teen speak, Neil, I don't think Sophie quite sees it that way,' Fisher states.

'I don't,' Demetriou says quietly.

'No?' Pemberton asks.

'No.' He sits forward, stepping into the space Pemberton has left for him. 'In many ways it's more of an opening. A gambit. Like chess. Check isn't checkmate unless the other player allows it to be. If they can't see their way around it, work out a counter move, they give in. Concede. It's down to us to understand what Sophie's saying and bat it back.'

'So you're saying Sophie is prompting discussion?'

'I'd say she's challenging it,' Fisher puts in. 'I mean, sorry Malcolm, but this *is* shit.'

'No,' Demetriou responds. 'It's not. And Sophie doesn't think it is either.'

'Don't I?' Sophie snarls, pushing up from her slump. 'What, are you the patriarchy police? Aren't I allowed an opinion? You have to mansplain it to me?'

'You know that's not what I'm saying.'

'What are you saying?' Pemberton prompts.

'To me, she's angry,' Demetriou decides.

Sophie pushes her tongue against her bottom lip, screwing up her face. 'Well duh...that's why we're here. Haven't you heard what they call us? *The Angry Brigade.*'

'That's nice. I'd heard *Angry Birds*,' Fisher puts in. 'Seemed somehow...sexist.'

'Broken wings,' Demetriou puts in. 'They call us broken wings. You know, the fact we're broken. We can't fly anymore. That we were once thought high-flyers. Now...not so much.'

'Birds, wings, all the same really. Like Sophie says, like I say too - we're angry. And again, for the record, - and again sorry, Malcolm - this *is* shit,' Fisher judges.

'But it's not all the same. Sophie's angry with herself. At least she is right now. You are, aren't you?' Demetriou pursues.

Sophie shrugs. 'What's it to you who I'm angry with?'

'Because it's me too. I'm there, I'm stuck too. Angry with myself, with the job, with everything – and for the record I think we all are, that's why you're saying this is shit. It's why we all are. It's everything. Everything's shit.'

Musgrove nods. 'I get it.'

'You do?' Demetriou asks.

Musgrove nods. 'Absolutely. My dad had a saying. *Charity begins at home until you're locked out.*'

Silence claps its hands and settles in. This is going to be good.

The drive through the winding roads of Wensleydale is clear. The village fetes have been and gone, the tourists with them. School holidays are in the rear-view mirror, and the farmers are busy collecting the summer's hay rolled as winter feed. Only the older tourists remain, hardy retired walkers, back-packs in place, plodding the Heriot Way decked in brightly coloured parkas, walking poles and compasses in hands.

'So, what did you make of it?' Demetriou asks.

'It?'

'Musgrove. His homily or anecdote or whatever. You know, the *charity begins at home before getting locked out.*'

'Oh, that? It was…very Musgrove. At least from what I know of him.'

'Do you?'

'…Do I what?'

'…Know much of him? Musgrove.'

She looks out of the side window, the dry-stone walls and

hedging zipping past, old, ancient, and solid. In the distance, across the rolling landscape, sits the hunch of Pen hill, to the right of the narrow road the thousands of acres of MoD land. 'Not so much,' she says to the window whilst gazing at the clouds shadowing the top of the hill. 'I've heard the stories. His legend. But given I know what they say about me, my own mythic story, so I tend not to put much store in them.'

'Gossip?'

'Gossip I can take, it's what's behind it. That people think they know you; have you all worked out and can pop you in one of their little pigeon-holes.'

'I get it.'

'Do you? I get *cold ice queen bitch*, *whore*, or *dyke*. What do you get?'

'*Paki*. Back in Brum they saw my olive skin and thought *Paki*. I'm Greek.'

'Really? I had it them seeing you as *stud*. Maybe *queer*,' she half-smiles.

Demetriou nods. 'And how do you see me?'

She turns to face him. 'Worse. *Brummie*.'

He smiles. 'Yeah. Certainly the outsider round here. Not like you.'

'Not like me?'

'…Well, you're from around here, aren't you? I heard-'

She turns to the side window. 'Like I said. Gossip. Innuendo. Pigeonholes.'

'But you are local.'

'…Ish.'

'…Ish?'

'Enough to understand the dialect. The way of thinking. The desire to be left alone.' She turns to the walls and hedges that follow the twist and turns of the tight bends that slope towards Redmire. The smeared blur of life. 'That's what gets me about our suicide.'

'Which one?'

'Both, now you mention it.'

'Both?'

'Suicide is almost normal round here. The statistics say three a week in UK agriculture. I looked it up. But lawyers and trafficked women...not so much. I read there are five thousand suicides a year in the UK. Do the math's, that's 18 a day. I mean, it's a lot, but to have two round here so close together. Odd.'

'Odd but hardly suspicious. I mean, statistically it's probably not much of an anomaly. It's just we've caught both, so it seems high to us. You know, we're more aware of it. Hyper-vigilant is what I think Malcolm calls it.'

'But they're both in lifestyles where it's low.'

'I don't know...Sofia was most likely trafficked. Certainly involved in drugs. Hardly the genteelest or safest of career choices.'

'Don't you go slipping into the comforting furrows of thinking like Crosby and Iverson. Tunnel vision, blinkered. Trust me on this. Too many coppers see what they're supposed to see, see what they think they should see. Makes life easier, sensible policing for sensible crimes - but not so good in detecting the trickier stuff.' She considers assumptions, the ease with which you could fool people into seeing what you want them to see. The Jedi mind trick, them wanting to see it that way, most of all the police...*Wet cobbles...Cold winds...Rusting stable door handles.*

Demetriou navigates the turn at the bottom of the hill, head craning to watch for traffic round the tight bend of the road they merge onto. 'So, what then?'

She shifts her thinking to now, not then. 'She was caught up in a bust, but she was homeless, looking for somewhere to sleep. I think it was just somewhere to be, somewhere she felt...free. She was getting out, making a fresh start. I think it's why she left the hostel. She was tired of being watched over.'

'A leap.'

'No. That was Wrigley.' Fisher turns to him. 'Ah, Sorry. I get you now. You meant...Anyway, think about him. It's like Sofia.

What do we actually know about what happened other than the assumptions we're making? All we know about Sofia is that she was homeless. No-one charged her with drugs after that raid because there was no evidence she used them or sold them or anything else. She was homeless. That's all we know. The rest is assumption. Fiction.'

'And Wrigley?'

'Same. He fell from the roof. That's it. No drugs or drink issues. No financial issues. No skeletons in his cupboard. We still don't know if he was up there by himself. We assume he was simply because we haven't found evidence of anyone else. But two of the hotel CCTV cameras were offline, technical issues.'

'Even so, the door was alarmed, and it alerted the staff the moment he went through. It would have tripped if someone else had gone through before him.'

'But not if they went through with him. Maybe met him by the stairwell and went through at the same time. Slipped back down and out of the hotel in the confusion.'

'So, you think it's not suicide?'

'I think it's not settled one way or the other. We need to see if we're missing something.'

'And Sofia?'

'We need to know where she was in the time between leaving the hostel and us finding her.

He allows a beat. 'You do know the chances are she's a suicide. Stranger in a strange land, mixed up and alone and all of those things. A suicide. Nothing more.'

'I know that's the smart money. But something's off.' She gazes out of the window. 'The method for one. The hair, too.'

'Crosby says both are suicide. Iverson too.'

'Yes. They do.'

'Is that why you're going in the opposite direction?' he prods as much as asks.

She turns. 'I'm not sure what you mean.'

'What you said before. They pissed you off, you want to prove them wrong.'

'That's harsh. And besides, they always piss me off.'

'Yeah, well, we're both in this broken wings thing for a reason. But we don't need Malcolm to tell us what our anger is. We understand it from the inside. Recognise it for what it is. The drivers. The triggers.'

'Everyone gets angry. Even Malcolm says so. It's…normal.'

'Not angry like us. Me, you, Doyle - even Musgrove. We understand it differently. Sometimes we channel it. The job. You know - *determination, aggressively career minded*. Sometimes it gets out of hand. Beating up suspects. Throwing punches at senior officers. A fine line.'

'Your point is?'

'What we know and what Malcolm doesn't is that we can't change it. Don't want to.'

'He'll be very disappointed to hear you say that, him all about the redemptive power of therapy.'

'We like it. We enjoy it.'

'Christ, Demetriou, you're sounding like some sort of Lecter psychopath.'

'Maybe we are. I've been doing a lot of reading the past few weeks.'

'Suspension does that. It's Jilly Cooper for me.'

'No, I mean…really? Jilly Cooper?' he stumbles, shocked.

'What's wrong with the Jillster? All that jodhpurs and posh bird bonking. What's not to like?' she bats back.

'Well, I suppose…I had you down more as…I don't know. Something…darker. Stephen King.'

She slaps his arm. 'Ouch!'

'That's for thinking I'm a nerd!' she states.

He glances at his forearm, watches her smile or at least the movement of her mouth that suggests one recently happened there. 'Anyway, I meant I've been reading about personality disorders.'

'Hardly Tesco or *Richard and Judy Book Club* fare.'

'No, but I've been trying to get my head around understanding the things that drive us. Drive me.'

'And?'

'You know, Malcolm's talk about a spectrum of aggression? It's classic Mizen or Harding or Lorenz.'

'Afraid I stopped at Freud and Jung. It's all about your mom though, isn't it?'

He shakes his head, determined not to be deflected. 'We're on it, all of us, the entire human race. Maybe some of us are…I don't know, maybe just a little further along than he thinks.'

'Is it me or has it just gone a little dark in here?'

'You've been through it, Guv, you said so. Therapy's all about understanding yourself, knowing who you are, knowing the triggers, understanding how to control it. It's surely more about how you use it. Recognise it for what it is. It's why you're looking at foul play for these suicides and not accepting the obvious. It's the anger that makes you good at all this, the investigating. You dig deeper than the rest of us because you want to shake things up. Unsettle the comfortable little world that Crosby and the rest live in. Make them feel some of what's in your head.'

She looks out of the side window, thinking to herself dear DS Demetriou you really don't want to know what goes on inside my head.

18

Hyland paces the room, disappointed. His sense of having dropped the ball offering an insight into what it must feel like to be one of the losers in life. Someone like…Musgrove.

He'd watched him in the Operations Meeting that morning, an ominous and depressing presence munching his way through bourbons and *Country Crunch*. It's bad enough that the Webb murder remains stuck in a rut of dull plodding enquiry without Musgrove sighing at every item on the agenda like the chief mourner at a particularly dull wake, a reminder of where promising careers might so easily end up.

Hyland slumps into his chair, thoughts of the enquiry pulling him earthwards, beginning to think it would have been better all round to have been left out of the operational loop of what has become an uncontrollable juggernaut of an investigation. It was over a week now, and it had become a runaway train of an enquiry, a Black Hole sucking in resources faster than he or his officers could find them. His role is now that of wandering the twilight zone, a place where his officers do the heavy lifting whilst he is put forward to field reporters who question the lack of progress. *Fucking Spooks*! None of the work and none of the accountability, agents carrying an air of assumed privilege, the presumption to do whatever it pleases them to do. The Downing Street card has been used over and over, a bottomless *Get Out of Jail Free* pass played to the point where he's given up trying to halt the stampede trampling his authority.

'So, where are we at with this?' Badgerman the Chief Spook had demanded five minutes into the meeting that morning, his usual first move in playing a political blame game he's adept at, adroit and slippery as fuck.

Hyland had applied his own tactic: straight bat down the middle, wary of the pace of a seam attack lining up to pound him with bouncers around his vulnerable bits. 'Our enquiries are proceeding. We've spoken to those present at the time of the attack and our tech people have scanned the CCTV. We've interviewed anyone involved in Webb's businesses who might shed light on potential perpetrators, and I've tasked senior detectives to talk with his wife and family. I think I can safely say, without fear of contradiction, that my force has covered all our bases.'

Badgerman had waved him aside. 'Yes, yes…I know all that. But that's the shop window, isn't it. The window dressing for our friends in the media. Far better for public morale if your little force is seen running around as though you're investigating it as a local spat between rivals rather than the calculated international terrorist attack we know it to be. An attack on the nation, an attack making us all potential targets and terrifying Joe Public.' He'd looked from side to side, the line of similarly dressed men in dark suits sat next to him, men who followed him wherever he went, men who hung on his every word. They'd nodded in unison. Satisfied at their affirmation of his logic, he'd pressed on, the light from the flush mounted ceiling lamps glistening off his ever-slick black hair. 'I'm talking about the real work. The tracing of hostiles. Those perceived as possible threats to the PM and the government. The dissidents and radicals. This stuff you've just told us has nothing to do with covering bases, Chief Constable, it's you covering your arse.'

Hyland had steamed. 'That's been taken out of my hands. Your own agents-'

'Yes, yes. Standard operational procedure,' Badgerman had interjected, stopping Hyland with another dismissive wave of the hand. 'We have oversight. We have insight. We have Intel. We have investigative know-how. I'm talking about the presentation of this investigation to the public. Our friends in the Fourth Estate. We have to consider how the narrative of this investigation is constructed for them. The potential for panic and doubt. The headlines. The Villains. The Heroes of our tale. I mean, do I have to tell you everything?'

Gina Hargreaves had spoken, a honeyed tone whispered through glossy red lips, a sheen that attached itself to her words, coating them as they slid by. Not for the first time Hyland had found the image of a snake slip into his mind, the broad narrow eyes and slight flaring of her nostrils. 'We have an...intimate relationship with the local media,' she'd almost whispered. 'It would seem they're accepting of matters as we've presented them. I've constructed a very acceptable *you scratch my back* partnership with most of them.'

'Well, that's lovely for you, especially with your election coming up, Commissioner. And I'm sure it plays well up here with the farmers and retired colonels and the like. But I mean the Big Boys. The nationals. BBC. Sky. Bloomberg. What about them?'

'A little...trickier,' Hyland had offered, re-asserting his own presence. 'They have an agenda.'

'Of course they have a fucking agenda!' Badgerman had barked. 'Right-wing, left-wing. The Greens. The woke. They've all got one. What about ours? What's our agenda? Who's getting it over to them? Who's making sure they play nice?'

'I've played a straight bat on it. No deviation from the line,' Hyland had pointed out.

Badgerman had groaned. 'What is it with you Yorkshire lot

and you're cricket metaphors and analogies? Are they buying in? Yes or no?'

'It would appear so.'

'Hallelujah! An answer! Christ on a bike, Harland - you could give my MI6 boys lessons on avoiding interrogation.'

'It's Hyland. Chief Constab-'

'What about the others?' Badgerman had interrupted, hand chopping the air.

Hyland, stopped in his tracks, had been genuinely puzzled. 'Others?'

'The Fifth Estate. The bloggers and vloggers?' Badgerman had sighed. 'YouTube.'

'I'm not sure I-'

'Oh, for fuck's sake!' Badgerman had dived into Hyland's sentence. 'Please tell me you know what I'm talking about.' He'd scanned the room, his team of dark-suited operatives smirking behind their hands. 'I mean the fucking internet has reached up here, hasn't it? You know, surely all the levelling up stuff has got you broadband at the very least.' The grins grew wider.

'I didn't think there-'

'Well, you got that right, Harland. Seems to me that lack of thought is what's been holding this investigation back. That bloody idiot pissing off the grieving widow, pissing off the influencers was the start of it.'

Musgrove had held a hand up. Tentative, really nothing more than just a lifting of his forearm, elbow still resting on the conference table. 'That was me,' he'd offered.

'Fully aware,' Badgerman snapped.

'I thought that-' Musgrove began.

'I think, uhm...sorry, you are?'

'ACC Musgrove,' Musgrove had helped.

'Musgrave,' Badgerman had nodded whilst his eyes appraised the ACC. He spoke as if he'd just had something confirmed about the man addressing him, something not very nice, some expected, yet still somehow unwelcome news. 'Just sit back, Musgrave. Finish your biscuits and leave the thinking to the those who have experience of such matters.'

'MusGROVE,' Musgrove had stated.

'Musgrove, Musgrave.' Badgerman had shaken his head. 'Hardly the time to be concerned about the niceties of rank or what have you, don't you think? It may have passed you by, Mus*grove*, but there's an investigation going on here. A major investigation.' He'd picked a packet of biscuits from the plate in front of him, tossing it across the conference table, the cellophane packet spinning round and round, stopping when it nudged against Musgrove's cup and saucer. *Country Crunch*. 'There you go. 'Enjoy!'

Musgrove had stared at the shrink-wrapped biscuits, its logo of happy farmers in a field of wheat. He'd glanced around; Hyland head down staring at the table; Hargreaves, face contorted into a snarl; the dark suited men from London grinning. He'd reached out and picked up the pack, the wrapper squeaking its protest as he'd opened it. He'd lifted a biscuit to his lips and bitten off a corner, crumbs showering the glossy tabletop.

Before the first crumb hit the table, Badgerman had turned his attention to the wider room. 'Now, Chief Constable, perhaps you can get your side of this investigation organised. We need you to shake the trees, see what falls out. We've looked into our watchlists, drilled down on informants. There are no active threats who could have committed this act, which means these terrorists are local. Home-grown, their feet deep in your God's Own County.' He'd looked along the row of dark-suited operatives. 'My men are a weapon, honed and hardened, but they need a target, and at the moment your efforts are frankly not good enough. Not by a long shot.' The address had ended with a definitive chop of the hand that became a wide sweep as if clearing the table of rubbish.

'But you side-lined us. Your men took over. We've been on the margins of all this,' Hyland had opined waving his own hands in the air, holding them wide as if defining the scale of *all this*.

'That's my point, and I might add, that of Number Ten, too. You're standing at the margins like it's some sort of game with you on the subs bench waiting your turn. Of course we took the lead. The bigger picture, the smart money, has it as a terrorist plot. National, maybe even global and certainly an investigation beyond your force's capabilities. But that doesn't mean your lot were supposed to stand around with their hands in their pockets. We expected you to be pulling your weight locally. Exploiting your sources, feeding us intelligence, making a difference. This lot must have stayed somewhere – local supporters, fellow travellers, maybe even a fucking Premier Inn! But they had to have stayed somewhere up here, and it's your lot's job to have found where.'

Hyland had turned to Hargreaves, his face a contortion of anguish and hurt. 'Gina, for goodness sake say something! This is preposterous!' He'd pointed across the table at Badgerman and the agents flanking him. 'They've benched us, and now, when they're struggling to find the culprits responsible, they're pointing the finger away from themselves towards us. Like we're the ones to blame!'

Hargreaves had shaken her head, the nursery teacher wading in to restore order, her tone that of disappointment. 'I think, gentlemen, that we all want a result. We're on the same side,' she'd stated in best political non-speak, words carrying the sense of indisputable truth whilst resolving nothing at all. She'd shifted in her chair, an action turning her from Hyland and his fast-breaking expression of betrayal. 'I'm sure you're as anxious as I am to find justice for poor Mr. Webb,' she'd continued. 'He was a friend. A man committed to the greater good of our region. Sitting around arguing the finer points of responsibility or whose ball it is gets us nowhere. Let's all of us work to get the result we want, the answers we simply have to find.'

'But Gina-' Hyland had begun, raising a hand for attention.

'It's Commissioner, not Gina,' she'd rebuked.

Hyland had slumped, bemused, beaten before he'd even had a kick, let alone resolved whose ball it actually was.

'Thank you, Commissioner,' Badgerman had replied, a smile and a nod in Hargreaves' direction. 'You're so right. This is about calming public anxieties as much as it is about finding the culprits - though the latter would clearly resolve the former. It's clear to Number Ten that this was a terrorist attack. The fact that we've been unable to find those responsible detracts not one iota from that operational assessment. These assailants are dissidents, radicals unknown to us because they've flown under your radar, Harland. Your force. Your people. Sleepers and infiltrators, passing unnoticed, awaiting their moment. A Lone Wolf cell.'

'Is that possible?' Musgrove had asked, brushing biscuit crumbs off the table into a cupped hand.

Badgerman had turned to him, annoyed at the interruption. 'Is what possible?'

'*Lone Wolf*. It means just that. *Lone*. By themselves, acting on instinct. A *cell*...well, doesn't that mean a group? Plots. Plans. People being organised.'

'What are you, the semantic police? Is that your remit round here?'

Musgrove had looked around for a receptacle for his crumbs. 'No. I just mean...Well, if it is a *lone* wolf then that's a different level of investigation to if it's a group. A cell.'

'So, you're what? *Planning*? *Operations*?' Badgerman had persisted.

Musgrove had shaken the crumbs into his empty coffee cup, wrapper screwed into an unfolding ball and popped on top. 'No. Not exactly.'

'Then just what *exactly is* your remit?'

'ACC Musgrove is currently *Refurbishment*,' Hyland had jumped in, wondering when it would all stop, just go away.

'What?'

'*Refurbishment*,' Hyland had sighed. 'We're decorating the HQ and-'

'I know what refurbishment is!' Badgerman had exploded, waving a hand to brush off Hyland's statement, a gesture ending with a finger pointing at Musgrove. 'I'm just at a loss to understand how it qualifies *him* to be in this meeting, let alone how it qualifies *him* to tell us how to do something he clearly has very little grasp of.'

'I've planned Armed Response before. Other posts,' Musgrove had responded.

'Armed with what? Paintbrushes? Ladders? Wallpaper catalogues?'

'I think-'

'What's your plan? Remodelling the terrorist den? Sort out their fucking *feng shui*? This isn't sodding *Changing Rooms*.'

'I don't think-'

'Ah! There we have it. You don't think.' Badgerman had nodded to the operatives either side of him. 'These men are seasoned agents who in the course of their work have prevented countless attacks, countless deaths of innocent citizens. They deserve their place at this table. They deserve that their ideas, their plans and judgements be heard. I know why they're here.' He'd pressed his index finger on the table as if pushing a button. 'Right now, I'm struggling to fathom just why it is that Chief Constable Harland and the Commissioner have extended that same invitation to you.'

'Hyland,' Hyland mutters.

'I'm ACC.' Musgrove had stated. 'The Chief Constable's right hand.'

Hyland's face, along with his spirit, had at that moment dropped, hand rushing up to meet it before it crashed to the table, Musgrove certain he'd heard a moan.

'A role that we've now established to be swatches. Paint and furniture. Which leaves me at a loss as to why you have a seat at this table. Maybe you do things differently up here,' Badgerman had said, addressing his remarks to Hyland and Hargreaves.

'ACC Musgrove is an experienced officer,' Hargreaves had offered in an attempt to protect the good name of a force she'd just realised was welded to her own reputation.

'I'm sure he is. And I don't mean to tell you how to do things, Commissioner, but...Well I'm wondering just what it is that he's so experienced at. More to the point, how it serves us at operational level in catching terrorists. Maybe if I talk to the Home Office or Number Ten.'

'There's no need for that.' Hargreaves had intervened. She'd looked to Hyland. 'I'm certain we can find the ACC a more suitable role. One, as you say, perhaps more in keeping with his recent experiences. I'm persuaded that perhaps his presence here could be seen as a waste of the many operational qualities he's evolved during his time with us, skills that might be better employed elsewhere in our work. Don't you agree, Chief Constable?'

19

'*Qualities he's evolved during his time here.*' Musgrove repeats the phrase, his facial expression a mix one part distaste and two of incredulity. To Doyle, it makes him appear…weird. Like an actor who'd indulged themselves in too much Botox. A mask of… oddness. Tony Curtis. That bloke married to Lisa Minelli.

'*Ones better employed elsewhere in our work…*What the buggering shepherd does she know about police work? Real police work? She's all about the election. Her own arse. And Hyland? He's just sliding into line hoping for it to go away.' Vitriol purged, he deflates into his chair.

Feeling some comment is required Doyle looks around the group, realising that as she's been the one stupid enough to have asked the question, she's now *it*. "Sounds like you were well and truly shafted,' she offers whilst Musgrove looks to the floor, unresponsive. 'Take it from someone who knows that feeling all too well,' she continues. 'Fucked…and not in a good, emotionally purging way. You know…not an orgasm. Not a release. I mean fucked in the figurative sense of being done over. Not one where-'

'I think we get your point,' Pemberton interrupts, cheeks shading crimson for the second or third time already.

'She's not wrong though,' Fisher adds. 'Well and truly fucked. Sorry, Neil.'

'Screwed. I think screwed gets the job done,' Demetriou states, eyes turning from contemplation of the clock. 'You know, the idea that it's really invasive. Pins you down and-'

'Okay, okay. Okay.' Musgrove looks up, hands gesturing in the universal sign of surrender. 'I get it. I wasn't looking for…' he pauses.

'What?' Pemberton asks. 'What are you looking for, Neil?'

Musgrove blows his cheeks out, as puzzled at his offering of these feelings as the rest of them. 'To share. To sound off.'

'Everything's shit,' Doyle states, in what is now the mantra of the group.

'Yes. That.' Musgrove shifts in his seat. 'The *everything's shit* thing. Because it is.'

'Do you want to tell us about it?'

'Where to start? The Commissioner. The Chief Constable. The Webb murder. It's just a great big pile of it. I'm not sure I can take much more, not after today's meeting.' He thinks of home, thinking he could just as easily have added that to his list, him and Jean.

'Sorry to hear that, Neil,' Pemberton says, cutting across his thoughts, the therapist's voice low, body language leaning him in to roost bird-like on the edge of his chair. 'At least you kept it in. Didn't lose it,' he offers.

'Better if I had. At least that way they'd have known what I think of them and their arse covering.'

'You sound fired up,' Fisher judges. 'First time I've seen that when it's not been pointing in my direction.'

'Fired up doesn't even start to describe how I feel right now,' Musgrove spits.

'Then use it. Use how you feel. Channel it,' Doyle suggests.

'Into what?'

Doyle throws her hands in the air. 'Isn't it enough that I come up with what you should do? I have to show you how? I'm not your mom.' She pulls her feet up under her thighs, arms folded, not playing anymore.

'What about our cases?' Fisher suggests.

'Sorry?' Pemberton responds.

'It's Demetriou's idea really.'

'What? What idea?' Demetriou asks, wondering why his name has been pulled front and centre.

'The other morning in the car. What you said about understanding ourselves. Who we are. Why we are. Doyle's right. We should channel it. Use it for good,' Fisher reminds him.

'What are we? *The Fantastic Four*? *Spiderman*?' Doyle asks, arms clenched around her.

'Maybe. Maybe we are. But it's about this stuff we have going on inside us.' Fisher looks around the circle. 'Why not find a use for it, this anger we have? Solve a crime or two - at the very least see if we can use it to find some answers about the cases that are troubling us, act on ideas we have that no-one's listening to. What do you say, Malcolm?'

'It's a cod diagnosis at best, Zara. Psychology 101. And on top of that, we're not supposed to discuss active cases. Data protection,' Pemberton instructs.

'Data protection be arsed. What about the idea. The... concept. Channelling things. What did you say it was Pan?' Fisher asks. 'You know, those books you've been reading, the internet Ted talks.'

'Displacement,' Demetriou replies wondering why his cookies and search history are being put on display by someone he'd begun to trust with his more intimate secrets.

'Displacement. Is it possible?' Fisher asks of Pemberton.

'There's certainly a couple of research papers I've read that say channeling fierce emotion is a way of learning to control them - but I come back to my point about data protection. This is a therapy group, Zara, not an active unit. You're on restricted duties, you and Pan. And as for Neil and Sophie, well, you're officers of the law. There are rules about this stuff,' the psychologist cautions.

'I think you'll find the reason we're in here, Malcolm, is the fact that we can't be arsed about rules,' Fisher responds. 'And apart from that and the anger, there's only one thing that unites us – like you said, we're coppers. It's what we know, what we do.'

'It's a grey area at best,' Pemberton states for any record.

She fixes him with a stare that pins him to the back of his chair. 'The question here, Malcolm, is do you want to help us get better or not? We've still got our skills. Doyle's brilliant with IT, Demetriou somehow asks the right questions, and Neil has access, official buttons and levers he can press or pull in the system.'

'And what about you?' What's your superpower?' Doyle asks.

'Me?'

'...Yes, you. What do you bring to this team of superheroes?' Doyle pursues.

'She was a great copper,' Musgrove puts in. 'The best, like her-'

'No, Neil! For once this is not going to be about him,' Fisher snaps.

'Sorry, I just...'

Fisher snorts. '...You see, Doyle, I'm a stubborn bitch, it's a sort of superpower. That plus the fact that Pan and I have got just the use for those powers. A good old-fashioned mystery, an itch that needs scratching.'

'It's like Spiderman,' Doyle says, sitting forward. '*With great power comes great responsibility.* We could have a badge, maybe a shield.'

'Whatever else happens,' Fisher judges, 'Neil has to avoid the Spandex and lycra costume.'

20

Musgrove can't sleep. Not that it makes it much different from most nights. Sat up in bed, he tries recalling the last time he's had a good night's sleep. By the time he's reached back past Easter, pretty sure he's heading for New Year's Eve, the heavy bout of drinking that to Jean's annoyance rendered him comatose some hours before the midnight chimes, he stops counting.

The bed's lumpy. How the hell Charlie slept in it all those years he isn't sure. Then again, he was a teenage boy with other things on his mind than how lumpy the bed is.

He gives in to the whole not sleeping state of mind. Swinging legs from under the *Star Wars* single duvet, he sits on the edge of the bed and raises a hand, flicking the curtains apart. He looks out across a ragged front lawn, recalling Graham Smart still has his mower, and watches as a fox emerges from a neighbour's leylandii. It walks unconcerned at the nearness of humans, the machinery of modern life, the sense of doing what you want simply because you can. The freedom to be.

He lets the curtain slip back, turning to the laptop sitting on Charlie's old desk. His novel.

He gets up, flips the lid, the screen flickering into life, the home page image of Bogey from *The Maltese Falcon*. 'Here's looking at you, kid,' he mutters out of the side of his mouth.

He opens the Word application and selects a new document. He sits, fingers poised, cursor blinking, mind running through the knowledge gleaned from weekend writing courses, the ones he'd told Jean were weekends of *"official police business"*, leadership conferences, chances for promotion. Instead, small retreats, the sharing of hopes with like-minded souls. Not that she'd ever bothered to ask about them. All the deeply convoluted excuses he'd constructed on each drive home, wasted other than practice for plotting his novels.

He stares at the screen. Nothing.

All he has in his head right now is shame and a little anger. Shame at the humiliation he'd suffered at Badgerman's hands; anger at allowing Hyland to once more throw him under yet another expedient bus as it hove into view. Hargreaves complicit as ever.

He sits for a moment, allowing the red mist to swirl, gather its power, curious to see if Demetriou's right about channeling emotions.

He guides the pointer to the tool bar that runs along the gutter and opens the trash bin, his previously discarded piece still there. What is it they say about computers? Nothing's ever really deleted. Nothing ever completely gone.

Maybe that's his inspiration?

He'd talk to Doyle; she seems a bright and more than capable young woman. He's seen her file. Her technical qualifications might be sparse but the reference from her previous employer is glowing, an employer known to recruit only the best. She's good enough to have the skills he might ascribe to a character. Maybe she could form part of a modern-day *noir*? After all, what would Spillane or Chandler be writing about today? Some things hadn't changed that much - there were still cops on the take willing to spill whatever information his own PI Rick Mangrove might try to get hold of - but as for the rest of it, they'd have to take account of mobiles, laptops and Google. No tearing out pages from bulky phone books. No door-to-door sleuthing. No dark-haired secretaries in shuttered offices. Now you needed *Google*. *Siri* and *Alexa*. Maybe *ChatGPT*.

He returns to the screen. Not just a new book, a new genre. He'll be acclaimed a pioneer, a visionary. The new Stieg Larsson or Jo Nesbo. They'd have to come up with a new term like they did for '*Scandi Noir*' or '*Cosy Crime*'.

He stares at the blank pane of the application. Okay. Here we go. The start is always the most difficult. Lee Child tells him it has to be gripping. He's watched the *BBC Maestro* course: *Crime Writing with Lee child* several times, at each viewing nodding agreement with the teaching. Lee's guidance struck home with him, all he's needed is a character - his big idea - and now he has one.

But he needs a crime. A crime enabling him to start the book with a grizzly page turner of a shock. Something startling the reader, compelling them to turn the page. Daring them to.

But what?

If his heroine – *no it was hero these days, irrespective of gender, and that was a can of PC worms of its own. Anyway, if she – yes, he was pretty sure he could say that, if not then the sensitivity editor would sort it out in the drafting* - is to be relatable, she has to be confronted with a crime so despicable and so morally repulsive that the reader becomes desperate for her to solve it. Cheer her on, hands covering their eyes. No that was watching films, eyes had to be free from impediment in reading, damn near essential. But he's being figurative rather than literal. The idea's sound. They have to be impelled to turn the page, yet at the same time dread what might be waiting for them. Like hands reaching for doorhandles in horror films.

So, it has to be a despicable crime, bloody and brutal – Chapter One, page one.

So, *who*? More to the point, *why*? And there's the *how*, not to mention the *when*, and the *where*, and the *what with*.

His eyes drift to the folders piled on the desk, the 'light reading' brought home in the hope of finding an hour or two to get his paperwork back on track. He flicks the edges as if preparing to shuffle a deck of cards, like the page flicker cartoons he'd drawn when a lad.

He pulls the top folder off the pile. Maybe working through a couple of cases might take his mind off his writer's block, immerse his thinking in the gritty reality of crime. The car thefts. The domestics. The...hmmm, what's this one? *Suicides*. Fisher's cases. The solicitor, the dead Bulgarian, the shaven-headed girl found in an old barn during the storm a week or so ago.

He looks at the image, the body dangling from a rope. Young. Not much older than Charlie from the look of her. What drove someone to this? To hang yourself in an isolated barn with a rope the case notes say was wrapped with human hair. Her own hair and that of others. He starts to read. It's grim. As grim as he's ever read.

Gritty and dark.

Bloody and visceral.

He turns to the laptop, the blank page that stares at him, and begins to type.

Doyle considers getting up, before just as quickly banishing the idea and then immediately giving in and getting up. She's been in bed less than an hour. The speed, the meth-amphetamine she'd dropped last night, still working, her mind whirring and whirling, bouncing from one idea to the next. From past experience it will do so for another three hours before spiralling her down, crashing face first into her office keyboard sometime – so she estimates - around morning coffee break. What would they think, her work colleagues?

She scans her bedroom, catching herself in the mirror, partially dressed, an outfit living somewhere between pyjamas and Club 18-30.

What had she been thinking?

A night out. Time outside herself, some fun, a night taking her out of the ever-deepening realisation of the mire her life has slid into. A club night. Except she doesn't do clubs. At least, hadn't for years, the lost years of her late teens, the years of amphetamines, uppers, downers, ecstasy, and anything else that came her way. It had only been what had happened to Ronnie that had finally cut through the fog of it, stopping her dead in her tracks. A vow to kick it for Ronnie's sake. Cold turkey.

And she'd done it, not that keeping her vow changed anything where Ronnie was concerned, but last night it had been five years, five years to the day. At AA she'd have had a badge by now.

She flicks on the bedside lamp. Then off. Then on. Then off. Then on before shaking free of the hypnotic pull of it.

Has she so easily forgotten all this? The physical ticks and rollercoaster ride, the sense of wonder at the little things in life that all too often simply pass by unnoticed, unremarked. Like switching on a lamp. She misses it, maybe will always miss it - but it doesn't mean she needs it. It doesn't mean she has to indulge those desires, fall into the washtub spin of it. All she needs is something...diverting.

She has an addictive personality, the tests all say so, both official and those in *Cosmo* or *Teen Vogue Online*, the ones that told you *how to get a man* before the ones the following month explained *why you aren't keeping your man*. At fifteen her therapist had said so, shown her the test results making it official. Like she didn't know. The Ed Psych at her school had told her, too. Told her parents.

'Sod that!' had been her mother's reaction before removing her from school, opting for home tuition for her A-levels whilst raging at the evils of the patriarchy.

But it was what happened to Ronnie that had stopped her. A great big Ronnie sized diversion from her own demons.

But maybe she hasn't beaten it. Maybe there's been no victory. That all she's succeeded in doing has been to cage it, chaining it up and shuttering it away. And now it was out. Last night she'd pulled back the shutters, unlocked the chain, and opened the door.

She'd thought about it a lot, the early hours, her mind freewheeling like riding a cycle downhill. She's certain it started with her boyfriend and the subsequent hack. What had that been if not the stirrings of her Beast in its cage? The rattling of its chains? Her forced transfer to Northallerton, to Forensic Computing, had irritated it, poking it with a stick, the sexual harassment dispute pushing it deeper into the corner of its cage. *The Angry Brigade* was just a final slur. *Broken Wings*. The deepest sense of what she was, who she'll always be. Wasn't that what Demetriou had said in the meeting? That we had to accept who we are. Well, she has. Last night proved nothing if not that.

She walks the room, flicking the spines of her books, tapping the edges of the desk, drumming on the walls.

She opens the curtains. Her parents' home is rural, views across the Dales towards Pen Hill. Here in the town, hers are rooftops. It's no inner city, but it feels contained, constrained, a little bit like a cage.

She slumps onto the bed, thinking about the therapy meeting and Demetriou's nailing of it, the freeing sense of accepting who she is, of what's happening inside her. And of course, he hadn't stopped there, that they should use their understanding of who they are, what they are. They should channel it, like they're… Spiderman. It was what she'd already told them, the whole *with great power*.

She doesn't feel like Spiderman or any other comic-book hero, but maybe Demetriou's right, that there's a better use for this…stuff she has going on inside, that there are things she could do.

She could be what her father strived all his life to be, what her mother always said Sophie herself has the power to be. *Be the difference, luv. Be the difference.*

21

'But I don't get it,' Musgrove responds to Fisher's statement.

'Which bit?'

'The fact that you haven't established anything beyond what the physical evidence and social history of that young woman tells us.' He raises a meaty hand, enumerates each point by flicking up a stubby finger. 'This Sofia died from hanging. Her head was shaven. The autopsy says suicide.' He drops his hand. 'I appreciate hanging's not the chosen method of most women, but maybe it was a case of needs must. No access to poisons. Shy of sharp blades. Dales traffic too thin for jumping in front of a speeding car. No bloody railways to speak of.' He shrugs. 'The only thing out of the ordinary is the fact her head was shaved. You said yourself she'd prior links to drug dealers. Maybe they did it, it's a…badge, like gang colours. A cult.'

'We're not talking *Bloods* and *Crips*, Neil. This is North Yorkshire, not South-Central Los Angeles. Why shave her head or any other woman's when it'd make her stand out a mile?' she states rather than asks. 'I sometimes wonder what passes for thinking on the top floor.'

Demetriou jumps in before Musgrove has the chance to explode a riposte about *those at the top having to waste their time dealing with all the crap from those below* that after just a few meetings he knows to be a favoured tenet of the ACC. 'When you say there's nothing out of the ordinary, aren't you forgetting the human hair in the rope?' he points out. 'When you add that in, surely it says something more than suicide, even if it doesn't say maniac predator?'

They'd been going round the idea for thirty minutes. It began when Demetriou and Fisher had entered the meeting deep in animated discussion, spilling out to the rest of the group when Musgrove had cut in, the ACC making observations about procedures that had fired up even Doyle who'd then proceeded to give full reign to her mother's ingrained readings on the exploitive behaviours embedded in the patriarchy.

Even Pemberton had been persuaded to throw in a short analysis of the state of mind of the suicidal. In particular, the impossibility of making sense of what message a suicide's death is supposed to have for those left behind. He'd been willing to let the discussion run, after all, they were talking. More than talking, they were animated, dynamic - particularly useful in throwing light on Fisher's state of mind. To his trained eye, this case of hers is provoking an inner conflict, something rubbing against deeply buried issues. Her sister's fragile mental state and the death of her father might be part of it, maybe the same issues that the Swanley trial had brought to crisis point before her breakdown.

He knows that it was the Swanley investigation that had triggered Fisher's Marie Antoinette Syndrome, the literal overnight whitening of her hair, a condition brought on by extreme stress and psychosis. He wonders if those same forces are gathering once more, for the moment a storm far out at sea, shadows chasing over an ocean, but one threatening landfall any time soon.

Most of all, he wonders if now, a year after Swanley and a few weeks since her return to duty, it's finally time to push at the now creaking doors she's previously kept so tightly sealed.

He sits forward, pen and clipboard lain on the chair. 'I hear what you're saying, Zara. But I feel there's more here. That maybe you want this to be something more than a mind numbingly routine investigation, the suicide of a sad, lonely woman. *The Stranger in a Strange Land* motif is a cliché, but that's because it's all too often true. Remember what you've told us of this woman's life. Trafficked. Violated. Depressed. I can understand why you'd want it to be more, that you might in some way transform her into the hero of her own story. But surely you see that in wanting her death to be more than a sad final act of desperation, you're wanting it to have been brutal and violent. The murder of a terrified young woman at the hands of a deeply disturbed individual finding sexual fulfilment in shaving a woman's hair and then strangling her with it.'

'Don't you think I've asked myself the same question?' she replies. 'Wondering what that says about me? But I can't change any of it. She's dead. Whatever happened to her happened. But if she *was* brutally murdered, then we owe it to her to prove it, to find whoever did it and to make them pay for what they did. You said wo*man*. Shaving a wo*man's* head. But what if it becomes wo*men*? There was more than one woman's hair twined in that rope. What if what happened in that barn was something clicking, like tumblers in a lock falling into place. That shaving isn't enough now. That he's not finished at shaving and strangling one woman. If it's a door that's been opened, then isn't it the experience that predators like that strike again and again, their cycle of attacks increasing in speed?'

Pemberton sighs. 'There's truth in what you say. If it was, of course, a murder.'

'But that's all we're looking for,' Demetriou adds. 'Bigger picture thinking, ideas getting us out of the ruts. There's websites offering all kinds of services out there. Women filming themselves shaving their hair and sending it to paying punters, sites we could check up on, find who was buying it. And I know it isn't the most extreme of it. It's like...the paddling pool end of what gets to be a very deep end. Olympic one.'

He smiles at Fisher, it's meant to be encouraging, the sense of their being aligned. In return he gets a nod, hardly Morse and Lewis, but something he can work with. The sense of an arriving thaw.

Musgrove elbows his way into the exchange. 'Look, I'm far from thinking you're right, very far. To me, it's suicide. Simple as that.' He looks around the group. 'But...just for a minute suppose it is murder. In that case, isn't it most likely it's someone at that farm that was raided rather than some demented serial killer getting his jollies from watching women shave their hair and keeping it?' he asks. 'I've studied this stuff. To me it stands to reason - opportunity and motive. Textbook. She was a working girl who'd had enough. I don't know...maybe she refused to work, annoyed her pimps, maybe angered them. She's Bulgarian. She'd been arrested, so what if this gang thought she'd been turned, promised immunity, maybe given citizenship. They might have thought she was about to inform on them, so they got rid of her. Expediency.' He sits back minus the *ta-dah* mentally ringing in his head.

Fisher wrinkles her brow. 'Why? Why would they kill her? She was profit. Merchandise. All that time and trouble to get the girls over here? It doesn't make sense. Why kill her if she earns good money? And why like that? The hair. The braided rope. The old barn.'

'Like I said, they thought she was an informer,' Musgrove replies, hitting his writerly stride. 'The barn was isolated, so no witnesses. As for the rope...well, it's silent. Plus, it makes us think she's a suicide. Confuses the investigation.'

Demetriou sits forward, hands clasped in front of him. 'Back in Brum, I've seen gangs do punishment beatings.' He closes his eyes; troubling images flutter across them. 'Worse. Maybe Neil... I mean the ACC, is right. She was an example.' He turns to Fisher. 'She was at the hostel over Swaledale, remember? Maybe she'd taken the chance to escape from that farm, and they found her. Dragged her back and made an example of her. Maybe they shaved the other girls' heads as a warning.'

'It's all possible,' Fisher agrees. 'It's why we have to push deeper.'

'Listen, I didn't say I believed it,' Musgrove remonstrates. 'It's just an idea, thinking out loud. Like I say, I like puzzles. Plot lines. I read a lot.'

Demetriou looks at Musgrove. 'But you see it, don't you?'

'I never said that.' He turns to Pemberton. 'I like crime novels. Plots...fascinate me. A bit like cryptic crosswords. I write stuff, ideas for books.'

'Some sicko shaved her head,' Fisher states, chewing her bottom lip. 'Then they twined it around a length of rope and used it to hang her. That's not gangs making an example, it's premeditated. It's...specific, it's not business.' She glares at Musgrove who sits arms folded, not playing anymore. 'If it was business, then why go to all that trouble? A bullet in the head. Slit her throat. Use a regular washing line or length of farm rope to strangle her or hang her. Any of those make the same point with the remaining girls. It was done that way for the killer themselves, not for anyone else.'

Demetriou takes a moment. 'I get that much of the evidence indicates Sofia's death to be the suicide common-sense holds it to be,' he states, aware Fisher now glares at him. 'Yet, there are things at odds with such a conclusion. *Why was the hair braided into the rope? Why all that time and effort?* There's nothing we've discovered about her life to suggest a woman making a statement about the cosmetic industry or the patriarchy persuading others to shave their own heads to wrap around the rope in some *TikTok* protest. An it doesn't suggest gangs.'

'You see it, don't you?' Fisher states.

He holds for a moment. 'Yes. Yes, I believe I do.'

'Oh, for goodness sake!' Musgrove sputters.

'Me too,' Doyle chimes. 'I see it. I mean, strip everything out and you've basic logic. All ones and zeros, it's binary. By that calculation, Fisher's right, given the evidence, murder by maniac is way more compelling a probability than suicide, greater even than that of her being executed by Bulgarians. You just have to be open to it.' She turns to Musgrove. 'Your plotting, Neil. You saw it straight away. The things I see in binary, in numbers and code, the writer bit of you sees too. Different paths, but comes to similar conclusions about the mechanics of it. Not the common-sense features everybody else sees, but the fact that it works as a plot. It's got something.'

'You're used to seeing things in a particular way,' Demetriou offers. 'The way we've all been trained to, the way the job conditions us to see things. It's the mantra we all know by heart - process and procedure. Organisations and big institutions do that to people, just ask Malcolm here. It's true, isn't it Malcolm? Institutionalised thinking. Hive minds,' he asks referencing yet another of the recent tomes he's read.

'A generalisation, perhaps,' Pemberton allows.

'...But the Met was institutionally racist and sexist,' Doyle puts in.

'Along with every other force in the country,' Fisher adds.

Ignoring her, Demetriou sticks to pressing his point, the one that's evolving even as he says it out loud. 'But it's like Sophie said, the other you, the writer part, that part sees it. Your ideas for motives flowed way too easily for it not to have been playing on your mind long before this meeting. Way before any of us said anything about it.'

Musgrove stares at them. He loosens his arms, uncoils, allowing them to flop onto his lap. He exhales. 'I...last night, early this morning. I couldn't sleep. I got up...wrote a couple of things. I...it's a hobby, really. Not that Jean sees it that way. More *a bloody waste of time*, she says.' He laughs, but they sit, listening. 'Bit like daydreaming. But...writing. Writing crime fiction...like I said...it's what I do. Like Sudoku. Relaxes me. Gets me out of myself, the stuff running through my day.'

'I hope your stuff's a bit more to the point. Maybe a bit of editing, eh Neil?'

'What? Erhm...Well, your case...cases actually. Some of the things about them were running round in my head.' He grunts. 'Percolating. Hardly surprising, really. You'd been so bloody annoying. I woke up and started thinking...'

'...Thinking what?'

'That's just it. *What. What if.* It's where all the ideas for my books start. Not that I've done anything with any of mine. Got a drawer full of them. *What ifs.*'

'...And?'

'It... flowed. It... wrote itself.'

'...And this idea...' Fisher prompts.

'No... it's...' Musgrove resists.

'...It's what? Demetriou asks.

'...Insane.' Musgrove judges.

'Try us,' Doyle encourages.

Musgrove looks at Fisher and then Demetriou. 'What if your suicides are linked.'

'Sorry?' Demetriou asks.

'Sofia and Wrigley. What if they're not suicides, but murders committed by the same person,' Musgrove suggests. 'The same motive. Wrigley was a solicitor. Sofia reached out to him. Involved him. Their deaths are executions. Business,'

'Bugger me!' Fisher utters. 'And there's me thinking I'm the crazy one.'

22

Why he's chosen to meet here is lost on Gill. Looking around, he thinks the platform of grey-white limestone's advantage lies solely in its isolation. Here, at this time of night, this season, there's little chance of being interrupted, even less chance of being seen by those who might know them. That said, there are thousands of such places littered across the county. So why has he chosen here?

Hands thrust deep in pockets, Gill shudders at the breeze gusting across the exposed escarpment. Maybe it has meaning for the man he's meeting. Maybe something linked to what happened all those years ago, the story Old Archibald had breathed on his death bed. Or maybe he likes Harry Potter.

He takes out his phone. No bars.

He slips the device back into the pocket of his Barbour, his eyes sifting the darkness for any shift in its shadows. Nothing. What had Archibald used to say? *Still as the gr-*...hmmm, maybe not go there. Not here. Not now. After all, if Jacob Strong is right, it's the reason he's here - deaths and graves, the unfinished business of the dead.

He moves closer to the edge of the natural stone terrace, the curved sweep of Malham Cove, the strange topography forming a cliff face on the southern edge of the county.

He looks across fields and paddocks towards Malham itself, comfort in feet planted on the stumps of limestone. He leans forward, looks down at the dwellings cradled in the curve of the landscape two hundred and fifty feet below.

He stands upright, stamping his feet and muttering. At first, it's a simple cursing of the weather, the wind. Then, he moves to cursing at the madness of allowing himself to be suckered into this meeting, conscious he's here not out of guilt but anxiety.

Webb. Webb's death had started it. According to rumour and popular media, Webb's death had been a matter of wrong place, wrong time - a miscalculation, the growing speculation that the police and intelligence services are convinced the PM was the target of an act of terrorism gone awry. Now commentators and analysts took turns standing in front of the flume - Clive Myrie and the rest, vox to camera, - the only talk now that of terrorist cells. Islamic State, Isis, Daesh, or whatever you were supposed to call them these days.

He's watched the nightly reports, the police claim of being on the brink of success, but after a week of investigation it appears they've no real idea of who was responsible. It left the gnawing sense that if it had been terrorist related, they'd have found someone by now. A *Most Wanted* list or something. At the very least, someone would have claimed responsibility.

Of course, that was part of the infection, the madness that has brought him here. That and the visit from Jacob Strong, the journalist who'd contacted him out of the blue a few days ago. A man who'd been an acquaintance of his father's telling a story matching that of old Archibald and of Wrigley. The story he'd pushed away as the ramblings of a dying, deluded old man and a drunkard, one of the many fictions *Archibald Gill and Son* had published over the decades. Hearing it told by Strong has been like touching cobwebs in a house you'd thought empty. Discovering there were things stirring inside, things that were alive and hungry. That monsters and demons are real. That nightmares move among us.

Strong had confirmed Wrigley's fears, that old Archibald, Wrigley, Webb, Strong himself and an associate whom Strong refused to name - were the target of a killer. That though Archibald had died naturally, he believes Webb's murder is not terror related, that Wrigley's fall is not suicide, that their deaths reveal a target on Strong's own back, possibly on Gill's.

Gill knows little about Webb other than he'd been a business associate of his father who'd earned a reputation for walking both sides of the street. *Running with the foxes whilst hunting with the hounds* as old Archibald used to have it whenever his name came up. Rumours abounded of Webb's activities, of ventures stretching the definitions of legality - but accusations of tax avoidance and dodgy dealings are levelled against many in his line of work. That he'd been the target of a murderer requires a different level of belief.

Despite his doubts, Gill hadn't slept well that night, nor those after. The press reported Wrigley's death as suicide, though the officers investigating it – so Strong had heard – are for some reason dragging their feet on a final report. Maybe Strong was adding two and two and coming up wrong. Wrigley was a loner verging on reclusive, a heavy drinker. A man who'd seemingly lived inside his own head for years, circumstances offering every possibility that Webb's death had prompted him to examine his conscience over the shameful venture that bound them. Thoughts pushing him, quite literally, over the edge.

Gill shivers. Why's he going over this now? Worrying himself with murderous thoughts whilst standing in darkness on top of Malham Cove waiting to meet a man whom Strong and Wrigley thought a killer? A man who at the very least knows of the secret that has bound Strong and the rest for the past fifteen years. The inclusion of the word *Gingerbread* in the message Strong received that morning demanding money for their silence had convinced

Strong his fears were real. The four men had all been executors of the Gingerbread Trust.

Strong had convinced Gill to make the drop-off of the money, that Gill's innocence made him the better choice as go-between. Gill had agreed because of something only he and the man he's about to meet with know: that years ago old Archibald had helped a man Strong and the rest had come to believe dead, a man who had threatened their enterprise. That man knows that not only is Gill himself innocent of anything these men did, but that Archibald had saved this man. It is a debt Gill is certain protects him.

Strong's suggestion is that the blame be placed on those already dead – Archibald, Webb, and Wrigley - for Gill to convince this man they'd been the real criminals. That Strong's role had been secondary, as was that of the unnamed other, the Fifth Man.

Gill's not sure he'll believe it, but he'll hand-over the hold-all. He is also to assure this man of Strong's continuing influence with someone whose own interests will ensure no-one will ever link these deaths. They will remain a suicide and a terrorist attack. They can all walk away, their crimes hidden forever: Gill's reputation secure, Strong safe from murder, the killer's own freedom secured, his vengeance complete.

He stops the train of thought. *What's he thinking*? Why had he agreed to be the one taking the meeting, the one negotiating, the one making the offer face to face out here? Suddenly aware that decapitating Webb in front of hundreds of family and friends and maybe tossing Wrigley from a rooftop are the work of someone pushing at the limits of any definition of sanity. How do you make a deal with the Devil?

He's still thinking about leaving, running, telling Strong to do his own dirty work, when a movement across the escarpment alerts him that someone else is up here. He calls out. 'Hey! I'm over here. It's me. Gill. John Gill. Archibald Gill's son.'

Squinting, he makes out a figure silhouetted against the rise of the ground, the grass covered terraces that undulate in steep rolling mounds into the distance. There are no bushes or trees here, the hostile wind and solid rock see to that.

'I'm alone,' Gill calls out, suddenly aware such an admission might not be the wisest. 'We need to talk. Put things straight.'

The figure doesn't move.

'I know why you're doing these things,' Gill says, unnerved by the figure's silence. 'Strong told me everything. He says to tell you that he never intended any of the things that happened. *Gingerbread* was Webb and Wrigley's idea.'

The figure appears motionless, though Gill thinks that possibly it's moved a pace or two closer. It's hard to tell from where Gill stands, his own back to the edge of the cliff, the man's outline set against the dark background of the terracing. 'I know you wanted Strong here, but I'm the go-between. I'm not involved in any of what they did. I only found out after Archibald died, but I know he helped you, gave you money to get away, covered up the fact that you were still alive. I just want to draw a line under everything. Strong says he can make certain the deaths are never linked, that everything stays hidden. Your crimes and his own. No-one will know.'

He picks up the canvas holdall that's lain by his feet for the past hour. He holds it out in front of him. 'There's money here.'

The figure steps forward. He wears a dark hoodie under a padded mountain jacket, his outline distorted by the bulk of his clothing. He is tall for certain, but other than that, it's hard for Gill to tell if he's thin or as well built as the layers make him appear. The man pulls the hood down, features masked by the gloom. Gill tosses the bag so it lands close to the man's feet, like he's seen in crime movies. 'It's yours. Take it.'

The figure kneels on one knee, hands unzipping the bag.

He appears to study it for a moment, even reaching a hand inside. Gill hears the sound of paper being flicked as he sizes up the amount. Tugging the bag fully open, the man turns it over, tipping the contents onto the ancient limestone. The wind immediately whipping the cash away.

'What?' is all Gill has time to say as he watches it blow past and out across the valley. The act has him half-turning, hands instinctively reaching to snatch the notes from the air as they sail by. The next moment he feels a blow against his chest, the impact winding him, as the onrushing figure crashes into him. The man's momentum - rising from the crouch, sprinting full power across the short space between them - knocks Gill upwards, literally off his feet, sending him staggering back. As Gill struggles to maintain his balance, light from the pale moon breaks through the clouds, falling across the figure's face.

Gill's eyes widen. 'You?'

The last thought that passes through Gill's mind as he tumbles the two hundred and fifty feet to the valley floor is how could they have been so mistaken.

23

Musgrove wakes with a start. What has he done? What had he been thinking? How can he have been so stupid as to have said the things he'd said? Shared the things he'd shared, those things better left in the shadows. The personal, the private, the *"you really don't need to know this stuff"* he's kept locked away.

Now they're out - and not because they'd broken through the bars or cut the razor wire of common bloody sense; he's simply left the gate open. More than that, for some reason – he thinks the warm runny sense of bonhomie he'd felt emanating from the others - he'd encouraged those thoughts to take a run out in the fresh air, trot around the therapy group conversation like preening show ponies. So why's he surprised that it got out of hand, that he's lost control, that deeply secret parts of him have taken off, stampeding away and carrying the last dregs of his self-esteem high above their heads like body surfers at a heavy metal gig?

He sits up, feels a cold sweat, hands reaching for the phone, checking the clock for the tenth time since jerking from a nightmare that's no such thing. It's real. It's what he's done. Right now, it's far worse than the one finding yourself naked in a meeting or whatever it is that the top five worst nightmares are.

He'd told them about his writing. Told them his idea.

He taps the screen of the phone. It isn't too late. He can stop this. Get ahead of the game, phone them – Fisher, Doyle, Demetriou - summon them to his office before they start their shifts. Get them there at the same time, make it appear official, a warning not to repeat anything said in the meeting, remind them of the consequences. He'd go over the sanctity of the therapy room, the whole *"what's said in therapy stays in therapy"* card. Hippocratic oaths and the like. Yes, that's his way forward, shutting it down before it has the chance to go any further.

But there's Fisher. Fisher who'll no doubt see it as a personal challenge to throw the whole cart load of apples as far and wide as she might. Cats among pigeons have little on Fisher once the mood takes hold. He'd seen it up close and it isn't pretty. She'll see it as funny, a lark, a stick to poke him with. Nothing will delight her more than to question him, undermine him in front of the others. Make him squirm. She's vengeful. The hellhound on his trail.

So, it's clearly better he sees them individually. Start with Doyle, then Demetriou, get them on board before confronting Fisher. Once they're in line he'll get her to see that any leak regarding his ideas about their cases are as much a threat to the three of them as they are to his own standing in the force.

Maybe start with dropping in something about Demetriou. He's noticed that even when they disagree she seems to have a warmer glow in her eyes when she talks to him. It isn't lust or anything sexual, and it certainly isn't maternal – both of which are elements of the woman he prefers not to think about. But he's caught the same feeling when she's spoken with Doyle. The acid words, the invective, is there, but underneath there's something else going on. Like...running hot water into an ice-cold bath. The whole remains essentially icy, in Fisher's case teeth chattering-*ly* so, but there's a warmer current at play, a thawing. In anyone else he'd have considered friendship or kindred spirits, but this is Fisher, so at present it's more of a UFO. Unidentified Fucked-up Object.

He could, of course, simply laugh it off, make a joke of it. The *"boy did we get carried away with it all"* approach of mates reflecting on a wild night out, the arm spread wide cheeriness of it, the whole *"what was I like"* jokiness of what he'd said. But they weren't mates or drinking pals, just a collection of broken people, unpredictable and with agendas of their own. In that case, it would come across as desperate pleading. And right now, he's no idea how that might go

The other way is throwing himself fully into it, embracing the madness. Testing the water in the cold light of day, push deeper into the swamp to discover what lies there. But he knows that can't happen, that his wild hypotheses days are behind him, that Hyland and Jean and his brother-in-law hold sway over that part of him. He's handed over the keys to any mid-life sports car dream of being a writer, that he now has to demonstrate sensible policing, manage the PR and protect the brand. Outside the box madness is the one option he can't put on the table, so better to remove the table completely.

He swings his legs out of bed. Whichever option he chooses – straight talking or matey jokiness – he's only a few hours to do so. Once the others arrive at HQ the chance of spillage, the leaking of his secret, the revelation of the well-hidden wildness of his thought processes, the Walter Mitty-*ness* of his life, increases by the minute.

He has to head them off.

He could of course take the nuclear option, threaten to spill the beans on them, the secrets they'd shared of themselves. Of Doyle's fear of her own redacted secrets finding their way into public knowledge, her parents' eternal shame. Of Demetriou's *ménage à trois* arrangement that would make him a cuckolded laughingstock. Fisher's…what? What does he have that Fisher would even care about becoming known? She'd laugh in his face, dare him. He knows that any mention of her father touches a nerve but he's not sure why and he's not sure it's a closet he wants to open, wary of the skeleton's he'll find there. The man died a hero, so he's unsure why she's sensitive to any mention of him. He knows something of her mother's troubles, a little more of her sister's addictions, but those are the very things putting them out of bounds. He's looking for her compliance, not an eternal vendetta being waged, his threats sparking the Hillbilly blood feud that Fisher would certainly send his way.

He looks at the clock. Time's running out and he's back to where he started.

The ping of a text arriving halts his thinking. He looks at his phone, a request to attend an urgent meeting with Hyland as soon as he gets in.

It's too late. It's game over.

24

'So, that's where we're at,' Hyland states. 'You've got your way.' It's a statement lacking grace or well wishes, more in the manner of a parent giving in to an intemperate child.

Musgrove's not sure what to think. At the moment it's very much along the lines of relief in discovering he's not been called in because Hyland's heard about the therapy session. His madness. At the same time wondering if it qualifies as escape or merely postponement of sentence, that once Doyle, Demetriou, and Fisher turn in he'll find his secrets graffitied along the corridor walls in left-over decorator's colour samples.

'Thank you, sir,' he manages, choking back the urge to scream in frustration at Hyland's ill-tempered pronouncement, a sign the Anger Management is going better than he's realised. He'll make a note to tell Malcolm.

Hyland's unconfined 'Harrumph!' cuts across any further comment. 'I can't say it's my idea,' the Chief constable reveals. 'Case of needs must. We're stretched thin by the Webb investigation, what with the Spooks demanding more and more of our time and resources. Manpower, you see.' He rolls a pen back and forth across the desk under the palm of one hand. Maybe it's some meditative yoga thing Musgrove thinks, that or that he can't even be bothered to look him in the eyes. 'I need my finest on deck, safe hands on the tiller and all that,' he continues. 'Frankly, I've no-one else left. No-one qualified, that is.'

'So what? You're telling me that I'm...what... *it*. Like *bottom of the barrel* it? The scrapings?'

Hyland snorts. 'A tad on the direct side. Makes it sound quite demoralising. Its more...we just need everyone pulling their weight.'

'And I'm not? I'm here every day putting in a full shift.'

'Yes, quite. I had a look at the Deployment Spreadsheet for the past few weeks,' he says lifting the pen, rolling it between fingers. 'These Therapy Meetings. There's been quite a few of those. More than planned. Having a breakthrough, are we?'

'With respect, sir. I'm there because you sent me.'

'Saving your bloody arse if you recall, 'Hyland states, slapping the pen onto the desk. 'That Webb fiasco at the pool. If it had found its way to Complaints it'd have been your head.' He stops short, both men chewing on the irony and at the same time inappropriateness of the analogy, given Webb's means of demise.

'Storm in a teacup, sir. It would have blown over,' Musgrove retorts.

'For God's sake, man, we're talking the internet. Social media. Nothing blows over. The internet never forgets. More to the point, Gina *bloody* Hargreaves never forgets. It was Hargreaves who insisted on removing you from the firing line. Her and that PR fella at her coat-tails.'

'Lawrence!' Musgrove spits. 'Harvey bloody Lawrence. That man makes my blood boil. He's so...' he stops, the realisation he doesn't know what it is about Lawrence that causes him to react this way. Maybe the whiff of shadows that follows him, the same feeling he has about Fisher, both of them like inner city building sites - the sense of things happening behind hoardings, an inkling of what's been knocked down, glimpses of things being built, but no defining sense of what that might be. He feels his hostility gathering a fresh head of steam, the crimson tide rolling in, the realisation he'd been premature in assessing the benefits of Anger Management. Maybe he'll not say anything to Malcolm just yet.

'Point is,' Hyland continues, 'I need you at Malham to run the checks on this unexplained death, a tourist from first reports. Some bloody overzealous Potter fan after a dramatic selfie toppling over the edge I don't doubt. For the life of me, I can't see it being anything else, you know, a protest against the Rowling woman's stand on trans or whatever it is she's said or done lately. I mean, three suicides in less than two weeks would be a record even round here. Some coincidence.'

'No such thing,' Musgrove states.

'What?'

'No such thing as coincidence. Einstein said it's God's way of remaining anonymous. One is happenstance. Twice coincidence. Three times…well he said at the time that it was enemy action. But that was during the war.' He smiles wanly at the realisation he's part way down another rabbit hole; bunny tail stuck up in the air. 'Anyway, the point holds.'

Hyland exhales long and loud, places the pen on the desk. 'At times, Musgrove, I do wonder how your mind works. All these…details, bits of stuff you dredge up. It's distracting. You do it in meetings. Miss the point. Its irritating, annoying.'

'I just thought it was…pertinent. You know, ways of looking at things differently. A fresh eye. Einstein was always coming up with statements that seemed relatively simple, straightforward, but they were the result of what business gurus call Blue Sky thinking. I just want to get us out of the ruts.'

'Frankly, I couldn't care less. Boxes, envelopes, blue sky or whatever other term the buggering PR gurus like Lawrence come up with. I need results, not waffle.' He rolls the pen once more, slowly, methodically, each roll halting at the same spot before rolling again. 'I have to say it's not what I thought we were getting when you were appointed.'

Musgrove senses bile in his throat, an irritation increased by knowing he has to bite down and swallow it. He stares at the carpet, *Berber, woollen twill, oatmeal. Twenty-five ninety-nine a square metre.*

'So, let's be clear. I'm seeing this as an opportunity for you to surprise me. Surprise us all. Get a bit of self-respect back. Erase a few of those blots on your career copybook, eh? Get yourself over to Malham and sort this out. Do the paperwork and get it ticked off on the crime statistics. Given the state the Webb enquiry's in, we could do with some simple wins. Get me a win, Musgrove. A simple meat and potatoes win. Not too much to ask, of my ACC, don't you think? A bit of support.'

Musgrove swallows. 'No, sir,' he says, teeth gritted. 'I'll get it done.'

'And by the book, Musgrove, by the book.'

Always Musgrove, never Neil.

He waits next to the stairs, trying to look casual, flicking through the rack of magazines, flyers about community action. Most are neighbourhood watch, aka the curtain twitchers approval scheme; Hargreaves's very own *Suspicious of Something? Ring Your Local Force* campaign plaguing switchboards across the county. Calls on everything from reports of shifty looking *Just Eat* and *Deliveroo* riders through to lost *Amazon* drivers wandering the streets looking for somewhere to leave a package.

A snack machine glows in one corner of the space, and he finds his hands twitching in trouser pockets for loose change, the desire for something sweet, a sugar rush to get him through the next ten minutes.

He scans the door, watches the polished glass and chrome pod popping out its cargo - senior ranks in dress uniform, civilian clerks in jeans and cargo pants that make it hard to tell them apart from the dress down plain clothes of CID.

Demetriou is first in, followed a few paces later by Doyle,

roll-top cycle bag hanging casually off one shoulder, headphones subduing the natural bounce of pre-Raphaelite curls. Fisher is nowhere to be seen, thus his course of action is decided by the pressing constraints of time and opportunity just as any good murder might be, certainly one in the world of *Rick Mangrove, PI*.

He calls them over, hustling them towards a quiet corner where his massive bulk pens them like sheep whilst he button-holes them.

'About the other day,' he begins.

'I can explain,' Doyle jumps in. 'It was a one off, won't happen again.'

'It won't?' Musgrove asks, taken aback and wondering what she means.

'No. Never.' She reassures. 'It was just...a bad day. An anniversary. I felt like I just had to let go...let stuff out. It won't happen again. I promise.'

'Is that a Pinky promise,' Fisher calls approaching them. 'Sorry, Neil, but I didn't get the memo for this sub-meeting of *the Famous Four*,' she states whilst sliding a HQ pass out of her trench coat pocket.

'It's not a meeting, as such' he adds.

'So, what is it *"as such"*?' Fisher asks.

'It's more in the way of a clarification,' Musgrove re-assures.

'...A clarification?'

'The rules,' Musgrove states, re-clarifying any misunderstood clarification.

'...Rules? What, are we talking like a VAR decision?' Fisher pushes.

'I...erhm...By I, I meant Doctor Pemberton. He says he wants to remind us that anything shared in the group is subject to a strict rule of silence outside the group,' he states.

'Like monks?' she suggests, flicking her pass against fingers.

'Like disciplinary proceedings,' Musgrove clarifies again.

'I thought the group was created because we're all pretty crap at that sort of thing. If we were good with rules, then the chances are we wouldn't be there in the first place,' Fisher judges. 'Anyway, I thought it was beyond all that. Rules and the like. Rank and hierarchy. I thought it was first name terms and trust. Real Libertarian hippy stuff.'

'Well, yes, there's that of course. But there's rules too,' Musgrove points out. 'Has to be.'

'What, like back-up? A threat?' Doyle asks, flicking her head from side to side as she ruffles her hair into shape.

Musgrove frowns. 'That's...' he manages before losing his way. He pauses, the sense that things are getting away from him.

'...That's what?' Demetriou prompts.

Musgrove settles on 'Harsh.' After a moment's thought adding 'Cold. Blunt.'

'You know me, Neil,' Fisher responds flicking at her own hair, wondering how Doyle manages to keep hers like that with all the cycling and the helmet. 'Cold and blunt are two of my better qualities on Tinder. Harsh is in there too, I think.'

'I meant that saying that rules are threats is too harsh,' he replies. 'They're there to offer assurance. Security, so that we know anything we say in the meetings is bound by the sanctity of the group.'

'Like church,' Doyle says, coiling the wire and dropping the headphones into her bag.

'Exactly. Like confession. We're like priests who hear what the penitent has to say but are sworn never to reveal it,' Musgrove nods.

'I'm hearing all this high church sinner stuff, Neil so I'm wondering if what you're suggesting is that we go in for burning incense and a bit of chanting when we next get together,' Fisher says. 'I mean, if that's what the rest want, I'm happy to give it a try, but it's not really my scene at all...though wine and bread might liven up things a bit more than those flasks of sluice juice they call coffee.'

'What like Hari-Krishna?' Doyle asks.

'No! Not at all. Nothing like any of that,' Musgrove snaps,

waving his hands up and down as if flapping washing. 'Look,' he pauses, aware of their faces. 'I said some things in the last meeting, things I'm anxious not be repeated outside the group. Are we clear?'

The three look at each other, thoughts expressed in arched brows, wrinkled foreheads and Doyle's last few flicks of her hair. 'Of course we're clear,' Demetriou replies. 'What, did you think, that we'd be blabbing to the rest of the force about what each of us said?'

'No, of course not...I just thought it was...good to reassure each other.'

'Neil,' Fisher begins, security card taking another tour of her fingers. 'For a start Demetriou here has no friends to speak of in these parts and frankly I'm not all that certain about back in Brum. The young Ms. Doyle no doubt presents to the geeks and twin set and pearls brigade she works with as an alien life form. And as for me...Do I really have to tell you of all people that I'm the last person anyone here wants to have a cosy chat with.'

'And there's the trust,' Demetriou adds. 'I wouldn't do that to anyone.'

'Nor me,' Doyle chips in still getting to grips with Fisher's alien comment.

'And for my part, only if you were Crosby. I'd dob the little wanker in at the drop of a hat,' Fisher judges.

'I...erhm...thank you.' He nods. 'Thank you, it means a lot... the trust.'

'Neil, it's the trust that binds us. It can't be broken,' Demetriou judges, prompting an exchange of looks with Fisher.

Fisher's lips purse forming a thoughtful half-smile. 'This is all getting a bit like *when a bell rings an angel's gets their wings* really isn't it? You know, *It's A Wonderful Life*. I wonder if right now Malcolm's not sitting at his desk wondering where that tiny tear forming in the corner of one eye's come from. A Christmas miracle.'

Musgrove shrugs, pats at topcoat pockets, checking for keys

and phone before slipping the jacket over his uniform. 'Well, now that's sorted, I've a job to get to.'

'What? A proper job? A shout?'

'Some bloke fell off the cliff at Malham,' he says stretching sleeves into place.

'Not another suicide, surely?' Demetriou asks.

Musgrove slaps his pockets once more, this time checking the bars of chocolate stuffed there aren't showing. 'Wouldn't think so. Most likely an accident so the Mountain Rescue are saying. Bloody routine that could be handled by a DS.'

'So why you?'

'We're short-handed. Seems they can't spare a DS but can send an ACC all the way out there to make sure we tick the right boxes.'

'A tourist then?'

'No, local. John Gill. The publishers over in Harrogate.'

'Can't say I know them,' Fisher shrugs.

Musgrove stops patting, turning to face her. 'Brightside. Gillian Brightside. You must know her. The children's illustrator. Folk brought up on her stories for decades. Anyone born after the seventies for sure. Mind you it was the seventies that finished her, the drugs and booze.'

Doyle shakes her head. 'Not my parent's thing, fairy tales.'

Demetriou shakes his head. 'No. Nothing. We had Jasper Carrot.'

'Tell you what, if it turns out to be suicide, we should share notes,' Fisher offers. 'Pan and I seem to be collecting them like Happy Families, actually, maybe Very Sad Families.'

25

Arriving at the scene Musgrove's struck by the lack of vehicles. He isn't certain what he's expected, but certainly more than an ambulance, a Mountain Rescue Land Rover, and the sole North Yorkshire Police patrol car. A little further back he notes a dark panelled van that awaits his say so to transport the dead man to Harrogate for the required autopsy.

He gets out of the car, reaching back to retrieve his outer coat from the rear seat. The morning air retains some of the previous night's chill and he knows better than to risk shivering at the site of an incident. His hands-on reputation is weak enough without providing canteen gossip of his *"not being up to it"*, *"weak stomached"*.

Shuffling the dark blue waterproof on, he makes his way down the path, struggling with his zip. Once the teeth engage, he manages a tug that tightens it, and it's only then that he looks to the far end of the track, the crime scene tape and loose assembly of uniforms and Mountain Rescue. The members of the Rescue Unit are easy to make out: bright orange suits, bandoliers of ropes and snap-on clips criss-crossing chests like Mexican bandits. They've gathered themselves around a mound of backpacks, and stand tight knit, dancers in a club around a totem pole of handbags.

The nearest constable, the younger of those present, manages a languid salute. The officer to his rear, clearly older and senior, opts for a nod of the head, a muttered 'Sir'. Musgrove decides now isn't the time to rail about the niceties of form and rank, an explosion that would find its way to the canteen before he even got back to his car. He wonders if this self-control is the result of Pemberton's therapy or self-preservation.

'So,' he begins in the time-honoured manner of detective procedurals. 'What have we got?' the clichés piling up at rapid rate.

The elder officer opens a notebook and flicks a couple of pages. 'I'm PC Verity. PC Metcalfe and I were called out this morning to attend the report of a body at the foot of Malham Cove. That one,' he states pointing at the hump of canvas covering the outline of a body. 'He was found by a woman out walking her dog. I took her details and sent her home. Didn't see much point in her hanging round, especially as the dog was a whining brute that didn't take too well to young Metcalfe here.'

Metcalfe shrugs. 'Aggressive little bastard,' he offers in support of what he clearly feels to be his colleague's precise assessment of both mutt and situation.

'Do we know anything about him?' Musgrove asks.

'Well, other than how aggressive he is,' the PC begins, 'Cock-A-thingy of some sort,' he states.

'The victim, not the dog,' Musgrove clarifies.

The Rescue leader nods at the tarpaulin. 'Gill according to his driver's license. John Gill. Male. Mid-thirties. Your uniforms called that in,' he states, voice dark and throaty matching weathered features and the day or two's worth of stubble. He shrugs his move to conjecture. 'Dressed like a tourist, but not a walker or hiker. Warm coat and jeans; boots leisure not walking. Fell off the top and hit every boulder on the way down.' It's the observation of a man who's brought more than his fair share of corpses and injured down from the fells, most of them ill-prepared and naïve in the ways of a county that, like its natives, doesn't suffer fools gladly. 'We haven't checked for other ID. Your lads said it was procedure to wait on the senior officer. Have to say, I wasn't expecting one so senior as yourself.'

'We're busy. The Harrogate thing. All hands and that.'

The man nods, exchanging looks with Verity.

Lambert hands over a leather wallet. Musgrove sees there's a few bank cards, a driving license and a piece of paper torn from a notebook, the word *'gingerbread'* written in pencil. 'Gingerbread?' Musgrove says.

'Sorry?'

'On the paper. It says *gingerbread*.'

There are shrugs all-round. 'Maybe it's a password,' Verity offers.

'Shopping list?' Metcalfe suggests. 'You know, him coming up here. Isn't that what walkers and climbers eat for energy?'

'That's Kendall mint-cake,' Verity corrects. 'Not that it's much use to him now. He's definitely dead. The para-medics over there confirmed it. Personally, I thought having his skull cracked open like an Easter egg was a decent enough indicator, but procedure says they have to confirm it.'

As he listens, Musgrove returns the paper to the wallet, nods in what he hopes to be a sage manner. 'Any marks up top?' he asks.

'Sorry?'

'I assume someone's been up top,' Musgrove clarifies, an outstretched arm indicating the cliff edge. 'Had a look around.'

'Look around?' the Rescue leader asks.

'Yes.'

The man looks to the cliff face and back again. He takes a pack of cigarettes from a zip pocket of his bright orange over trousers and knocks a smoke out of the pack. He rolls it between his fingers before replying. 'For what?'

'Well, some indication of what happened up there.'

'He fell is what happened. Not sure what good it'd do, going up there. What it'd add to that fact.'

'It might be a crime scene.'

'A crime scene?' the man asks, lighting the cigarette with a disposable lighter. He takes a long breath, pulling the smoke deep into his lungs. He exhales slowly, his words spread wide on the breath. 'You think so?'

'Possibly.'

'What sort of crime would we be talking about?' the man asks.

'Did he fall? Did he jump? Was he pushed?' Musgrove offers.

Police and Rescue look from one to the other, a Mexican wave of furrowed brows and puffing of breath. Long sighs are exhaled in passive dismissal. The Leader wrinkles his top lip, his nose coming along for the ride. 'It doesn't happen that much. Pushing off cliffs and that,' he adds. 'They usually slip from getting too close. Selfies kill more tourists than anything, trying to get that Instagram shot. Harry Potter's a lot to answer for in that regards,' he adds, idly moving his helmet from one hand to the other. 'You know, getting them up there at the precipice with their Hufflepuff and the like.'

There is a nodding of heads, mutters of assent.

Musgrove notes the word MARTIN stencilled across the man's helmet. 'Now then, Martin, don't get me wrong. I'm not saying this is anything other than what it appears, a distracted tourist stumbling off the edge. But there's procedure to follow. That's something these officers know all about. They're trained, see?' He points across the track. 'I can see there's tape down there, but there should also be an immediate investigation of the place from where he fell. I assume that's straight up there above us. That he hasn't rolled away from where he hit?'

'There's blood and stuff here. Nowhere else,' PC Verity observes in answer to what he presumes to be a question. He shuffles a little more upright, a nod in the direction of the improvised shroud. 'We did the tape to stop folk coming up here. Thought it best to wait for senior officer before anyone went up top. Procedure.'

Musgrove nods, a gesture ending with a striking clap of his hands. 'Well then, I suggest that whilst we wait for the pathologist's lot to get here we make ourselves busy. Take a look up top. What do you think?'

Verity looks around. The Rescue team shrug, he's Verity's boss, not theirs. 'Yes, sir,' he agrees, turning to his partner. 'You wait here, Metcalfe. The ACC and I'll get ourselves up there, see if we can find anything that might be of assistance in ascertaining what happened.' Metcalfe notes the key change in Verity's speech pattern as it moves from colleague to official police speak mode. He hasn't heard his partner use a word like *ascertaining* in months, and even then it had been some word play involving the '*ass*' part of it. Not that he can recall the actual topic, but he knows he'd laughed at the time.

Musgrove turns to MARTIN. 'Maybe you'd like to come with us. See if there's anything you might cast some light on. Your knowledge. The rock. The sort of signs you might expect to find in such circumstances.'

MARTIN shrugs a shoulder twitch of agreement. 'Yeah. No problem.' He nods his intention to the members of his team who settle to packing the equipment.

The walk to the top is steep, a series of steps - part stone, part mud - carved into a rock-face that takes them up a track positioned at eleven o'clock to the straight up of the limestone cliff face. In places hands are necessary to steady their stride onto the steeper steps, the only means of preventing slipping on the tufts of grass and wet mud that in places fill the track. Musgrove climbs in silence, unwilling to show just how short of breath he is. He assumes the silence of the other two is down to their unwillingness to say anything that might drag them further into what they obviously believe to be a fool's errand.

Walking out onto the platform of limestone stumps, he's

struck by the scope of a view that stretches miles into the distance along the entirety of the 180-degree panorama.

'Gorgeous,' he mutters.

'Sorry?' MARTIN asks.

'The view. Spectacular, isn't it?'

MARTIN shrugs. 'Don't really notice. Spend a few nights up here in the pitch black looking for numpties and you find you've mixed feelings. Find your mind's fixed on things like getting them and yourself back down in one piece.'

Musgrove nods. 'Suppose. Still, it is magnificent.'

MARTIN grants a reluctant nod before continuing his search of the platform. 'What precisely are we looking for?' he enquires.

Verity ceases kicking the scrub of bushes, awaiting guidance.

'To be frank, I'm not sure. Just anything...odd. Out of place.'

'I'm uniform not fucking Bear *bastard* Grylls,' the constable mutters to MARTIN once Musgrove has turned his back and begun scouring the edge of the platform. 'I wouldn't know if anything was odd up here or not. I mean, what is there? Stone. A few tufts of grass. A bush or two. Gravel.' He watches Musgrove sink on one knee to begin staring intently at the ground. 'Is he doing what they do in the westerns? You know lie with an ear to the ground and tell us how many Apache have ridden by.'

MARTIN grunts. 'Not sure what he expects. Not sure he knows what he's doing.'

'I think he went over here,' Musgrove calls, peering over the edge of the cliff. 'The body's pretty much right below me,' he clarifies before looking at the surrounding stone. 'Tell me if I'm wrong, Martin, but this looks like scuff marks. Like rubber's been scraped off the sole of a boot. I'll take a picture, get the SOCOs up here. Get them to see if the rubber's a match for his boots.' He pulls out his phone and snaps away, fiddling with the macro setting to capture what he thinks is a tread mark.

MARTIN turns to Verity. 'Who does he think he is? CSI Harrogate? Is he always like this?'

'Can't say. First time I've worked with him. I've heard stories but never met him. I mean, ACC, it's all desks and paperwork. They say he's a bit soft. You know, his head's all over the place. Someone said he reads a lot. Crime and that.'

'Well, he's acting like he's buggering Agatha Christie. You know *Poirot*.'

'I saw that. The one with Branagh, not the old fat bloke in the white suit. It was alright, but I preferred that *Knives Out*. *Netflix*. Daniel Craig with a weird accent.'

'Anything?' Musgrove calls, halting Verity's critical flow.

'Nothing sir. Not a thing,' Verity responds.

Musgrove grunts and returns to his investigation.

'When you said not a thing,' MARTIN asks in what amounts to a stage whisper, 'Were you just saying that or not?'

'No, there's nothing. Why?'

'There's nothing you were keeping quiet about? Nothing you were planning to keep to yourself?'

Verity takes off his cap, scratching his head. 'No. Why?'

MARTIN leans to one side, pointing. 'Have a look at that bush behind you.'

The constable turns and shuffles his way over. The bush is mottled, dark green where the leaves hadn't yet succumbed to the brown blight covering much of its foliage. Some blue/grey stuff oozes from a few of the spiky fronds. It is only when he gets closer that Verity sees just what it is he's looking at. The bush is full of money. Bank notes. The brown of Tens, the blue/grey of Twenties. Lots of them. 'Bugger me!' he exclaims. 'My old man was wrong. It does grow on trees.'

26

The house to house had not gone well. The knocks on doors followed by enquiry as to whether the occupant had recently come into possession of wind-blown fifties, tens, or twenties. A question eliciting either a puzzled "No", followed by an enquiry of "What's going on?" or shifty denials and the rapid closing of doors.

'I mean, what were we expecting?' Verity asks. He stands with Metcalfe at the end of the second street that Musgrove, with the aid of a weather app, calculated to be in the direct path of last night's gusts. Despite the rain that is once more starting to fall, he pushes his peaked cap further back on his head, fingers rubbing the brow line of his scalp. 'No-ones' going to own up and hand them over, are they? Would you?' he asks.

'Yes,' Musgrove jumps in, joining them. 'I would. Especially as it might be crucial in understanding what happened to our faller. Also, for the record, I assume you would, what with you being officers of the law and all that.'

'Just not sure how finding it helps,' Verity responds snapping to attention and re-adjusting his cap. 'Strikes me he most likely dropped his money and fell off the cliff chasing after it. Either that or he was up there and found it. Decides to scoop up as much as he can, maybe reaching for a tantalising bunch of fifties and... splat!' The slapping of hand on palm added for emphasis.

'Well, interesting a spin as it is, it's not something I'd give much credence to. For a start, why was he up there with a big bag of money?'

'Could be all sorts of reasons.'

'Most of them nefarious. A drug deal, a ransom drop-off, buying illegal firearms or contraband,' Musgrove points out. 'All of them criminal and meaning someone was up there with him.'

'It's all what you'd call speculation though, isn't it, sir? I mean, that's CID, not uniform.' He checks his watch. 'And our shift ends in fifteen minutes.'

'You must be curious?' Musgrove asks looking from one officer to the other.

'I've little need of curiosity, sir' Verity states. 'I've less than a couple of months to retirement, and I've seen the movies. I've fifteen minutes left on shift and we've a long drive back to Ilkley.'

The smart money is that Gill had fallen. The rubber tread marks coming from scrambling for a foothold as he'd slipped whilst chasing his own dropped cash. Hyland has refused Musgrove's earlier request for more officers, the reason for Gill having the cash not felt worthy of investigation, given there's no evidence of anyone else having been there. Maybe he'd been to a cashpoint on his way home, was the view passed on to Musgrove. Maybe he distrusted banks or credit cards or both, kept it under a mattress. Given they'd been unable to establish how much he'd dropped other than the two hundred pounds or so they'd recovered, it doesn't help the theory of a massive drugs deal or any other illicit activity. To top it all, Hyland had indicated that Gill's family name carried weight in the county's business world, a son having recently lost a father, the pressures that may have affected a young man struggling to keep the family business afloat. Gill's tragic death coming so soon after Webb's murder and Harrison Wrigley's suicide was not going to play well with an already grieving County set or the local business world. It would play even less well if a whiff of disreputable activity was attached.

Having been privy to that particular to-ing and fro-ing over their Airwave devices, Verity and Metcalfe had found little enthusiasm for Musgrove's insistence they should undertake a house to house. And now time is up on that too.

'PC Metcalfe and I have to get back to the station, sir. Sign out. There's a good deal of paperwork attached to all this. Wouldn't want to get any of it wrong. Wouldn't look good, what with you being ACC and all.'

Musgrove nods. There's little he can do, no loyalty he might call on to put in another hour for the sake of justice. The truth of it: another hour to satisfy his own curiosity, the tick nagging somewhere in his head like a buzzing fly that there's something he's missed.

'You'd better get off to the station. I'll stay. Maybe give it another hour or so.'

The two officers leave, Musgrove watching as they go, leaning into each other, shoulders touching, chattering, certain he hears the words *sad* and *pratt*. It's a story that will crown them canteen legends at tomorrow's shift change.

He looks at his notebook, compares the houses ticked off with the Google map of the village on his phone. There weren't that many. Holiday lets for the most part and mainly empty at the end of the season. He checks his watch. Another hour or so ought to see him done, maybe two, depending on the response he gets from each household he talks with, part of him thinking Verity is right, no-one is going to offer up any wind-fall bounty. Word has already spread round the village, news passed on by the Mountain Rescue boys in the café that served as local shop. A tourist had fallen. Not a word of anything suspicious or untoward. It was familiar news, just another of many such incidents each season, a footnote in passing conversations, along with a shake of the head at the stupidity of outsiders who thought they knew better. The risk to the men whose job it is to hike out and find them.

Little wonder he's encountered blank looks from those who'd bothered to answer their doors. It was a non-event. So what if a few banknotes had blown across from where he'd fallen? The strength of the wind up here last night, there's as much chance of them ending up in Ilkley or Skipton as down in the village.

What is it he's looking for? What's the itch bedevilling him?

Maybe he's more like Fisher than he credits, unwilling to settle for the mundane. Wanting it to be more like one of his novels, the chance to show what he can do, that what he does counts. If it doesn't, then what does it amount to, this life he's built?

He turns a page of the notebook, on impulse scribbling a reminder to ask Doyle to look into Gill, use the hacking skills he's more than aware she possesses. Tells himself it's procedure, something he'd do for any such unexpected death. That he's not about to dive further down the rabbit hole he started, the one that Fisher seems intent on excavating further, boring her very own Channel Tunnel to la-la land. The caution to himself that it's a madness he needs to take control of before it finishes all of them.

He shakes his head, closes the notebook, and slides the phone into the pocket of his coat. He lets out a breath, emptying his lungs before breathing deep, filling the hollowness gathering in his chest. Mindfulness. *Become aware of who you are. What you are.*

He sighs, exhales, lets the breath go. Maybe that's why they're in the same therapy group, him and Fisher. Both needing to heal, both unwilling to admit to it. Maybe it's where they belong. Maybe he'll tell her that. Maybe it will help them both. What was it Malcolm said? *Anger is an addiction.* A drug, like drink to alcoholics, a slot-machine to gamblers. The first step is admitting to the anger, acknowledging you have a problem.

He stands on the corner by the car park entrance, draws in

another long breath, holding it a beat before he shouts. 'My name's Neil! And I'm an angry man!'

'Now then, Neil,' a voice calls. He turns to see an old man on the other side of the road walking a whippet. The animal, draped in a thin grey blanket, head bowed, tail between legs, looks as tired and unfit as its owner. They shuffle, wrapped up despite the morning sun that's breaking through. The man raises a rolled-up newspaper from under an arm, waving it at Musgrove. 'I'm Brian,' he calls. 'Nice to meet you, Neil. Have thee sen a nice day, lad!'

27

Jacob Strong sits in the calm of a third-floor room of *The Post* offices. He's a long way from home, deep behind enemy lines. Leeds. West Yorkshire. Bandit country.

Those outside talk of *Yorkshire* as a single organism, when in reality it is four very distinct nations: the rugged industrial South; the multi-cultural West; the rural East; the isolated beauty of the North. Strong himself having grown up in the assertive gentility of Harrogate, a town where he still lives, knows some living there who won't deal with anyone from the South or West. Friends refusing to sell their homes to *arriviste* from Leeds or Sheffield in an effort to keep them out. The Ridings remain tribes more often to be found pouring scorn on each other's region whilst sipping a pint of their county brew – *Black Sheep* for the North; *Stones* for the South; *World Top* in the East; *Timothy Taylor* in the West.

For Strong, a foray to Head Office, is rare, usually in response to a summons. Today is different, he's hands on and digging up the bodies.

He sits in the clippings room, his view across the road one of bruised red girders, the framework of yet another new build piercing the skyline. Like *The Post* itself, the design on the hoardings shows it to be a clone of every other development, the kind making Leeds more and more a city forgetting what it once was, a city losing sight of what it might be. Economy and efficiency hold sway, each new build lacking the tingle of those they replace. He misses the old *Post* building, the thunder of the presses, the smell of hot oil and newsprint, the whirl of metal rollers spinning out the day's news. *Titanic. The Great War. VE Day. Kennedy's Assassination. Sinking of the Belgrano. The Miners' Strike*, stories that had been told there. *What does he have?* Digital files and laptops. Stories of the petty corruption of grey-suited men, the irony that he himself is one of them. Corrupt.

His had been a bargain struck with the Devil, but not a Devil appearing at some rural crossroads - no midnight rendezvous, no deal struck in blood under the light of the moon. His Devil had first made himself known in forms unexpected and underwhelming. Webb, Gill, and Wrigley. The thought now that maybe it had been just that – the sheer implausibility of the men who'd been sent to tempt him - that had pulled him in.

He looks at the page he's copied. *June 2009. The Harrogate Rotary Club Summer Ball*. A mention in that day's *About The County* section, a fluff piece accompanied by a black and white photograph. A photograph of the meeting that began it all, this grand design of his damnation.

He recalls every detail of it, black ties, four men sitting in dwindling light, a warm breeze gusting the patio, swirling the summer air. A half-circle of sorts, cigars and brandy glasses in hands, men lamenting the financial crash, the paucity of cash flow, the plans they'd been forced to put on hold. Webb's grand ideas of expansion, of building a water park, Wrigley's notion to develop a London office stacked with showbiz clients, Strong's own stalling career in PR, and Archie Gill's determination to resist the aggressive takeovers circling his business. All of them aspirations the crash had strangled.

Looking back, he's certain it had been a blue-sky thought. The sort of *end-of-the-night-craziness* that inebriated men are wont to throw out. It may have been Webb with his dark secrets and lofty ambition who'd first suggested it. It might have been Strong himself; an idea dredged from his journalistic mind. A *'what if'* thought, whilst he carelessly waved a cigar in the air. The idea for a novel or a screenplay taken beyond the point it should have stopped at.

Whoever's idea it was, the opportunity seemed timely, a pact siphoning the wealth of Gillian Brightside's estate. The perfect crime because these men would be the only ones to know a crime had been committed. Not that they'd intended to take it all. Just enough, sufficient for their needs.

For Brightside, those were still the good years, years where her books rose to the top of the best sellers. Reliable, a sure thing. A cash cow, quite literally according to old Archibald Gill who knew her acid temperament best, her brusque manner and selfishness, her oh so solitary nature, her weakness. On reflection, it had most likely been Archibald's suggestion.

Keeping her sweet had been easy. Webb knew people, his Bulgarians, the men who'd provided his finance, the cheap labour on his construction projects, along with the muscle to secure such contracts. Such men were only too happy to furnish the drugs Brightside was soon habituated to. At first old Archibald had seen in it a means of fuelling her creative imagination, *opening up the Doors of Perception*, so his sixties mind had schooled him. Drugs opening brave new worlds where Brightside's art might weave its patterns whilst dulling awareness of the contracts she signed. Contracts presented by her trusted publisher, legal papers drawn up by his trusted friend, Harrison Wrigley.

Each had played their part.

Gill making regular visits to her studio, reassuring and assuaging her doubts, trips making certain her cabinets were well-stocked with the drugs Webb's contacts provided.

As newly appointed executors of the Gingerbread Trust, they controlled the books, wrote the contracts, managed the network of off-shore companies and accounts channeling her money overseas before funnelling it back, clean and ready to use. The Bulgarians had proved helpful in such matters, investing the laundered money in Webb's Water park, a venture promising rich dividends long before anyone might think to question its origin or the part played in it by the financial affairs of Gillian Brightside, well known addict of the town.

And should anything be suspected, there was Strong himself who, on Archibald Gill's recommendation, had been installed as her attentive PR, the sole gatekeeper to Gillian Brightside. On the one hand, he saw to it that Brightside and her work were widely promoted whilst on the other leaking tales of a bizarre recluse. *The Howard Hughes of Harrogate* was one of Strong's own tags that he saw to it was freely distributed amongst the media. He made certain stories of her eccentric behaviour leached out - tales of oddball ideas and her Dali-like complexes. Stories that Strong publicly denied whilst ensuring everyone got to hear them.

Her sudden fall in sales took them by surprise. They rode it for over a year, sure the money would flow again, money they depended on to enable a safe retreat from their conspiracy, an exit leaving their trail well-hidden.

Things got worse.

Gill admitted there was little hope of a pick-up in sales. Brightside was out of fashion, cancelled, effectively finished as a marketable asset. There was nothing could be done, they were in too deep, the coffers empty.

There was only one safe exit. Brightside had to die.

Later they would recall that no-one had disagreed. There'd been no horror-struck expressions, no gasps, no melodrama. In the end it had simply been a matter of business, and, after all, they were businessmen. Men with reputations to think of.

It helped there were no heirs, no strange bequests, and that Wrigley himself had personally drawn up the will. With her death, the estate remained in the possession of her executors, its secrets sealed forever.

The more they'd discussed it, the better a plan it appeared. They would keep the money they'd taken but now with no thought of repayment. Better still, with Brightside's demise they might yet cash in on a resurgence of interest in her work.

It had been Webb who'd suggested the method. After all, with motive established it became all about the means, every crime fiction aficionado knows that much. Overdose, he'd suggested. A kindness in its own way, he'd said.

The others had nodded. Webb knew people. People who'd make it work.

He places the photograph back in the file.

Four men. Black ties, brandy and cigars, smiling at the camera, destined for great things.

Now, only he and one other remain. The one not in the photograph. The one who'd kept them safe, prevented the stones from being turned over.

Closing the folder, he tosses it onto the pile for return to the library. It's a file recently accessed by another. Research for a book, is the reason scrawled on the access slip.

But Strong knows there is only one reason for the file to have been accessed: a killer's hunt for the identity of the one not in the photograph, the one whose presence would be suspected but whose involvement remains unknown and undocumented outside the four conspirators. Strong has to contact him, convince him that Webb's death is not the act of a jihadi terrorist cell, or Wrigley's fall a guilt-ridden suicide - John Gill's death itself must be proof enough of that.

And Strong now knows who their killer is, that the name on the request slip is that of a hunter scouring the files to find his prey. Frustrated by what they'd found there, he's certain to have used other means to achieve that objective. Knowing now who they are, he's certain they have the means to do so.

He stares once more at the slip. It's a name that has more than surprised him. It shook him to his core.

28

'The point being that a murder, even a hint of the faintest possibility of it being a murder, impacts all our futures. Yours as Commissioner, mine as Detective Chief Superintendent.'

Gina Hargreaves runs her tongue round her teeth. It isn't beguiling, and Crosby doesn't think for a moment he's supposed to see it that way. It's more the feel of a lioness noting the arrival of a herd of antelope into her bit of the savannah.

Personally, he has no great feeling one way or the other for the future of Gina Hargreaves, be it as Commissioner or back to whatever it was she did before her elevation. He does, however, have great interest in his own future in the North Yorkshire force. 'What I don't understand is that this attachment of yours to the investigation came from your office. It was your request,' he states.

'Bloody Harvey! One of his ideas.' She thumbs her intercom. 'Harvey! Get the fuck in here.'

Harvey Lawrence's voice comes through the speaker, a bone China tone made even thinner by the device. 'Ah, Gina. Truth be told I'm a bit stuck at the moment. I've got to arrange-'

'I don't care. Now.' Letting go of the button she drums her

fingernails on the desk, an anxiety measured by her own insensitivity to the damage meted out to perfectly polished nails. She spits the words out. 'It was supposed to be just shots of me with Fisher,' she says gazing to the near distance. 'Maybe looking at a folder. Pointing at something. The story was my intervening in a tragic death; a desperate young woman pushed to the edge by the patriarchy. I was bringing light to such matters, something Harvey says plays well with mid-thirties women voters, the swing demographic according to the focus groups. Instead, you're telling me I'm tied to a mad woman's delusion of serial killers.'

Crosby nods. A summons to the Police, Fire and Crime Commissioner's office after office hours is the harbinger of one of two things, neither of them good. Either she wants you to do something she can't do herself, something illegal or transgressing the accepted line of her own authority, or you'd already crossed some other line, a line you might not even have known to have been there, and she's about to exact the cost of it from your career. Given the chaos around Webb's murder - Hyland's mental frenzies, the man acting more and more like a tribute act to Hitler's Berlin Bunker period - he is relieved that tonight it concerns Fisher's fate rather than his own.

'DI Fisher has something of a reputation,' he relates.

Lawrence taps the door and enters, crossing to where Hargreaves and Crosby sit either side of her desk. 'Have you heard this?' Hargreaves asks of her still standing PR guru. 'That photo opportunity for the suicide we went to?'

'The barn?' he clarifies.

'Of course the barn, how many other bloody suicides have we been to?' Hargreaves snarls, part disdain, part charmless teenager. 'Seems you've teamed me up with Norman Bates's sister!' She picks up a pen from the desk caddy, twirling it round and round in her fingers whilst staring at the far wall.

'But, surely, you must have known,' Crosby puts in.

'How? How could we have known?' Lawrence asks. 'And known what, exactly?'

Crosby looks from Lawrence to Hargreaves and back again. 'The awards ceremony? A year ago? The female officer decorated for an operation she'd been involved in. The Swanley murders? Surely you remember. *Wensley's Lizzie Borden.*'

Lawrence shrugs.

Crosby turns to Hargreaves. 'You gave her an award.'

'Christ, Crosby, I give out awards all the time. Why would I remem-' She stops, realisation sweeping across immaculately applied make-up. The fire engine red of her lips grows noticeably paler, more the insipid pink of supermarket meat. She twists the pen, the device snapping with a crack. 'Oh Christ!' she howls. 'The woman who went on about institutional misogyny in the police. She picked up her award and then stood next to me trumpeting the merits of Hussain. Bloody Hussain! The man's been campaigning for a public enquiry into sexist attitudes in the force for years. It's the bloody keystone of his pamphlets and speeches.' She ponders the broken halves of the pen, recalling her humiliation, the months of work spent recapturing ground lost to her political rival. 'But she looked different. Didn't she have blonde hair?'

Crosby nods. 'She cropped her hair after it turned white overnight. Some French syndrome thing…Marie somebody.'

'The PR fall-out from that event was a bloody nightmare. She hijacked the entire ceremony. How the hell could you have paired me up with her?' she asks of the room.

Crosby looks from Hargreaves to Lawrence and back again. 'It was your office's idea. You told the Chief Constable you wanted to be hands on in Fisher's investigation.' He shrugs. 'A distraction from the fall-out from Webb. As for it being Fisher, I just assumed it was part of your campaign. You know, that slogan of yours…*Fresh Start, New Beginnings.*' He smiles, nervously. 'I mean, you're on the record saying you're determined to root out old attitudes. I thought things had been…

I don't know, patched up between you and her, that maybe Harvey decided the pairing made you the bigger person. Bygones and all that.'

'Fuck fucking bygones! She's bloody stitched me up!' She throws what's left of the pen onto the desk and turns to her PR man. 'You're supposed to know stuff like this. I mean, she must have known. She's hardly likely to forget, is she?'

'Hard to see Fisher forgetting anything,' Crosby affirms. 'Hard to see her forgiving either. It's why I thought it...odd.'

Lawrence puts a finger to his chin. 'This was all before my time, Gina. I don't see how I'm expected to know things like that if I wasn't here.'

Hargreaves takes a breath. 'Let's think this through. As of now there's no damage done.' She turns to Crosby. 'This is just in your email to me, the feedback you had from Musgrove about what was going on with this therapy lot. I mean there's no pictures gone out just yet. There's no real trace of any of this.'

Crosby shakes his head. 'Your office put out a statement. You saying how this case made you realise the need to create a safety net for young women like Sofia. You say it's why you're keen to work with Fisher's investigation. It quotes you. You saying you're going to find something good to come out of this young woman's suicide. I think *Determined* is the word you used.'

Lawrence nods. 'It plays well with the post-Met enquiry. Pushing back against perceptions of misogyny in the police.'

'So it's too late? It's out there?'

Crosby nods. 'There's a picture of you and Fisher.'

'Ah, yes. It came out rather well considering the lighting. Very *Scandi-noir* and atmospheric if I say so myself,' Lawrence chimes.

Hargreaves rounds on him. 'Jesus, Harvey! This idea of yours about a change of direction, one promoting the emotional intelligence side of me!' she shakes her head. 'I think it was better when I was all *tough on crime and on the causes of crime*. Not only does it turn out this dead woman I'm championing is

Bulgarian - something alienating the PM's rabidly Brexit anti-immigration demographic who'll no longer vote for me once they discover that fact – but according to Crosby Musgrove's convinced Fisher is intent on pushing the idea of it being a murder. A predatory killer on the loose in the run-up to polling day!' She slams the report on the desk. 'You two have put me in direct line of responsibility. I'm going to be seen as not only pro-immigration and sex workers, but actively involved in Fisher's insane Ripper investigation, supporting it even! And to top it off - the cherry on my shit trifle - once they dig into their clippings and find out who she is, they'll have her down as my biggest bloody critic.'

'Surely not your biggest critic?' Crosby suggests, aware the Swing-ometer of blame is tracing an arc towards him.

'Oh, thanks! What, she's in a big fucking queue is she?'

'Hardly a queue...' Lawrence begins.

'Listen, both of you need to shut up right now - unless, of course, either of you have a way out of this mess you've gotten me into.'

Crosby and Lawrence dip their heads to the floor, contrite schoolboys withering under the headteacher's admonishment, wanting it to be over so they can get back out to the playground.

'Nothing. Not a whisper of an idea?' she asks.

'It's not easy. She's already in Therapy along with her DS, Demetriou.'

'Hang on. She's on psych evaluation isn't she?' Hargreaves asks.

'It's as I said,' Crosby offers. 'A lack of self-control.'

'You're saying what? That she's...delicate? Disturbed?'

'Delicate isn't a word I'd use to describe Fisher. If anything, she's-' Crosby pauses. 'Oh, I see...Hmmm. Yes, now I come to think of it, the idea that she's somehow...fragile is certainly one way of seeing her actions. That she's maybe not fully recovered, that her judgement's clouded...unreliable even. Her personal struggles are quite possibly what's shaping her assessment of situations. It's certainly an interpretation the media might conclude if they had the facts of it.' He stops, walks around the notion kicking its tyres. 'There are stories, well-known ones. Things that happened when she was younger, a teenager in fact. Her father's tragic end. And of course, there's her recent breakdown brought on by the Swanley trial. She had a good deal of media coverage at the time.'

Harvey nods. 'Your recent discovery of this - her over wrought imagination, the impact of this recent investigation on her recovery - has you, Gina, now stepping in to see she's stood down from all investigations. It's further example of your compassionate leadership, you putting others' well-being before your own reputation. Something especially good if we ourselves were the ones to remind the world of the trouble she caused you in the past. You'll be *Saint* Gina, romping to polling day!'

Hargreaves tilts her chin towards the ceiling, fixing what she feels to be a beatific expression in place. Something religious, a Renaissance painting. 'Tell me more,' she coos.

'She's a woman under emotional stress,' Crosby puts in. 'They're calling her therapy group broken wings. You know, damaged goods. Not up to it.'

'Surely grounds for desk duties,' Lawrence suggests. 'Take her away from her stressful investigative caseload.'

'I'll confer with the Chief Constable. Get her out of the spotlight. Get the therapist involved, too, get him to tie things up medically.'

'This may help solve a few more of our birds with just that one stone,' Lawrence suggests.

'How so?'

'Well, you say that Musgrove's in the same therapy group. If Hyland rests Fisher, well, surely, he's duty bound to stand Musgrove down from the rest of his duties, especially after the whole Badgerman row. Maybe more than that, we could lean into the idea, find him culpable for the recent failings there've been there'

Hargreaves smiles. 'Which, of course, would necessitate the need for appointing a temporary, untarnished officer to ACC. One with recent experience of high-level cross-service investigations. Someone maybe like yourself, DCS Crosby?'

'Really?' Crosby replies. 'I hadn't thought of it like that.'

29

'Why mention it to that twat in the first place? What were you after? A blessing?' Fisher snarls. 'You might have guessed how he'd react; I bet a good deal of rubbing of palms in glee was involved.'

Musgrove sits forward. His revelation that he's made Crosby aware of the subject of their discussions, their theory of serial killers, hasn't gone well. Demetriou sits eyes to the floor, Doyle satisfying herself with staring ahead, a trauma reaction he's seen when delivering news of the death of a loved one. Fisher has of course exploded. At least he has a full-house on his checklist of how they'd take the news. 'I'm ACC, in case it'd escaped you,' he replies. 'He asked why things were delayed on Wrigley and the Bulgarian woman, said he thought that feet are being dragged, that he's not seen progress. Said he's under pressure from Hargreaves, what with her being actively involved in one of them. She was bound to find out what was going on sooner or later, Crosby too. What did you want me to do, lie?'

Fisher's look indicates she did.

Musgrove deflates. 'It didn't help when I told him I thought we should look deeper into all recent suicides. That I'm myself looking further into Gill to see if there's anything in the idea of three suicides occurring so close together being linked.'

'You're throwing Gill in as well? What did he say to that little bombshell?' Demetriou asks looking up.

'He didn't. He just stared at me. Went a bit pale, if I'm honest. Elephant's Breath White. He hadn't heard about Gill, no doubt the shock of another fellow Mason dying so prematurely upset him. These were prominent businesspeople, - Wrigley and Gill, - and he's also got the Webb murder to deal with. It doesn't look good us going public suggesting things are being rushed, that we think details may be being overlooked. Makes the force look bad.'

'Him, you mean. Because if there is more to it, well, it implies culpability on CID. Him.' She sits back, takes a breath. 'But I still don't see why you had to go and tell him.'

'It may have escaped you, DI Fisher, but I've a command responsibility beyond my own needs or wants'

'Would it have killed you to have kept quiet a few more days? At least until we'd something concrete.'

'Concrete? What the bloody hell have we got that's anywhere close to being concrete? I mentioned it for the simple reason that once I'm outside these meetings I panic. Think *what are we doing*? *This is crazy. Mental.* We should be committed let alone be having therapy. What do you say Malcolm?'

Pemberton shrugs, sits a little straighter in his chair. Before he can speak, Doyle wades in. 'I agree with Neil. Wrigley and Gill, a publisher and a solicitor might have had dealings, contracts or something. But the rest...well, it's bat-shit stupid. The fact this solicitor had dealings representing some Bulgarians, I mean, we've looked and there's nothing beyond the circumstantial - Harrison Wrigley maybe represented some Bulgarian drug dealers at some point in his career. The other suicide you wanted looked at is a Bulgarian woman with an equally loose connection to a drug ring. That's it. End of. You might link two at a push, but not three.'

Fisher jumps in. 'She was trafficked. You do know that don't you, Sophie? That the drugs and the sex weren't part of a job description she applied for back home. It wasn't consensual. It wasn't what she wanted or wished for. She's as innocent and naïve in that as young Demetriou here.'

'What's that supposed to mean?' Demetriou asks, irked at Fisher's method of dragging him into her disputes.

'Well, Pan, let's face it your track record with the opposite sex suggests a certain credulity. An openness to being fucked over, if you pardon the expression, Malcolm,' she spits, leaving Demetriou wondering what was igniting this particular blue touch-paper and why he's finding himself suddenly holding this particular explosive.

Malcolm waves a weary hand in the air. All fight has long since left him when it comes to correcting Fisher's manner, Musgrove's ever-present bluster, or even Doyle's truculence. Demetriou is his only hope, and despite the hurt look on his face even he appears to have bought into Fisher's madness, her impish interventions in anything that takes her fancy.

'Anyway,' Demetriou wades in, gesturing towards Doyle. 'I'd have thought someone with decent IT skills could offer something more than vague *sometimes* and *someones*. There must be something a little…fuller. A little more detailed. You know, facts – dates, times, or clients that you could find in your searches, something useful, something we could hang a motive on.'

'I'm going off crumbs Pan. The name of a solicitor who's no doubt handled hundreds if not thousands of cases with the chance that one of them might be Bulgarian. It's computer science, not computer magic.'

'Surely you write some algorithm or worm or trojan or whatever it is to do it?' Demetriou pushes.

'You've watched too many films,' she retorts. 'You know shots of fingers racing over keys and folk jumping back from screens shouting *Eureka*! It's not like the movies, in the same way these cases aren't like Neil's books. I'm dealing with facts, not fairy tale nonsense like those stories this Gill bloke published. I mean, if Neil thinks it's not an accident, him falling, then it's likely a suicide. You asked me to look at his company finances, Neil, see if I could find anything explaining him carrying a lot of cash. From what I saw the whole lot was going down the toilet. That dead author woman of theirs hadn't seen decent sales for ten years. Her own estate's in a trust that's a busted flush let alone the publisher's. No happy ever after there, I can tell you. Decent reason for him deciding on ending it all but not a motive for murder.'

'Crime writing isn't nonsense. It's plausible, based on truths,' Musgrove murmurs.

'And what would those be here? These truths?' Demetriou asks.

Musgrove shrugs. 'I don't know, you'd have to dig deeper.'

'Looking for what?'

'Connections. It's all about connections.' He feels the tug of their special madness pulling him on, decides that right now he's too tired to resist. 'If there is a killer there's a reason why they're targeting these particular people. Something linking a Bulgarian sex worker, a solicitor, and now I think maybe a book publisher too, Gill. We have to connect Wrigley to Sofia and maybe the Bulgarian mobs. As for Gill... all I know is there's something we're missing.'

'Our sanity?' Fisher suggests.

Demetriou looks up. 'You do know that if we can't find a link, then we're likely wrong about everything. That they're just what Crosby says they are - three sad deaths that happened within a short space of each other. Sofia seeing no other way out of a sad desperate life; Wrigley a sad lonely drunk, and, from what Sophie says, this Gill was beset by his part in the failure of a family business.'

'We'd have to let go.' Doyle says.

'Nothing else to do.' Demetriou states. 'Going on what Zara's told me about the man, I don't see DCS Crosby sitting for long on what he's been told about what we're up to. He's bound to be furious, do what he can to stop us.'

'And that was my point,' Fisher offers. 'He'll be straight to Hyland and Hargreaves and anyone else he can hitch his revenge to. We've got days, maybe hours.'

Musgrove sighs. 'Unless there's another death soon. You know, one that offers another point we might find some link to.' He looks at them as they stare back at him. 'The more there are the more chance we have of narrowing down the similarities, a common thread,' he states defending his seeming insensitivity.

'The more killings, the narrower the search for a connection,' Doyle adds. 'It becomes obvious.'

'Hardly the most noble of wishes.,' Demetriou says. 'More murders in the hope of proving we're right. And it has to be soon.'

'Maybe there's another way,' Fisher offers. 'What if we look backwards. Maybe I'm wrong. Maybe Sofia isn't the first and Wrigley and Gill aren't the second and third. Maybe There are others, ones before Sofia. She might be the second or third or fifth. We look at other recent suspicious deaths to see if we can link any of those to these cases. If we can, Crosby will have to give us more time because then we'll know for sure we're not mad, that we've got ourselves a serial killer.'

30

DCS Crosby sits forward, allowing himself a shake of the head. When he speaks his manner is level, direct. 'We need something, Doctor Pemberton. Need it sooner rather than later, if you get my drift.' It is a statement rather than a suggestion, non-negotiable, a drift that if not caught threatens to wash the therapist away in its undertow.

Pemberton sits on a visitor's chair next to Crosby, considering how best to respond. His summons to a meeting with the Chief Constable, DCS Crosby, and the PR guru, Harvey Lawrence bestows him a status akin to hostage. 'I understand what you're asking,' he begins, lips pulling tight, a grimace he hopes expresses his professional dilemma. 'But it's not how therapy works, and certainly not one involving a group. Certainly not one with the dynamic of the one we're discussing.' He turns to Hyland, hands spreading in a gesture of willing hopelessness. 'You see, Chief Constable, it's as much a matter of practicalities as it is of being ethical or moral.'

Crosby and Hyland exchange a look that suggests neither thinks ethics or morality was ever part of the meeting's agenda, not even as an AOB.

Crosby fixes his best cold-eyed smile. 'Doctor, let me assure you that none of us wish in any way to be seen to rush such... sensitive and crucial work. But you must see where we're coming from.' He shakes his head to underline their helplessness in the face of seemingly insurmountable odds, ignoring the fact that he's done most of the boxes of odds stacking. 'We're reasonable men, Doctor – intelligent men, worldly. We know that after just a few sessions, we can't expect a cut and dry verdict on DI Fisher's state of mind, no definitive medical conclusion as to her fitness for duty. What we're looking for is more in the way of a staging post. A marker. Something we can in good faith offer to Police Fire and Crime Commissioner Hargreaves. The Mayoral election is but a few short weeks away, and she rightly feels a close link to one of your patients is somewhat compromising for herself and the force, PR wise.'

He looks across to Lawrence who sits semi-sprawled on the Chief Constable's couch. The Commissioner's PR guru nods agreement at the potential for media-based difficulties should word get out. 'Maybe there's some little detail we might use. Nothing major or compromising for you.' He shrugs as a measure of his blue-sky thinking. 'Maybe something enabling a little more...distance be put between DI Fisher and her caseload. Something keeping her at arm's length from the case of that unfortunate Bulgarian woman's suicide that Gina has identified so closely with in her recent campaigning. Something reducing Fisher's front line duties,' he clarifies, 'Ease the pressure on her. Win-win, so to speak.'

Hyland decides it's time for one of his famous stating the bleeding obvious moments. He's good at this sort of thing. Many are the meetings he's sat in listening to the genius of others and then, judging the moment right, stepped in to summarise what had been said. Applied correctly, it often left the impression that those ideas are his own, a career enhancing Jedi mind trick of Derren Brown proportions. 'In short, Doctor Pemberton, what

DCS Crosby and myself require is a medical reason to remove DI Fisher from active duties, specifically her investigation of the suicide of the Bulgarian woman. Word has reached us that she's intent on treating it as a murder.' He pauses, shakes his head. 'Because of Fisher's instability, what began as the Commissioner's personal interest in a case of female abuse and suicide now risks exposing both her office's good name and those good causes to ridicule. Not to mention how it reflects on the force as a whole when the eyes of the intelligence services and the global media are on us. You do see that don't you?'

'I know it's something they've talked about.'

Hyland halts his summation. 'Sorry. What? Who? More to the point; why?' he demands.

'ACC Musgrove and DS, Demetriou. And the young woman from Digital Forensics, Sophie Doyle. DI Fisher's case came up during our sessions. It attracted...well, discussion. Ideas.'

'So, you're telling us your therapy group has turned itself into some mutant *Famous Five*?' Hyland summarises. 'That instead of sorting out their own troubling personal issues they've formed themselves into what, *Crime Fighters Anonymous* or something? Vigilantes?' His irritation is palpable.

'No. Not really. But, well...I suppose some might say.'

'What? What would they say?' Hyland asks, irritation rising.

'That they're exploring ways of dealing with their issues. They're in new territory.' He smiles nervously, the impression of a chimp from the old TV tea adverts.

'Some might say you've overstepped the mark, Doctor,' Hyland judges.

'No...I can't see that as the case,' Pemberton offers. 'One could say that we've certainly pushed into new directions. You see, your three officers – Fisher, Musgrove, and Demetriou – discovered they'd each been given a suicide. With everyone so absorbed in the Webb investigation, it's easy to see how they've come to feel themselves cast outside the force and its work. But through discussing these cases they've found a shared objective.

An identity. A place they're starting to feel they might belong. It's a good thing, therapy wise.'

Hyland waves a hand dismissively. 'Doctor Pemberton, it's one thing them talking about their mommies and daddies or whatever you therapy people do. It's quite another for them to be discussing active investigations.'

'Why are these suicides of such interest?' Lawrence asks.

'ACC Musgrove feels there might be something to Fisher's idea of a murder. He's suggested that...well, that Gill and Wrigley's deaths may have things in common.'

'Musgrove? The last good idea he had was...' Hyland trails off, unable to weigh up either when or even what that might have been.

'What sort of things?' Crosby asks.

'Musgrove's a writer. It's an interest he has. He had some hypothesis. Like a sort of *what if*. The rest joined in and it... spiralled. There's talk of finding a link between them,' Pemberton replies. 'The suicides, I mean.'

' Like what?' Lawrence asks.

'They don't know.'

'But isn't Fisher investigating a sex worker's suicide?' Crosby puts in.

Pemberton nods. 'Yes. But as you know, she thinks there's more to it.'

Hyland's face is ashen. 'This has gone far enough! Christ only knows what the press and TV boys would make of it. It has to stop immediately. I'll see to it Fisher is suspended pending an assessment of her fitness for duty. I'll have Musgrove suspended too. The man's way out of line here.'

Crosby stands. 'I'll pass on the news.'

Lawrence rises from the couch, mobile phone appearing in his hand. 'I'd better get onto Gina. Get her up to speed. You have to get a lid on this and see to it that it stays on.'

'I intend speaking with Musgrove straight away,' Hyland states, before turning to Pemberton. 'Doctor, I need a report recommending DI Fisher and ACC Musgrove be removed from all active cases forthwith.'

'But-'

'There's no buts. The way this is going, we'll be lucky if we're not all looking wistfully at what were once promising futures.'

31

Cars. It was always sitting in cars when she started to think of the things she's been doing her best to avoid. Arriving when she woke, they tap at the window demanding attention.

That morning she'd shaken them off whilst brushing her teeth, only to find them waiting in the shower, slashing *Psycho*-like at her conscience when she's at her most vulnerable. The dark times before morning espresso.

The drive to work hadn't been too bad, the concentration on traffic, the tourists towing giant caravans like migrating snails, the cyclists who think that because it's North Yorkshire they're Bradley Wiggins and that padded lycra shorts make them immortal, at the very least places them above the normal rules of road users. They rode, side by side and in groups, each yellow shirted team a peloton of potential brain trauma at every tight bend in the road.

At work she can focus. Days like this whole shifts might pass before her mind found space to fix on the issues she buries under her day's routines. But here, in the car, a passenger, there's nowhere to hide.

Wet cobbled yard. A cold wind. Rusting handles of old stable doors.

She watches the dry-stone walls slide past in the rain. It's hay baling time, vinyl wrapped sausage rolls littering the fields. In the distance tractors scythe through the last of the grass whilst others gather it into rows. There will be a day or two of drying before it too is ready for the baler.

She's to be stood down, end of the week, Demetriou and Musgrove assigned to restricted duty whilst she herself is officially on sick leave awaiting yet another tribunal. Doyle remains untouched, yet for some reason seems more uncertain of her future than the others, the sense there's somehow more at stake for her.

Almost three days have passed since they'd embarked on a last hurrah of looking for suspicious or sudden deaths that might link to what by his own admission is Musgrove's crazed theory of connections. Musgrove himself still vacillating between fervent certainty and abject denial of its credibility, has added John Gill to the mix, Demetriou exploring any business connections to Wrigley whilst Doyle is busy filtering reports of suspicious deaths in the past two months. At one point yesterday afternoon she thought she'd found something. She'd decided to widen the search criteria to include missing persons and had come across the disappearance of a retired detective - DS George Townley. According to his wife, her Georgie went out one night following a phone call and never came home. That was more than two weeks ago.

Fisher had remembered him, Musgrove had too. A DS, his had been a forced retirement two years previously under the cloud of sexual harassment of young female officers. He'd left on full pension; the charges not pursued because of Hyland and Hargreaves' concerns at not tarnishing the police image - though in the period since then the Met had stepped up to do the heavy lifting on that sort of thing. Doyle was currently going through his files looking for connections, whilst Demetriou was contacting the officers investigating Townley's disappearance. Neither were optimistic of any connection to Gill, Wrigley, or Sofia. Sofia hadn't been in the country when Townley was on the force, and there seemed little chance of him having come across Wrigley who had been a commercial rather than criminal lawyer. Even less so of him having met Gill. But with so little else, it was worth a look.

'Do you ever get tired of it,' Demetriou asks. 'The view,' he clarifies.

'Some days,' she responds, grateful for distraction. 'Especially when I'm stuck behind one of those things,' she says, flicking a hand in the direction of the fields to her left. The giant tractors.

Demetriou risks a glance across, eyes immediately fixing back on the narrow road ahead with its sharp turns and dips. 'Yeah. I've had a few shocks coming round bends the past few weeks to find one of those barrelling along in the other direction. Not to mention the milk tankers.'

'The public must have milk for their tea,' Fisher finds herself agreeing, relieved at a topic of conversation moving her thoughts from darker places, the shadowed alleyways she's been sidling towards. 'Got to have their morning cereals,' she says, mustering enthusiasm for the topic. 'Nothing stops the tankers getting through. They're like the Pony Express. *Neither wind nor rain*...you know the saying.' Her mind thinking that even the Wild West had branded mission statements.

'Can I assume it gets better in the winter?' he asks. He knows walkers and cyclists are not the sort to be put off by dark evenings or the chill of winter, but harbours hopes of the disappearance of those making a wrong click on *holidays.com* – no doubt guided by the power of *the Yorkshire Shepherdess* or *All Creatures Great and Small* and finding themselves here in late autumn rain rather than late Majorca sun.

'Yeah,' Fisher says, face turned to the side window, eyes following the silvered grey lines of stone walls snaking off across the slopes. 'Then it's the rain and the storms. The snow and ice. But the tourists are less. Or is it fewer?' She wonders why she can never get her head around that particular grammatical concept. Maybe a linguistic workout for the rest of the journey might keep the memory wolves from the door. *The Hounds of Guilt.* Maybe Sting or someone could write a song about it.

The pool car rounds a bend, a right so sharp it has the satnav warning *'make a right turn'.* If it can fool the Great Geo Co-ordinates in the Sky it must be a tight one. Demetriou shifts down the gears, a large *Winnebago* ahead of them lumbering its way round the curve, rolling on protesting suspension before righting itself as the road straightens out, if you could call the series of tight S bends for the next mile and a half straightening.

How long has it been since she could hear anything by *Sting* without finding herself thinking of her mother? The music that haunted her childhood. *Ghosts in the Machine.* The irony that it's exactly what it's become for her mother, locked into herself in the old house, all her certainties ripped away, the doubts that gnaw at her like rats in a sack. Each day she sits in her chair, bottle close at hand, dust and gloom piling about her, sealing her in like a tomb, like those ancient civilisations where once the king dies the queen is interred with them. That's how it feels when she visits. The quiet desperation, the wringing of hands, the bile and bitterness that rises up to drive her away. And all of it accompanied by a soundtrack of Sting.

'Constable Burton,' Demetriou calls out, finger raised off the wheel and pointing at the village sign. 'I heard a story that one of the old ACC's finding a Chris Burton had joined the force whisked him down here for a PR shot. Stood him by the sign. Constable Burton was made Constable Burton's constable.' He smiles, Fisher sensing rather than seeing it. 'Makes me smile,' Demetriou confirms as if he's looked inside her. 'I love those things, the village names. The next one's Patrick Brompton and Thornton Steward's up over the hill. Sound like old black and white film actors.'

'In real life they were in colour,' she observes. 'But I get the point.'

'And it's like I'm listening to *Lord of the Rings* when the satnav's directing me.' He begins to list them, eyes scanning the road for a place to overtake the hulking motorhome sticking leech-like to its forty miles an hour. '*Arrathorne. Hutton Hang. Spennithorne. Finghall. Crakehall. Akebar.*'

'I get the drift, Pan. I do,' she sighs, thinking he's a puppy locking hold, refusing to let go. At times it's a distraction, endearing. At others it's fingernails down a chalkboard.

'*Tunstall. Barden Moor,*' he chimes on.

Better than the alternative. The dive into her own head, a scene stuck like a broken video tape, the ones her mother plays when she visits. The same ones, over and over: family holiday; the beach; the river; collecting fallen leaves from the paddock. The voices: her father's and her own when she was what... seven? Each autumn when the leaves fall, piling up along the roadside, she thinks of a moment that has for some reason scratched its way into her head. The series of random images that lead to the moment that always comes. The climax of her fever dreams. A day of thinking too much, a day of not being able to shake it, to divert herself from it. *Wet cobbles. Cold winds. The handle of the door, rusting where her father never got round to sorting it. The creak of the hinge as she pushes his study door open, stepping inside. A sobbing. Livvy. Words repeated again and again...*

'No! No! No! No! No!' Demetriou shouts, pointing at the flashing blinker of the motor home in front. 'This wanker's going to go all the way to the A1. We're going to be following him for the next three miles. Maybe I can get past him at the longer stretch into Bedale. What do you think?'

Fisher studies the blinking indicator, glad she doesn't have to think. 'No rush,' she replies. 'Nothing's going anywhere before we get there. Embrace the moment, be glad of where we are. Trust me, there're worse places to be stuck, places you never want to find yourself in.'

32

They'd pulled into the car part of the ice cream parlour a short while ago, the four of them agreeing to keep further investigation to themselves. They were already thought to be mad and bad, so the last thing they needed was the idea to take hold in Hyland's mind that they were crazy dangerous too.

The Chief Constable was somewhat pre-occupied with frying fish of a far larger portion. After weeks of intense investigation, the lack of any progress in the Webb murder meant there was pressure for all hands to be at the pumps, Hyland now clinging ever tighter to the belief that numbers were the answer. If they couldn't solve the murder, then at the very least he'd be seen to have allocated overwhelming resources to it. It was a hearty shove of the wheel of fortune, a move designed to nudge the fickle finger of fate and responsibility further round the dial of complicity away from himself. Let Whitehall and Downing Street make what they would of the investigation, Hyland would be in the clear. It was a Vegas gambler desperately slapping all their remaining chips on red.

Hyland's exhortations to the rest of the force meant that a group of officers about to be on sick leave, suspension, or restricted duties –

through their failure to clear investigations which any remotely effective investigator ought to have closed, stamped, and filed days ago - could fly low under the radar for a few days more. It was the last chance to get any ducks they'd corralled into a sort of orderly row rather than the current chaotic gaggle. It's why they were sitting in the *Wensleydale Ice Cream Parlour*, a converted barn steeped in stunning rural isolation on the road between Aysgarth and Hawes. Meeting here placed them far from the eyes of Headquarters, and winter opening meant they'd room to work undisturbed just as long as they kept buying cakes, ice-creams, and coffees - a problem Musgrove is considering taking on single-handed.

Demetriou is head deep in a folder, reading details of the autopsies. Opposite, beyond folders stacked in the centre of the table, Musgrove eyes up the iced delights on the menu. 'These are the best ices. Folk come from miles around,' he observes, finger tracking the list of flavours in mind-numbing wonder. The delights of the chilled cabinet display downstairs had caught his attention as they'd entered, him mumbling the flavours out loud like a mystical incantation to the Spirit of Desserts as they'd passed through.

'Well, if we get a few hours in on these folders I'll treat you. All of you,' Fisher offers, hand waving over the files.

The thought took root. Musgrove's attention fixed on making the right selection.

Fisher sighs. 'They do take-away,' she adds. 'Any you can't handle today you can take home for later. But let's get this done first.'

Musgrove harrumphs. 'Doubt Jean would be too happy. The diet and everything,' he says. The raised eyebrows of Fisher, Demetriou, and Doyle pass him by. 'Steamed fish tonight,' he opines. 'Second time this week. Fish is supposed to be battered, like chips are meant for bread and butter.' Finding no takers, he settles to sliding another folder off the pile. 'Not even certain what we're looking for,' he grumbles.

'A link of some sort. A trail of breadcrumbs,' Fisher answers. 'Anything tying these deaths together.'

Musgrove slaps the cover of the folder. 'It's just a story. You know a bit of fancy. I never meant for you to take it literally. It's not a sustainable theory…It's…whimsy.'

'We understand that, but we're here because weirdly it fits better than anything else we've got,' Doyle responds, looking up from a spreadsheet she's constructed on her laptop.

Fisher nods. 'You must know the old Holmes thing about once you've discounted all the logical stuff then whatever's left, no matter how buggering-*ly* mind-blowing it is, must be the truth. We just have to find it.'

'But that's only if we start off by assuming these suicides are other than what everyone tells us they are: suicides. The logic says they're suicides, all three of them. It's statistics, these are just one of those anomaly things.' He shakes his head. 'Don't get me wrong, I'm…touched. I mean, I appreciate the fact you all think it's a decent idea for a plot, and maybe I'll write it one day, but that's all I it is. A plot, a bit of fiction. You lot grabbed hold of it like it's some sort of life raft, clinging to it like it can save you from all this,' he judges waving an arm in the air.

'We know that. We know if it was down to following process anybody else would have filed reports days ago,' Demetriou states passing a hand over the files. 'I mean, if ever they get AI in on stuff like this, it's finished, no-one taking a second look. No ChatGPT Sherlock Holmes or AI Poirot finding it worth more than the nano-second of the time it would take to assess and dismiss. The logic is compelling, everything we've got goes against anything other than suicide. Wrigley for sure, Gill probably, even Sofia.'

'You do know you're talking us out of this, don't you? That there's nothing that says they're murders let alone linked in any way?' Doyle puts in.

Fisher sighs. 'If he wasn't so obvious, I'd be thinking it's all a Pemberton ploy, keeping us occupied so we're not punching each other's lights out. Kids in the backseat of a car on a long journey.'

Demetriou nods. 'Maybe it's why Malcolm's indulged us, why he didn't shut it down as soon as Neil suggested it. Zara's ideas too, and mine. And now, well, it's all got out of control, a shared delusion we can't row back on, us being in too deep. Rather than help us, he's got us chucked out.' He looks around the table, their empty faces, a sheepish expression sliding across his own. 'But still...Something's not right. There's...I dunno...a smell about things. Instinct, if you like. Neil stumbled on it, what Sophie called his inner crime writer, his subconscious working away underneath the surface. Zara too, except being a real detective her working out was up front, loud. Even you Sophie, you can see stuff in the jumble of code, all the ones and zeros. Something out of place, things not belonging. A glitch. A kink. A ghost in the machine.'

Fisher shakes her head: *wet cobbles...cold wind...rusty doors.*

'And what about you?' Doyle asks. 'What's your superpower of deduction saying?'

'He was the one beat the game bird out of the brush so the rest of us could shoot it,' Musgrove states.

Fisher grunts. 'Christ, Neil, you're so bloody Yorkshire.' She tosses a file she's been flicking through onto the pile, her torso quickly following as she slumps forward, arms outstretched across the table. She sighs dramatically, raising her head though her arms remain resolutely stuck across the table. 'That's what Hargreaves said that night in the barn.'

'Sorry?'

Fisher, pushes herself a little more upright, wrinkles her face. 'She turned up at Sofia's crime scene. She and that PR bloke. Lawrence. He said he thought police work was all about instinct. She agreed. Said I was Joan of Arc or something.'

'There's some would happily see you burn,' Musgrove murmurs.

Demetriou ignores him. 'See, they got it. It's not always about logic, the obvious. Not that I'd vote for her,' he adds, wondering if approval of Hargreaves is something anyone would want on their CV.

'I told him it was bollocks,' Fisher states, bursting his balloon. 'It's not all Poirot. Look at us. Misfits, *The Broken Wings* going all Agatha over it.' She glances round the table. 'Maybe Pemberton's right, I'm hoping for something to wrap myself up in rather than face up to the mundanity of what we're really all about - sweeping up the dead souls, the wasted lives. Maybe I do just hate the thought of that poor girl living a life so destructive she can't go on, grasping at anything that might give her death some meaning. Maybe she did just shave her own hair and knot it in the rope with the rest she'd collected in a final protest at toxic masculinity.'

Demetriou shakes his head. 'No. You're wrong. I mean, I understand why Malcolm says that, he's interested in getting inside your head, pushing you to think about what drives you. But he's not one of us. He's like the linesman or something. Us, we get it. Of course it's a bit...

'...Batshit crazy?' Doyle offers.

'...Batshit crazy,' Demetriou nods, accepting her baton. 'An idea that means we're way outside anyone's idea of suspicious death investigations. We're talking madness – seeing murders and serial killers where everyone else sees suicide. But we're here because we understand that sometimes there are things that set off alarms. That buried deep in what to everyone else appear simple events can be answers that are...deeper.' He screws his face in recognition that his words aren't the flowing speech he's envisaged, appalled at the clunkiness of what was supposed to be a rallying cry, his Henry the Fifth moment.

'Complex things,' Musgrove agrees, bailing his point out. 'Disturbing things.'

Demetriou nods. 'Yes. Like Neil says. Disturbing.' He turns to Fisher. 'Worst case, end of the day, we've given it a shot. If there's nothing, we let it go. A false positive.'

'What do you mean, false positive?' Musgrove asks.

'Indicating something's there when it's not,' Doyle says. 'You know, sets off all the right alarms and checks in a system, but in reality is nothing. A glitch. You reset. You go on.'

'Unlike our careers,' Musgrove mutters.

'Reset. If only life were like that,' Fisher says. *Cold rain...wet cobbles...rusty doors.* 'Anyone for an ice?' she asks, standing and scattering her thoughts.

'Oooh yeah,' Musgrove replies. 'The stem ginger. Or the black cherry. Oh...there's lemon meringue, too. Tell you what, surprise me.'

'Dealer's choice,' Demetriou says.

Fisher picks up her bag and makes her way to the spindled staircase. Watching her go, Demetriou turns to Musgrove. 'So, do you really think we're onto something?'

'Not a chance,' he responds with a snort, cradling the menu. 'Not a bloody chance.'

33

It took another hour of fruitless checking, of sifting and grading, of cross-referencing and noting. An hour of possibilities and of those possibilities' dead ends.

Musgrove broke first, a severing of the synaptic connections linking his mind to the hypothesis. 'I need a bloody coffee,' he notifies the group, at the same time slapping shut the folder he's been reading - a movement sending it skittering across the table to join the pile of identical manilla folders. The edifice crumples inwards, folders slithering across the table to end at odd angles to the core.

Doyle raises her head from her spreadsheet, a digital algorithm of connections. 'Might be helpful to put it back on the correct pile,' she comments, contemplating the slurry of displaced folders. 'You know, in the interests of keeping some sense of order. Respecting the process.'

'It's all a bloody mess, anyway,' he snaps back. 'A wild goose chase after some...'

'...Wild geese?' Fisher suggests, looking up from her own spread of folders, yellow Post-Its scattered over them like a dreadful disease, a vicious bout of puss-coloured acne that has broken out across the white of the paper. 'I thought we were trying to get ducks in a row.'

Musgrove's eyes narrow in distaste. 'Might as well be using a buggering Ouija board. You know, all link hands, contact the three dead people and ask them direct: *did you commit suicide? If not, who killed you and why? Will any of us still have a career next week?*'

'So, you're suggesting a Zoom meeting for the undead.' Demetriou summarises. 'A spiritual FAQ.'

Musgrove wrinkles his nose. 'Be just as much a chance of getting an answer as carrying on with this,' he states pointing at the files. His words are delivered in the manner of a verbal foot being put down in the way those who say *I'm putting my foot down* do. 'Needles and haystacks,' he judges.

'I always had you pinned as more of a *process and procedure* type rather than the antsy restless sort,' Fisher observes. 'You know, *The Sweeney*. You as Haskins to my Regan. You always demanding it be done by the book, wanting us to be *i* dotting, and *t* crossing-*ly* thorough. You, insisting we wade through the paper chase of it. You, certain the answer's here if only we looked. Never had you as the one sitting there dismissing it as a waste of time.'

'If that were the case I'd hardly be here, would I?' He shakes his head, somehow managing to shrug his shoulders at the same time as holding his hands out. It's an Olympic gold gymnastic routine of physical despair. 'I mean, look at it. Look at us. This is hardly textbook, is it?' he states rather than questions, thinking that maybe Hyland's whole rhetorical thing's more contagious than he'd considered it to be.

'You're here because you're terrified to tell your wife what's happened,' Fisher judges.

'Of course not…I mean of course I've told her, that's not why I'm here.'

'Ah, I get it' Fisher states pointing her pencil in his direction.

'You're out of your depth and starting to panic, wondering where the bottom of the pool is. Face it, Neil, despite all the writing and dark plotting, you're a *by the manual* type. A *by the book* sort of copper. This is you slumming it, crime solving wise, wanting to see how the other half lives - our intuitive leaps. You're fretting over what you've got yourself into, you a nice Catholic girl finding herself at a party where there's booze and drugs and wondering what had possessed her to come here, - though admittedly not any Catholic girls I know. Wild as fuck!' she observes.

'It's Neil's moment of scepticism. Like in the films and his books, the moment of crisis.' Demetriou offers.

'You're talking about *the Long Dark Night of the Soul*,' Musgrove replies. 'But this is real life, not a book.' He sits back; the dismissive head shake re-appearing. 'Problem is none of you are listening.' He drops his voice a notch, moving it more in line with his mood of weary exposition. 'It was an idea, a blue-sky writing exercise meant for my writing group. Nothing more. I'm not a believer in any of this. In truth, I'm only here to try to pull it back, see to it you don't end up dropping yourselves and me along with you deeper into something stupid and career-ending for all of us. Damage limitation, I think they call it.'

Fisher sighs acceptance coloured with a tinge of defiance. 'I think we're all a little too exposed to be thinking about careers, Neil. Face it, the reason we're here is because we *have* no careers. Not anymore. Not proper ones, anyway.'

'What would your hero bloke do now?' Doyle asks, interest piqued. 'Not that he has to be a bloke. Could be a woman. Maybe gender neutral. A *they/them* detective. That'd be good. Probably *Gen Z* good, though. Not one for you *Boomers* or *X*'s really, is it?'

Musgrove exhales, deciding the path of least resistance to be compliance. 'The *Long Dark Night of the Soul* is the point in the story when everything seems hopeless – lost causes and dead ends.'

'Just like now. Us,' Doyle puts in, her expression closer to bright eyed comprehension struggling out from under her default look of resting-truculent-face.

'Pretty much,' Musgrove agrees.

'What does *he-she-they* do?' Doyle pursues.

'Well, they have a moment. An epiphany.'

'A *what-any*?'

'Epiphany. It's where the hero hits rock bottom but looks inside themselves, faces their darkest fears, finally realises the lesson the story's been trying to teach them.'

'The lesson?'

'Yes. The lesson.' He sits forward, picking up a discarded pencil, twirling it in the air. Soon it's a baton leading his words along the path of a narrative arc he knows by heart. 'You see; to truly resonate with your reader, a story has to be about change. How your hero is changed by what happens to them and those they have grown to care for. Without change there's no heart, no emotional core. You need the reader to root for them…the hero, that is, want them to win because in winning comes the hero's own salvation You see, by this point they've shown us a glimpse of their true nature by saving the cat. Now comes the point where they realise for themselves just who they are. The caterpillar becomes the butterfly if you like.'

'Bloody hell! And I thought it was all just Poirot gathering suspects in a room and telling them who it was. You know, *it was ze butler that did eet*,' Fisher observes via offensive cod Belgian-French stage whisper.

Musgrove turns to her. 'Yes, well, cosy crime's a bit of a genre to itself. An exercise in logic and problem solving. More like a cryptic crossword.'

'What's this cat then?' Doyle asks. 'What's happened to it?'

Musgrove waves the pencil. 'It's just a term for the hero doing something earlier in the story that shows us they're likeable. You know, deep down, beneath all the outer shell of themselves they've been showing the reader up to that point.'

'Okay then,' Doyle says.

'*Okay what?*' Musgrove asks, wondering what bit he's not made clear. He knows from experience the whole Zak Snyder's *Save the Cat* idea can be troublesome.

'So what happens then? After this *Long Night* they've had thinking about their souls.'

'Well, depends. For the most part, they get energised by realising there's something they've missed. Something staring them in the face all along. But now they can see it. They've changed. They see things differently. It's a sort of analogy.'

'So?'

'So what?'

'What's ours?'

'Our what?'

'Our epiphany thingy. The nanny-ology thing you just said.'

Musgrove laughs. 'Look, it's a plot device. It's for stories. Not real life. It's what I've been saying for the past god knows how long. This fiction we've been blindly pursuing is just that - a fiction. A fairy tale.'

'A fairy tale?'

'Make believe.'

'Make believe?'

'Christ if all you're going to do is repeat everything I say we're not going to get very far. It's a nursery rhyme, Doyle. Fake news. Not real. A story to frighten the kids with. And like nursery rhymes, it's for children, not grown-ups, and certainly not grown-up detectives and nerdy geeks who should know a damn sight fucking better!'

34

'Christ, Neil you were out of order back there.'

Musgrove looks round, breaking off from perusal of the display of serving tubs. 'How so?' he asks.

Fisher shakes her head. '*Doyle*,' she pushes the name out through gritted teeth. 'You damn near bit the kid's head off,' she rebukes.

Taken aback, he flusters a response. 'She was being…you know…she was…'

'What? What was she being, Neil? Naïve? Innocent? Looking for some hope?'

Musgrove sighs, shoulders slumping in harmony. 'What's she expect?'

'From you? Clearly nothing.'

'That's unfair,' he says turning to her, cheeks flushed. 'Why's it on me? What about you? Where's your great detective mind when its needed, eh? Where's DI Zara Fisher, the *Great White Hope* of CID?'

She waves a hand dismissively. 'No-one expects anything from me. Haven't you heard? I'm *the Great White Fuck Up*. Where've you been the last year?'

'More to the point where have you been?' he snaps. Aware of

a member of staff busy topping up the metal bowls, he drops his voice to a whisper, still fierce for all its carefully tended volume. 'You, DI Fisher, had the lot. Best clear up rate. Champion of just causes. When I first arrived here...Christ! I envied you. Your reputation. Your capabilities. And then, *pssst!*' he pinches thumb and forefinger together in front of his face. 'Out of the blue, you toss the lot. You're surly. Aggressive. Cold and uncaring. You know the names. *Elsa. The Ice Queen.*' He stands staring her in the eyes. He's never stood this close to anyone other than Jean. From here her eyes are even more ice-blue, cool like sapphire. Not hard to understand the ease of the leap to frosty nicknames. It's then he notices something moving deep in them. Something shadowy stirring, something moving up from the depths towards the surface, dark yet fiery.

She grunts, not quite a sigh, but nearly a breath. A sound his inner writer can't find the words to describe. She shakes her head, relenting, letting something go. 'Life happened, Neil.' Her voice is low, intimate. 'Death. Things that go bump in the night. All the nasty stuff you think you've securely walled inside you.' She pauses, releasing something recognisably closer to a sigh, a half-smile forming on her lips, lips through which her words suddenly ungainly tumble. 'It got out. It got out and I can't put it back. My dad. My mother. My sister. Swanley. Things you know about and plenty you never will. The job. The shit I see, all the stuff you tell yourself you'll get round to dealing with but never do. It gets inside, like a...virus, an infection. And you carry it with you - you walk around with it, and you don't even know it. And then, one day...one day something hits you, touches you. Nothing special, nothing so shocking or so terrible that you haven't seen it a thousand times before. But it's different...it changes something, something inside. You feel it like you haven't before...it's somehow more shocking, more dreadful... maybe in some strange and twisted way, even awe inspiring. And you realise just how awful it is, this stuff you've found inside you, this thing that's part of you. And you start to wonder about yourself. What it is that you've become to be able to carry such things. That in walking with monsters on your back, you've become one.' She shakes her head, the shadows in her eyes receding. 'And out it comes. A trickle, a wave, a flood.' She snorts, 'You're the writer, Neil, take your pick. But however it comes, you lose sense of who you are. So you keep people away, hoping they won't notice. But they do, no matter what you do, no matter how hard you try, they sense it. Smell it. They treat you differently. Not that anyone ever gets that close anymore, just in case they catch it too.'

'So, you push back,' he says.

She nods.

'That's what you're doing. Pushing back,' he judges.

'Not that simple,' she snorts. 'But I'm sure Malcolm would love to have a go at it. I've read the course books: *A psychotic personality disorder, a mix of self-protection and self-harm* or something like that. I like to think of it more that I'm suicide bomber and target all in one.'

Musgrove shakes his head. 'Demetriou was talking about you, wasn't he? About anger being something you need.'

She grunts. 'It understands me, Neil. Defines me. I can rely on it. Like you, just now with Doyle. For all the patient explaining, you just wanted to tell her to fuck off.'

'You think so?'

'Well, you sort of did, actually,' she smiles.

'I did, didn't I?' He stands a moment, hand rubbing chin. 'Maybe I should go back and say something.'

'It'd be nice. But that wouldn't be you, would it? Someone else would, and it would be the right thing to do. But not you. And she certainly wouldn't want it. It's not her either. She gets it.'

'You think so?'

'It's in her as much as in me or you. Demetriou as well. That's why he gets me. Gets us.'

'What should I do?'

'Well, you could start by seeing if we really have a case we can solve. Make it worth the effort. One last charge...you know into the valley. Go out with a bang not a whimper. Tom Cruise in that Samurai film he did.'

'Yeah,' he smiles, allowing a chuckle. 'Would be good, wouldn't it? Show them.'

'Make your fairy story come to life.'

'What?'

Fisher indicates young parents with a small child, a toddler all wide eyes as his mother points to the pictures in the book of nursery rhymes she holds in front of him. Each parent taking it in turns to distract the child whilst the other seizes a moment to drink their coffee, gulp down a forkful of cake.

'Charlie had that one,' he says. 'Gillian Brightside. A classic.'

The mother gets up, returns the book to the rack set next to the counter.

'Let's get these ice-creams,' Fisher suggests.

Musgrove looks at the display of ices, his appetite waning. *Blackcurrant. Rum and Raisin. Pistachio. Gingerbread. Jaffa cake.* A world of flavours and him suddenly with no appetite... *Gingerbread.* ...What is it about gingerbread that caught on his thinking, pressingly inviting? Maybe it was seeing the nursery rhyme book. Brightside's illustrations. Witches and gingerbread houses. Gill's death, his dad old Archibald being her publisher. *Gingerbread.*

He turns to Fisher, fingers snapping. 'Gingerbread!'

'What? Well, I suppose. I was thinking pistachio myself.'

'No. *Gingerbread*! Gingerbread!' he repeats, his feeling the surprise at a match struck in darkness. Small yet febrile, it starts burning up the blackness that's obscured his understanding. 'That's it!'

'*It what?*' Fisher asks.

Musgrove turns to the rack of books, tugging out the recently returned Brightside volume. He starts flicking through it. 'The answer. The thing we've been looking for. A link. The link. The three deaths. Well, Gill for sure, Wrigley too. Somehow Sofia. Harder for her, but it's there.' He slaps the palm of his hand onto the open page of the book held in the other. 'Oh Christ it's so obvious! Her hair! Her bloody hair!' He turns another page, face becoming ashen. 'Oh, my God!'

'What is it? To be honest, Neil, I'm still struggling with the hair thing.'

'Oh, good fucking grief!' He cries at the turn of another page. 'Webb! Webb too. They're linked. Wrigley, Gill, Sofia, and Webb too. Paul bloody Webb! We've been looking in the wrong place, the wrong man! It's not terrorists. It's…well, I don't know… something else…But we're right…we're bloody well right! It's not a fantasy, they're linked.' He looks up from the pages. 'They're murders. Diabolic and evil and ever so wonderfully plotted - admirable in fact - but murders all the same.'

Fisher holds out an arm to steady a man almost bouncing on the spot. 'Maybe you don't really need that coffee and sugar boost.'

Musgrove pushes past, racing to the stairs. Part way up, he turns, waving the nursery rhyme book and calling over his shoulder. 'Coffee, Fisher! Plenty of it! We've a killer to find!'

35

The looks on their faces say it all. Looking at the group squeezed around the small table, he tracks their expressions like a movie camera. They range from Demetriou's incomprehension, Fisher's bemusement to Doyle's appearance of someone with the asylum on speed dial, finger poised ready to push the button labelled *come get the crazy man*.

'Well?' he's pushed to ask. If nothing else, it breaks the silence they've been swimming in since he's outlined his idea. His latest insanity.

Fisher is first to respond. She's had time to accustom herself to the fiery glow emanating from the ACC, though she's as taken aback as the rest at the extravagance of the idea he's put before them. It's an Aladdin's cave of thinking, a merchant throwing down a rug on which he's laid out his most exotic wares, arms widening, beckoning them close, asking them to buy his intricate pattern of an idea. She can't help but think it's only an idea if by idea you mean a raving jumble of coincidence and leaps of logic sitting mid-point on a continuum somewhere between David Eyck and Yuri Gellar. Maybe David Blaine's in there somewhere too, him and the bloke who wonders round the centre of Ripon shouting at traffic.

BROKEN WINGS

'It's a lot to take in, Neil,' she offers. It's some way from a judgement, more a statement offered as place-marker for debate. Something to come back to after he's had a lie down in a dark room and a little medication.

Musgrove bounces in his seat, enthusiasm undimmed. 'I get it. I really do. But you of all people must see that it fits.'

'When I say *a lot to take in*, what I actually mean is *what the fuck are you saying*? You know? One minute you're stood next to me queuing for Jaffa cake ice cream, the next you're off on one, presenting an idea that's some rejected script from the *X-Files* telling us there's not only a murderer on the loose but an especially maniac serial killer. And this after you'd all but told us you think the whole thing is bollocks and that we should go home and forget about it.' On reflection she's decided the direct approach is best. It's uncomplicated, although one not always finding favour with those on the receiving end. On the plus side, it quickly gets to the heart of things, on the negative, it's the most cited reason for her being in therapy in the first place.

Musgrove sits forward, agitated. 'I know what I said, but this is what we've been looking for, something way beyond report filing and moving on. You started it, Fisher. Your idea that there was something we weren't seeing in Sofia's death, something making her and then Wrigley more than suicides.'

'Neil, what I thought was that maybe there's a chance the deaths are linked. That your idea of a story suggesting that possibility had some merit, scratched the itch Pan and I had about our suicides, that it wouldn't hurt to take another look for anything beyond the usual, the out of place.' She looks to Demetriou and then Doyle. 'I thought maybe a pact of some kind, Sofia and Wrigley, the sex worker and the maudlin drunk. Maybe they'd crossed the same gang, Sofia's Bulgarians are notoriously violent, all full of eastern sadism. I could see how Wrigley as a solicitor might be involved...maybe contracts he'd drawn up or some legal advice he'd given - something shady and off the record that made him a weak link. Maybe they were cleaning house.' She holds her hands up. 'Gill...well, Gill was always a bit of a curve ball that you threw into the mix, but I thought we could sort of play with it. See where it led. But this new idea...Webb. A serial killer...' She shrugs, a gesture she hates the most in anyone's response.

'I know it's a bit of an ask,' Musgrove relents, letting the line play out from the spool.

'Bit of an ask? It's a whole season of *Only Connect*. It's not a blue-sky question, an outside the envelope idea...it's...mind-blowing.' Demetriou adds.

'But if we include Webb, it works,' Musgrove persists, unshaken despite the silence that follows Demetriou's summation of what they'd heard.

Doyle licks her ice-cream, twirling the cone to catch drips threatening to escape her tongue, her piercing slavered in vanilla. 'This Webb? You do mean the businessman bloke? The one who got his head chopped off?' she asks.

'Yes. The same.' Musgrove clarifies wondering what other decapitated Webb she's been considering

'Weird,' she responds, tapping at the keyboard of her laptop.

'But that's terrorists, not criminals or serial killer,' Demetriou puts in, demanding Musgrove's attention stays fixed on the point at hand. 'It's all over the news. They tried for the PM and missed. Bad timing. Wrong place, wrong time. They're hoping for a breakthrough,' he points out.

'You sound like a Hargreaves' PR hand-out,' Fisher states. '"Hoping for a breakthrough soon".'

'That's as may be, but it's the line they're taking,' Demetriou responds. 'These are agents, not coppers. Experts - *Spooks*.' He holds his arms out wide. 'I like a good theory as much as the next, think that all ideas are worth consideration, ideas as *outside the envelope* and *blue-sky-whatever* as you can make them. But it has to have at least one foot in reality. It has to be grounded in something more than...fancy. Maybe it's got to you, Neil - the group thing. There's papers been written about it, a shared madness. Like Zara, you want it to be something more than what it really is. It offers purpose when you see Hyland locking you out of major investigations. And now there's the threat of suspension. You need it to be worthwhile, worth the sacrifice. But aren't you maybe grasping at straws?'

Musgrove shrugs. 'I understand why you're saying that, but don't you think that I find it's mad too? I mean, it's a lunatic idea!' He sighs. 'I'm hardly likely to be pushing this theory to Hyland or Hargreaves any time soon, am I? Don't you think I know that to do so screws my career for good? That outside this group there's no-one I'd even begin to think I could put this to without being laughed out of the room?'

He stops. The dawning realisation that he means what he's just said. That there really is no-one outside these three he'd say it to. No-one else he'd let in, no-one else he'd trust. The sense they too were coming to the same realisation, a momentary opening in their defences through which he might yet get his idea across. He looks around the group. 'You just have to let go,' he says. 'Just for a moment.' He scans the three. 'Close your eyes, all of you,' he instructs. 'You as well, Fisher. Let your mind see it. What if there's the smallest sliver of a possibility that Webb's murder *is* linked to Sofia. To Wrigley. To Gill.'

Demetriou, closes his eyes a moment, a blink that lasts a lifetime. A conclusion he's certain Fisher and Doyle are arriving at. 'Then yes, we'd be looking at a serial killer. Like Zara said, a warped and deranged one.'

'Aren't they all?' Doyle asks, eyes still closed. 'Serial killers, I mean. Warped and deranged. Isn't that the job description?'

'My dear Sophie,' Fisher says, voice cool and steady. 'You have much to learn about the ways of the psychopath.' Her words sound like a line from a Jedi training manual. The Darth Vader edition.

'You said it yourself,' Musgrove says. 'That it was like a fairy story. And you Fisher, you told us about that council bloke's reaction at the barn – *Rapunzel*, a rope made out of hair. Wrigley, big and fat like *Humpty Dumpty* having his great big fall. And Gill, John Gill failing off the cliffs, John is also Jack. He's also known as Jack Gill. *Jack and Gill*. Jack Gill went up the hill.'

'Hardly for a pail of water,' Fisher states.

'But he did fall down and broke his crown.'

'Okay. I'll give you that.'

'And that means Webb too. Webb…well, that's a spider, isn't it? Sliding down the spout of water. Washed down the drain.'

'What, *Incy-Wincy Spider*? Can't see Badgerman jumping on board with that,' Fisher says. 'And technically him not going back up the drainpipe is way off the mark. What with him not having a head.'

'Technically, okay. But it's a link. Gillian Brightside's books. It's what we said, another murder might give us our connection. It's Brightside's death. Gill links to Brightside, Brightside links to Wrigley, and Wrigley links to Webb. I'm sure of it.'

'But what connects a Bulgarian sex worker to any of it? It's a wild enough theory even before you try to fit Sofia into it.'

A silence descends like private prayer at a funeral - the squeak of a moving foot; a cough; the distant sounds of the world outside the veil of their thinking.

'I don't know about Sofia, but Neil's right about the link between those three men,' Doyle throws into the silence.

She spins her laptop so that the screen faces them. She leans a hand over the top, pointing at a listing part way down the page. 'I *Googled* it, The note he'd found in Gill's pocket that he'd thought was a password or something Gill needed to remember. I ran a search of *John Gill* and *gingerbread* and came up empty. But I've just run a search cross-referencing those three terms with Webb and Brightside added in. It came up with a link to Company House. *The Gingerbread Trust*. Brightside's estate was managed by Webb, Wrigley, and Archibald Gill. I mean the Gill is different, but the rest…'

'It's a family firm,' Musgrove says. 'Archibald Gill was John

Gill's father. It's what I said. They're connected to Brightside and her rhymes.'

'Let's not get carried away. It's a connection, a place to start. What it doesn't do is offer a motive for killing them. And it doesn't tell us how Sofia, despite her hair, is connected.'

'But it gives us somewhere to look,' Musgrove states.

'And there's this bloke, Jacob Strong,' Doyle adds. She swivels the computer back to herself. 'When I googled Brightside it found her obituary, *The Yorkshire Post*.' Turning it back to them, she points to the article's by-line. 'Strong wrote the obituary, and it says in italics at the bottom that he worked as PR for Brightside. Maybe he can offer an idea of who or why.'

'He might be a target himself,' Demetriou says.

'Or the killer,' Fisher judges.

'Well, there's one person who could shed light on that,' Musgrove states looking up from his own laptop and the police file he's just accessed. 'I'm looking at the case notes, the officer who signed off the investigation as unexpected death.'

'Brilliant! We can ask if there's anything not in the report,' Fisher says. 'Maybe a suspicion they weren't sure enough of to include.'

'You can't speak to him.'

'Is it this bloody suspension? Because if it is I can-'

'It's George Townley.'

'Townley?' Doyle says.

'The retired DS who's gone missing,' Demetriou tells her.

'The same,' Musgrove confirms.

'Maybe there's a link, him being missing,' Doyle suggests.

Musgrove shrugs. 'He was always a bit of an oddball.'

'By oddball you mean letch,' Fisher adds. 'Early retirement on grounds of all the multiple complaints of sexual harassment finally catching up with him. The Harvey Weinstein of North Yorkshire CID.'

'Whatever, old Georgie's been gone a couple of weeks now.'

'Maybe he's the killer, Doyle suggests. 'He's gone off grid and now he's killing these others. That or it's coincidence'

'I'm beginning to think there's too many of those happening,' Fisher judges.

'Well, you can always speak with the DI who supervised Townley's investigation into Brightside's death,' Musgrove tells her.

'Who's that?' Fisher asks.

'Your best mate, DCS Crosby.'

'Crosby?' Fisher frowns.

Musgrove looks at the screen. 'Seems he was in overall charge of what the Brightside investigation judged to be nothing other than a *sudden unexpected death,* something not worth additional investigation. Townley was simply delegated to do the paperwork. Townley who signed it off.'

"Georgie Porgie,' Doyle says quietly.

'What?' Fisher asks.

'*Georgie Porgie pudding and pie, Kissed the girls and made them cry, When the boys came out to play, Georgie Porgie ran away.*'

'Christ!' Demetriou says.

36

The building is just as Crosby remembered. Yorkshire stone, the red-brick extension jutting out like a raw growth, the sort of scab impelling a desire to pick it away. From where he sits - car on the crown of the road contemplating turning onto the drive running alongside the property - he sees the blue lamp fitting has already been removed, leaving just a filigreed bracket to indicate where it had been. His gaze moves along the frontage, metal security shuttered doors and windows, the early seventies light box slick with a film of green moss, its blue Perspex pane cracked and torn, lettering faded to a less than informative P_L_CE. To the left of it a large noticeboard remains fixed to the wall, its own Perspex shield dulled and faded, wooden frame blistered, varnish flaking and peeling to expose greying timber under the dark oak stain.

He puffs out his cheeks. The road is empty, little more than a cut through for local farmers anxious to avoid busier tourist roads that in summer months are choked with caravans and motor homes. Late autumn the traffic is as occasional as the nearby railway line and its fortnightly gin rides and Steam Train outings.

He makes the turn, driving to the rear and the small car park, a pad of cracked tarmac shot through with weeds. Here and there odd shards of concrete and roof tiles have been scattered by demolition crews stripping the carcass. Left for others to dispose of, it's all part of the evidence of just how long it's been since the premises saw active duty, not that he recalls action here being anything more than a few bicycle thefts with the odd rustled sheep or barn break-in thrown in for a change of pace.

Around the perimeter are an array of demolition company signs in varying condition. Some are new, commissioned for the job, others re-used, edges battered, graffiti tags for *Leeds Posse* or *Bradford Ultras* still visible. Some are red, others a garish blue and yellow, plastic placards warning of the danger of intrusion. Attached to the largest is an order from the council informing interested parties of the demolition later that week.

He gets out of the car, standing for a moment to take in the views. Stunning as the landscape is, it's abundantly clear why this particular outpost of the North Yorkshire constabulary has come to its end. Surrounded by the ruins of a once vibrant Victorian hamlet, it gives fresh meaning to the idea of isolated with no other dwellings between it and the village some five miles further along this section of the Dale or the one he'd driven through five minutes ago in the opposite direction.

Times changed. Things move on. The station house became surplus to needs in the Seventies when patrol cars replaced the village bobby on a bike. From what he knows of its history, it had been kept on as a symbol, flying the flag of law and order. In recent times it served as little more than a presence appeasing a once wealthy parish council's need to feel itself relevant. Now, in the digital age where the watchwords of costs and spending restraint hold sway, time has caught up with it.

Like the nearby railway, the police station house has run its useful course. Unlike the railway there are no quick fixes repurposing it as a distillery, a café, or maybe a tourist walking destination. For the past ten years its function has been more like the police box in *Doctor Who*. Once a week a passing patrol car

BROKEN WINGS

checked in and two constables would set up a community response desk - in reality, bored uniforms' passing a morning reading the newspaper and topping up the community notice board. The poster for Hargreaves' election with it's felt tip moustache and blacked out teeth seems to fly in the face of the project's intention of a local police presence deterring crime and anti-social behaviour. The passing thought that it would have taken a highly motivated graffiti artist to travel all the way out here to commit such an act. That or a couple of bored uniforms with a magic marker and a couple of hours to kill.

Walking to the rear of the building, he stoops, fumbling in the weeds for keys left where they'd always been, set in a hollow stone, wondering what the Crime Prevention Boys would make of it. Rolling up the security shutter and unlocking the door, he steps inside, one glance reassuring him they'd have little to worry about. It's empty, stripped of everything beyond the original fixed counter and the security screening installed during the IRA bomb scares of the seventies. At the time, such screens had been mandatory for all stations, a requirement complied with by a puzzled yet grateful local builder.

The smell, however, is very much present. Damp wood, a musky aroma of mould ripening in dark corners where the sun rarely shone. It is the definition of musty - a cocktail of dry dust and rotting timber that catches in the throat and sticks in the nostrils.

Lungs acclimatising, he walks the space, hands reflexively dragging along the dark oak of a once familiar counter, his thoughts drifting to early career years of life as a constable and the few months he'd served out here in what even then had been termed *Fort Apache*, the locals almost as reflexively hostile to outsiders as Geronimo and his boys.

Even in the semi-darkness of its shuttered windows, the room is smaller than he remembers, about the size of the lounge of a modern semi. Off to one side, a galley kitchen had been installed in the red brick extension. Through a tiny passageway running the width of the building is access to two small cells built, so he'd been told, as part of Peel's unification of magistrates and local yeomanry in the 1840s, probably its last meaningful act. Behind the waiting area with its wooden pew style bench is an office and storeroom.

He stands rubbing hands together, brushing away dust accumulated from door handles and countertop before taking his mobile from an inside pocket only to find the *No Service* logo flashing. He considers standing outside, wondering if the signal might be better, when he hears an engine revving as it rides over the sleeping policeman that lies across the car park access. He wonders just how many policemen passed their shifts here in such a useful manner.

He thinks about what he's going to say - threats, quiet advice, maybe a sharp punch in the face. For a moment he's torn between threats and act of violence, but the minute Jacob Strong appears in the doorway, the option of an act of violence starts to contemplate a victory lap at what it sees standing there.

Crosby focuses on Strong's creased light grey suit, a look akin to it having been slept in, the sense of louche disarray added to by the open collared white shirt and no tie. He hadn't seen him in person for almost a decade, but the impression of a man embracing to the full his cultural image: journalist as media icon, a rebel wrapped in trademark disheveled stylings, poster-boy cool testimony to the results of a life lived wildly is as present as it ever was. He carries a copyrighted Keith Richards-like sense of wasted-ness, darling of the Harrogate social and literati scene. A punch in the face feels about right, but Crosby takes a minute.

'About time,' he states as marker of his feelings.

'Apologies. Unavoidable,' Strong replies, yawning and stepping into the room. His tone strikes Crosby as no apology at all. Punch in the face starts limbering up with a few quick squats and thrusts, ready for the call to action that is surely coming.

'That's as may be, Crosby retorts. 'But I've better things to be getting on with than hang around doing all this *Secret Seven* clandestine spy bullshit,' he spits. 'It's hard enough getting away, let alone dragging myself all the way out here,' he concludes, annoyed at the casual brusqueness Strong wears like a badge of achievement. They'd met only a few times, but as ever he's aware of Strong getting under his skin, pulling levers and pushing the buttons of his dislike of the man, his calling, and his lifestyle. He knows that to men like Strong people like him are 'other', unworldly and uneducated and to be reminded of that fact whenever possible. Punch in the face awaits the call.

Strong takes in the room. 'Must say, I like what you've done with the place. What is it? Early Dickensian hovel?'

'And I've no time for jokes or playing silly buggers. I've an investigation to oversee,' Crosby states, fists twitching.

'Again, apologies,' Strong offers. He fiddles with his hands, picking at a nail.

Crosby takes a moment. 'You look dreadful,' he observes. 'Even more a sack of shit than you usually do.'

Strong flicks a hand at the front of his jacket, looks at a sleeve, runs a hand through his hair. He smiles his best goosh smile and shrugs. 'You know how it is. Late nights. Not a deal of sleep. Trying to get my head around everything that's happening. Wrigley. Gill. Webb.'

Crosby shakes his head, knows where this is going. Putting a punch back in the box, he instead gives in to his desire to cut things short, the urge to head it off at the pass. 'Don't you think you're letting your imagination run a little wild? Stuff like this is the last thing I need, what with the Webb investigation stuttering when it ought to be in full swing. There are eyes on all of us. Me in particular.'

'I understand that,' he says, Crosby staring at him, silent and unmoving. Strong taking it as permission to say what he has to say continues. 'But even if no-one else has seen it, there must be something nagging at you about these deaths? We both know there's a connection that CID are missing.'

Crosby maintains a silent stare.

Strong shakes his head. 'Look. These deaths happening in such a short space of time can't be coincidence. You of all people must see that, knowing what you know.'

Crosby steps forward, closing the gap between them. 'Knowing what I know? You mean knowing what I did. What you pushed me to doing.' He stands a pace apart staring into eyes that remain unblinking. He allows a beat before stepping back. 'Like I said on the phone, all this speculation, it's madness. These deaths *are* coincidence. Webb *was* murdered by a jihadi terror cell. Wrigley couldn't face the sad world he'd forged for himself. And Gill, well, he wasn't even part of anything, was he? That alone should undermine your crazy idea of a serial killer. Now's not the time to be drawing attention to things better left where they were.'

'You mean better for the two of us that are left.'

Crosby ignores the point. 'You losing it, shouting down the phone about murders and bogey men isn't helping. You need to get your shit together, Jacob.' He fixes him with a disdainful glare. 'Maybe help if you eased off the booze.'

'It's not the booze. Not this.'

'No? Maybe not. Not this time.' Crosby looks him up and down. 'But right now there's just one thing stopping me simply telling you to fuck off back into whatever bottle you came from. You and your ravings.'

'Is it what I know about you?'

Crosby snorts. 'Jacob, neither of us are any position to turn the other in. We'd both serve time. Lots of it. If I tell the Spooks what I know, this crazed theory of a vengeful killer, I run the very real risk of the spotlight being turned on me, that or being laughed out of the building. Neither are decent career options.'

'But they'd know what they're dealing with. They wouldn't simply dismiss it. They'd investigate. Make the connections.'

'I wouldn't be so sure of that. Seems your special madness is contagious, either coincidence or a shared melodrama. *A shared madness* Malcolm Pemberton calls it in his report. You know him? Pemberton, the psychologist?'

'The profiler, the one your lot used on that serial rapist? Caught *The Sedbergh Stalker*?'

'Of sorts.' He allows himself a chuckle. 'He's got himself a therapy group. Washed up officers, whose careers are in free-fall. ACC Musgrove, DI Fisher and a couple of newbies.'

'Musgrove? What's he got to do with it?'

'Our esteemed ACC fancies himself a writer. Somehow he stumbled across an idea for a story, a hare-brained tale plucked out of the air linking the deaths of Wrigley and Gill. He's got them down as victims of a serial killer wreaking havoc on capitalists, some Marxist zealot killing off the Masons and Rotary Club Members like a Sherlock Holmes villain.'

'So, you're telling me he's investigating what he found. That he knows about Wrigley and Gill being linked. Does he know about Webb? Us? Our arrangement?'

'ACC Neil Musgrove is a second-rate officer. Probably third-rate even. A man so ineffective that the Chief Constable and the Commissioner have had him on refurbishment and PR for the past six months. Thanks in no part to me, Hyland and Hargreaves are convinced it's an act of delusion, an idea so crazy that if word of it got out it risks undermining the credibility of the force. They're about to suspend him. Fisher too.'

'They don't believe him?'

Of course not! It's... fantasy. Comic book shit.'

'But we know there's more to it. Surely, if Musgrove and these others start asking questions they'll find the connection. I remember Fisher, her reputation, her clean up rate. She caught Swanley. If she's involved it's only a matter of time. Once they link Gill and Wrigley to Gingerbread, they'll find Webb, then me. After that there's a clear link to you through Townley.'

'Of course there's a link. They're local businessmen. There's got to be hundreds of possible connections between them and you and hundreds of other similarly successful businessmen. It would be against the odds if you didn't know each other. What they're claiming about Wrigley and Gill - this maniac capitalist killer - means they've shot themselves in the sanity foot. No-one's going to listen to anything they come up with, especially from what is an off the book investigation by a bunch of damaged investigators based on some writer's whimsy.'

'But Musgrove, if you get rid of him and Fisher, it's a story.'

'The minute they open their mouths they won't have any platform at all. Think about it. In an act of group delusion, they started a fantasy crime fighting group of losers and failures hell bent on proving a spate of deaths are the work of a serial killer bumping off local businessmen. They're mentally disturbed is how they'll be painted. If they try to link Webb's death into it they'd be going against Downing Street's theory of terrorist cells. After what's about to happen to them no-one will dream of looking any deeper. It puts us in the clear.'

Strong looks to the floor. 'I don't know, it seems...maybe.'

Crosby takes a moment, stands by the front door poking a finger at the edge of the sealed shutters, wonders why they're pretty much airtight when the whole place is being demolished in a few days. 'Have to say that you had me wondering if you'd gone a bit potty yourself,' he tells Strong. 'You know, the drugs and the booze. Even crossed my mind it might be you killing off your fellow conspirators. I came out here thinking maybe you were trying to set me up. You know, going to bump me off and maybe drag me into getting the blame. Especially with Townley missing.'

Strong looks up. 'Townley? Townley's missing?'

'Thought you were a reporter, though I suppose what with Webb and everything, even the story of a missing ex-detective's been pushed down the news agenda. Few weeks now. Seems Old Georgie went out for a paper or something and never came back. Makes you wonder.'

37

Demetriou looks out of the window of the service station restaurant. From where he sits in a booth close to the door, his view is of a quad of tarmac. Across it, a scattering of cars are haphazardly assembled in an area enclosed by a two storey red brick building to one side, the McDonald's he sits in on another, with unkempt hedges on the other two. It has more the feel of a greasy transport stop than a services, a step down even from the tawdry gloss of the stops on what he thought of as the real national motorways. The M1s and M5s and M6s, the proper ones with *WH Smiths* and *Waitrose* outlets, *Costa* and *Starbucks*. Not the wannabe M62s or A1 bracket M close bracket, the structure of the name itself an indication of the afterthought it is.

Sitting contemplating the wreckage of his life choices, he finds his fingers occupying themselves in peeling the sticker off the bright red fries carton. The poster on the restaurant wall promised *Fifty thousand pounds or a Big Mac* as the prize. He turns the sticker over. Surprise. He's won a Big Mac he can claim on his next visit, an offer you couldn't refuse. Not him or the sprinkling of punters chomping their way through meals whilst idly scrolling down phone screens or staring into the distance, all no doubt open to the idea of being lured back by the siren promise of a free meat patty.

This morning, the urge to taste a burger has been irresistible. Like the Force, or those things folk on Desert Island disks say they'd miss - maybe ex-pats pleading for a suitcase full of Bovril when you next visit, maybe Marmite, possibly brown sauce, or cheese and onion crisps.

His stop here is part undeniable craving and part calculated reasoning. The location is half-way between Leyburn to the west and Northallerton and CID HQ to the east. It was as good a place as any, he'd thought. And there were burgers.

The stop lurks down a pitted access ramp, pot-holes full of standing water, that takes drivers past a *Holiday Inn* inspired rest stop. He wonders who'd choose to stay there. If you were travelling to Newcastle it was only another forty minutes further north. And to the south at similar distance were Leeds and Harrogate and the charms of York. Why would even the weariest of travellers not take one look and decide to press on? The peeling frames of the windows and the moss on the signage was surely enough to urge one last push north or south, giving a miss to what at first sight appears to be the Bates Motel of the Dales.

Tucked around the back of it, like some shadowy drug dealer is McDonalds. It was there, but only if you really wanted to indulge, if you really couldn't control those feral urges, a location designed to make you feel dirty, ashamed. Admit it, you're an addict, one some way from the Twelve Steps. Looking down at himself, the slight protrusion of a paunch pushing against the cotton of his shirt, he recognises that as far as steps of any description went he's probably not even up to three or four of them without chest pains and the associated wheezing breath.

Not that he's unfit. Far from it. He still weighs close to what he's always thought to be his fighting weight. But the last few weeks, what with the move and the comfort issues around pining for Jessica, he's lost some of the physical edge that his weekly gym routines back in Brum had kept in trim. It was temporary, one look at Musgrove had determined him on that. As soon as he finds somewhere local he'll sign up. The issue was that round here "local" meant twenty miles, and after the long shifts Fisher has them pulling there's precious little time left for drives to gyms let alone the desire to work-out.

He bites into the bun, the roll yielding like the soft pillow of sugary dough it is. The taste of the fat on his tongue delivers its greasy promise of mainlining the odours he'd queued in. Fried meat, fried potato - all the flavours of his imagination. He opens his eyes, realising he'd closed them as he chewed.

After a few more mouthfuls he sits up from the almost foetal bend he's been locked in whilst he ate. He begins the unthinking tick of wiping away the crumbs of fries and salt that have slipped through his fingers onto the tabletop. The bun itself, bound tight with sugar and fat, gave no crumbs.

Wiping his fingers before dabbing a napkin to the corners of his mouth like a Michelin starred afterthought, he sets about flicking the lid off his flat white. Mind unfettered by hunger and cravings, he finds his thoughts returning to the text he'd received earlier. Jessica's news.

Pregnant. Her and *the wanker formerly known as* DI Addison.

Addison. The reason why he'd transferred out, Addison who'd moved himself in with barely a day's grace of Pan's own leaving. She's pregnant. He was no expert in biology or female cycles, but even he knows it means if it isn't his child that Jessica and Addison had been much more closely acquainted for longer than she'd told him. Given that for months they'd not had anything in the way of relations beyond the most civil or platonic, let alone the good sexy ones, it means she's lied to him. Played him for an even bigger fool than he'd thought. That whatever they'd had – whatever he thought they'd had – meant even less to her than he's imagined. She hasn't even been honest about her deception.

And whatever else it means, he's sure her next text will be to tell him she'll now be putting on hold her agreement to sell the flat. That she and Addison couldn't afford to buy him out. That he'd be saddled with paying his share of the mortgage for the next year or more to enable her and Addison's game of Happy New Family Home to play out. It was agree or stop his payments, something putting him into default with the bank. It isn't a sensible financial prospect for any of them. No good choices. No good outcomes.

He fiddles with the lid of the coffee. One thing is certain, there's no way he'll be telling Fisher any of this, at least not anytime soon. The last thing he needs right now is another of her fulminations on his too-niceness. The listing of reasons why in her opinion he's what she'd termed so decisively to be a man who was *"naïve. Ooh, and a bit of a pratt"*.

As far as Fisher goes, he's certain he's lumped into the pigeon-hole labelled *Victim*. Stuck in there with the trafficked and the weak. The addicts and users, the terminal losers. And even there, he'd find himself to be among the worst sort. Self-inflicted, shooting himself in the foot and a good few parts anatomically north of it.

But most of all, it's the way she'd say it. Her drive-by riposte of *"factions speak louder than words,"* had been a comment she'd used a day or so ago as a put down of a *'wanky DI'* from a local force who bent to whatever wind his superiors saw fit to blow on them. A comment fixing him forever in terms of how Fisher sees him. It was how she would fix him, Demetriou. It would be a reinforcement of the image he's sure she's shaping of him: a two time loser - personal life and career.

At least it was an instance of an effective work-life balance. Him being a prat in both.

He tries to think of what he's contributed to their cases these past few weeks, the manner in which he's conducted the enquiry into Wrigley's suicide that he technically leads on. Wrigley, his first real case since his move. The chance to show what he could do. Efficient, focused, determined - all of the qualities his last professional review in Brum had listed in assessment of him

BROKEN WINGS

prior to his transfer. All of them true - at least before everything good went Addison-shaped.

What had he managed with Wrigley? None of the paperwork or anticipated actions had been completed, nothing like. So much for his efficiency. He'd been drawn into this strange Mad-Hatter's tea party world, first by Fisher's delusions about her own suicide case and then Musgrove's even more bizarre writerly fantasy about Kovalenko and Wrigley, and now Gill and Webb. Ideas of serial killers and nursery rhymes. So much for his focus. And as for his dogged determination, well the scepticism he'd maintained around Fisher and Musgrove means he's tackled their theories with reluctance and foot dragging of the highest order. Stuck between two worlds: the real one and that of the Broken Wings.

And, on top of everything, he's found himself sucked into it. The mass hysteria and self-delusion of the group. Fisher even crediting him with inspiring it all through his call for her to channel her inbuilt anger, an idea he now finds less convincing in the reality than in the telling. Musgrove had been right the first time - things had gotten out of hand, everything rolling downhill with a gathering speed and with little thought about whether they'd included brakes in the construction of their clown's jalopy of a plan.

Here, in the cold light of day, things look different. Like the funfair in daytime, the gaudy lights and music and smells and the sounds of the crowd replaced with reality.

Away from the thrall of the others, away from the sealed in meanderings of their hive-mind thinking it looks so different. Leeming Bar rest area: people going about their business, stopping for a burger with no thought of murder or suicides or serial killers. No fanciful pondering on nursery rhyme inspired mayhem unless it was firmly locked inside whatever holiday book they'd scooped off the shelves in *Tesco* or *Sainsbury's*. A story to titillate. A story to pull you in from the anodyne cycle of work and domestic routine. A compelling page-turner, a gripping thriller. But at the end of the day, a story. Not real. There were few if any hit-men stalking the Dark Web waiting for your call. There isn't a disturbed psychopath running your local *Kwik-fit* or *Costa* or *Halifax* building society, sizing you up each time you popped in. There are no twisted serial killers dreaming up ever newer and inventive ways of killing their prey. Multiple murderers are few and far between - strange, lonely people incapable of loving. Badly wired souls. But they aren't *Psycho*.

This will be the last act of his madness.

Finding Crosby and asking him about the investigation of Brightside's death. An interview he knows will be conducted to the tune of Crosby's outrage at the questioning of his stewardship of a case of a drug overdose, Crosby lumping him into the fiery pit of ire he reserves for anything Fisher related. Demetriou is Fisher's DS, her boy. They are linked, chained and shackled. No matter how hard he might saw at the bonds binding them, he'll never be able to change that. As far as DCS Crosby and promotion were concerned, after this upcoming meeting he, DS Pan Demetriou, will be a marked man.

Maybe this was what Iverson and the others had warned of, Fisher's true nature breaking through. *Elsa, the Snow Queen, Frozen*. Despite his sense of her thaw, she's hanging him out to dry. Maybe it's because of what Musgrove has hinted at, her breakdown, her father's murder, those dark clouds from her past.

He gets up, shoving the waste of wrapper, cartons and cup onto the brown plastic tray before walking to the door and sliding the rubbish into a wide mouthed bin.

The sooner he catches up with Crosby, the better. He'll make him aware of the necessity for him to carry out his Inspector's wishes even though he knows the weakness of her theory. It's what a good DS does. Crosby would understand. It was about being the good soldier, following the line of command.

He would tick the boxes.

Efficient. Focused. Determined.

38

'It makes sense,' Strong exclaims, hands moving up and down like he's shaking an empty box of cornflakes in front of him trying to rattle the last piece free.

'No, it doesn't. How does it make sense? Did you not hear what I just said about *therapists* and the whole *insane group that are roped into it*? What are you talking about?'

'Brightside's death.'

'A death you dissuaded me from investigating beyond the obvious conclusion of her well-known appetite for drugs and alcohol.'

Strong shrugs the point into agreement. 'We knew the politics of it, the implications for the pathologist's budget if there was no request from the investigating officer to delve deeper.'

Crosby grunts. 'And everyone knowing the reluctance of Waddingham to poke any kind of a stick into a deep dark hole of controversy. His eagerness for a quiet life. His knighthood.'

Strong pushes hands deeper into his trouser pockets, eyes fixed on the toe of a shoe sweeping a dust angel into dirty floorboards. 'And with your good self on board, the power behind your very own Townley shaped puppet, we were secure.'

'If I'd known the whole of it…'

Strong looks up from his artwork. 'Superintendent, I can't believe you didn't suspect there was something more at play than the executors' desire to have proceedings expediently dealt with. Why else did you insist on having Townley sign it off if it wasn't to obscure a paper trail leading any later enquiry to your door?'

'Wrigley told me any hold up in declaring a cause of death would hamper probate. The town's economy and reputation needed a misadventure judgement. As for Townley...he was a liability, but I let him have his dignity, his name appearing on the report.'

'And the fact you knew Gill to be a close friend of the Chief Constable, of Wrigley's connections to local political figures, and Webb's personal connection to the man who would go on to be Prime Minister had nothing to do with it,' Strong observes. 'Men of standing and influence in the community, not to mention with the police promotion board. Men who'd be grateful to someone helping their cause.'

'I expedited matters. I didn't know she'd been...'

'Murdered?' Strong tuts. 'You took the promotions, and with Wrigley's backing you even joined the Masons. You haven't done badly out of turning a blind-eye, so it's a little late to be getting squeamish about the details.' He moves to the counter, leans against it, toying with the latch of the fold-up opening. 'But that's in the past. It's the present I'm concerned about. These deaths - Webb, Wrigley, and Gill, maybe Townley too,' he says, finger sketching a hangman style platform and noose in the dust, a stick figure dangling from it before he rubs it clean. 'When they started dying, I thought I was going mad. Webb's murder was a shock, but appeared a random act, you know, terrorists, a symptom of the sick world we live in. The Spooks were clear on that fact, but I couldn't fully buy into it, what with the shadow of the Bulgarians over so much where Webb was concerned, arrangements that maybe even Special Branch with all their contacts know little of. Wrigley's suicide coming so soon after was similarly disconcerting. We all knew that Harrison lived with a troubled conscience, that he and old Archibald had qualms from the start, ones that greed and vanity and the fear of imprisonment kept at bay. But, lately with the increase in his drinking...well, who knows where his mind may have wandered. A sudden urge to end it all seemed unlikely, yet was within the odds of possibility, even probability. The more I thought about it...I reached out to Gill's son, told him about his father and our secret, a secret it seems Archie had passed on to him on his death-bed. He said Wrigley had told him the same story the night he fell.' Strong shakes his head. 'I'd had a message from someone claiming they'd information about Brightside's death. That they wanted money to keep quiet. That they wanted me personally to bring it to them. They said to use *gingerbread* as a password. It meant they knew.' He sighs. 'Gill went instead. We thought the fact he hadn't been involved offered credibility as a go-between. He was to hand over the money and to find out what they knew about Gingerbread. But when he fell...it meant I'm right. The deaths are connected; it was the killer he met. It's why like you I thought it a risk to meet out here.'

'What? You think I killed Wrigley and this Gill? Killed Webb? Kidnapped Townley?'

'Not once I'd been to Leeds and realised that Gill was killed not because of who he was but because he didn't have what the killer wanted. It was never about the money. The killer wanted to meet me for a reason.'

'And what's that?'

'They know someone else is involved. They took Townley, probably killed him too, but at some point must have realised he was just a front man. They'd need access to the files or me to find out who it was who'd conspired in Brightside's verdict. I'm the last one alive who knows about you. He can't just kill me, he has to meet me to find out for certain who it was signed things off, the name of the person who'd protected us.'

'You're insane. Certifiable. I'm a DCS, I've got the inside track on each of these investigations you've mentioned. What you're talking about is coincidence. Webb, Wrigley, Gill - they're not murders. They're a suicide, an accident, and a terror attack. It's what all of the evidence points to. It's bad luck, that's all. Theres nothing to see.'

'Just as you told everyone with Brightside.'

'You're as mad as Musgrove, a fantasist watching too much TV and reading too much pulp fiction. Why? Why would someone want to kill them, and why now? It's been ten years.'

'I thought maybe you were cleaning house, but then I found something in *The Post's* cuttings library. A name on a slip of paper.'

Crosby, unsure where to send the anger and irritation he's feeling, his emotions fuelled by the nonsense he's hearing from a drug-addled drunk, storms to stand a foot or so apart. The urge to poke Strong's chest is irresistible. 'What the hell have you got me into?' Prod. 'The only reason I agreed to meet all the way out here is to shut you up.' Prod. 'To stop you calling me day after day with your insane ideas about serial killers.' Prod. 'To tell you to sober up and stay quiet.' Prod. 'The entire force are looking for Webb's killers. They're looking for terrorists - Islamic, Irish, Right wingers, Left wingers, Mumsnet - whoever the fuck might have wanted the PM dead. And by the way that's a very long list. And with all their attention fixed on that, we're safe. The only fly in this - apart from your incessant phone calls - is Musgrove's band of misfits. But I've sorted it, sidelined them - hell they're doing it for themselves.'

Strong stares at him. 'What did you say about agreeing to meet here?'

Crosby furrows his brow. 'Your paper said to meet here. Your idea for a feature about changing times and old Yorkshire landmarks. You asked for me by name. I just assumed it was-'

'They told me you'd asked for me.'

'What?'

'Northallerton. This idea for a feature, for us meeting, came from there.' He stops. 'Oh, of course it didn't! It came from the only person it could have.'

A clang of metal from the rear door stops both dead. 'What's that?' Strong asks, turning from Crosby to look down the passageway. 'Is there someone with you?'

Crosby shrugs. 'Of course not, last fucking thing I'd need. The door's just blown closed. Bloody winds up here.' The sound of a key in the lock and the security shutter rattling down, changes his mind. 'Christ! Someone's locking the fucking door!'

Both race down the corridor. Crosby, arriving first yanks at the door handle with one hand whilst hammering a fist against it with the other. 'Oi! What's going on? There are people in here! Can you hear me? Open this door!'

Beyond the door and its shutter, they hear the dull clunk of a padlock snapping into place.

Strong steps back. 'There's no point.'

'What do you mean? Some silly sod from the security company or the builders has seen the door left open and thinks they're doing a good turn by locking up.'

'Why would they do that? Our cars are out there. They'd have known someone's in here. They'd have called out. We'd have heard them. There's nowhere we could be other than in here. It's deliberate. A trap.'

'What?'

'It's them. The killer.'

'You're saying they've locked us in. Like a dungeon?'

A half-smile verging on appreciation plays on Strong's lips. 'No, not a dungeon.' He slides down the wall, coming to a rest on his haunches. He laughs. 'Don't you get it? It's Brightside. The thing I couldn't see. The nursery rhymes. You're the detective, think about it, what have all those deaths got in common? Wrigley's fall off a very high wall; Gill's tumble off Malham and rolling down the hill; Webb's head being chopped off.'

Crosby narrows his brow, shakes his head in puzzlement. 'What?'

'...Nursery rhymes,' Strong states. 'Fucking nursery rhymes.'

'...What?'

'This is an old police station house, remember.' He nods in the direction of the door. 'They're the Big Bad Wolf. And you, DCS Crosby, you're the little piggy that couldn't be found. They've used Townley's disappearance to get to see the files they wanted. The killer knows it's you. The little piggy he got to run all the way to here to where you once worked, all the way home, so to speak.'

'What? But...' Crosby's face screws in thought. 'What about you?'

'Me? I'm an investigative crime reporter. The one who's supposed to expose the corruption of others, the one who sold out the truth about Gillian Brightside for a profit. I'm the little piggy who went to market.'

'So that means...'

'...They're going to blow down the little piggie's house. Blow it down with us little piggies inside.'

39

Demetriou stands by his car door fiddling with the fob, puzzled. There are two cars in the parking area. One he knows to be Crosby's pool car, the other he doesn't recognise.

Dropping the fob into a pocket, he walks to the rear door, the nearest and most obvious means of access. The security roller shutter is down tight and padlocked in place. Walking to the front of the building, he finds it too shuttered and locked.

He steps back, eyes scanning the frontage for some clue as to where Crosby or the other driver might be. 'Hello!' he calls. 'Anyone there?'

With no response, he returns to the rear looking for any access he's missed. Finding none, he turns his attention to the cars, a hand placed on each bonnet finding both warm.

He bends, hand shielding the reflected glare of the windows, and scans the interiors, first Crosby's then the other. It is then that he sees the card propped on top of its dashboard, a laminated sign placed from force of habit as the driver exited. PRESS it reads. JACOB STRONG printed underneath.

'Strong,' he whispers.

He takes out his mobile, but there's no signal. 'Shit!' he

exclaims, popping the phone into a pocket whilst wondering what Fisher would do.

He's now certain Crosby can shed light on the idea of a motive connecting Strong and the three dead men, maybe Townley's disappearance. But the fact Crosby's here with Strong offers no sense of his role in it all. He might be here to ask Strong questions of his own, either that or he's unwittingly about to become Strong's next victim or may possibly himself be Strong's killer. You take your pick...

He turns, scanning the parking area, certain there must be some sign of the two drivers, at the same time wondering what his ploy will now be. He can hardly play his previously agreed approach of *'I was just wondering about that investigation you were involved in a few years ago, the one where all those involved suddenly seem to be being murdered.'* He certainly can't go that way if at the time of asking Crosby is stood next to Strong, himself either victim or killer or accomplice. Especially not in an isolated building when he's holding nothing more than sheer bravado as a weapon.

Maybe the better option is to withdraw, regroup. Consider his options.

It's only the thought of Fisher's look of smug disapproval at further evidence of his lack of balls that stops him. That and the thought of Musgrove - despite his recent bout of manic enthusiasm - chewing his way through a Lion bar whilst shaking his head and bemoaning how it had all gone too far, his pension disappearing. And Doyle, wrapped inside her puffa jacket thinking him a prat, a weak and cowardly one at that. It's a combination of group disdain that stops him from jumping in his car and racing away.

Instead, he turns to the building and begins considering just what it is that's going on in there.

'What do you mean, you can't get hold of him?'

Iverson stands in the doorway of the cupboard serving as CID office. 'There's no signal,' he explains, hoping a simple statement of the facts is sufficient to hold Fisher at bay whilst he picks up the file he has to get to the CPS and slips away.

'So where is he?'

Iverson shakes his head. This is clearly going to take time. 'It's the signal, Ma'am. The transmitter. You know, the dead spots.'

'So he's in one of those.'

Iverson rolls his top lip in consideration. 'Most likely. But they're all over the place. No rhyme nor reason to them. Dips and hollows. The odd valley top getting in the way. Sheep. He could be in Wharfdale. He could be in Swaledale. He might be anywhere between Muker and Settle if I'm being honest.'

'Fuck,' she states.

He clears his throat, hesitates. 'If I might ask, Ma'am. Should you be here, looking at files,' he asks nodding at the folder spread across her desk. 'Your suspension.'

'Effective midnight. Clearing my desk, which thanks to the shit you lot have piled up on it will take a month. So just fuck off and let me get on, there's a good DS.'

When he leaves, she returns to what's been on her mind since Doyle had first pulled up the file of the Brightside investigation for her.

A suspicious death generated an enquiry, most simply a matter of reviewing the circumstances with maybe the odd interview or two adding a little local colour to the coroner's report. Open and shut was invented for such cases, and Townley's report was exactly that. But even though Townley's name was on it, she's certain Crosby would have interviewed the executors of Brightside's estate himself – Gill, Webb, and her lawyer, Wrigley - probably followed up with an interview of her PR man, Strong.

All were men of good reputation, the definition of solid

citizens. Masons. Men whose questioning would have demanded the unwritten protocol of a senior officer's involvement.

She'd read the report, each telling the same story. Exactly the same. The fact they were exactly the same was the first itch she'd needed to scratch. No case has exactly the same interview findings. The art of the report writing of an unexpected death lay in interpreting the disparate truths of the witnesses, all of whom would have had different ideas and agendas and relationships to the dead person. In doing so, a coherent whole emerges, one enabling a rational conclusion to be reached. A conclusion satisfying Waddingham, a coroner with little inclination to look further than the summary pages.

From what she'd read, the report had been a matter of writing up the same ideas four times. The same expressions four times. The final conclusion was little other than a cut and paste requiring no interpretation of the unanimous views of the four men. The same phrases occurred in each one. *'A troubled soul…a woman of feral urges, hard to restrain…'* Each one using the same telling idiom: *'her mind was a tangled thread'*, a comment Crosby had clearly been at pains for Townley to use in his summation of *death by misadventure*. And that troubled her. In all her years on the force she's never seen such unanimity in witness reports, of the same phrases being repeated in each. It was if they'd been written by the same hand.

She knows Crosby to be a man limited in imagination. Things like *troubled soul, feral urges* and especially *tangled threads* were not in his or Townley's lexicon. It had to be Jacob Strong, his inner journalist and feature writer making itself known.

It meant Crosby and Strong had colluded in the writing of a report that Townley then signed off. From what she knows of Crosby's aspirations, his golf club buddies and links to the Masons, she could guess the price for such collaboration.

She stopped. What if Crosby is more than complicit? That he's cleaning house, a corrupt officer with ambitions of ACC, a

BROKEN WINGS

man who with Musgrove's suspension that he's worked hard to bring about, is about to be promoted. It's certainly motive, a corrupt officer shielding himself from the worry of conspirators telling what they know.

It means Crosby is either the killer or himself the next victim among a group of men Strong has marked out for murder. Whichever it is, Demetriou's desire to find Crosby, to confront him in an effort to put things right regarding Fisher's own suspension, means he's walking into a situation that puts him between a possible killer and their next victim.

———

Demetriou's convinced himself of the rightness of confronting Crosby, and if necessary, doing so in front of Strong. He doesn't think either poses an imminent threat to his safety. He's hardly Musgrove's nursery rhyme material. Conspirators or not, the odds are he'll find himself on at least one of their sides against the killer - though right now he's not sure who that is.

He's driven here because Crosby's Day-Sheet has him signed out for an interview, a feature for *the Post*. Strong being the interviewer is a complication to his plan of finding a moment to talk to Crosby away from the glare of HQ.

He wonders whether Crosby came here knowing who the interviewer was going to be. Would it not have set alarm bells ringing? Was it part of his own murderous intentions?

He stands, hands on hips, thinking things through.

He feels that the building being padlocked from the outside rules out the two being inside, but it leaves few other places where they might be. If it was a feature interview, surely the idea of coming out here would be to have the station house itself as backdrop?

He walks to the road and looks west in the direction they'd have had to have taken otherwise he'd have passed them on his way here. There is no sign of anything before a bend takes the road out of sight. At the same time, he wonders why they'd have walked. What would be the reason? If they'd arranged to meet here clandestinely then surely the best choice was to have remained close to cars tucked away from sight rather than taking a stroll down a country lane. If they couldn't get in the building, the cars offered comfy seats and discretion.

The more the thinks about it, the more he sees the decision to take a stroll unlikely. And the more he thinks about that, the more certain he is that it's a meeting arranged to discuss something other than the closure of a local landmark or to be part of a feature article on the erosion of Dales life that's been recorded on Crosby's Day-Sheet. Neither requires the DCS in charge of a major murder enquiry to appear for interview in the middle of nowhere.

He ponders any places he hasn't yet considered. With no barns or outhouses, it leaves only the building itself. As it's padlocked from the outside, it means he's missed something, maybe an unnoticed access, an open door. Something.

He begins another turn around the building, starting from the front and inspecting walls and access points more closely. He begins rattling the shutters that cover the windows and doors in case they're stiff rather than locked, maybe just requiring a firmer tug.

'Hello!' he calls out. 'Hello! DCS Crosby! Are you in there?' He steps forward and jiggles the shutter across the front door. 'It's DS Demetriou! I need a word!' He stops, suddenly aware that whilst he's been focusing on the whereabouts of the two men, something else has been troubling him, something nagging at the back of his mind. There's no flex in the shutters. When a PC back in Brum he'd dealt with similar security measures checking industrial units and jewellers for break-ins. Usually roller shutters cover the doors and windows but always with a flexibility that means they rattle in their runners.

Closer inspection reveals lines of plastic beading sealing the gap between the shutters and the metal frames of their runners.

The beading is clear, thin, hard to make-out unless you look for it. The fit of security shutters is designed to prevent the ingress of any sort of crowbar or lever behind them which means they didn't require sealant. He steps closer, puzzled, rubbing an index finger along one of the vertical lines of translucent plastic.

Why?

He'd seen the council notice as he'd parked, aware the building is scheduled for demolition. Though he hasn't taken in the actual date, he can tell the place has been empty for months, meaning there's nothing of value still inside. Knowing there'd be slim pickings, the shutters themselves were surely sufficient to deter vandals or thieves let alone desperate kids looking for mischief. So why seal them? Why make the building airtight?

It makes no sense.

40

What passed as a knock on Musgrove's door is more the result of Fisher's fist bashing into a panel as she bursts in.

'Fisher!' Musgrove calls out, hand sliding a half-finished *Yorkie Bar* and an open packet of *Cheese and Onion* crisps off the top of his desk into a hastily opened drawer. 'What the hell's going on?' he demands, sweeping flakes of chocolate and deep-fried potato from his hands.

'Demetriou!' she blurts out, recovering from a dash up two flights of stairs.

'What about him?'

'I can't get hold of him,' she says, slumping into a chair.

'What do you mean?'

'I mean I can't contact him.'

'The masts are-'

'No, it's not that. I know all about the masts and intermittent black spots or sunspots or whatever. He's not answering his mobile.'

Musgrove snorts, the reasserting of control arriving belatedly over the hill of his shock at a violent intrusion into what had been a world of quiet contemplation. He picks up a remote, fumbling to mute the sound of meditative Japanese *Honkyoko* music drifting from the portable speaker. 'So, your DS's not answering his phone.' He shakes his head, hands fiddling with the buttons of the device. 'Do you mind telling me why that's a reason for barging your way into my office? I'm not EE technical support and I'm not *Find My Friend*. He's not here and I'm only here myself by the skin of my teeth writing a statement for Complaints.' He looks at the wall clock. 'And shouldn't you be gone by now? You're suspended.'

'Midnight...But this is important. Last I had was a text to say he'd stopped at the MacDonalds at Leeming Bar.'

'McDonalds', eh?' Musgrove replies, music muted, mind freed to migrate to thoughts of Big Macs, go-large fries and hot apple pies - plus a rumination on where he'd put the prize-sticker from his last visit. *A free Big Mac. Result*!

'He's tracking Crosby,' she tells him.

'Tracking Crosby? Why's that?'

'He's following up on what we talked about. That with Townley missing, he thought we needed to ask Crosby about the Brightside enquiry, see if there's anything Townley missed. As I'm being suspended, Demetriou's decided to do just that. Seems Crosby's off into the Dales, some sort of PR thing for the Commissioner.'

'None of us are supposed to be anywhere near operational matters,' Musgrove mutters. 'You know that.'

'Hardly operational. Asking a superior about paperwork connected to Wrigley's suicide that Crosby himself directed Pan to oversee. It's routine. At least, Demetriou will spin it that way.'

He looks from her to the chocolate bar peeking out of the draw. 'Why would Crosby open up to a DS?'

'Think it's some sort of a blokey macho thing.' She shrugs it off as an irrelevance. 'Demetriou sees things differently to us. He's got this whole karmic thing going on. Some inner Peaky Blinder. Feels that everyone wants to do the right thing. You just have to help them see it.'

'Jesus! How did he ever get into the force? And how did he get promoted?'

'Buggered if I know, but it's not the concern right now. I've looked at the Brightside report. Read it cover to cover which, by the way, is something the Coroner evidently thought better of doing. Maybe it was all those high-profile businessmen involved, his fellow Masons and the like. Most likely he scanned it, went straight to the summary and ruled accordingly. Death by misadventure, case closed and everyone moves on. No foul, no harm. Townley did the same, barely bothered with anything above the most basic, took whatever Crosby told him at face value. The interview statements are a joke - sloppy at best, downright criminal at worst.' She shakes her head. 'And sloppy as Crosby can be, I'm tending to it being the worst. A suck-up to men who could shower benefits on his career - which of course they have. His getting Townley to sign it off and take the credit, well that's downright suspicious in itself. Crosby's not the sort to offer helping hands.'

'I hear what you're saying,' Musgrove responds. 'But I'm not sure why it's got you storming in here. We're out of any investigative loop even more than we were before, if that's possible.' He looks directly at her, then averts his eyes to the desk. 'We have to stop, let it go. All that stuff I said… There'll be a Disciplinary hearing. Us having to swear to stuff under oath, so whatever it is you think you have, don't tell me. Take it up with Professional Conduct. Not that I think it'll get you-'

'Our theory, you idea-' she begins.

Hand help up, he stops her mid-flow, shuffles uncomfortably, a longing for the half-eaten Yorkie waving from the open drawer. 'No,' he says. 'I've had time to think about what I said in the ice cream parlour,' he finally says. 'You know, the nursery rhymes.' His fingers fiddle with his forehead. 'I've sat here all morning writing my statement for Complaints. Seeing it written down on paper…Cold light of day…it's…madness. We can't tell them anything about that. Bad enough we've been saying those deaths are linked, even without the Brightside nursery rhyme idea we come across as crazy lunatics. If they found out what we talked about the other day...We'd look like *Q-Anon* conspiracy theorists. Lizard people and *Illuminati*. We're saying stuff that even Trump would think twice about saying.' He shakes his head. 'If they hear my Brightside idea, the nursery rhymes, then all we'd be doing is proving why we're in therapy in the first place. If word of that gets out, we never get back in. We'd be finished.' He waves a hand in the air. 'We have nothing, not a thing other than a book of rhymes and two dead men who happened to be executors of a crazy sick junkie woman's estate. We've no money trail. No evidence of murder. Everything about it screams coincidence, and once it goes to formal tribunal everything about us and what we've done comes out, comes out for nothing. We'd be laughed out of the force. I couldn't sleep last night thinking about Charlie's tuition fees, telling Jean, the pension, the mortgage.' Giving in, he pulls the Yorkie from the drawer, disappearing it in one bite. 'We're done, Fisher. Dead in the water,' he offers through the munching. 'Even without telling them the nursery rhyme theory we'll be lucky if it's just suspension and loss of pay.' He enumerates on the fingers of one hand. 'Loss of rank. Out on our ears. Christ knows what Jean's going to say when she finds out, especially with it starting with my writing. I can't do it.'

Fisher lets go the tensions holding her together, opens the valve of everything building inside since she's realised what they'd missed. She needs him to come with her: see what she sees, understand what she sees. 'I get it, I really do. Your mortgage, kids at uni. I know you're worried about the fallout. But I know what I saw the other days - something I'd not seen for a long time. Christ, I'm about to sound like one of your stories, but there was a spark in you! A flicker...something different, something changing in you. Even when you were reigning us back...your caution had a sense of, I don't know... life, flesh and blood, real feeling. You wanted to believe, all of us saw it.' She sits forward, fixing him with the fire in her eyes. 'Listen, Neil, I'm not asking you to put your neck any further on the line.'

'But?'

'...But what if we're wrong.'

He frowns. 'Are you telling me you now agree with Hyland and Hargreaves? That Crosby's complaint about us is right?' He shakes his head, trying to re-order the jumble of thoughts and half-musings rattling inside. When he speaks his voice softens. 'It's been a mad time for all of us. The therapy group, the suspensions, the wild-eyed game of *Cluedo* we've been dragged into.' He pauses. 'Maybe pulled each other into.' He looks her in the eyes. 'Whatever happens, it's not your fault we ended up here. The whole thing was a crazy idea from the start, an idea that was never supposed to see the light of day. I let myself get carried away, you know, having an audience willing to listen. It was...intoxicating. Whatever happens, you're a great detective. It's not your fault we've nothing concrete proving murder.'

'No, not that. None of that. I mean what if it's Crosby?'

'It's Crosby what?'

'It's *Crosby who* actually,' she corrects. 'But my point is, what If the killer we're looking for *is* Crosby?'

'Are you insane?' he splutters, holding up a hand, mood shifting from affable to irate in a millisecond. 'No, wait, I know the answer to that. You are. You're in Anger Management because you go off at half-cock! You're under suspension and probable expulsion from the Force, and yet again here you are doing your best at dragging the rest of us with you.' He pulls out the remaining drawers, searching for something sweet, chocolatey. Coming up empty, he stops and looks at her. 'Listen to what you're saying. I get it, I really do, what you told me about all the tiny little things piling up in the day, all the shitty things adding brick by sodding annoying brick to a wall you want to tear down.' He pauses at the minefield he has to cross. 'There's your father's murder.' He holds up a hand. 'I know you won't talk about it, but maybe that's the problem right there. And the Swanley thing.' He watches her nostrils flare, eyes narrowing, their ice-blue growing colder. 'You're not over these things; they've been set off by some seemingly tiny irritation that's now become all about straws and camel's backs. I mean Sofia's death. The waste of her life.' He holds the other hand up. 'God knows I'm his biggest sceptic, but it's what he said, Pemberton. We have to find ways of stopping that wall from getting built. You know, ripping out the foundations before it gets too high to deal with. Before it falls and crushes us.'

She leans forward, hands pinning the desk as if she thinks it's about to rise up *Exorcist* style. 'What are you, Neil? Bob the bloody Builder? Where my father's concerned, you're as ignorant as the rest. You know nothing about it, any of it. And as for Pemberton, I've read the books, been in the room, bought every fucking Tee-shirt there is. I know it by heart - emotions… anger…repression…paranoia. I'm a barely walking check list of psycho-therapy methods and strategies for coping. I get the career in jeopardy stuff, the shit coming from the top with their worries about reputation, concerned about brands and elections and medals that all adds up for us to *shut the fuck up*. But what if we're right? I mean really fucking right. What is it they say, about a broken clock's right twice a day? What if there was a conspiracy? What if Crosby covered it up? What if it's him killing these men? I mean, think about it. He's in the perfect place. He knows how we work and what we'd look for. He knows how we go about determining cause of death, and most of all he knows Waddingham's ambition for a quiet life and a knighthood. Knows Hargreaves, Hyland, Crawley, and the coroner won't want the boat rocked. He'd know that it's the perfect time to get away with murder. For Christ's sake as DCS he even had the say in who gets what case. He assigns whoever he likes, knows who won't question things, knows the ones who'll take the easy route in an investigation. The ones who won't turn over stones. The ones who'll follow whatever path he's laid out for them. Not to mention that he knows who's vulnerable to threats about careers. The new boy, Demetriou, worried about fitting in. Doyle with her paranoia about everyone watching her. For god's sake even you, Neil!'

'If that's the case, then how does it explain him giving you the suicide in the barn? He of all people knows what a stubborn bugger you are. Can't see you following anyone's path unless it's in a bulldozer with you intent on ploughing a better, bigger route of your own.'

'That's the thing. We're still not sure how she's linked to the others, but he didn't assign me. Remember? It was Hargreaves. Commissioner Hargreaves insisted on it being me. She told the Chief Constable, who told you, who told Crosby, and then me. Direct order. Much to the annoyance of that bloody PR guru of hers, too as I recall.'

'Lawrence. He was here earlier today. Wanted to know what was going on with the Webb enquiry. I mean, why ask me? I'm the last one who'd know. Sticking his bloody nose in. He was the one so insistent on you and Demetriou being taken off those suicides, yet he's demanding to be kept in the loop on both of them, on Gill too. Gill! My own bloody case and he's demanding access to my files. Gloria says he's had Townley's files for a while now, wanting to know if we were close to finding him. You see? It's obvious!'

'No, I don't quite see...'

'He's spying for Hargreaves, looking for something to revive her campaign, quite possibly doing that by getting rid of us. Your spat with her that time, me being in this group with you, enabling you to poke around in those deaths. It's the election. It's political. When I told Gloria to sort out access for him, she found out he'd already looked at other files. Bastard's been keeping tabs on us for weeks looking for dirt. It's why we've got to stop the nursery rhyme idea getting out and giving them more ammunition for the tribunal. Him and Crosby and Hyland and

Hargreaves wanting us gone. Crosby's all but measured himself up for my desk.'

'What other files?'

'God knows. Gloria's got the list.'

Fisher gets up and exits Musgrove's office. He watches through the open door as she goes to his secretary's desk and picks up a sheaf of paperwork. She flicks through it, discarding one after the other before stopping at the one she's looking for. 'Lawrence's case file request list for the past six months,' she calls out. She runs a finger down the files that Hargreaves' office requested access to.

She stops at one to look up at Musgrove who now stands in the doorway. She presses a finger against the paper, Musgrove watching it whiten. 'Why would he ask for the Brightside file?' she asks.

Musgrove sags against the door jamb. 'Oh bollocks! Someone's been bloody well talking. Pemberton watching his back, bloody Hippocratic Oath – more like hypocrite! I knew this would happen. We're too late. It's over.' He shakes his head. 'This is Lawrence getting ready to be rid of us, getting ahead of the fall-out if news of what we've been doing gets out.'

'I'll say he's getting ahead. It was the first file he asked for. Six months ago.'

41

That the building is sealed adds to Demetriou's puzzlement. They couldn't have got in without breaking the security seals.

His mind sets out on a Holmesian quest, the whole Conan Doyle thing, the *ruling out what was impossible* train of thinking. That whatever remained, no matter how improbable, must be the truth. It was the crime mystery variation on Occam's Razor, the idea that when there are competing hypotheses to explain a phenomenon, the simplest explanation is often the best.

So what remained? What is the simplest explanation?

He moves to the rear door and runs a finger around the shutter. It's tacky, very tacky, his experience of sealing the shower at his and Jessica's old flat suggested it had been applied within the past hour. They had to be in there, Crosby and Strong. There was nowhere else they could be. He's looked in every conceivable direction, considered every variation of where they might be if not inside.

That both cars are here means neither has left. If they are in there, someone has locked them in.

But why sealed? If the idea is to imprison them, why seal it? He supposes that it might make things uncomfortable – the stale air; maybe sound proofing – but doesn't see how it prevents them being extricated. People know they are here. It's how he'd found Crosby himself.

What was the purpose?

They hadn't responded when he'd called out, even with the thick walls of Yorkshire stone and the sealant he's sure he'd have heard if they had. They'd have heard his shouts, and he'd have heard them calling back. And he hadn't. So they hadn't.

Couldn't. They couldn't call out, they were gagged or unconscious, most likely bound. Which means they'd have had to have been taken by someone inside waiting for them, someone who knew they'd be there. It could wait, right now he has to focus on getting inside, finding out for certain that they're in there, and freeing them.

And in focusing on that, he's pushed towards considering the reason for the sealant. If you're not sealing something out, you must be sealing something in. A gas, an asphyxiant, something keeping them unconscious or worse.

Basic chemistry suggests carbon monoxide, which in turn meant there'd be a source, a means of regulating the flow. It would be too risky to have it inside, bound or not, they might be able to turn it off.

He looks around, sees the chain-link builder's cage at the far end of the building and close to the wall, the type used for secure on-site storage of construction materials.

He crosses to what is essentially a series of wire mesh panels padlocked together. Closer inspection shows the end panels are attached to heavy chains fixed to hooks bolted into the wall, the chains themselves then padlocked in place. The whole forms a compound a few metres wide on each side, three metres high with a section of the same chain fencing covering the top.

He pulls at the gap between the nearest panel and the wall. It doesn't budge more than an inch or so, a gap leaving no space to squeeze through or for him to be able to reach the green tarpaulin sheets pulled over something tall and thin, a glimpse of red metal between the folds.

Finding a length of fallen branch, he pushes it through the gap he's created and towards the nearest tarpaulin.

It takes a couple of attempts before he's able to dislodge an edge. A few more prods and gravity does the rest, the topmost tarpaulin slipping down to reveal what he's expected. Propane. Big red tanks of it, chest high, stood next to the wall. The sort used on camping sites, caravans, building sites, factories, and domestic heating. It's impossible to reach, but he sees flexible tubing extending from each cylinder and disappearing through holes drilled into the brickwork of the extension. The gauge on the nearest tank is falling, the gas channeling into the building. Not only its own gas, but that of the five other bottles it is chained to.

Propane. Not only a powerful asphyxiant, but explosive and flammable. Enough to blow up the building and anyone close to it.

'Fuck!' he whispers.

Time. It was all about time. And right now it's a calculation he's no idea as to the elements involved. Usually it was all if x is *whatever* and y *something else* then the result of x times y *over yet some other letter* gives you your answer.

But he's no idea what x is. No idea how long they've been in there. He'd no idea of y. No idea of the potency of the mix of propane and oxygen building inside. No idea how long the taps of the noxious gas have been opened. No idea if they're merely unconscious or already dead. But he does know one thing: that attempts to get inside will generate sparks, an ignition of the gas -oxygen mix sufficient to blow them to kingdom come.

He's no idea of how he might even begin to go about getting in. It was the thing about sealed buildings. They were literally sealed.

He sinks onto his haunches, hands cradled either side of his head and contemplates the dilemma.

He can't get inside a sealed building filling with explosive gas, and he can't turn the gas off. His phone has no signal. The nearest village is five miles in either direction. Even then it's a couple of farms with only the remote possibility of the farmer being home and able to help rather than off in some far-flung paddock tending his flock. At most it would be a farmer's wife and the hope of a landline, though he's been told that even the line on those can be intermittent in some hamlets. And if he got through, how long for the fire brigade and other services to get here? Half an hour? Maybe a little less, possibly a little more. And they'd face exactly the same problem. The building is sealed, and they wouldn't be able to use specialist cutting equipment. He'd seen them at pile-ups, chainsaws and dedicated levers generating arcs of blue-white sparks. Even the snap from bolt cutters or a skeleton key grating in the lock might prove sufficient to send them sky high. Even if they get to the cylinders and stop the flow there's every possibility the gas will have done its work and it still being too dangerous a mix to risk entry.

'Fuck!' he exhales. 'Fuck, fuck, fuck, fuck, fuck!'

He wracks his brain. There has to be a way. Something he's missed. Something the killer neglected.

At some point the previous day the killer had sealed the shutters in readiness, creating the wire mesh cage for the gas bottles and drilling holes for the pipework. Nothing about what they did would have looked out of place. Pick the right 4X4 and trailer and anyone passing would simply assume you were part of the demolition crew preparing the site.

They'd have waited their moment for the two men to arrive, somehow knowing Crosby would be here today. Strong too. *How had they known? How could they have been sure?*

He shakes his head clear. Stuff like that had to wait.

Once the two were inside, they'd either overpowered them or

seized the chance to trap them, locking and sealing the remaining shutter and turning on the gas. Their victims would have quickly lapsed into unconsciousness, and sometime after that their breathing would stop.

No. It doesn't fit the pattern.

Whatever else, it now looks as if they'd been right - Musgrove, Fisher, Doyle, and himself. They'd identified Strong as a possible victim which means the other deaths are linked - certainly Wrigley and Gill and possibly Webb too, the logic still out on Sofia's part in it all or of Townley's fate. If that's the case, then maybe Musgrove's also right in assuming the motive is linked to Gillian Brightside. Whether it be revenge or greed or jealousy, the killer is obsessed with Brightside's illustrations, the nursery rhymes. If so, it doesn't require much of a leap to see Crosby and Strong as little piggies trapped in a Police House. Crosby's job making him literally so.

It means the house has to be blown down - not suffocated and not burned down. It means the killer will have taken steps to ensure an explosion. A grand finale.

With no phone signal it rules out the movie cliché of a bomb maker's call triggering the explosion. Out here, they'll have to rely on a timer of some sorts, a means as old time and analogue as the region itself. Demetriou's early years as a PC had involved a case investigating allotment fires. Kids breaking into sheds. Candles sat on the valves of the propane canisters that the growers used to brew their cups of tea. Canisters going off like rockets, explosions ripping through shed walls and roof alike.

Somewhere inside, possibly in a cupboard, will be a smaller canister attached to an initiator of some sort. A simple battery-operated circuit. It doesn't help his calculations, but at least it alerts him to what he faces.

He looks at his watch, a pointless action given he has no idea of the time frame he's working to, but an action impelled by habit. All he knows for sure is there is now less of whatever time it was he'd started with. The whole if x is *something* and y

whatever calculation reducing second by second whilst he sits around trying to work things out.

He stares at the second hand of the watch. The soundtrack of the classic Guinness surfer ad pushes forward from somewhere in his head, the watchers with their pulsing drums. *Tick followed tock and tock followed tick.* A line cycling inside a head already full of melting Dali clocks. The whole mind-numbing-action-freezing nature of it roots him to the spot. The realisation he's afraid. Terrified.

He shakes it off, throwing his head from side to side to clear it, a *ctrl-alt-delete* reset of his functions. He pauses. Nope. Nothing. No Fisher insight. No Musgrove big idea. No Doyle gung-ho action. Just white horses pushing through foaming waves whilst somewhere a melting clock ticks to the pulse of tympani.

But it shakes him from the rut he's taken shelter in. He stands. Movement.

He paces back and forth pushing himself to think, to run through what he knows. There's nowhere he's not already looked and looked again, no side of the building he's not scoured looking for a way in.

Side.

He's checked the sides, the walls. But he's not checked the roof.

What demolition company secured the roof? Answer: *none of them.* It was pointless. Overkill. Anyone looking to get in that way needed a ladder and there were none on the site. With the security shutters padlocked on the outside, then even if they succeeded in getting in, they'd face the likelihood of not being able to climb back out. Besides, there was nothing of value to professional thieves, those gangs are more interested in raiding unsecure barns. And there's nothing to pique a passing vandal intent on mischief that would have them clambering onto the roof.

No-one shutters skylights or Velux windows.

He runs to the front, crossing the road to stand opposite the building. By standing on the soaking wet grass verge close to the dry-stone wall of the paddock, he sees the late autumn sun's rays flare off what can only be a large pane of glass. A skylight. A glare confirming there's no shutter.

He's found his way in. Now all he has to do is pray he doesn't run out of time before he is able to reach it.

42

The climb was challenging but not the worst he's attempted. Late night lock outs from flats in Brum offered more challenge. Modern buildings had smooth bricks, plastic drainpipes and guttering held in place with thin fixings. Buildings like this were built in the Victorian era, made of sterner stuff. Massive stone blocks with recessed mortar, solid cast iron drainpipes and guttering secured with strong fixings, and out here, builds meant to withstand the driving Dales westerlies.

Using the guttering, he scrabbles over the edge, pulling himself onto stone roof tiles the size of tombstones. He lies on his back for a moment catching his breath and looking up at the sky.

Breathe.

He rises to his knees, scanning the rooftop. A few metres directly below the old chimney stack is the skylight he'd seen from below. The first thing he needs to do – or so he's decided on the way up - is to get air inside, the hope that the chemistry of mixing air with the gas already in there worked in his favour. The optimism of the added oxygen displacing the gas rather than mixing with it to form a more flammable mass. From what he recalls of GCSE Science, gases like propane are heavy and will gather closer to the ground, the mass only rising as more is added. Heavier than oxygen. Though what it means for any plan he might form, he's little idea.

He scrambles to the skylight and looks down.

What he sees stops him. In the office a few metres below are the huddled figures of Crosby and a man he assumes to be Jacob Strong. They're alive. Conscious.

They wear improvised masks of torn cloth wrapped around mouths and noses. For a reason he can't understand they've taken refuge close to the windowless outside wall where they sit on the floor, sideways on, heads close together nuzzling each other. When Crosby moves his head, placing it closer to the wall, Demetriou realises that what he'd thought to be peeling wallpaper is in fact strips of broken plasterboard that surrounds a roughly hewn hole a little larger than a man's head. He realises they're taking it in turns to push their heads into the hole, buddy breathing using an old chimney as a snorkel, a covered fireplace most likely boarded up decades earlier. Like the skylight, the killer had ignored the chimney, maybe thinking it had been capped once the convenience of electric fires had arrived, oblivious to the boarded-up fireplace in the rear office.

Having served here, Crosby had no doubt recalled the old fireplace and somehow found a means to open it up, of using the flue as a Victorian airway keeping them alive.

In addition to the breathing hole, Demetriou makes out bits of tarpaulin stuffed against the door that have slowed the influx of gas.

Whatever the formula might be, he knows they're running out of time. That despite their efforts, the two are running out of air, noxious fumes finding their way in through cracks in floorboards, loose set doors, and the countless other chinks in the room's crumbling solidity. But their measures have not only bought them time, but the probability of making the mix of gas and oxygen weaker than elsewhere in the building.

Demetriou pulls out a large piece of stone liberated from the wall opposite the station, a stone carried on the climb swaddled in the jacket he'd fashioned into a sling over his back. It's around six kilos in weight, more than sufficient for the job he's got in mind.

Grasping the edge of the Velux, he hefts the wrapped stone above his head, smashing it in a downwards arc into the glass. Leaning over the edge, he watches the shards tumble to the floor of the office below, much to the shock evident in the eyes of the two men.

Quickly, he lowers the length of discarded nylon rope retrieved from the site, at the same time calling down. 'DCS Crosby! It's me. DS Demetriou.'

'Demetriou?' The word is muffled, but even so Demetriou detects puzzlement and confusion. 'How?' Crosby asks.

'Never mind that! You have to grab the rope and climb up. Quick as you can!'

'I'll never make that,' Crosby states before taking his turn at plunging his head into the chimney's void. 'It's too far,' he continues once he re-emerges.

'Use the bench and desk to get higher. I'll tie it off around the chimney breast. There's not much time. I think there's a device set to blow the whole lot up.'

'A device?' Strong asks.

'Attached to batteries. Something closing a circuit and creating a spark!' Demetriou shouts, aware he finishes talking to the back of Strong's head now taking its turn in the chimney's void.

'Maybe we should find it. Pass it up so you can get rid of it!' Crosby shouts.

'It could be anywhere! You'll be dead the minute you step outside that room. You have to take the rope and get out!'

Strong and Crosby swop places, Crosby breathing whilst Strong drags the desk to where the nylon rope swings invitingly three or four metres above it. 'Not much rope,' Demetriou calls. 'I've had to wrap it around the chimney stack or I'll never be able to hold you!'

Strong waves understanding and crosses to the fireplace. It's clear to Demetriou both men are weakening by the minute.

Crosby takes Strong's place beneath the dangling blue rope and clambers onto the desk, leaping for the end. The first time his hands slip, Crosby shouting out in pain at the rope burn. As he stands on the desk preparing for a second attempt Strong appears behind him. This time, as Crosby leaps Strong grasps him around the waist, holding him steady whilst Crosby rolls a section of the rope around one hand to prevent sliding back down.

Demetriou leans back and pulls, Strong somehow finding the strength to lift Crosby. At first he grips him around the knees, then his feet, each time Crosby wrapping the slack around his wrist, hanging tight to each upward gain.

Metre by metre he rises towards the skylight. Every few seconds Demetriou pausing to alter his grip, the better to take up each slackening of the rope before hauling on it once more. At each pause he wraps the newly gathered lengths around his forearm, locking them in place like the ratcheting of cogs on gears. Leaning back across the slates, he's no longer able to look into the room, his feet now braced against the thick stone tiles that surround the opening. With each intake of breath, he pushes his shoulders back, hauling as hard as he can, hands shifting along the shortening rope as he twists it around his wrist and forearm.

After a few minutes Crosby's head appears above the hatch, one hand on the rope, the other clutching desperately at the side of the opening as he seeks purchase, somehow ignoring the pain of the jagged shards of glass that he grips.

When both of Crosby's hands are levering him out, Demetriou risks letting go the rope and grabs him around the shoulders, hauling him onto the roof like a fisherman landing some beast of the seas.

Both collapse onto the tiles, Demetriou on his back, Crosby on his stomach gasping for breath.

Demetriou forces himself up. There's no time to waste. He and Crosby have to return the rope as soon as they can if they are to get Strong out.

It's then that he hears the ringing of a bell. For a spilt second he's puzzled, then understanding sweeps in. It's the sound of an alarm clock, a battery-operated device completing its circuit. His world suddenly turns bright orange and then black as the roof he sits on disappears beneath him.

43

Fisher sits to one side of Demetriou's hospital bed staring out of the window at the rain, the shock of her reflection – paler; partial; transformed – takes a moment to land, the whole distorted by the glare of lighting on grimy double glazing. It's to do with refracted light, like the cover of that Pink Floyd album - an illusion, a chimera. She knows it, yet each time she sees it she stops, chastened.

She's sat for hours, her vigil conducted to the soundtrack of medical machinery clicking through cycles of scrutiny. It's late. There's no voices, no squeaking of rubber-soled shoes, no rattle of trolleys, no muffled chatter. An odour leaches into the room – bleach and institutional cleansers. Long after she leaves she knows she'll carry the sense of it, a bouquet of despair and last chances. Bad things happen here, happen to those undeserving of such fates. Broken wings, she thinks, unable to fly.

She glances down. Under the raised scaffold of sheets, her DS of but a few weeks has been reduced to a mass of bandage and tubing, something between the Mummy and Frankenstein's monster. Walking into the side-room, she'd been overwhelmed by the urge to laugh, him swaddled like an extra from a *Carry-On* film. Knowing he'd be the first to see it himself, to laugh.

And laughing is okay; you deal with grief the way you need to. Sometimes you make it your friend, sharing the joke of death with it down the pub. Sometimes it follows you whilst you walk, unbidden, hand on your back, an arm round your shoulder. Sometimes it holds you whilst you sob. Sometimes it screams with you, binding itself to your pain forever.

She isn't the drinking type, nor is she the hugging or screaming kind either. Most of all, she isn't the hand holding type. Instead, she watches the readout of the equipment, a focus broken only by staring at her reflection in the window, wondering how they'd come to be here, the two of them. It's tough to answer, but a thousand times easier than dealing with emotions she's finding slippier than wet fish.

She has a list. Two columns: *Facts* and *Speculation*.

Fact: Jacob Strong is dead. *Eviscerated* is how Crawley put it to those gathered around the crispy remains of the journalist in the car park of the shattered police station house. Knowing how these things work, the punishing effect of explosions on human flesh, she'd thought he'd been reaching for *evaporated*. Now knowing what she does, eviscerated does the job just fine.

Whatever the word, Strong is gone, leaving a shed load of questions behind.

Fact: with Demetriou busy doing his Boris Karloff impersonation it means Crosby is the sole source of what happened, the only one capable of providing a story linking the deductions of the on-site forensics team to the drama that had played out.

Fact: Of the three men involved Crosby is the only one physically capable of talking. A hairline fracture of one wrist, cuts to both hands and second degree burns to arms, legs, face, and scalp. Other than that, he's okay. A fact the first-responders found truly astonishing, attributing it to the fact he'd literally been blown off the roof by the explosion whilst Demetriou had fallen into the flames.

Fact: Thus far Crosby's offered nothing in the way of an

explanation. Rushed from the scene by the ambulance crew, there'd been no time to ask the burning questions she had. On reflection it had been a poor choice of words to have used earlier in the hospital waiting room in front of his doctors. And his waiting wife and family.

Fact: Crosby is sedated, cocooned in the protective embrace of doctors determined there be no upsetting questions. No push requiring him to replay traumatic moments.

Speculation: Suspended or not, she, Musgrove, and Doyle had found a moment in which to put their heads together. All they'd come up with was more speculation in search of solid evidence.

They know Demetriou went there to ask Crosby about Townley and the Brightside investigation. They know Crosby was there to meet with Strong. That the fire crew recovered no other bodies, leaves Townley still missing, the possibility he may be the man they are looking for, the man who Doyle has tagged the Nursery Rhyme Killer.

The three believe Strong was the target, his death in the explosion fairly convincing proof of that. They're also confident that Crosby is not the killer, is in fact another intended victim, the explosion a twofer giving flesh to their theory of the link to Brightside. An explosion that follows the pattern of the nursery rhymes. *Three Little Pigs. The house blown down.*

The fire officer's conclusion is that if it hadn't been for some ventilation – he supposes through the old chimney and skylight - none of the three would have survived. He'd explained how the ventilation created a thinner propane mix, making the explosion weaker than it might otherwise have been, the succeeding fire less intense.

The fire-crew could only assume these men had somehow become trapped inside, their current theory is that of a demolition crew security shutter slipping closed and preventing their exit from a building rapidly filling with gas. Them clambering to get out through the skylight. They didn't yet know how the gas had begun to leak other than thinking it being a faulty valve damaged during the demolition work. For their part, the demolition company didn't know how so much propane came to be there in the first place, the firm's duty manager wondering if someone had messed up in clearing the site of equipment.

She has other ideas. Mostly questions. So many questions.

Was Strong really there for an article? Why ask for Crosby? What did Demetriou discover about the meeting? How did the killer know they would be there?

They needed answers, but with Demetriou out of the picture Crosby is the only one who might provide them, but of course neither she nor Musgrove are allowed anywhere near him. Not only is she suspended, but she's also tainted, the bad blood between herself and Crosby sufficient to preclude her from involvement. Hyland would never allow it.

As for Musgrove, he's equally tainted - though not through bias or personal grievance but Hyland's perception of his competence. More precisely, his incompetence. He'd made him ACC Refurbishment for just that reason, a reluctance to trust his eccentric thinking anywhere close to an investigation. And of course, he too is stood down from active investigations with Crosby his probable successor.

They're stuck. They'd thought they were building a case, close to finding solid ground in what they'd come to think of as their delusional craziness. Instead, they're even further down a rabbit hole of Alice like proportion, one that they themselves have dug.

On the other side of the James Cook Medical Centre, Crosby sits flicking through the channels of his TV. *Men and Motors; Storage Hunters;* re-runs of *The Professionals* and *The Sweeney.*

He loves *The Sweeney*. Regan and Carter; Haskins; Ford Capris. *'You're nicked, sunshine!'* Better times, times when you got on and got the job done. Slaps on the back, drinks in the boozer. No-one asking too closely how you'd done it.

He changes stations, grazing the late-night channels that lurk deep in the *Now TV* menu, hidden from the daylight world like strange sea monsters, their blue-white light shimmering across the room at each tap of the remote.

He's in a private room, though unlike that of Demetriou, his is set closer to a nursing station. He's conscious, sitting up in bed with only a single gauze bandage wrapped around one wrist, unguents and emollients smeared across exposed burnt flesh. He's sore, strong painkillers dulling the pain of a seared scalp and the burns on legs and arms, and he remains 'under observation', a status preventing him from walking out and spending the night at home, but one holding at arm's length interviews from Complaints or the Chief Constable's specially appointed investigators who will soon require he provide evidence regarding the 'unexplained death' that he's learned Jacob Strong to be.

The current situation suits him fine. A chance to get mind and story straight, to see what can be salvaged from the wreckage. It depends on what they know, what they can prove, and what he might convince them to be true.

At shift change, he'd listened to the gossip of the nurses clucking around the ward station. Strong was dead. Demetriou teetering on the brink of joining him. Saving the recovery of the Brummie officer, Crosby himself is the sole source of what happened.

His problem is that he is unclear as to just what did happen.

Within minutes of the security shutter dropping they'd smelt gas. As best he could, Strong had begun sealing the doors with old tarpaulins, Crosby himself had begun tearing at the flimsy covering of the old chimney, a fortunate confluence of his recall of the old Victorian coal fire and his GCSE Chemistry. *Air pressure. Ventilation. The snorkel effect.*

He recalls the shock of Demetriou's sudden appearance, head

poking through the skylight. The leap to safety propelled by Strong's surprisingly sturdy and muscular frame. The sound of a bell ringing followed by the sense of being hurled through the air. Of waking to the sound of ambulance crews and fire engines.

Before he constructs his story, he needs answers to his own key questions. The most pressing being what anyone knows of the nature of his connection to Strong and the rest, whether they believe the reason for his being there, which raises the concern of why Demetriou had turned up.

The first part is straightforward. He'd complied with a request from the Commissioner's office for him to be there as part of Strong's supposed article on rural crime.

He's an obvious choice, nothing remotely suspicious about a senior commander versed in media relations who'd once served there complying with the Commissioner's wishes. Of course he knew of him. They'd met years ago when he'd overseen Townley's investigation of Gillian Brightside's death. Just like he'd met so many other businessmen.

These are simple answers rooted in truth, concealing the fact that the meeting had offered the chance to put the reporter straight, to curb the irrational calls and text messages that might incriminate them both in any cold case investigation of Brightside's death that Musgrove's little lot might try to force.

As for Demetriou's appearance, he's certain that's down to the same speculation, the suspicions he himself had encouraged be laughed away as indicative of the reason why the four were in therapy in the first place. With Fisher's suspension, the newly arrived DS's misplaced loyalty had no doubt pushed him in seeking answers to help at her tribunal; either that or he'd wanted somewhere far from HQ where he might beg his DCS to save his own career.

And there's the matter of the explosion. Strong's death and his own close call have put Strong's paranoia in a different light. He'd been scornful of both Strong's paranoia and Musgrove's wild theories, but now neither are so easily dismissed. He needs time to think. To strategise. To see if he might re-arrange the facts to form a better truth. Better for him, that is.

The one thing he's clear on is that for Hyland and Hargreaves, any PR fallout is something they will want to draw a veil over, no matter how thin that veil might be. But he also knows that whatever they tell the outside world, they might privately wonder about the linking of these deaths. Instead of the derision he's worked to make happen by appointing first Demetriou to looking at Wrigley and later ensuring Hyland's assignment of Musgrove to Gill's investigation, their wild theory now has credibility. The explosion brings the possibility of more considered attention to Fisher and Musgrove's ideas, and with it the possibility of Musgrove's vindication and his own career nose-dive. If he is to escape culpability, he has to ensure the credit for resolving this mess is his and his alone. Played right, the circumstances he's been dealt might yet offer the chance to re-shape his role in the original Brightside investigation, turning it from one of guilt to one of redemption.

It's all about the story. The story he might himself might weave. Webb, Wrigley, Gill, and Strong. A group of desperate men anxious for riches conspiring with Townley to dupe a naïve DI whose only failing had been his anxiety to help his native county prosper. Now more worldly wise, an investigator holding a hand up to his younger self's inexperience.

The outline of his tale is simple, based on facts and truths: recalling the connection between the recent spate of deaths of these prominent businessmen, he'd taken it upon himself to quietly re-open the Brightside case. His now more seasoned eye had grasped the motive that might lie behind their deaths. He'd taken the chance offered by the feature article to meet Strong, by then the sole survivor of the suspected crime and thus the most likely killer of his fellow conspirators. He'd met Strong for the interview and had confronted him about his crimes, unaware the journalist had already laid a trap for him. With Townley's disappearance, Crosby was the only one who might make the connection that would lead to Strong's apprehension. The two men had fought, and with Demetriou's help, Crosby had escaped, Strong perishing in his own trap.

All things considered, it worked. A narrative leaving him the hero, an officer possessing a new-found maturity and strength of character in recognising his younger self's flaws, his youthful mistakes. The man risking his life to correct a miscarriage of justice that he felt in some way to blame for.

If Strong was correct – and the explosion suggests he is – the real killer remains undiscovered. Whoever they are, by Crosby publicly owning his own error, telling the story of his effort to right that wrong, the killer will see that his only misdemeanour is to have been an unwitting dupe, a young officer guilty of nothing more than naivety in trusting the word of evil men. He would be in the clear with everyone - the killer, Hyland, the public.

As for Musgrove's merry band…Well, theirs is a less worthy tale. The story of shared madness: *Foile á plusiers* is how Pemberton's report had described it. He'd looked it up. The *Madness of Many*, a group delusion, each pulled deeper by the others. Somehow they'd stumbled on the truth, followed the breadcrumbs, and discovered the original Brightside investigation. But their trail ends with the meeting at the Station house, a meeting where he will say Strong tried to kill him. His alibi for confronting Strong there is perfect: after all, the interview had been arranged by the Commissioner's office.

All he needs is a narrative implicating Strong as the killer of his fellow conspirators, the well-trodden plot of thieves falling out, of greed leading to a murderous spree. The ludicrous nature of the deaths can even be ascribed to Strong's writerly nature, his tendency for the theatrical flourish.

He knows how the hive mind of Hargreaves and Hyland works. Hyland's bid for a knighthood, Hargreaves' election ambitions. He also knows that Webb's death slotted into the mix creates considerable embarrassment for Whitehall, something with much appeal for Hyland and Hargreaves, not least of which would be the satisfaction of sending Badgerman off tail between his legs. But it has to be played carefully. The idea of the waste of public money and security service foul ups would be resisted, might lead to awkward questions from Special Branch that risk exposing the truth of his own role, unless, of course, he offers them credit in his finding the solution.

He stops channel hopping. *Murder She Wrote* fills the screen. Agatha had it right. It's all in the story.

It's about control, no longer keeping secret the link between the deaths, it is now a matter of when and to whom to reveal it to, of offering a happy ending. Hyland, Hargreaves, Badgerman, and all their political advisors are biddable. They will want to believe him, it's simply a matter of constructing a narrative that lets them, a tale clearing him with Complaints that removes any temptation for Cold Cases to go nosing through the original enquiry. A post-dated slap on the wrist is better than twenty years in jail.

But such a story requires a seasoned eye, and right then it strikes him that Harvey Lawrence - Hargreaves guru of PR - is just the person to turn to. After all, with the Webb enquiry stalling and Hargreaves' increasingly beleaguered reputation, the tale of an officer involved in an heroic rescue whilst solving a series of murders surely plays well just a few days before an election. What better in these trying times than a "good news" story? A *Post* exclusive.

He picks up his mobile. He'll call Lawrence and pitch his idea. With Lawrence on board comes Hargreaves, and with the PFCC in tow inevitably Hyland follows. He, DCS Crosby hero of the hour, will be untouchable, the story of his oversight all those years ago buried from public scrutiny, interred forever amid the backslapping and cheers of present success.

He sinks into his pillows and dials.

44

The scales fell from their eyes.

The more you thought about it, the more obvious it was. Like *Wordle*, there was a Holmesian purity to its solution. You exclude everything it can't be and whatever is left, no matter how absurd, is the truth. It was almost a law, like gravity or *if you pop you can't stop.*

And what a truth it is.

'You can't be serious,' Hyland states in the smoothy reassuring manner loved by TV newsrooms, the one that made you feel safe at night. The one that said *this is god's own country. Nothing bad happens to good people on my watch.* It was the sound of *Brexit.* Of *Red Walls* tumbling.

He scans the faces gathered in front of him: Musgrove, Fisher, Doyle. Faces saying *we're more than serious,* we're very serious indeed. Blocked, he changes tack as smoothly as the keen amateur yachtsman he is. 'You must know I can't allow you to say any such thing.'

'*Allow?*' Doyle asks mustering her super-power of feisty belligerence. 'What do you mean *allow*? It's the truth. People deserve the truth.' Her father's speeches course through her, the indignation of a just cause, of barricades to be defended or walls to be brought down.

Hyland slaps a hand to his forehead, an action taking Musgrove and Fisher as much by surprise as it does Doyle. 'Oh of course, how stupid of me!' he exclaims. *The truth will out,* won't it. *The truth will set you free.* Is that really the gist of your point? Erhm...'

'Doyle,' Musgrove states helpfully.

Doyle takes a moment, smoothing the pad of a finger across her eyebrow. *Yes,* she thinks. *Yes.* She's sure that is precisely her point. She says so. 'Yes. That's precisely my point.'

Hyland relaxes, the back of his designer chair reclining to the point on the fulcrum it's locked to. A push of the heels and the whole thing scoots from the desk, castors rolling silently across burnished parquet flooring. *Summer Oak,* Musgrove recalls. '*A right buggering bastard to lay,*' being the fitters' rationale when billing for additional hours. Hours sending the cost of this particular office's refurbishment spiralling over budget. Recalling Hyland's dismissive wave of a hand at Musgrove's concerns over the growing expense. The CC got what he wanted, and just as then, he's determined to do so now.

'I have to say I'd expected a more polished argument,' Hyland responds, settled in reflective pose, chin resting on a pyramid of steepled fingertips. 'You know, something a little more than the mindless recitation of what amounts to the chanting of slogans. The sort of things you see on placards. The stuff scrawled in felt tip on brown cardboard and waved around for the cameras. An embarrassment for everyone.'

Doyle stares at him, non-plussed. Hyland returns his best *One Show* smile. Capped teeth: a crease of tanned laughter lines, just like his PR photo in the CID room, the one Fisher likes to throw darts at.

'Maybe the fact they're slogans is because people believe they're true,' Fisher offers, stepping into the fray and offering a far more conciliatory viewpoint than anyone might have anticipated. 'They say cliché's are clichés because they're true. Clichés tell us that things work the way we want them to. Truth and justice. Good people winning. The idea that no matter what happens things are going to be okay.' It isn't going to end the debate let alone win it, but it's an intervention designed to stop Doyle either waving the white flag of sulkiness or punching the CC in the face whilst rummaging about for a better option as to where she might shove that proverbial banner's proverbial flagpole. Right now, Fisher's not sure which is the more likely, but she credits herself with at least recognising such a tipping point has been reached.

Hyland turns from contemplation of Doyle's unease, her clenched and whitening knuckles, to Fisher. Fisher is the bigger prize. Despite Musgrove's seniority, Hyland knows convincing Fisher to fall in line offers the best chance of shutting the whole thing down, of stones being put back where they belong. Of the rest of this ragged troupe falling into line.

'Well,' Hyland begins. 'I'm pleased to find at least one of my senior officers recognises how the world turns. Someone able to acknowledge *"the things that have to be done to get things done".'* It's a familiar line of his, one much used in conference speeches and radio and TV interviews, a line polished to logical and lexical perfection.

Fisher's thin-lipped grimace frustrates his expectation of the response of an officer who right now ought to be wallowing in the glow of her senior officer's praise. He changes tack. 'It's not easy being me, you know. Being Chief Constable, I mean,' he clarifies, at the same time reflecting that being him is something he personally finds headily intoxicating. 'CID and uniform think all the tough stuff goes on out there,' he says, nodding at the window. '*The streets*,' he again adds for clarity. 'But there's toughness required here, too,' he continues, arms taking in the space around them. 'A toughness of the mind. A toughness in taking decisions. Decisions with consequences far beyond these walls. Far beyond this force.'

Fisher nods. 'I'm sure that's true, sir. I mean DS Demetriou all swaddled in bandages and braces in hospital might take umbridge as to who comes off worst, you know, you here in your office or him on the streets being blown up by a maniac killer and all - but I'm sure the rest of the force is on your side. Maybe on DCS Crosby's too, him being old school gym-locker solid in his thinking. His moral compass.'

Hyland bobs his *One Show* nod. 'DS Demetriou is a fine officer. A brave one, too.' He opts for a dramatic pause, Churchillian, yet one that says *what I just said is nothing more than polite and deferential bollocks to appease you*. He sets about fixing his gravely concerned media expression in place. 'But there remains the question of what he was doing there in the first place. Off the books, so I understand.'

'Not exactly how I'd put it,' Musgrove responds.

'Well how exactly *would* you put it?'

Musgrove has been wondering that himself. In truth, *Off the books* is precisely how his fictional *PI Rick Mangrove* gets things done. But that was fiction. In this room he's outside the pages of his hero investigator's maverick personality. In this world, ACC Neil Musgrove feels safest colouring inside the lines, whilst *Rick Mangrove* doesn't even recognise such lines exist. They're back to Fisher's point about moral compasses. They'd been following their own, and it had gotten Demetriou all but killed. Maybe it was time to let go, to get back on the path. *Process. Procedure.* Time for *PI Rick Mangrove* and his fantasy plotting to return to the drawer of unfinished manuscripts, the world where he belongs.

'Well...I'm...erhm, that's to say...'

'I think you're making my case very eloquently,' Hyland snorts, watching Musgrove's words fall like dead leaves onto the burnished oak flooring. It's easier than he'd thought. *Musgrove. Fisher. Doyle.* Two were beaten before they'd arrived. Doyle's childish, directionless fury; Fisher's guilt over Demetriou. Now that he's prodded Musgrove's sense of his own inadequacy, the man's virtually holding aloft the carpet for it all to be swept under. Forgotten.

He'd send them back to Pemberton. *Broken Wings* he hears they're called. And that's precisely what they are. Broken. Unfit to serve, chickens running around with their heads cut off, unaware they're already dead. They'd tried to fly, but now he's about to cage them. 'This story of yours,' he begins.

'Do you mean my report?' Musgrove asks taking a last stand.

'*Story*,' Hyland repeats. 'As in *fiction*. As in *fantasy*.' He shakes his head whilst he stamps over the final barricade of opposition. 'It can't stand. It just can't. And to be clear, I mean it *won't* stand. If you choose to persist in these wild allegations you leave no other option than a recommendation that all three of you be discharged with immediate effect.'

'But sir!' Doyle opines, wondering how that impacts her agreement, thoughts turning to black sites and whether they allow parental visits.

Hyland swivels, fixing her with a stone-face stare. 'You're not going to tell me I'm being unfair, are you?'

Doyle stops, wonders how he knows.

Hyland drops into conference rhythm - pace, certainty, the gloss of truths being told. 'If the Met has shown us anything, it's that modern-day policing relies on consensus. A consensus maintained by the fact that we appear to know what we're doing. That we have systems and processes; we apply methods that work. Methods, plans, and strategies that get results. If all else fails, we have the voodoo of DNA we can wave at Joe Public and the media whenever they question whether we've got the right people banged up. The fact that most of the criminals we catch are so stupid that they convict themselves with barely any input from us is neither here nor there. In the eyes of the great mass of the public, we arrest the right people. We know what we're doing.'

It's a darker version of a mantra trotted out at conferences, the talk he reserves for late night drinks in bars after keynote speeches. An after-hours *Black Mirror* variation of ideas long ago honed to oven-readiness for local and national media.

He shakes his head. 'How do you think they'll react when we tell them we've invested hundreds of thousands of pounds worth of man hours, resources, and equipment in a search for non-existent terrorists? A search puling in *MI5, MI6,* and *Special Branch*. Actions risking that the real terrorists and bad guys were getting away with all sorts of *Isis* stuff elsewhere whilst the *Spooks* joined us in blundering around the Dales on a wild goose chase? That deaths we'd tagged as suicides turn out to be three horrifically brutal murders? One in the centre of Harrogate outside a congregation of said *MI5, MI6,* and *Special Branch* and another at the biggest natural tourist attraction in the whole of the bloody county! A location beloved of *Harry Potter* fans? Oh, and of course, not to mention the decapitation of one of the country's leading business figures in front of hundreds of the great and good and the PM. Or how about your other idea, that the head of North Yorkshire CID gained his position through at best incompetence and at worst several very specific acts of corruption through covering up the swindle and murder of one of the county's most celebrated artists, herself a national fucking cultural treasure? And that's before we add in the bit that tops it all: a group of officers in therapy solved it in their spare time with only the aid of a child's book of fairy stories.'

'It was actually the killing of Sofia. That's what really started everything,' Fisher offers. 'All a bit strange and not quite right.'

'And Neil's story. Without *PI Rick Mangrove* we'd be sitting in therapy with a serial killer roaming free,' Doyle feels she has to add, a variation of a condemned person's last meal.

'Whatever,' Hyland snarls, sweeping their comments and his previous civilities aside. 'This will not stand. Will-not-fucking-stand! You will each of you accept the official report into these events, either that or suffer the consequences.'

'Sir,' Fisher begins. 'What you're asking is that we sign up to the idea that DCS Crosby, the man who couldn't find his own reflection in a room full of mirrors or his ass in a bag of elbows, somehow managed to solve a quintuple murder enquiry on his lonesome. That he saved DS Demetriou's life. Anyone who knows the man will see it as the tissue of lies it is, not to mention that it pegs us as idiots for saying it's true.'

'What I'm telling you, DI Fisher, is that this force needs a win. Not just a simple *aren't we wonderful putting the bad man in jail* win, but one restoring faith in the system. A win reminding the public that process and procedure and agencies working together gets the job done, not some maverick group of outsiders clinging to their careers by the skin of their teeth. It's not Hollywood! Not one of Musgrove's books!'

Musgrove tosses his copy of the draft report onto the Chief Constables' desk. 'I'm all for being a team player, sir, but this... what you're asking is beyond that.'

'How so?'

'For a start there's the very good chance that DCS Crosby is up to his Mason's cummerbund in the Brightside conspiracy and murder,' Fisher offers helpfully.

Hyland spins between the two. 'Utter garbage! I don't see it like that, and neither do *Special Branch, Five,* or *Six*. Certainly not the Home Office. DCS Crosby risked his life to bring the serial killer Jacob Strong to justice. Having been involved on the original case, he was the first to see the connection between these deaths. He realised he'd made a terrible error; one put down to his then lack of experience. Him going alone to confront Strong at that isolated spot is not the action of a man knowingly complicit in such things.'

'The Spooks! What do they know?' Fisher snarls, waving the report. 'They're covering their own highly exposed arses. Them having Crosby attached to their investigation means they'll claim credit for solving Webb's murder. They've already trumpeted that the hunt for his killer uncovered other planned terror attacks. It's going to be spun as a win rather than as a cock-up! It even says here it was their *"unflagging efforts"* to find the killer that inspired Crosby to make the connection we know he never really made - or rather, a connection he knew about all along but was too scared to admit to for fear of incriminating himself. When all's said and done, it's a lie built on a fallacy, built on bollocks.'

Hyland stands, an action sending his chair rolling further back. Like the man himself, the movement is smooth and well-oiled. 'However you choose to see it, whatever delusion you are operating under, I'm telling you that you have to sign off the official findings.' He tugs the cuffs of his sleeves into place as if underlining his rank. 'This operation requires a hero, someone we can stand in front of the Great British public. A chest we can pin a medal on in the hope it washes away the mis-steps of the past few weeks. We agree - Hargreaves, Badgerman, myself, the PM's office - that the chest cannot be that of officers in therapy responding to a wild fever dream.'

'Even though we were right,' Doyle puts in.

Hyland looks at her, then Musgrove, and finally Fisher. 'Look at yourselves. One the daughter of communist sympathisers, another the disgraced, sad, and isolated daughter of one of the finest officers to have served this force. And you, ACC Musgrove, an officer unable even to organise the decorators, a man struggling to separate reality from fiction. Not exactly anyone's idea of heroes.'

A silence lies across the room.

Hyland nods. 'This is what will happen. I'm going to leave this room for ten minutes. On my return I expect to find that you've signed the official report. However, before I go, I want you to be clear that it must be all three of you. Any of you electing to be a martyr for this cause, means all of you – including Demetriou – being dismissed to face charges of obstruction of justice, jail time. The full force of the law would be arrayed against you, broken wings or not.'

45

'So where does that leave us?' Doyle asks biting her bottom lip, a question addressed to no-one in particular. They stand in the fading light of the Police car park - Doyle, Musgrove, Fisher, - a knot of bodies like those outside hospital entrances. A stunned gathering sifting the words they'd just heard, the diagnoses delivered, wondering what tomorrow might hold.

'Where we always were,' Fisher judges, slumping against the bonnet of a patrol car one foot playing with a puddle. The formation shuffles, unwinding itself a little to accommodate her.

'Up shit creek. Paddle-*less*.' Musgrove clarifies, pulling a Twix from a pocket whilst offering his assessment of the political geography they find themselves in.

'There has to be something we can do. Has to be,' Doyle responds, teeth clenching her lip so fiercely it whitens at the edge.

'What did you have in mind?' Fisher asks.

Doyle sighs, flails her arms in the air. 'Go to the media. Tell our story.' She looks from Musgrove to Fisher and back again. 'Like what I said up there. The truth sets you free.'

'It's not *Day of the Condor* or *All the President's Men*,' Musgrove explains biting into a finger of the caramel bar and wondering why all the good political movies had Redford in them. Wondering whatever happened to him, was he dead, how old he is now.

'Day of what? The Condo? And which President's men?' Doyle asks, eyes narrowing in confusion as she attempts to batter a way into his pondering.

'They're films. Classics,' Fisher responds, taking pity and putting Doyle out of pop culture misery.

'Films? What's films got to do with anything?' Doyle demands.

'Well,' Musgrove says, emerging from musing on who Redford married and that if he'd had shares in Paul Newman's salad dressings they must be worth a bit now. 'They're not just films. They're ones where the good guys save the day by using the press to expose a conspiracy.'

'See. That's it then,' Doyle replies, face brightening. 'We expose them.'

Musgrove wrinkles his face. 'I think you're now the one confusing fiction with reality. All that "the pen is mightier than the sword stuff". Great line, but it won't work,' he adds through hefty chews. 'Politically naïve, you see. Swords are a lot stabb-*ier* in a fight, anyway.'

Doyle brushes past the comment in full charge mode, banner waving high *Les Miserables* style. 'But it will. My dad used the papers all the time, turned people against the government, against the bad guys. Got the word out direct to the people.'

'Again, you're confusing the past with now. You know all that "hold the front-page stuff". It's influencers now. Like that woman at the water park. The blogger or vlogger or whatever she calls herself. The busybody whose complaints landed me in this stuff in the first place.'

'What about the BBC? They're still mega. Supposed to be all honourable and everything. We could go on *Look North*. Tell them what really happened. The murders. Demetriou's part in solving it. Most probably him saving Crosby's life.'

'It's all BBC Verify now. They'll want hard facts. No way Hyland gives them that. Not that there's anything to give other than it being our idea. As for Crosby, he's pleading inexperience and lack of judgement at the time. On top of that, you heard what Hyland said, who's going to listen to us now that Crosby's being made the hero? Man of the moment restoring the good name of the Force.'

'So we give up? Is that it? No wonder you're refurbishment. Maybe Hyland's got something right, maybe that's why they don't let you loose on real policing anymore,' Doyle sneers, turning from him.

'Weren't you just in there?' Musgrove snaps back, pointing at the building with the remaining chocolaty caramel finger of Twix. 'Weren't you listening?' he demands, face reddening. 'What was it this time? Off in one of your moody sulks where you shut it all out?' He steps forward, forcing her to turn to him whilst herself taking a step back towards a parked car. 'You know, the way you usually get when we start talking, when we start telling each other about ourselves or when we're trying to solve these murders. There's you, slumped in your chair lah-lah-laahing to yourself, fingers in ears trying to drown out all the nasty things happening in the world. The things that don't interest you because they aren't about you or your issues. Policing, proper policing, is about helping others, Doyle. Them with no voice of their own. I mean, is it that you just can't be bothered because you can't selfie it or Tik-Tok it. You and your Generation X or Z or millennials or whatever you are! Fucking snowflakes!' He pauses. 'Let me be clear now that you've woken up to what's going on. We're-finished-Done-Period-The end!'

Fisher watches Sophie's knuckles turn pale, her face flushing. 'Alpha!' Doyle spits, leaning into Musgrove, her chin pointing upwards. 'It's Generation Alpha! Not that I'd expect an old ham like you to know that. What is it grandad? Pissed off the world's passed you by? Suddenly realising you've fucked it all up – your career, your life, your cold, tired, marriage. Feeling guilty it's your kids who're left to sort it out, this world you've broken, leaving us to shovel up your shit!' She shakes her head, face twisting to a snarling grimace. 'Like this case really, isn't it? Us putting flesh on the bones of your idea while you hummed and hawed about your precious fucking career. Your bloody pension! Us making it work. Pan ending up where he is because he believed what you told him. Him sucking it up, sucked in like a bloody fool, like we all were. Still are. Still stood here, listening to you and your whining shit!'

Fisher levers herself from the bonnet and steps across. 'Maybe we need to step back a little.' She puts a hand on Musgrove's chest. 'Literally, Neil. Step back.'

Musgrove looks down at her hand, noticing he's somehow moved three or four strides to pin Doyle against a parked car. Doyle looking down seeing her own hands balled into fists.

Musgrove steps back three paces. 'Oh, Christ!' he gasps, dropping his hands to his side. Sophie, I'm sorry. I don't know what got into me. I should never have said any of that.' He closes his eyes, the crimson mist blowing back out to sea. 'I know you care, all of you, I know that. And I know you believe we're right, and that you're angry…that you want to fight. We'd never have got here, not even close without you, Sophie. What you did, your passion. I know it's why you're here, why you're angry with it all, with me. And I know it's why Pan's not here, that him almost dying is on me. Just me. All of it…'

Doyle straightens her jacket, fists relaxing to open palms. She steps closer, flinging her arms around him, holding him despite the fact her arms reach no further than his sides. 'You're really an old softie, aren't you?' she says into his chest.

He looks down, uncertain what to do. 'I don't know about that. My Charlie would give you plenty of reasons I'm not.'

She stands back a little and looks up, taking him in. 'Charlie?'

'My son. Charlie. He's not much younger than you. Maybe that's my issue. My issues with you, I mean.'

'What do you mean? Are you saying I bring out the dad in you?'

Musgrove stands stock still, arms pinned to his sides looking to Fisher for a rope.

Fisher exhales and throws him one. 'Well at least we know why we're Broken Wings. All that anger still festering away. Might have to have words with Malcolm at the next meeting. Let him know that though we're talking there's work required.'

Doyle loosening her grip, steps back and nods. 'Yeah. You can say that again. Think we'll be there a while yet. That's if we're still here to have meetings with Malcolm.'

Musgrove stops the readjustment of his coat, his post-hug tidy-up. 'Pemberton!' he announces.

'Yeah. Like I said. Malcolm.'

'No, not him. It's *what* you said about him. About us.'

'That he's not done that well? Time to turn in his Blue Peter Therapy badge,' Fisher offers.

'In a manner of speaking, yes. Just that. That he's got work to do. On us.'

'So?'

'So Pemberton's work applies to any officers returning to duty after trauma.'

'So?' Doyle decides it's her turn to ask.

'Crosby!' Fisher snaps, clicking her fingers.

'Crosby,' Musgrove concurs.

'Why are you both saying Crosby so dramatically?' Doyle asks.

'Crosby has to undergo a therapy session with Malcolm. It's mandatory.'

Doyle thinks things are getting more than a little repetitious but finds herself asking. 'So?'

'So we arrange for it to be with us. You see, part of Neil's HR remit is staff welfare. His suspension from active investigations is one thing, but he's still in charge of HQ logistics, which in the Kafka*esque* Catch-22 manner of the Northallerton protocols and management structure puts him with direct oversight of Pemberton's work whose patient he is. Before a return to duty any officer involved in operational trauma undergoes a meeting with the Force therapist - Pemberton - for an assessment of their mental and emotional fitness.'

'We're suspended, with no access to a formal questioning of Crosby,' Musgrove says. 'But we can still ferret around in his head during the circle time I'll mandate him to attend as part of his rehabilitation.'

'But we're Anger Management. Why would Crosby be directed to a session with us? Why would that ever happen?'

'Because I get things wrong,' Musgrove states raising his hands in the air in surrender. 'Hyland of all people believes that. Christ, I think these days he even expects it. Human error. I might just direct him to the wrong group.'

'So,' Fisher elaborates. 'It's our chance to interrogate him. He has to be there. We have to be there. It's the rules. We have him to ourselves for an hour. An hour to break the bastard. Even if only for an hour, DCS Crosby is about to find himself the newest member of The Broken Wings.'

46

The house is smaller than he'd remembered. Less imposing. Like its former owner's reputation, the years haven't been kind to it – windows covered with dust, paintwork faded, once remarkable gardens overgrown and running to weed. After a decade of abandonment, it's even more of what it always was - a Hollywood set designer's fantasy of an English country house. *Grey Goose House*, stone walls smothered with gnarled wisteria and infused with faded grandeur. All it lacks is a gargoyle.

Crosby stands in front of it, flexes each arm, hands held tentatively away from him, the slow sting of ointment tingling on burnt flesh. The drive was harder than he'd imagined, and despite the car being an automatic, the twist and turns of the last few miles have him thankful for the heavy dose of painkillers taken before setting off.

There's a car on the gravelled driveway, Lawrence beating him here. He wonders if the photographer travelled with him. Then again, there's the possibility Lawrence will shoot it himself. Times are tough for print media, and he knows most cell phones shoot a quality of image better than many cameras, has seen *Post* reporters using them at media briefings. He snorts. Matters of newspaper industry demarcation really shouldn't be his concern right now.

Right now, it's the story, and in that respect Lawrence's idea to hold the interview at *Grey Goose House* - Brightside's old home - is a stroke of genius, a literal return to the scene of the crime. It offers evocative images, shots re-shaping the narrative. Maybe him stood next to the carved fireplace, arm outstretched along the mantelpiece in full Poirot mode. Even he knows the hearth is legendary, the centrepiece of a lounge holding an arts and crafts notoriety befitting Brightside's quirky reputation. As well as a striking pose, it would remind readers of Brightside's taste for the bizarre, her rapacious nature, her drug fuelled unworldliness. It sits well with the intended narrative: a young and naïve detective caught in the thrall of monsters who'd deceived and exploited him. Like all good stories, Lawrence's PR genius will ensure it ends with Crosby's redemption, a hero dragging into the light those same monsters. Men who in turning murderously on each other had revealed their true natures.

Arriving at an already open front door, he pushes it wider. 'Lawrence! Are you there?'

His voice echoes through the hall, reverberating off oak panel walls.

He stands for a moment before calling out once more. 'Lawrence!' he shouts. 'It's me. DCS Crosby!' He pushes further inside. 'Lawrence! Are you there?'

'Of course I'm here, Detective Chief Superintendent.'

He turns to face a pair of sliding double doors that have opened without his noticing. He is still pondering how such unmaintained fittings could move so silkily - part of him thinking he really ought to sort out the patio door Carol's been on at him to fix - when Lawrence, stepping to one side, beckons him into the room.

'And of course I know who you are,' Lawrence continues. 'Even if I weren't expecting you, we've sat in enough of those joint task force meetings, eh? And lately what with the Webb murder and all those *Spooks* cluttering the place up...Well, let's just say Gina and I make a point of knowing who our allies are in there.'

Crosby enters the salon, eyes adjusting to the dim light, the bizarre splendour of the space, whilst his good hand accepts the handshake the PR man extends in his direction. 'Really? There's usually so many top brass there didn't think...you know.' Crosby finds himself stumbling over the idea of his newfound standing in the Commissioner's eyes. He looks from side to side, eyes overflowing with the strange carvings on the fireplace, the intricate moldings carved into the plaster of the ceiling. 'I didn't realise. Feels like many of us locals have been a little...erhm...' he stutters to a halt.

'Undervalued?' Lawrence prompts.

'Maybe,' Crosby replies dragging his mind to focus on the conversation. 'Maybe more, I don't know - unappreciated. Like you say, squeezed out by the *Spooks*. The politics of it.'

'Oh, I quite understand why you might see things that way,' Lawrence offers, placing an open palm on his chest. '*Mea culpa*, there I feel. My trying to keep the Commissioner's career and priorities secure and on track. We can't afford to be seen upsetting the political Big Boys. Whitehall wields considerable power even up here. It's been more a case of, you know, needs must.' He waves his other arm in an all-encompassing arc, eyebrows raised. 'And those *Spooks*! Men like Badgerman, well, they're certainly some kind of devils when it comes to getting their way!'

'Control freaks,' Crosby judges.

'Precisely!' Lawrence gushes. 'I'm so glad you understand. I'd hate any bad blood to linger longer than necessary between valued officers like yourself and the Commissioner. Not on my watch, anyway!' he adds, text-book PR smile fixed in place, carved there Rushmore-like. He steps closer, extending an arm that he places lightly on Crosby's shoulders, encouraging him further into the room. Crosby allows himself to be led, guided sheep-like to the centre of the space.

'It's a little dark in here,' Crosby observes noticing the thick floor length curtains are drawn. 'A little gloomy, don't you think?' he states, noting the slivers of outside light funnelling their way into fall on the plaster carvings of nymphs and woodland folk.

'Ambience, Superintendent. Ambience.'

'The photos.'

'The photos.'

'I thought so,' Lawrence says, pleased at the shared vision. 'Like you said about selecting here for the feature. I can see how it lends itself to atmospheric shots.' He nods at the carvings of scampering demons on the mantel-shelf. 'That and showing the world what a bloody *weirdo* Gillian Brightside really was.'

Lawrence pauses in his stride. 'You think so?'

'For sure. I mean just look at this weird shit.' He spins around, good arm waving at the scene. 'Who has goblins and forest folk scampering around a dado rail? Nutters and black magic,' he answers himself, adding, 'It's the drugs. Addles the mind. Seen it before.'

Lawrence nods and then walks to a briefcase laid on a drop cloth currently imitating the shape of an old chaise-lounge. He produces a hip flask and unscrews the top, offering the flask to Crosby who accepts with a smile. He sniffs the top. 'Whiskey?'

'Single malt. Filey Bay.' Lawrence responds. 'Gratitude for a little work I did on their brand.'

Crosby dips the flask in acknowledgement and swigs. He smiles, lips clenching appreciatively. 'Damned good. Nice and peaty.'

'Damned good,' Lawrence echoes taking the flask and screwing the top back into place.

Crosby watches him return it to the briefcase. 'Are you not joining me?'

Lawrence wrinkles his face. 'After. Need to keep a clear head.

Find it helps relax the subject though.' Depositing the flask, he returns his attention to Crosby. 'Going back to what you said of Brightside. Her...situation. I assume that means you knew her. Personally, I mean, before you were put in charge of investigating the circumstance of her death.'

'Me? No. Never met the barmy old cow.' He slowly spins; head tilted up to the carved ceiling rose.

'Yet you talk as if you knew her.'

Crosby lowers his head. 'The type. I know the type. The *weirdo* junkies and the like. The ones that ought to be locked away. Kept in secure care rather than left out for the rest of us to step-over in doorways, having to deal with their madness.'

'Left out? Step-over? You make them sound like the recycling. Stuck on the side of the road,' Lawrence observes.

Crosby smiles at the thought. 'Maybe just that,' he nods. 'Except of course for the fact that you can't remake those sorts into anything approaching useful. Nothing like. Un- reclaimable empties. Used up. Finished.'

'I can see why you were so willing for DS Townley to sign off her case,' Lawrence notes. 'You know, so readily accepting it as an overdose. Why waste good taxpayers' money on an investigation into *someone like her*, eh?'

'Well...that's not quite right...Townley's role. I mean...' he stumbles. Recovers. 'It was a decision based on good evidence.'

'Oh, and what was that?'

'Well, for a start there were witness statements. Her PR man, Jacob Strong. Her solicitor, Wrigley and her publisher, Archibald Gill. And Paul Webb too. They all made statements as to her mental state at the time of her death. Open and shut.'

'And they turned out to be such reliable men, didn't they,' Lawrence mutters.

Crosby stands by the curtains draped across the windows. All part of the man's taste for the dramatic shot he supposes. All mysterious lighting. Black and white too, no doubt. He turns, uncertain. 'Erhm...have we started? The interview I mean. I thought we were just...you know, chatting. Off the record sort of...so to speak.'

'It's how I work, I feel my way into a subject. Background.'

'But shouldn't there be a...signal of some sort. You know, I assumed we'd be...' he laughs. 'I don't know, sitting down. There'd be notebooks or a recorder or something. A sign,' Crosby says.

'Ah, sorry. Of course, perfectly understandable. No need to worry, I'm not recording you. As you said, we're just two men talking. Getting a sense of each other. Feeling each other out. Our character. Our natures,' the PR guru replies.

'Ah, got you. Get a sense of the man behind the story. The bloke behind the headlines.' Crosby pauses, considering his words. 'It's just that, well...I wouldn't want you to think that I was in anyway...you know, culpable in her death. Well, not her death. That of course was before I was involved. I mean the idea that there was any sort of...cover up on my part. After the fact, I mean. It's like you said over the phone. I was naïve. New to the job. First big case. Unknowing. I trusted those men. Townley too. There was nothing...criminal regarding my conduct. There was no conspiracy, just...naivety.'

'Chief Superintendent, I fully understand why you'd not want such an idea to get out. How it might appear to others more cynical than yourself. Those who might feel there was some...incentive for you to have signed her death off as misadventure. A bribe to head off a murder investigation,' Lawrence concedes.

'Of course not. Like you said, I was naïve,' Crosby states for the record. 'Those men – Webb, Strong, Wrigley, and Gill - were monsters, murderers. We know that thanks to my uncovering of their conspiracy, done no matter the risk to my reputation. Sadly, there's no Townley around to verify everything that happened back then. But I'm the hero here. It's a redemption tale. Like in books. The films.'

'That's true,' Lawrence agrees. 'Such tales usually reach a

point where the hero suddenly realises what they have to do, no matter the cost to themselves. It's about sacrifice, you see.'

'Sacrifice?' Crosby asks.

'The hero giving up something they treasure. The thing they hold dearest. Maybe their own life.'

'A bit extreme, but I get it. Like you said. I'm the hero of a redemptive tale. Almost died myself,' Crosby reminds.

'Ah, but you see the problem that leaves us, don't you? The conundrum.'

'Conundrum?'

'The challenge,' Lawrence clarifies. 'The problem. The thing that's missing from your tale.'

'Missing? Missing how? What? What's missing?' Crosby asks.

Lawrence stands by the hearth; arm extended along the mantel. Classic Poirot, Crosby thinks, wondering whether it shouldn't be him standing there rather than Lawrence. Lawrence takes a pause before meeting Crosby's gaze. 'Since we spoke, I've given a great deal of thought to it, this story of yours. The flaw in all this is that there's been no real sacrifice. You've suffered nothing other than a slur on your reputation. There's nothing to stir the public imagination. Nothing to catch fire, so to speak.'

Crosby looks at the burns on his hands and arms. 'But my reputation is everything. What people think. What they might think.'

'What? That rather than acting out of what you claim to be naivety, they'll believe you were part of the conspiracy? That you played a more than significant role in enabling murderers escape justice? That in your eyes her murder counted for nothing? That it wasn't worth the bother of your time? That you were perfectly happy for Townley to take any blame,' Crosby offers.

'No! Of course not. How could anyone think that?'

'But that's what you just told me, wasn't it?' Lawrence responds. 'She was a *weirdo*, you said. Someone *not worth recycling*. That people will assume you attained your meteoric promotions and wealth through protecting men whom you knew to be guilty. Men you knew to be complicit in a murder serving their own ambitions and ultimately yours. Men guilty of destroying Gillian Brightside's reputation in order to protect their own. A reputation your report was integral in ensuring was rubbed in the dirt.'

Crosby stares at him. 'What is this? Some sort of journalistic tactic? You know, provoking me to see what I'm made of? How I'll cope under the media spotlight. What makes me tick? Like those celebrity *SAS TV* shows or what have you?'

Lawrence exhales, shaking his head. 'I feel the world knows only too well what makes a man like you tick, Detective Chief Superintendent. Isn't it more a case of what the world will come to know of your part in these matters. What we'll tell them? What secrets we might uncover? What stones we'll help them look under? The truth we can provide?'

Crosby moves from the window and looks to the now closed doors. 'I'm not sure this is such a good idea. It's not what I thought I was signing up for. It was to be my redemptive story. That you'd help in its shaping. Shoot some nice images.'

'Be honest Chief Superintendent, what you believed was that you were signing up to getting off scot-free,' Lawrence declares.

'Sorry?'

Lawrence smiles thinly. 'You came here with the intention of using me to ensure you escape justice for your part in the robbery and murder of Gillian Brightside. Exploiting my talent and reputation in exactly the same way you did hers.'

'No! That's not true!' Crosby protests.

'You're right, of course. It's more than that. It's the audacity of your ambition. That you not only think you'll get away with it, but you want to make yourself the hero. The champion of a dead woman whose murder you covered up.'

'I think it's better that I go,' Crosby judges. 'This is clearly a mistake. A gross intrusion of the press. I came here, seeking support from the Police Commissioner's office, to safeguard the force's reputation and the Commissioner's as much as my own. I was looking to provide a good PR story, one to help her win the election. But you can forget all that now, forget about exploiting my story.'

'Don't you mean *alibi*?' Lawrence corrects.

Crosby moves towards the doors, a growing mushiness in his movement. The floor appears spongey, his head murky. He stumbles. *Christ all he's had is a sip of whiskey. Maybe the painkillers...But hardly enough to...*He turns, a smiling Lawrence has closed the gap without Crosby having any sense the man had moved at all. 'What?' is all he manages.

'A sedative, Superintendent. I assume that's what you were about to ask. *What have you done to me*? Ironic when the real question surely is *what have you done to me*?'

'To you?'

'To me, Chief Superintendent Crosby. To me and to my mother, Gillian Brightside.'

47

'What do you mean he's not around?'

Iverson stands bemused, pondering on the many ways he might respond, the lexical choices, the different nuances or shaded tones he might apply to his words. In the end he circles back to his first instinct, his father having always told him, *if it ain't broke don't fix it.* 'I mean, he's not around,' he repeats, maybe a little slower than the first time, like talking to foreigners on holiday. 'DCS Crosby, that is,' he clarifies hoping it might be the fix he's looking for. 'DCS Crosby's left the building,' he throws in for good measure.

'What? Who does he think he is? Bloody Elvis?' Fisher asks, her face arranging itself into an expression of scorn to better match her tone. Belt and braces, as she always tells herself. No room for equivocation as to her mood at any particular moment.

'Sorry?'

'Yes you are, DS Iverson. A sorry specimen of a useful officer.'

She swivels on her toes and makes off down the corridor to the meeting room, its circle of chairs and wheezing coffee flask. Musgrove looks up mid pour of an especially brackish brew. 'So, where is he?'

Closing the door, she lifts open her jacket. 'Well, as I'm neither David Blaine or Dynamo, and given the fact he's not up a sleeve, I think you can safely assume he's not bloody coming.'

'But he has to,' Musgrove replies, selecting a tone of outrage to colour inside the lines of his reply. He slams the cup on the table with as much emphasis as you might a Styrofoam beaker. 'It's procedure. He can't ignore it. I helped write the by-laws on it. He has to be here.'

'Well, clearly he's not. On top of that, no one appears to know where he is. Seems he's left the building.'

'What, like Elvis?' he asks.

'Sorry?' Doyle puts in from her default position cross legged on a chair. 'Elvis who?'

Fisher and Musgrove share a look, Fisher selecting a pitying head shake. 'I don't get it,' Musgrove opines, disregarding Doyle's interruption. 'He can't just choose to ignore these things. It's not optional. He's a buggering DCS. He should know better,' he adds, the back of one hand slapping into the palm of the other as a measure of affirmation.

'Maybe he had a better offer. Something a little more suiting his taste for self-aggrandisement and self-interest,' Fisher puts in.

'Such as?'

She blows her lips together, motor-boating. 'Hyland. Hargreaves. Maybe they got wind of our plan. Maybe one of them is cleverer than we thought,' she offers before screwing her nose up. 'No. Scratch that,' she decides. 'I mean, we're not in one of your books.'

'Maybe I can find out,' Doyle suggests, retrieving her laptop from the roll-top messenger bag.

'Can you do that?' Musgrove asks, head inclining towards the device whilst desperately trying to get the image of Fisher and motor-boating out of his head.

'Find him?' she asks.

'Use an off-the-books laptop. You know, your violations,' he says.

'Best you don't ask,' she replies, fingers dancing across the keypad. 'More to the point, best you don't know.'

'She's a hacker,' Musgrove states.

'I got that already,' Fisher states.

'It's why she's here. This group.'

'What Neil means is that I hacked my way into somewhere I shouldn't,' Doyle states without glancing up. 'The Black Hats found me, and for my sins sent me here.'

'Here? Why here?'

'Suits me and them. Close to home. Close to where they can keep an eye on me. I think they feel being near my roots stabilises things for me. Emotionally.'

'I don't mean to sound ungrateful, but why not prison?' Fisher asks.

Musgrove clears his throat. 'Because I suspect like fraud, if its big enough you pass out the other side of regular sentencing. Too hot to handle. Too big.'

Doyle nods as she taps at the keys. 'Something like that. Mutually Assured Destruction so my handler tells me. Looked it up. It's all about Cuba or something.'

Musgrove clears his throat. As ACC he's read the file, at least the bits not covered in black sharpie redacted-ness. 'To put you away, there'd have to be stuff they don't want coming out in a trial. But should you use what you know, they'll put you away irrespective. Trial or not. Probably not. Hence M-A-D. Kennedy and Khrushchev. The Cuban missile crisis.'

'A deep dark hole was mentioned by someone,' Doyle adds. 'Might have been my solicitor.'

'So, you end up here,' Fisher states. 'Off the radar where, should they decide you're not playing, they can whisk you away with the minimum of fuss or *habeas corpus*.' She sits close to where Doyle is running her fingers over the laptop's trackpad. 'It makes sense now. Explains why you kicking a senior officer in the balls didn't end with you being fired. Why you were sent here, us.'

'Something like that,' Doyle says barely lifting her eyes from the screen. 'I suppose that technically and practically I'm pretty much un-sackable. Equally, I'm also un-quittable. At least for the next few years. Stuck.'

'Aren't we all,' Fisher offers, eyes meeting Musgrove's who grimaces back.

'I'm in!' Doyle states.

'In?'

'The Duty roster. Where the Senior Team are at any time of the day.'

'Hargreaves' HQ Day-Book!' Musgrove spits.

'Well for once it might prove its worth,' Fisher responds, wondering when she'd last found cause to approve any part of the bureaucracy the Force runs on.

'Weird,' Doyle says as she scrutinises the list.

'Weird?' Musgrove asks, peering over her shoulder.

'According to this, DCS Crosby's out of office, something to do with an article for *the Post*.'

'*Deja vu*, eh? No doubt the powers that be are rushing to get his version of what happened made the official line. You know, Holy Writ delivered straight from Mount Crosby,' Musgrove judges.

'Ironic, given that's what he was supposedly doing when he met Strong at the old station house,' Fisher observes, her mind struggling to contain Musgrove's image of Crosby dressed like Moses holding up stone tablets. 'And look how well that ended.'

'They're getting the early PR out there, setting an agenda, you know, covering everything under uber-thick layers of positive spin. By the time they've finished it'll be like it was Hyland's personally sanctioned operation all along.'

'Who approved it?' Musgrove asks ignoring Fisher's musing. 'This interview.'

'Hargreaves.'

'No surprise there. She'll have Crosby putting out the party-line, make any dissent from us look like whinging.' He strops his way to the table, scooping up a pack of *Country Creams*. Tearing open the wrapper, he stuffs the first biscuit into his mouth in one go swiftly followed by a second. Not his first rodeo.

Fisher snorts. 'Didn't think he could put much of a sentence together.'

'Well, it'll be ghost written, won't it.'

'What do you mean?'

'He's meeting Lawrence. There's a note attached to the Day-Book. Lawrence is meeting him at some old house.'

'More PR bollocks,' Fisher says with a curl of her lip.

'Hmmm,' Doyle murmurs. '*Grey Goose House*. Where's' that?'

'*Grey Goose House*. Isn't that-' Musgrove begins.

'…Gillian Brightside's old house.' Fisher replies. 'It was in the files Demetriou was looking at.'

'Oh, that's where I've seen it.' Doyle says, finger tapping the trackpad. 'That's weird.'

'What calling a house *Grey Goose*? Suppose it's better than *Dun-writin* or *Abide-a-wee*,' Fisher observes.

'No. Not the house. I get why it's a smart choice of location. I'm looking at Demetriou's notes.' She taps her finger a few more times. 'There's an unopened email in his inbox, a response to an enquiry he made. Seems he was looking at Brightside herself.'

'That's Pan. Real boy scout, dotting the *I*'s and crossing all the *t*'s,' Fisher replies.

'Can you access everyone's mail?' Musgrove asks, finger working at his shirt collar.

'Of course I can.' She wrinkles her nose, free hand waving in the air. 'Stuff like that's Hacking 101. But this...' She spins the laptop to face Fisher. 'One of his searches was for her death certificate.'

'Yes, well, he'd be checking the cause of death that Townley signed off. Like I said, him doing his usual dotting the *i*'s and *t*'s of it,' Fisher states.

'But his search engine criteria was too broad,' Doyle judges. 'He didn't refine it enough. Lots of people make the same error. It looked at all the *Brightside's* in the county.'

'So?' Fisher asks.

'Well, the results came back after the fire so he hadn't seen them. There's a birth certificate.'

Musgrove grunts. 'Well, stands to reason if there's a death certificate there'd be a record of her birth. Top and tail.'

'This one's not hers,' Doyle says. 'It's for a boy, Gillian Brightside's recorded as the mother.'

'But there's nothing in the file about a child,' Musgrove says. 'We'd have known. Not to mention that any heir would have come forward to claim the estate. Maybe he died at birth.'

Doyle shakes her head, fingers pinching the trackpad as she scans the file. 'There's' no record of a death. But there's a note in the email from the records office. An adoption.'

Musgrove stops chewing, scrunching the biscuit wrapper in a fist. 'Which means maybe no-one knew about him.'

Fisher sits forward. 'This boy-child would be a man now, someone with motive for revenge.'

'It's possible,' Musgrove agrees. 'Adoption would mean a change of name. Is there anything in the files?'

Doyle skims the Record's office email. 'Harvey,' she says. She stops, finger pressed against the screen. She looks up. 'Oh God! The adoptive father. His name was Harvey. Lawrence Harvey.'

'Like the old film star,' Musgrove says.

'Lawrence Harvey. Harvey Lawrence.' Doyle says.

'Harvey Lawrence. I mean that's the same as…really? Lawrence, a serial killer?' Musgrove ponders. 'I mean, have you met him, he's…well he doesn't look like a killer.'

'I bet if we dig into it we'll find it was Lawrence who set up the meeting at the Police house,' Fisher says. 'It came from the Commissioner's office.'

Doyle opens a series of windows on the laptop. 'You're right. Theres an email here Hargreaves' office suggesting the idea for the feature. They insist the newspaper send Strong to the meeting.'

Fisher stands. 'We're wrong about Crosby, the same way we were off-target about Strong. It's Lawrence, not Crosby. He's Brightside's heir. He's our killer. Think about it, he's had his fingers into every one of our investigations from the start – Sofia, Wrigley, Gill, Strong, Webb. He's not only tracked every move, he's even directed some.'

Musgrove runs a hand through his hair. 'And he's meeting the last of the men he blames for robbing and murdering his mother. Meeting him at her old house. He's going to kill again.'

48

He wakes to a blurred vision of the world, a grey-white haze swirling across his eyes, a fog rising like the inverted clouds of a Dales' winter mist. He screws them closed and open, now dimly aware his chin lolls against his chest and that he's looking at the floor from a height greater than he's used to. The dawning realisation that he's standing on a wooden dining chair, arms bound behind him, torso sensing the squeeze of a rope pulled tight under his armpits holding him upright. Although he can't see it, lowering his chin to his chest he feels the touch of another rope looped loosely around his neck.

'Ah, there you are,' Lawrence's voice says from somewhere behind. 'I was hoping you'd be awake soon.' He hears footsteps slap the floorboards as the voice moves further away. 'Now, I need you to be clear on this, Chief Superintendent. I'm about to slacken off of the rope that's running under your armpits. It's the means by which I've been holding you up whilst you dozed. If you don't brace your legs, then the rope I've tied around your neck is going to do its work a lot quicker than I'm sure either of us want. Do you understand what I'm telling you?'

'Why are you doing this?' Crosby asks.

'Not the answer I'm looking for, but good enough,' Lawrence

responds. He slackens the knot tying the rope to one of the iron light fittings attached to the wall, returning the business of keeping Crosby upright to the DCS's body. Crosby feels himself sag, feels the rope bite at his throat. He locks his knees, an action that stops him from falling or the rope around his neck from tightening. 'That's the boy!' Lawrence calls. 'Just the job!'

It takes a moment for Crosby to steady himself. A moment before he can trust that he's stable, that the chair is wide enough, secure enough. He takes a breath, calming himself. If he keeps still he'll be okay, at least as long as he keeps awake. 'What's going on?' he asks, head twisting to find his tormentor.

'Well, a detective like yourself can see it's not good. Not for you, that is.'

Crosby tries turning his head to the other side, searching for his persecutor. 'What do you want?' he demands.

'What do I want? That's as they say the sixty-four-thousand-dollar question. Although I'm sure sixty-four-thousand dollars is nowhere near the sum your friends swindled from my mother.'

'They're not my friends!' Crosby shouts at the gargoyle's carved into the wood paneling before a wobble makes him stop and focus on balancing.

'Co-conspirators then. Those whom you joined in a criminal enterprise. Extortion, murder.'

'That's not true! I did none of those things!' he twists his head, this time much slower, legs wobbling the chair.

Lawrence slides into sight holding a folder. 'That's' not what it says here. This report tells a different tale.' He tosses it to the floor, the pages tumbling out stark white against the blackened oak. 'Being PR to the Commissioner has its perks, one of which is access to relevant service records and active files. Your little adventure with Jacob Strong at the old police station offered the opportunity to get my hands on your file. I blame myself for not having worked it out sooner, especially after Townley proved himself so obviously incapable of such a conspiracy, but I had to be sure. Be certain that it was in fact you who'd covered things up, protected men you knew to be fraudsters and murderers, merely using Townley to keep your hands clean. You did it for advancement, for greed.' He nods at the papers he's scattered around the chair. 'Not quite the heroic tale of redemption you were thinking, eh? Grubby and tawdry might be more fitting.'

'No! That's not true. I was deluded...duped.' *Wobble.* 'It's like we said on the phone.' *Wobble.* 'I was naïve, yes, but nothing more.' *Wobble.* 'I wanted to do the best by them, by everyone. I thought I was doing the right thing.' *Wobble, wobble.*

'You mean for your own ambition.'

'I'd no idea what they'd done. Not a clue,' he insists, aware of the impish carvings laughing at his denial. 'They said closing an investigation without complications was good for business, preventing everyone getting tied up in months of paperwork and questioning.'

'And, of course, for such a service there'd be a reward.'

'No...It wasn't like that. There were...suggestions, nothing more.'

'But look at you now. From middling Inspector to Detective Chief Superintendent in a few short years. Or do you really think you're that good?'

'What do you want?'

'Isn't it clear?'

'Revenge,' he says, eyes looking into the faces of the grinning carvings.

'I feel *revenge* sounds so...frontier. You know, *eye for an eye*. I find the idea of *justice* to be so much more...Civilised.'

'You killed them.'

'Webb and Gill and the rest?' he nods, smiling. 'Townley too, though I doubt anyone will find poor Georgie anytime soon. Not that he'd been much use to anyone for years, at least not since filling in as your stooge.'

He sighs, relaxing into his task. 'Oh, and of course there's the poor Bulgarian girl - Sofia I believe Fisher said her name was.

Sadly, a woman as easily forgotten in death as she no doubt was in her sorry little life.'

'Why? Why do this?' Crosby pleads rather than asks.

Lawrence busies himself in flicking the upturned papers with a foot, arranging a scene he clearly has in mind. 'I won't bore you with the minutiae of what happened all those years ago. Simply put, after my mother's death I found a birth certificate telling the truth of my biological mother's identity. When I made my existence known to her executors - Wrigley, Gill, Webb and Strong - Webb's Bulgarian thugs grabbed me and made clear the fate about to befall me for interfering with their plans. I was sure I was going to die, but in a moment of what passed for conscience, old Archie Gill helped me get away, even gave me a large sum of money to keep quiet. I fled to London, changed my name, had extensive surgery on the broken cheekbones and jaw I'd received courtesy of the Bulgarians. I can only assume that Archie told the others that the Bulgarians had done their work, something the Bulgarians themselves seemingly felt disobliged to deny. After all, they'd been paid to make me disappear and they too have a reputation to preserve.'

He stands back, checking the impact of his design. 'Once I'd recovered, I considered what I might do, but by then I had little in the way of evidence backing my claim. On top of that, the Bulgarians are men known to hold grudges. Men better left alone. After all, I'm merely an amateur. A talented one, I grant you, but little more than a novice. This present venture is more in the way of a quest - an interest rather than a calling. Despite what you might think, I'm no Hannibal Lecter. I've no unquenchable thirst or appetites. I intend to walk away.' He looks up at Crosby, checking he's understood. 'So, that being the case, you can see that I wouldn't want to spend the rest of my life looking over my shoulder to see if any feral East Europeans have worked it all out. The girl was more in the way of a cipher. A symbol. A scratch on the flanks of the drugs and violence merchants whom Webb had relied on for the nastier parts of his conspiracy.'

He scans the room, checking this work. 'She was something of a trial run. It's why I made certain Gina and I went to that call - easy enough to convince her of the merits of one of her little "trips" that night. A trip enabling me to see close-up whether your lot could be fooled. Braiding other women's' hair in the rope, the isolated location, plenty of enigmas. Easy enough to sideline anyone who might be a threat to my plans, someone such as the returning Fisher. I knew of her reputation, her maverick thinking, but having Gina keep her at arm's length from the good stuff I was planning dealt with that potential pitfall. It left me free to get on with the rest of my plan unhindered. Webb, for example. As the Commissioner's PR I knew early on about the PM's withdrawal from opening the water slide. After that it was a simple matter to use my position to access the site the previous night, knowing that once I'd set the wire in place Webb's death would be linked to an attack on the PM, a theory sending everyone off on a wild goose chase. The swirl of distraction blinded you to the actual target and motive. As a bonus, it punished the Bulgarians, them having their lucrative operations terminated by the presence of all those security forces, not to mention occupying the very thugs who might otherwise have been looking into the issue of who'd defiled and murdered one of their sex workers.'

He looks about, nods. 'Of course, Gina being so hands on enabled me to influence so many other things. It was really all too easy, accessing the files, ensuring that it was the Force's investigative fuck-ups who were put in charge of scrutinising my ventures. Persuading Hyland to have Musgrove assigned to Gill's death, and you yourself so helpfully assigning Demetriou to the Wrigley enquiry and saving me having to expose myself further. Fisher, Demetriou, and Musgrove. I mean, no matter what they found, who'd take them seriously?'

'Broken Wings,' Crosby murmurs, calf muscles twitching.

'Apt really. Though I have to admit to underestimating their determination. Strong almost got away because of that. After John Gill's fall, seems he'd worked most of it out, at least the link. He was going to tell you what he'd discovered, him stumbling across my trip to the *Post's* cuttings room, him knowing your head was so far up the arse of the *Spooks* and the Chief Constable and Commissioner you'd have never worked it out for yourself.'

'He saved me,' Crosby moans.

'I wondered about that. Once I read the reports - how you'd used the chimney flue - I realised I'd missed something. Not that it mattered. I figured you'd scrambled over him.' He shakes his head. 'From what you say it appears Jacob found a touch of nobility at the end.'

'He knew I wasn't to blame for your mother's murder. That it ended with him.' Crosby feels his legs stiffening, muscles straining at being held in the same position. He's got to keep him talking. The eternal hope of another miracle rescue, maybe a chance to get through to him. 'You're Brightside's heir.'

'I never had the chance to meet her,' he replies, thoughts drifting, held like the motes of dust in the light through the gaps in the heavy drapes. 'Once my nose and cheekbones were fixed I started a new life. I became terribly successful, public relations. My mother's story telling is clearly something she passed on to me.'

He shakes his head. Biology.

'After a few years, my newfound success purchased the skills of Dark Web hackers more than capable of discovering the secrets that men like Webb, Wrigley, Strong, and Gill want kept hidden from the world. I knew they'd never be punished. Not properly punished. Men like that, men with money and influence never are. I knew that I had to be the one to punish them, punishments fitting their crimes. I bided my time - watching, waiting. Finally re-locating up here, poor Gina so desperate to have me on board to resurrect her failing campaign that she skipped so many of the usual checks, not that they'd find anything, I've the best identity money can buy.'

He holds his arms out, palms upturned as if carrying an unseen tray. 'And now we have the finale. A happy ever after.'

'What are you going to do?' Crosby finally asks.

Lawrence shakes his head. 'I'm going to do nothing, let nature take control. The natural laws of physics offering the natural law of justice. Your muscles versus gravity.' He pauses. 'But there has to be a rhyme, otherwise it's not complete. For you I've chosen *The Bells of St Clements*. I assume you know it? *When will you pay me? Asks the Bells of Old Bailey*. Did you know it's a reference to Tyburn, to the gibbet that once stood within earshot of the bells, the place where the law courts now are? It was a moral tale, one that reminded children that they hang debtors. And you, Superintendent, have a debt to pay. The man supposed to offer justice, supposed to punish the guilty. Instead, you've forced me to do that for you. It's you who is to blame, forcing me to end Wrigley, Gill, Webb, and Strong. Sofia too. That is your debt, Superintendent, payment now due.'

He walks out of Crosby's line of sight. 'It shouldn't take long for them to work out where you are, but of course by the time they get here all they'll find is your dangling corpse. I myself will be long gone, maybe sat on a beach somewhere reading your story in *the Post*, though not the one you'd imagined. Certainly not once the files I've lain around the room have been read and understood. Files documenting your complicity in extortion and murder. *Overwhelmed*, is how they'll describe it. Full of guilt at all you'd done, you found yourself unable to live with the consequences of murdering those you blamed for your disgrace. Your corruption eating away at you. Having punished them, well, you were left with only one outcome.'

He steps back, wrapping a scarf around his neck, raincoat draped over an arm. 'Farewell, Detective Chief Superintendent. Or, as my mother always ended her stories, *Good night and sleep tight!*'

49

'What do you mean, they're not to be found?'

Iverson feels another touch of *Deja-vu* coming on. Wondering could you have double *Deja-vu*? Having *Deja-vu* about having *Deja-vu*? A bit like wearing double denim. 'Well, sir...I suppose what I mean is...well, the thing is, I can't find them. Any of them. Well, none of them I suppose is what I meant...mean, I mean.' Feeling a recap is required, he wanders back the way he'd come along the winding path of his response to Hyland's initial enquiry. 'DI Fisher and ACC Musgrove aren't here,' he summarises. 'They've left the building.'

'Who do you think they are? Fucking Elvis?'

Iverson shrugs. Wonders why everyone's so keen on this Elvis bloke. A shrug is the best he can manage right now, his lifetime of carefully compiled non-committal words and phrases having seemingly deserted him, fleeing like pheasants in a field in front of Hyland's combine harvester of ire.

'Someone must know where they are,' Hyland fumes, slamming the fleshy side of a fist against the corridor wall.

Iverson can't fault the logic. At the very least both Fisher and Musgrove would know for certain. He stares at the floor for a moment, like respite care. On looking up he finds himself still confronted with Hyland's glare, the demand of a fuller response. He opts for yet another shrug, thinking that at the very least it offers the idea that he's trying to comply with a senior officer's expectations.

'Do you have some sort of twitch or something, Detective Sergeant?' Hyland asks, watching the tremors undulating wave-like across Iverson's shoulders.

'No sir. I'm fit as a fiddle.'

'In that case, I suggest you use that fitness to bugger off and find someone who does have the faintest of ideas where my ACC and one of my senior Inspectors have got to. Find out why the hell they're buggering about the building when they're both suspended. They can't have vanished. Musgrove for one would find that particular trick difficult to pull off given his BMI issues.'

'Sir,' Iverson responds, before hightailing down the corridor, tripping over a roll of dust sheets and almost tipping a decorator's step ladder over in his rush to get away.

'Shit!' Hyland breathes watching Iverson's impression of a lobotomised mime artist, all waving arms and twisting of torso and legs. He's certain the reason Musgrove and Fisher can't be found is because they don't want to be. That they've gone '*off the reservation*' as one of his unreformed Reform Party supporting brother masons would have it. They were up to something, something flying in the face of his directions to them, something creating waves of hostile PR of the shit-stirring-career-threatening kind. Whilst it might offer the satisfaction of helping put the final nail or two in Commissioner Gina *buggering* Hargreaves' election coffin, he knows such things bring collateral damage of the buggering-up-the-Chief-Constable's-career kind. He's determined not to let that happen, not when he's closer than ever to retirement. A retirement where thanks to all that's happened - the gratitude of Number Ten in keeping everything *sotto voce* re the bumbling mis-steps of security services and political advisors - he's on the promise of a knighthood, regular appearances on *Newsnight* as the BBC's go to observer of all things police and crime related dangled as an added bonus. And despite all her bleeding-heart BBC liberal leanings, he loves Kirsty Wark.

So right now, he needs to find his command's very own Laurel and Hardy and fix them on a tight leash. If it should strangle them in the process...well accidents happen.

'Christ, Neil! Can't you go a bit faster? You know, put your foot down. You drive slower than my grannie, and all she's got is a Zimmer frame.' Fisher says staring out of the rain-smeared windscreen, frustrated and anxious. 'Mind you, she did once customise it with go-faster stripes. Didn't make her any faster, but it did offer the illusion she was whooshing by, especially if you squinted out of the corner of one eye as she shuffled past.'

Musgrove bites his tongue. The thought of Fisher having a grannie is somehow shocking. Admittedly, he's little idea of her family background beyond the myths and legends, the rumours picked up along with the stuff he'd read in her file. Bits and pieces, aftermaths of overheard conversations and tittle tattle, the stories of her father. Musgrove once saying he'd liked to have worked with her dad had been met with a stare as cold and shadowed as her patented *Ice Queen* label. He's not sure what's going on there, but once again he has the sense that there's definitely something, a stone waiting to be turned.

'Maybe we should have taken a pool car,' she offers, biting her bottom lip, mouth tightening in frustration. 'You know, one with bells and sirens and flashing lights. The good stuff.'

'No this is better,' he replies, eyes fixed on the road, hands gripping the wheel, the tension in the upper arms pulling his torso upright, and his head close to the windscreen. 'Remember this is off the books. We're suspended, access to the building only to pick up personal items. No way we hijack a pool car without having to explain why we need it.'

Fisher jabs a finger in the direction of a tractor lumbering ahead of them, its trailer piled with teetering bales of hay, shrink-wrapped rolls that sway at every bump and pothole, of which there are many. 'Maybe you should try a bit of Pemberton's visualisation. Manifest us getting there. See yourself as Lewis Hamilton or whoever. At the very least get past this daft bugger!' She leans to the side, head craning to see across the turns in the road. 'Go on! You're clear!' she urges.

Musgrove looks from road to Fisher and back again. Gripping the steering wheel ever tighter, he accelerates hard, swinging the car out into the other lane. Swerving just as hurriedly back as a milk tanker hurtles towards them in the opposite lane, air-horn blaring 'For Christs sake, Fisher! Are you trying to get us killed?' he shouts as the tanker thunders past.

She turns to the rear window to watch it hurtle by. 'Sorry about that. Blind spot.' She cranes her head to the side again, eyes scoping out the bends, hands lain on the dashboard. 'And what I'm doing is trying to get us to Brightside's place before our serial killer PR guru does the job of getting rid of Crosby for us. Admittedly, on the *no bad thing in itself scale* of things it presents as a win-win, but not terribly lawful or moral - which in itself has issues, us being the police and all that. I'm also thinking we really ought to get there before we grow too bloody old to do anything about it,' thinking she can't quite visualise Musgrove skidding to a halt and sliding over the bonnet Starsky and Hutch style. 'Can you not go faster?' she appeals.

'I'd rather get there in one piece than end up splattered across the Dales like those bloody pheasants back there. These roads aren't built for harebrained driving, no matter what those bloody bikers seem to think each weekend.' He risks taking a hand off the wheel to wave in front of him. 'I once met a tank coming the other way down one of these. An actual *tank*. Just outside of Catterick it was. Damn near put me in a ditch. All the squaddies did was laugh!'

'Strikes me we'd be quicker in a tank,' she murmurs to the passenger window.

'Trust me, Fisher. *Softly Softly catches monkey.*'

She turns to him. 'Bloody hell, Neil. You really are straight out of the bloody ark, aren't you? Who says stuff like that anymore? And what the hell does it mean anyway? I'm pretty sure it's offensive. Most likely racist. Certainly sufficient enough to get you cancelled - that is if you weren't already after all that stuff at the water park.'

'It's not racist. I even changed the *catch-ee* to *catches*. You know, took out the Pidgeon English. I did Hargreaves' course. You know, *PC Pc's – A New Model Force For A New Century.*'

'Which one was that? The Nineteenth?' she snorts. 'Maybe just focus on the driving, eh?' She twitches, shuffling in her seat, watching the dry-stone walls pass ever more slowly by. 'Maybe I should drive?' she suggests.

'You're not insured,' he snaps.

She folds her arms, shaking her head. 'At this rate by the time we get there yours'll be up for renewal.'

'I'll get us there,' Musgrove insists. Ahead of them, the tractor brakes for no apparent reason before stuttering forward. 'Eventually,' he concedes.

Unfolding her arms, she waves a hand in the air, gesturing at the windscreen. 'Neil, of that I have no doubt. You drive like a textbook, a living Highway Code! My point is that like comedy, it's all in the timing. And right now, yours is about as far off as bloody Micheal McIntyre. We're running on empty here.' She slaps the dashboard as the tractor brakes again. 'And this bloody wanker's not helping!' she cries, at the same time slamming herself against the back of her seat. 'Lawrence or whoever he is has likely done the deed and is half-way to wherever it is he's planning to spend the rest of his life. A life where he'll be calling himself something other than Harvey Lawrence.'

'You're sure it's him? That he's our killer?' Musgrove asks ignoring the vitriol.

'Who else? You're the wannabe Agatha Christie.'

If his shoulders weren't so tense, he would have shrugged. If his eyes weren't so focused on the tractor in front he'd have been unable to contain the urge to put Fisher straight. He's a Spillane man. Chandler. Pelecanos even. Christie's a different beast altogether. A little too prim for his tastes, too English Country House and cucumber sandwiches. Murder and cream tea just aren't his thing. He likes his fictional crime bloody and raw, along with raven haired *femme-fatales*, a little jazz and neon lighting thrown in for good measure. Maybe a trench coat or two. A ceiling fan and slatted blinds. Despite that, he ventures down the path she's lain out for him. 'Well, if we assume it's not the butler who did it, then yes, it points to Lawrence. The mystery man. Roger Ackroyd. The unreliable narrator. The man no-one knew existed - the man who was never there. He mentally notes the phrase as a future title. *'The Man Who Wasn't There'*. A bit clunky, but a promising starting point. All he'd need is a plot.

Fisher speaks to the wing mirror, pulling Musgrove from his musing. 'Of course, we also have to ask the question: *why now, not then*? If that sealed record was available to him after the death of his adoptive parents, he'd have most likely sought out Wrigley, the estate's lawyer years ago.' Staring in the cobweb draped glass of the wing mirror, she thinks about it. A young man approaching established figures of business. She considers her own experience, a teenager, thirteen, sifting through her father's affairs for a mother grief deep in a bottle. The things she'd instinctively known had to be kept hidden, the legal tripwires she'd had to negotiate, the secrets and lies, the sidestepping of insurance brokers and pension funds anxious to escape liability. Guilt and attached itself to everything of his she'd touched. *Rain wet cobblestones...cold whisper of a Millennium wind...The creaking of an old stable door...the sound of sobbing...the smell of fresh blood.*

'What if he did?' Musgrove suggests. 'What if they fobbed him off. Tricked him. Threatened him.'

She thinks of Sofia Kovalenko, of shady Bulgarians and muscle for hire. Her mind fixes on motives for Lawrence exacting a young woman's death. *Sending a message? But who to?* She had to be something more.

'They couldn't have recognised him when he appeared as Lawrence, could they?' Musgrove asks of himself, taking up his own unanswered musing. 'None of them made the connection. And that's odd in itself, knowing what a small social and political world it is round here. They must have crossed paths - and Lawrence is hardly a retiring soul! I'm just amazed none of them were asking questions once they'd all started dying.'

'Sofia's murder would have gone under their radar,' she offers. 'As far was we can tell, there's no obvious connection to any of them, so there'd have been no alarm bells at her death. Archibald Gill died of natural causes. Townley retired years ago and had disappeared weeks before any of the murders. In any case, his role was peripheral, so maybe he wouldn't have been a consideration. Wrigley was a melancholy drunk who everyone accepted had topped himself during a downward spiral. The PM's involvement meant Webb's murder was linked to terrorists. When John Gill fell off Malham...Well, yes, maybe they'd have woken up to what was happening. But by then there was just Strong and Crosby left, men who more than likely - just as we did - suspected each other. And as of now only Crosby can tell us what happened when they met - maybe it was to check each other out, or maybe they'd realised what was happening, who was to blame.'

'But it wouldn't explain why Crosby would meet Lawrence now, unless he's got a death wish, thinks he can bring him in by himself. You know, cement himself as the hero,' Musgrove suggests.

Fisher chews her bottom lip. 'Maybe he doesn't know there's an heir. He wasn't part of the original group, so maybe they didn't tell him. Maybe there just wasn't time for Strong to warn him.'

Musgrove exhales. 'It's all maybes again, speculation.'

'Which is why we have to get a bloody move on. Get to *Grey Goose* before a particular goose is cooked.'

Ahead of them, the tractor signals a right turn and trundles through a farm gate. The road ahead, as much as a Dales route can, opens up. Musgrove pushes hard on the accelerator.

'Can't help but wonder,' Musgrove says, eyes on the road.

'Wonder what?'

'What nursery rhyme he's got in store for Crosby.'

50

The house is in darkness, Crosby's car sat on the driveway. Musgrove brings his own car to a halt on a gravelled parking area at the front of the house, Fisher leaping out before the engine has died, passenger door left open. 'Hoi!' Musgrove calls. 'At least wait till I've stopped. Maybe got the handbrake on.'

'No time,' Fisher says, stopping, turning, leaning head and shoulders back inside. 'We have to get in there!'

Musgrove reaches a staying hand in her direction. 'We should at least have a plan, don't you think?'

'Save Crosby – though it goes against my personal instincts – and catch the bad guy, Lawrence. Then you phone for back-up and we go home heroes.'

'No signal,' Musgrove informs her, tapping a finger against the display screen of the car's digital console.

'Surprise! What else is new?'

'We can't just go barging in,' Musgrove argues, levering himself out of the car. Standing, he looks across the vehicle's roof to the impatient Fisher who stands waiting despite the downpour. Seeing the expression fixed across her face, he experiences a mounting sense of alarm. 'There's protocol. We might contaminate the scene. Might create issues for a prosecution. Not to mention the fact that we don't know who's in there, or if they're armed.'

Fisher meets him at the bonnet, raindrops running down her forehead. 'Well, the paperwork sorts itself once we've established there's a crime occurring. And given his track record, I don't see Lawrence as the man for a shoot-out. But knowing what happened to Pan, I take your point. There might be traps.'

Musgrove nods. 'Anyone in there's going to have heard us arrive,' he says suddenly crouching down low.

'What are you doing?' she asks, bending to speak to him, turning her collar up against the increasing rain that the wind is whipping around them.

'If Lawrence is in there,' he whispers, 'then maybe if he looks out and can't see anyone he'll think there's more of us. That we've surrounded the building. He'll come out to give himself up and we grab him before he's had a chance to realise it's just us two.'

'Brilliant!' She says. 'Maybe we should start shouting out in different voices, make him think there's loads of us. You could do your Irish accent, your Frank Carson you did at the Crimewatchers Charity Ball last Christmas - but for God's sake keep off your Lenny Henry or he'll be the one arresting us.'

'Can you not stop being so sarcastic even for a minute?' he snarls.

'Can you not come up with a decent plan?' she asks, wide-eyed.

'Okay, in that case, what's your big idea?' he demands

She picks up a piece of crumbled stonework from the weed strewn flower-bed, pushing it towards him. Involuntarily he reaches out a hand to take it. It's wet, slimy. 'When you hear me shout "*now*", throw that in there,' she instructs, pointing to the French windows that sit to one side of the portico entrance. 'Should suffice as a distraction long enough for me to get in and grab him.'

'That's it? That's your cunning plan?'

'Unless you have a better one. I never said it was cunning. Just workable.'

Musgrove weighs the stone in his hand. He looks to Fisher. 'I'm not sure.'

Fisher exhales. 'Neil, face it, you never are. It's what makes you a nice bloke, a good neighbour and husband and all that. I'm sure your wife loves you for it. That you're never loud or demanding of your own infallibility. I'll bet you're the toast of the neighbourhood watch, lending your lawnmower to all and sundry.' She points at the house. 'But if we're right, a man is about to die in there. There's no time for being sure or second-guessing ourselves. We have to act. Do something.'

Maybe it was Fisher's reference to his wife. His neighbours. His attitude to life. The years of being the nice bloke. The years of being passed over. The lawnmower loaned to a neighbour at the end of the cutting season and still not returned. Whatever the cause, she would later swear that at this precise moment she heard something snap. Maybe it was the sound of the weeks of Pemberton's good work on self-control and counting to ten breaking, the weeks of deep breathing and serenity that could be heard running screaming from the building that held the last of his good sense. 'Sod it!' he shouts, standing upright and heaving the lump of stonework as hard as he can at the French windows. The glass shatters on impact, a large hole appearing in its person sized pane.

Fisher stares, stupefied. 'You were supposed to wait for me to be ready at the front door!' she yells. 'And you were supposed to create a distraction, not re-model your own *Grand Designs* entrance.'

'Bugger it!' Musgrove shouts, swallowing hard before charging as fast as he can after the stone, forcing open the now shattered frame of the doors and disappearing inside.

Fisher stands for a beat contemplating her plan of using the main door. In the end she merely shrugs before following him through the wreckage of the garden doors with its now

Musgrove shaped gap and plunging into the darkness of the room.

'He's choked to death.'

Fisher stoops, placing a hand to the side of Crosby's neck checking for a pulse. The fact that to do so she has to push her fingers under a tight coil of thick nylon rope isn't the most promising of starts.

'Looks like the rope was tied off to one of those old iron wall lights,' Musgrove says stepping over the vague circle of plaster and bits of ceiling scattered around the prostrate DCS. Leaving Fisher to her medical explorations, he goes to the far wall, poking a finger into the exposed lath and plaster. 'Yeah, definitely that,' he confirms over his shoulder. He turns, looks at the shattered ceiling above where Fisher works at Crosby. 'Looks as if the whole section around the central light fixing came away. Shoddy work, really,' he judges, cowboy builder complete with sharp intake of breath.

Fisher, gaining a little leeway under the noose, presses her fingers firmly into the flesh of Crosby's neck, uncertain whether Musgrove's comment of 'shoddy work' is directed towards the plasterer's workmanship or Lawrence's efforts at killing Crosby.

'I've got a pulse!' she calls out.

Musgrove halts his *DIY S-O-S* analysis and crosses to the kneeling DI. 'Are you certain?' he asks crouching next to her.

'Well, I'm no doctor, but there's something. Weak but definitely something.' She begins loosening the line and working at the knot. 'And by *"weak but definitely something"* I mean his pulse, though I agree it could equally be his Tinder profile. Can you get a signal?' she asks.

Musgrove takes out his phone and stares at the screen. After a moment of waving it around as if performing a mystical incantation, the sense of some pagan 5G devil being summoned. He shakes his head. 'Nothing.'

'Of course, if we'd brought a pool car we'd have a radio,' she snarls.

'Nothing for it,' he judges ignoring the rebuke. 'We'll get him to hospital ourselves.' He starts getting up, groaning at the effort. 'I'll get the car.'

'Jesus Christ! In that case you'd better let me drive. Your speed's more like the hearse he'll be needing if you drive.' The rope now loosened, she feels Crosby's neck once more. 'His pulse is stronger. Now the rope's off his airways are clear, but I don't know about lasting damage, depends how long he was dangling before the ceiling fell in. His brain's most likely been starved of oxygen and his heart's taken punishment. His lungs could collapse.' Medical dictionary exhausted, 'We need to get help as soon as possible,' she concludes.

Musgrove passes her his keys. 'Fine,' he relents. 'You drive. Just don't hit anything. My insurance broker would have a heart attack if he knew.'

Fisher taking the keys, nods. 'We'd better see if we can lift him first,' she says, shifting position to get her hands under Crosby's shoulders. As she moves, she notes the position of the rope burn, the bruising blooming around the throat. 'It was meant to strangle rather than go for a quick neck break. Nasty stuff,' she comments. 'Same sort of botched job that decapitated old Saddam. End up with a neck like Naomi Campbell.'

Pushing aside the shards of plaster, Musgrove moves to Crosby's legs. He pauses, nodding towards the nearest wall. 'Look at the design of the plaster.'

She turns, following his gaze. 'This is really no time for a refurbishment lesson, Neil.'

'Look at the motif on the dado rail. It's newer than the rest.'

Fisher screws her eyes, concentrates on where the light floods in through the broken French window and laps against the wall. 'Fruit,' she says.

'Not just fruit. Oranges and lemons.'

'So?'

'*Oranges and Lemons. The Bells of St Clements.*'

'The nursery rhyme?'

'Not just any old rhyme,' he says. 'Remember?' he asks before chanting:

> "*Oranges and lemons*
> *Say the bells of St. Clements*
> *I owe you five farthings*
> *Say the bells of St. Martins*
> *When will you pay me?*
> *Say the bells at Old Bailey*"

'Get it?' he asks.

'So that's the connection to Crosby,' Fisher says.

'The bells of the Old Bailey is where Tyburn stood. ' Musgrove states. 'The bells were rung whenever a prisoner was taken to the gallows.'

Fisher eases her grip on Crosby's shoulders. The recumbent DCS sagging in the middle like an old hammock. 'So it fits,' she says. 'You were right. The rhymes.'

Musgrove nods. 'A murder made to look like suicide.'

Fisher looks around, one foot shifting the pages from the files scattered across the floor. Lowering Crosby's shoulders, she picks one up. 'These files. They're from the original investigation into Gillian Brightside's death.' She picks up more of the pages. 'And there's newspaper clippings. This one's a photo of Webb, Gill, Wrigley, and Strong. Looks like a party or something.'

Musgrove lays down Crosby's legs, instead picking up a handful of the papers. 'Makes it look like Crosby tried to kill himself. The shame of things coming out. All this evidence makes it clear he was part of it. That he knew all along what they'd done.'

'No way Hyland gets to ignore this,' she declares. 'It's a

storm of evidence and all of it incriminating. With Crosby here still alive, they'll prosecute. Have to. It'll be public, which means we're off the hook, old jobs back and Demetriou a bloody hero. Bye bye Broken Wings.'

'Hmmm,' Musgrove murmurs. 'At least it shows you've got your investigating chops back. Your stubborn-assed desire for the truth.'

'I'll ignore that passive aggressive excuse of a compliment. And cheer up, Neil! Any investigating officer worth his stripes sees this for what it is. A conspiracy. A series of murders. I mean, they'd have to be an idiot or corrupt themselves to miss this. You'll see, this time next week we won't just be back at our old desks, they'll be shiny new ones!'

Musgrove grunts. 'As long as it's someone else picking the carpets and colour scheme, I don't bloody care!'

51

'There's no other way to say it, is there?'

'Not really. No.'

Fisher scuffs a tuft of coarse grass, watches the dark brown of her boot turn black with disturbed moisture. Welcome to late autumn in North Yorkshire, she thinks. Only just October yet frost already smears the top of Swaledale with a shimmering white paste. 'Are you sure there's nothing can be done?' she asks.

Musgrove shakes his head before turning towards Wensleydale and the haunch of Pen Hill. He'd asked the same question many times himself since his meeting earlier that day with Hyland, a meeting overseen by the brooding presence of Commissioner Gina-*bloody*-Hargreaves. He'd expected Hyland to be annoyed, irate even, but he just as certain he could ride it out. Whatever their transgressions, they'd rescued Crosby from becoming the sixth victim of a serial killer, uncovered the corrupt DCS's involvement in fraud and murder, and in doing so solved five other deaths, not to mention Demetriou's near death.

Of course, even whilst driving Crosby to hospital Musgrove had sensed it was an operation whose success would never be triumphed. It was a secret win, a victory veiled through fear of attracting unwanted media scrutiny of the deeper issues - the linked intelligence operation that had burned through millions of tax-payer pounds, upset tens of thousands of voters, and angered every ethnic community. Not to mention the issues of corruption and of masonic fingers found being dipped in so many pies.

Yet it remained a triumph, no matter that Hyland saw it as originating from their disobeying of his own direct order. Yes, they'd disobeyed, but in what way was that an issue in the light of the result? And what might a disciplinary panel make of a case brought in such circumstances? Not to mention the afore cited media, should they get wind of it.

He understood that news of a second rescue of Crosby would, unlike the first, not be one paraded across the pages of *the Post* or feature as a segment on *Look North*. But everyone involved knew it for what it was: the triumph of good policing over bureaucracy, of instinct and street smarts over strait-jacketed thinking. It would keep them in their jobs. More than that, it was a shoo-in understanding of Musgrove's that it would herald a return to front-line command, books of carpet samples and colour charts banished to his past.

But then Hargreaves had stepped in bearing gifts from Badgerman and Number Ten. The price to be paid for their transgressions.

That the public could know nothing of what had gone on was a given. There were elections, Hargreaves running for the newly created Regional Mayorship and a general election in which a beleaguered PM needed news of the criminal conspiracy of one of his oldest benefactors like he needed yet more of the Blonde Fat Boy's public-school chums crawling out of the woodwork parading details of their own tawdry goings on.

And there would be no backing down on claims of terrorist links to Webb's death. *"For fuck's sake there's talk of a fucking statue of him!"* Hargreaves had announced at one point. *"Those mad dog rabid nationalists on the PM's right are insistent on pressing for one. If the PM opposes the idea there'll be questions. Questions impossible for him to answer. If he agrees to it and later this serial killer stuff gets out, well, he's screwed that way too. Right now, the Cabinet's got a big fat 'D' notice slapped on everything. Sealed for fifty years. By which point no-one's even going to remember who the little toe-rag was."*

For a moment Musgrove had wondered whether the *toe-rag* in question was the PM or Webb, a thought cut short by the realisation she was steering towards other shores, shores where he, Fisher, and Doyle were about to be washed up. Literally.

'So nothing gets out. Crosby's taken care of,' she'd stated, folding her arms in the universal sign of matters concluded. 'He's fully on board, enthusiastic even - not that he's much choice in the matter,' she'd counselled.

Crosby was absent from duties on medical grounds. Grounds keeping him that way for some time. There was to be no arrest. No charges. No prosecution. The idea that at the time of the conspiracy he'd been a naïve dupe was the political and legal line. There was talk of a move sideways, something less exposing to scrutiny of the man's professional and personal life. Some years down the line there'd be quite a push out of a side-door, a giant *'We'll all Miss You'* card in one hand and padded pension in the other. It was an arrangement ensuring his silence, enforced by the threat of the Public Prosecutor's office ever deciding to pursue post-dated charges of corruption and the obstruction of justice. He was getting off lightly, though Musgrove wondered whether Crosby's side shuffle put him in line to pick up his own soon to be discarded mantle of refurbishment. Not something he'd wish on anybody.

'There are other matters, too - loose ends,' Hargreaves had continued.

'Loose ends?'

'Yourself and Fisher.'

'We're loose ends?'

She'd nodded. 'We can't just let you all back in as if nothing's happened.'

'But a lot has happened. We've solved five murders. Saved a man's life.'

'And each involving things we can't disclose,' she'd sighed. She'd much to teach men like Musgrove about the ways of a world they seemingly drifted through. 'The Chief Constable and I conclude it best that although we'll lift your suspensions, all four of you must continue to meet with Pemberton. What is it they call you?'

'Broken wings,' Musgrove had said dully.

'Yes!' she'd smiled as she'd contemplated the name. 'Broken wings. Exactly that. You must see that it's far too awkward for you to suddenly return to duty, cured so to speak. There'd be questions. Explanations wanted. Good as Pemberton might be - and there's so very much conjecture as to that – he's no miracle worker, his therapy getting all of you sorted for duty in a matter of a few weeks…It's out of the question. If you want to stay in the force, then the arrangement remains as before - and it goes without saying that you must all agree to this.'

'So nothing changes? I'm still refurbishment. Fisher's still under suspicion. Doyle's still tainted.'

Hyland had shaken his head. 'Not everything remains the same. That would be ridiculous. We've had to change details of some recent operations. Although we're not prosecuting Crosby there's no way we're letting the little bastard be the hero of that explosion at the Station House. As far the media are concerned, DS Demetriou is the hero there. Demetriou rescued Crosby, not the other way round.'

'But that's what happened,' Musgrove had interjected. 'Demetriou rescued Crosby.'

'Glad you're on board with it,' Hyland had responded with a conspiratorial wink.

'But I've always…' he'd shook his head. 'Fisher's already said …' He'd let it drop. If ends and means were to be the order of the meeting, then at least they'd got one bit right. Demetriou was a hero.

'Damn right!' Fisher had affirmed when they'd met in the cafe in Muker. 'It's at least a start on putting things right,' she'd agreed.

They'd talked in hushed tones at a small bay window table, the last of the autumn tourists shuffling in and out, dropping backpacks to the floor, exhausted voices ordering the cheese scones and Swaledale Welsh rarebits that were house specialties.

Afterwards, they'd walked up the hill out of the village, crossing the wildflower meadow that blossoms each spring and walked along the bank of the Swale. Cresting the rise, each found they were a long way from Kansas.

Fisher turns to Musgrove. 'I've the feeling there's stuff you're not telling us,' she says. Musgrove shrugs. Nods. Shuffles. The silence is awkward, pooling, finding its way into whatever it is they've managed to construct between themselves in the way of friendship, comradeship, - at the very least a truce.

'It's more the fact that there's nothing else,' he says.

'But what about Lawrence? Finding him. Going after him or whoever he's turned himself into?' she asks.

Musgrove shrugs. 'Not going to happen.'

'What?' Fisher's tone reaches towards incredulity. It's a steep climb, higher than she's scaled before, but she makes it with a little room to spare. 'They can't!' she splutters.

'Can and have,' Musgrove says turning to look at the ominous clouds brooding over the tops of Swaledale, clouds sliding their way towards the deep drop of Buttertubs to the west. Clouds that hover over the back of Fisher's head like a monk's cowl.

'Why?' she asks.

Musgrove shakes his head. 'Expediency. Arse covering. Call it what you will. Nothing's to be done.'

'He gets away?'

'Of sorts. I mean, if you think of it, in one way he's rid the world of some very despicable people.'

'And that way would be what, the Old Testament Way? Eye

for an Eye? Or maybe it's the Sharia Law way, you know, chopping off the hands of thieves. Gouging out eyes. It's what Trump thinks we've become,' she asks.

Musgrove snorts. 'It's a sort of justice,' he ventures.

'Neil, he killed people. Murdered them in cold blood. Decapitated Webb, threatened Wrigley knowing he'd jump off a roof, chucked Gill off a cliff, blew up Strong and we've still no idea what's become of Townley. Not to mention trying to hang Crosby and putting Demetriou in the hospital. I mean, Pan's in for months of recovery, not to mention leaving me without a decent DS,' she adds.

He shrugs. 'What can I say?'

'Bad people or not, I hadn't realised we condoned vigilantism, not even up here in wild North Yorkshire,' she says, waving an arm, encompassing the hills.

'It's the cost of pursuing him. It's deemed too high,' he judges.

Fisher shakes her head, eyes looking to the distant slope of the Dales. 'You mean that the PM and Number Ten think the price they'd personally have to pay in the way of reputation and credibility is too high. Their cosy world of cronies and kickbacks.'

'Maybe,' he shrugs. 'Definitely. There's to be a press release. Hargreaves is putting one out stating that Lawrence left his post for personal reasons. Pressure of work, whatever. Seems he's listed as travelling abroad. *Camino de Santiago* or whatever. She'll say it's it's always been his ambition. Him being a spiritual being.'

'And the murders?'

'They officially go down as the Force has always pegged them. Two suicides. An unclaimed act of terrorism. A missing person and a dreadful accident at the old Police House.'

She turns to face him. 'And Sofia? What about her? How does her death fit into this shoddy little narrative of Hargreaves and Hyland's? What's the PM and Number Ten line on that?'

Musgrove looks her in her eyes. He thinks it's the least he can do. 'She was an illegal. We know that. A victim of gang life. Trafficked. They'll say he took her own life rather than face what she'd become. What they'd made her.'

Fisher turns once more to the distant line of the Dales, lifting her head to the skyline that sits above the hunched landscape. The sun is setting, dropping towards darkness. She scans the shadowed incline of fields and paddocks and trees, realising the barn where it began is but yards from where she stands. She wonders about Lawrence, the man who boasted he could make her *more famous than Joan of fucking Arc*. The man who'd stood in the churned mud of the barn that night whilst Sofia hung from its blackened rafters a few feet from him, rafters he'd only hours before strung her from with the rope of human hair he'd created. Her rainbow's end. No bluebirds and lemon drops. None of the dreams of the life she'd thought was waiting her in the Dales.

She wonders about dreams and hopes. Demetriou's hope of reconciliation with his ex-partner; Doyle's hope of an act worthy of redeeming her poor choices; Musgrove's search for purpose; her own search for closure with her father. Guilt. Atonement. All he'd done. All she herself had done.

She wonders what Musgrove might write about it all. In so many ways it's the story he's looking for. Truth disguised in a fiction, a fiction hiding in plain sight, a fiction that will be made a truth. Fake news.

She turns. 'Neil,' she begins. 'This idea for a novel of yours. How about you work on the ending. Get it finished and maybe get it out there. I mean, there's nothing that says you can't write a novel. Maybe even one *"based on actual events".*'

'You're mad, DI Fisher, do you know that?' he says, smiling, the red mist building since that morning's meeting wafting away.

'I'm not mad, I'm mad as hell,' she tells him.

He nods. 'Maybe I'll call it Broken Wings.'

ACKNOWLEDGMENTS

Rebecca Millar, my fabulous editor with whom I look forward to working with on many more books to come.

To Cat Yaffe - a wonderful crime writer and the inspiration for my taking the 'Indie' path and re-igniting my writing passions.

To my Beta readers:

Jo Pardoe: Derek Rainsford; Howard Parr; Huw Morgan; Nick Rainsford; Andreea Piciu; Al Pardoe; Isla Straupmanis; Vicki Allison; Jan Croft; Ian Whitehouse.

To my ARC team and to all those on my mailing list who find not only the time and interest to open them each month but to offer the feedback that sustains me on my writing journey.

To Stefan and the team at Spiffing for the amazing cover art and the digital design of my website and promotional material.

June at Tennants Auction Rooms for believing in the need for a local Dales crime festival and helping launch *Blood in t' Dales* up here each June.

ABOUT THE AUTHOR

What critics say about Barry N Rainsford's writing:

"…A master-class in storytelling…"

"… the very definition of a page-turner…"

"…A stonkingly brilliant read…"

"…Clever, unsettling, and brilliantly done…"

"…irresistibly gripping—his sharp hooks, atmospheric settings, and believable characters keep you utterly invested…"

"…impossible to put down…"

"…as good as some other books I've read…"

KEEPERS OF SOULS:
BROKEN WINGS BOOK 2

If you enjoyed Broken Wings, the next book in this North Yorkshire crime thriller series may be of interest:

"With a politically sensitive NATO conference occurring in the North Yorkshire region, the last thing Chief Constable Hyland and Commissioner Gina Hargreaves need is for the anger management therapy group dubbed the Broken Wings to wreak the kind of mayhem experienced a few weeks previously.

The discovery of the long buried body of a young woman missing for almost twenty five years appears a sufficiently harmless enough distraction to occupy the social and professional hand-grenade that is DI Zara Fisher. But as those linked to this cold case begin dying, Fisher once again draws upon the wayward skills of her outcast therapy group to find out why. Their investigation soon connects to the NATO meeting, and through it to powerful figures in the military and intelligence communities, men with a great deal to lose and who are prepared to kill to protect both themselves and their secrets."

ONE

Harrogate, North Yorkshire Millennium Eve

It's cold. Only a few minutes into the year and it's already deep January cold, knife-sharp westerlies, and freezing rain. North Yorkshire cold, bitter and chill. Winds that sweep between narrowed buildings, unreliable pavements, slick and shiny with night-time frost that by morning will be white paste. She's starting to think she should have stayed at the stop, waited for the last bus. Maybe taken the taxi and bugger the expense.

But she hasn't. Impatient like her father and stubborn like her mother, Naomi reflects, if she is honest with herself, a New Year resolution she's already teetering on the edge of breaking. And there's the fact that money is tight. Despite the promises made in October, Christmas has drained her accounts, more than that, her credit card is maxed out. Spending more than she has is her norm, spending more than she can afford, less so. But she's done just that. Another case of her being driven by whims and rash decisions – like tonight, her spur of the moment decision of not waiting for the bus. Walking home.

It means January will be Tupperware left-overs, lunch on a bench. Baked potatoes, beans and cheese for dinner with the

ONE

thermostat turned down, much to Marcia, her flatmate's complaining. It isn't Marcia's way to go overboard with fancy gifts or new party-wear leaving her unable to pay her share of the bills. No, it's Millennium Eve and Marcia's sat at home on the couch, shoulders wrapped in a duvet, satisfied at having lectured Naomi on just such things before she'd left to meet up with friends.

Broke or not, she's needed to let off steam. She's not been anywhere since Christmas Eve, the nights since then spent at her parents', *Trivial Pursuit*, *The Great Escape* and *the Sound of Music*, all topped off by her father's annual James Bond Festival of VHS tapes, boxes of Celebration and Quality Street. She's needed to get out, and it is Millennium Eve, knowing the question in years to come will be "where were you Millennium Eve?". Even the sainted Marcia can't expect her to live like a nun just because she does.

She looks over her shoulder at the road. Even for so early in the morning the traffic is light, the earlier sleet seen through the bar's windows no doubt keeping drivers off the road. She hunkers into herself, wishing she'd opted for the puffa and fleece her mother would have suggested rather than the stylised merits of her thin cotton jacket and PVC raincoat. But the club had been hot, and she hadn't planned on this walk.

A van passes. It is close. Close enough to make out what she sees as the leer in the driver's eyes as he stares back at her in the wing mirror. She pushes her head down, pressing on a little faster. After a few paces, she glances up, aware the van has slowed to a crawl. It doesn't look like someone struggling with directions, it slows with purpose. Something inside her finds the word "menace". Danger.

She thinks about turning around, crossing the road, but the vehicle is too close. It would look all too obvious in that embarrassing way of avoiding a fellow worker at the office party. Her mind for some reason flooding with memories of Colin from sales and his oh-so-obvious leaning across her at the

ONE

Christmas buffet of the solicitor's practice where she's worked as a temp in the holiday. No-one gets that excited about salmon quiche or a Fat Rascal.

She smiles before becoming aware she's drawn much closer to the now stopped van. She hardens her expression, the last thing she needs is a smile spreading across her face when passing a stranger. Anything more than eyes ahead, face set to anodyne, could be seen as inviting trouble. She's read the reports, had the experiences. The way you dressed, the come-on of a smile, a kind word. Asking for it.

Face fixed to indifference, she walks ahead, drawing closer to the parked vehicle with its still running engine. She waits for the door to open, a window to slide down, the comment, the invitation of a lift home, the request for directions - the things inevitably requiring her getting closer to the van and its driver. If she ignores any request - the hailing voice, the demand for contact and recognition - it looks rude, provocative, the sort of response in its own way making the driver angry. Whichever way she plays it, she understands she'll end up wrong.

She closes the gap, walking past head down, eyes glancing to the side. The rear windows are tinted out, the front window fogged up, windscreen wipers slapping lazily across the glass. The sense there's more than one person inside.

She passes the van, each ever-widening step extending the distance between herself and the vehicle, breath held until she's a good ten paces away, her body relaxing, the muscles in her shoulders easing, aware of just how tight she's been wound by the experience.

She comforts herself in knowing it's merely the power of imagination, her mind allowing her fears to take flight. Her English lecturer had talked about it in a seminar before Christmas, how Hamlet's obsessions shape his actions, Hamlet telling Rosencrantz that *"There is nothing either good or bad but thinking makes it so"*.

It's an idea that's fixed itself in her head. She thinks that

ONE

maybe it's her recent breakup, her mind working to shape the angry and painful experience of her ex's intimidations making her ever more sensitive to threat, his rage meaning she now sees the world as meaner, darker, a far more threatening place than before.

She crosses the road glancing both ways, the panelled van still stationary, engine running. Maybe they were lost. Maybe they were phoning someone. Texting, it's the new thing apparently or so her friends who can afford mobile phones tell her.

She walks on, on impulse making the decision to cut across onto Elgar Walk, the footpath that runs through the city centre gardens. Down here she's sheltered from the road, a route not only taking her away from her concerns about the parked van, but on a night like this it's quicker, less chance of ice, less risk of tottering off her heels - her other bad fashion choice for the season.

The sound of a car door closing somewhere on the road behind her prompts her to walk a little faster, head swivelling, hopeful the shadows of the hedgerows and trees now hide her from the road. Soon the only sound is of her own footsteps. the black water of the nearby ponds dulling their echo off the tarmac of the footpath.

She knows the route well enough, the nearby embankment is a favourite of summer tourists for picnics, sandwiches from Montpellier, scones from Betty's. She knows it brings her out further along Cold Bath Road and much closer to her flat than following the main road.

She's walking along Harlow Moor Drive when she's suddenly sure that the shadows of the bushes ahead are moving. Not as they might by the cold wind sweeping across the grassy slope, more in the manner of being held apart, held steady. The thought someone is hiding there sweeps through her senses, eyes now certain she sees the vehicle from earlier ahead of her.

She stops walking. It's a natural reaction to the perception of

ONE

a threat. A chance to think, to consider options. Going back. Pressing ahead. But she feels it maybe also makes her vulnerable, weak, maybe marks her as prey. She has to decide what to do. None of her options appear inviting.

It could be her ex, certain that if it is him there can be only one reason why he's tracked her down tonight. The thought that he'd been there, stalked her, followed her from the bar to the club, Marcia no doubt telling him where she'd said she'd be spending Millennium Eve.

Naomi's seen him when he's fired up - drunk, aggressive, and impossible to deal with. It was why she'd finished things, something he's been having a hard time accepting judging by the notes he's stuffed in the letterbox of the flat whilst she's been away at her parents'.

She can't face him right now, a decision that sees her dart to the side, plunging through to the small path that goes deeper into the bushes and trees that line the road, certain she hears a voice call out after her. Though she can't quite hear what's being said, whoever it is seems upset, angry.

She moves off the path as soon as she can, cutting through a line of bushes, not caring at branches that tug at her sleeves, or the thorns and sharp leaves that tear at legs and arms. Within minutes she's out in open ground, quickly recognising the slope that leads up to the bowling club. She moves as fast as she might, even considers discarding her shoes but rejects the idea, aware of the harder ground she knows lies ahead, not to mention their cost.

Arriving at the trimmed lawn of the bowling club, she goes straight to the clubhouse pavilion, trying the doors in the hope rather than expectation of finding a place to hide. They're locked, but she finds a secluded space behind the clubhouse where she can crouch down, hidden from the path behind some old wooden pallets, heart pounding, breathing heavily.

It's then she hears them. Voices, a group walking in a line, chattering, safety in numbers. She steps out, arms waving, 'Can

ONE

you help me, please,' she calls out, head turning from side to side scanning the slope behind her. 'I think there's someone following me,' she says as she turns to the line of men that have fanned out across the path to from a loose semi-circle.

The taller of the five steps forward. Even in the gloom she can tell that like the other four he has tightly cropped hair. As he steps into the light she has the clear sense she's seen him somewhere before, she thinks maybe earlier at the bar or in the club, maybe he's the guy who'd waved and smiled at her and her friends, the one who'd sent them a drink. 'Of course we'll help,' he says. 'We know how to treat a lady n distress, don't we lads?'

TWO

Sleeve tugged up, checking her watch, DI Zara Fisher walks towards the thin glow of the tent sat on top of the ancient mound. *Six o' clock,* the yellow-white of the lamps leeching little more than a pale light into the murk of the rising early-morning mist.

Letting the elasticated cuff snap back, she grits her teeth, composing her expression into the required mask of seriousness. Business-like. What one boyfriend once remarked on as her *resting bitch face*. The fact that it had been followed by her fist slamming into what became his own *screaming with pain face* is beside the point, though now, as always, it provokes a momentary upturn, the thin wisp of a smile.

She lets her imminent appearance play out in her head: everyone watching her, looking for signs they are certain will be there, some indication of queasiness, a little shading of green around the gills, a pale face - anything indicating she's about to throw up. That she can't cut it. After all, six or more months on the sick, a career-wrecking nervous breakdown, is a sure sign she's out of her depth. The rumours of what had happened between her and the now disgraced DCS Crosby on her return

TWO

are rife, not to mention her own recently hospitalised DS, Demetriou. Anyone who comes near seems doomed to some Jonah-like fate.

Whatever they see, they'd exchange in the pub, the canteen, the *WhatsApp* groups - the titbits of gossip posing as insight that are bartered for credibility. The chance of being thought *a good lad. One of the gang.* A story like that would be confirmation of everything they believe about her: she's weak, something she covers with spite and cruelty. It's what she's learned to expect, balled fists grasping tight to a version of masculinity they'd spent decades shaping themselves around - the magazines they read, the films they watched, the social media they fed. It was Institutionalised, Met-Approved.

Whatever she does today, there are some who'll claim they'd seen those signs even if they aren't there. She has no say in that. No right of reply. Not that anyone ever says it to her face, these are revelations that tick the box of keeping themselves shadowed, behind her back.

And if she doesn't show the weakness they sought, doesn't break down at the sight of the body, doesn't gag at the blood and gore, it merely confirms the other stories attaching themselves to her, the barnacles of baggage shaping her in their minds. *The Ice Queen. DI Elsa. DI Frozen. Captain Birdseye.* She's cold. Heartless. Unfeeling. *After all, she had that incident, Swanley wasn't it?* A year later and she's still in therapy, psychological support mandated by Hyland, the Chief Constable himself. It mixes fantasy and truth in distorted measure. It is rumour, gossip, and innuendo, a Holy Trinity that has acquired the faithful across the force.

She knows the idiot PC she's just reprimanded at the police tape is thinking it, doesn't take a mind reader to know that. It was written all over his face as she'd left him and his fellow officer. The seething indignity. The assault on his manhood.

Not that she'd been well-liked before her breakdown, it just offers a better excuse.

TWO

Standing on top of the westerly of the two earth mounds, she stops at the flap of the small tent she assumes has been set above the access hatch to the underground bunker. How many is this? *Twenty? Twenty five? More?* When had her victim-dead merged into a faceless, uncountable mass? Had there been a single moment? An occurrence? Some singular instance triggering it without her realising it happened? A tipping point of anxiety. An exhaustion of compassion. Kira Swanley, the *Leyburn Lizzie Borden*, was that it, the moment? She thinks not, things had been shifting in her head, loose cargo, even before her arrival to a blood-soaked Kira.

Truth be told, she hasn't a clue.

The first ones had been there every night, her originals, the first eleven, an undead Teams call gathering them together as she waited for sleep to arrive, faces etched in her mind, details sharp and remembered for months. Every time she'd closed her eyes she'd seen distended faces, twisted bodies. *Jane Holland. Anna Burns. Chloe Fellows.*

Now they are a blur.

Maybe it goes back to her father. Didn't everything? Maybe he's the reason, the numbing of it all. Millennium Eve.

…Wet cobblestones…Cold wind…Rusting door handle…

She shakes her head clear. Repressed, or so Pemberton would judge if she'd ever reveal it, both knowing she never will. It would be textbook for the Force therapist. Open goal for a Jungian fanboy. She likes to believe she's better than that. More complicated and layered than daddy issues. An enigma rather than an open book, but maybe she's just deluding herself. After all, wasn't it all really about her issues with her father, his brutal life, his equally brutal end.

…the iron smell of blood…the sound of crying…a muted scream…

She shrugs once more, this time busies herself in tugging on the Tyvek suit pulled from the boot of the pool car. Extra-large, no delusion there. Like body bags, one size fits all. She totters on

TWO

one leg, the strong winds of a brewing storm making it heavy going, hands jerking at the cotton-plastic folds as she hauls it over trousers and fleece lined coat - no way she's forgoing her *Fjälräven* in this cold, it was staying. The plastic fibre overshoes prove equally tricky, the heels of her walking boots catching on the material. Even for a cold, wet November in the Dales, the day isn't starting well.

The sound of echoing voices reminds her of her focus. Creepy's voice, the senior pathologist's dulcet tones reverberate up the access shaft and out through the now-widening gap in the flap of the tent along with the expanding slice of light that precedes the emerging face of DS Iverson. The pale yellow light heralds his appearance like a heavenly optic fanfare, except Iverson's pockmarked cheeks are, as ever, more gargoyle than cherub.

'Can't go on meeting like this,' she states, face-mask dangling from one hand. 'As bad for my image and reputation as it'd be good for yours. Unless maybe you wore one of these,' she says as she jiggles the mask up and down in front of his face, a puppet on a string.

The look of shock on his face is palpable. He stands upright, eyes averted, stripping off the over suit as swiftly as he can, an operation fraught with as much difficulty as Fisher had found in putting it on. He undulates his shoulders, shaking his overcoat into some semblance of a fit, hand disappearing round the back to tug at the hem. 'Ma'am,' he utters in demonstration of the fact he's trying to conjure a reason for his being here. Desperate to be away.

'Don't tell me that they've assigned you as my bagman whilst Pan's off?' she asks, straight away considering her use of the term 'off', as if it's a holiday or a dentist appointment, not the whole life-changing burns and dreadfulness of what had happened to Demetriou that day, the psychological and probably deeper emotional stuff, an aftermath designed to cripple and embitter him.

TWO

'What? No. Not at all. Not me. I'm here to...to erhm...Can't really say,' he tells her, a hand smoothing unruly hair into shape, his prematurely wrinkled face seeking the appropriate look of innocence from a poorly maintained mental dressing-up box.

'Can't really say? Who is it you've got tucked away in there,' she says, pointing at the tent flap the embarrassed DS has now flicked shut. 'It's not Lord Lucan is it? Been looking for that bugger everywhere.'

'What? No. No it's not. It's just...'

'...Just what?'

'It's the PFCC.'

'Hargreaves? The Commissioner? She's the victim? Blimey, that means Crawley's having to hammer a stake through her heart to make sure the job's done properly.'

'No. Not her,' he scrambles. 'We don't know who it is. The corpse I mean. What I meant was that it was the Commissioner who told me to get here,' he at last gets out, relieved at having a direction for his thinking to go in. 'Yes. Her. The FPCC. Since the Webb thing she's been a bit more... circumspect. She's all about getting a heads-up on anything that's a bit, you know, odd, out of the ordinary, especially now her PR bloke, Lawrence, has disappeared off to wherever it is he's gone. Some spiritual awareness thing I heard. She told me from now on she wants to be ahead of the curve.... a bit like a racing thing, I think. But I'm sure she means things that might upset her campaign for the mayorship. She wants a hands-on report ASAP, horse's mouth.' He finishes, taking a breath, relieved to have gotten everything out, though he thinks he might have ordered them better if it hadn't been for Fisher's elfin stare, the X-ray-*ness* of her ice blue eyes that always troubles him.

'So you're what? A scouting party?'

'Sort of, yeah,' he responds, wishing he'd thought of that.

Fisher steps forward, and even in the cold of the moors he feels the sweat-line forming under his collar. 'Well then, Tonto, now that you've put the required tick in Hargreaves's box, what do you say to you fucking off so that this particular dog can get to see this particular rabbit? And I'm using *dog* in a very particular non-sexist non-*hashtagmetoo* manner. Clear?'

Iverson isn't. He's busy trying to calculate if she means is he clear about her role or the dog bit. Bewilderment spreads across his face like a nasty rash.

Fisher reaches out a hand, gently easing him from her path, fixing an expression on her face that strangers might mistake for sympathy, but one that experience has taught Iverson is simply pity.

Entering the tent she's confronted by the raised surround of the hatch, a metal box, grey and rusting, rising some four feet from the concrete platform in which it's set. Accessing the shaft itself requires stepping onto a raised concrete step and then lifting a leg and swinging it into the opening, the foot then finding purchase on the metal ladder fixed to the shaft wall. She then lifts her other leg up and over and begins her descent of the fifteen feet or so to the solid concrete of the shelter's floor.

'Fisher,' she hears Crawley's voice call at the appearance of her legs and backside, an identification she finds troubling. Turning around she finds herself in a small access room, off which a doorway offers entrance to the main room, a space she estimates to be some eighteen feet by eight. Space is at a premium, her eyes falling on Crawley crouching next to what she assumes to be the body whose presence she's been sent to investigate. The pathologist waves a gloved hand in the air as if spinning a plate. 'Find yourself an opening if you can. I think I can squeeze you here next to me,' he invites, patting the yellow carpeted floor with a leer.

'Didn't Argos have the adult size?' Fisher asks nodding at the tent above the shaft. 'That looks more like a ridge tent I spent a forgettable week on Skye in.'

'Biggest they could risk up here. The wind and all. Storm Circe or Diva or whatever they're calling her this week,' Crawley states. 'And the work's down here anyway,' he adds, an arm

TWO

encircling the confines of the small shelter cramped even further by the addition of Crawley, two SOCOs, and a tripod stand of arc lamps powered by the generator she'd heard rattling away up top. 'We really just need it to keep the generator dry, that and shield against any nosey back-packers with their binoculars, them and the alt-media citizen journalist nosey bastards. Without it they'd be posting everything to Twitter or X or whatever before we even got her back to the lab.'

'They lost a tent over at Nidderdale a couple of days ago,' one of the masked SOCOs squatting the far side of Crawley offers. Even masked, ill-disguised acne erupting around eyes and forehead indicate it to be Ramsay, Crawley's newest intern. 'It was one of the big ones, too. Fair whipped it up and over the Nidd. Found it in Swaledale yesterday morning. Torn to shreds. Damn near took two of the SOCOs inside with it.'

'There's probably a moral in there somewhere. Damned if I can find it, though,' Fisher offers as the other of the masked SOCOs squatting next to Crawley shuffles back to create a space for her. At his movement, a foul odour fills the air. Fisher picks up a second surgical mask from the box and holds it over her nose and mouth. 'Please tell me that's the corpse,' she gasps through the additional layer of covering.

'Sorry,' Dublin responds. 'Beckie did one of her dhal's last night. Always has this effect. Bloody lovely though. Nadiya's recipe.'

'Jesus. Next time maybe give fair warning. Better still, get up top and waft a flap,' Fisher admonishes, holding the second mask tighter against her face.

'Think it was his flap wafting did the damage in the first place,' Ramsay states, tugging his mask tighter.

'Anyway,' Crawley continues pulling his own mask down as the odour dissipates. 'Dublin's the main reason for wearing these.' He nods at the body, at least the leathered outline of what once passed as human. 'This one's been gone some while. Decades. We've maybe no need for the Tyvek either. All that

TWO

time, there'll be precious little trace evidence left. Little of use anyway.'

'Any idea who it is?'

'Female. Young by the morphology – the look of the pelvic bone. From what I can make out, there's no fusing or thickening of the bones. Twenties at most. Certainly less than thirty. The coat's plastic. You know, the PVC things they wore in the seventies. Bloody stuff never rots. Means she's been here less than fifty years. Thirty at most. Know more once we get her back to the lab. Get some of those archaeological fellas in from the university. There's ventilation through the old air shafts over there,' he says, a hand indicating the slats of a vent tucked in a corner, 'but looks as if they were sealed some time ago, most likely when the place was decommissioned. Once you get that date it ought to give a better time frame for you. Whenever it was, the trapped air has sort of mummified her rather than the decomposition you'd expect if she'd been buried in a shallow grave up above. Whover put her here saved themselves all that digging. Most likely a quick thinker, too, you know, someone capable of functioning under pressure.' He smiles his oily smile. 'Though that's the speculative Poirot realms of yourself, Fisher. My humble report will stick to our rigid line of demarcation, yours the ethereal and speculative, mine the physical. You know how keen I am on the physical, Fisher.'

Fisher's thankful the bulk of her *Fjälräven* masks a shiver. Cause of death?' she asks, hopeful of diverting Crawley back to the task in hand.

His manner shifts a gear. 'Do I look like Derren Brown?' With balding scalp and Bobby Charlton comb-over he doesn't. Not to mention the claret blotches on his cheeks that are actually blotches of claret, a man used to the finer things in life, at least where food and drink are concerned. But that was where notions of refined taste ended. Shiny designer suits, spectacularly colourful shirts and ill-matching ties and waistcoats suggest a personal shopper inspired by Jackson Pollock retrospectives. A man obsessed by being 'now', who all too often appears simply as 'not'.

'I'm assuming you found something to indicate it's a homicide rather than some terrible accident leaving her trapped in here. If not, why would I be here rather than a DS?'

'What, you think I had other designs in mind when I asked for a senior CID presence, that I asked for you, Fisher?'

'Look Doc, I'm just trying to speed things along.' She looks around the space. 'We need to find out if's there anything indicating who she is and how she got here – a purse or wallet, walking boots, cycle clips – if she's a walker who got lost, was she on her way home or if she was meeting someone here. But before all that, I need some early idea of the cause of death. I can see there's no knife sticking out of her ribs, so what is it – blunt force trauma? Strangulation?'

'You're no fun anymore, Fisher, not that you ever were,' he simpers. 'Her shoes are over there,' he says indicating a bench table fixed to one of the longer walls, the items they've already recovered lain out on plastic sheeting ready for bagging and labelling. 'As for speeding things along, I think we can safely say this poor girl's in no great hurry. She's likely been here thirty years or more, I can't see a day or two more in sorting out such matters being an issue.' He sighs, relenting under her glare. 'However, as it's you, Fisher, her hyoid bone's been fractured,' he says pointing at the corpses' throat. 'An occurrence most often perimortem and associated with strangulation,' he adds, tossing her a proverbial bone. 'But it's early days. We don't know what we might find once we have her in my lab,' he states, Fisher finding a definite metaphorical if not actual lick of the lips in his manner.

The obvious relish is disconcerting. She appreciates that some people love their work. Nurses. Some of the teachers she'd had. A calling. But Crawley's obvious excitement at a freshly discovered corpse - even one as leathery and worn as this one -

TWO

takes matters to the extreme. Could he ever wonder at the epithet so easily attached to his name? *Creepy*.

'Thanks, Doc. Appreciated.' The idea of throwing in an *I owe you one* is a statement she's learned to avoid. Crawley took such promises seriously, seeing them as akin to a blood pact. She'd already made one trade too many with the devils in her life, none of them delivering much in the way of a decent return on her investment.

She shuffles closer for a better view, aware of the danger of a misplaced thigh brushing against the still-squatting pathologist. She leans in as far as she dares. 'How did you find yourself ending up here?' she asks of the leathery corpse.

'Good question,' Crawley responds, head nodding, turning to shuffle closer, a little more personal, his knees brushing a little too long against hers as he twists. 'Hardly on the bus route, is it? Clearly no transport of her own unless there's an abandoned vehicle or, as you indicated yourself, a bicycle somewhere. Given the location, I'd think such a thing would have been found and reported at the time, don't you? If you find there's no such record, then it'd be clear someone brought her here. Either that or she's your walker or hiker.'

Fisher looks closely at her. The shape is human. Not skeletal, yet also not fleshed out, a figure trapped in some half-stage. The *'here's one I did earlier'* part of a demonstration of how to strip a body of its humanness, either that or how to make a skeleton into a person. It was as if whoever was doing the making had for some reason decided against carrying on. Bored. Depressed. Frustrated at the lack of progress towards the required standard.

The body lies facing the ceiling; looking up, Fisher sees Styrofoam tiles of the kind she remembers from her grandmother's old house, wonders at their efficacy in holding back the anticipated radiation should the site ever have been called to action.

She scans the space: small, inconsequential. If it is murder, it seems a tell as to how the killer had seen this woman in life.

TWO

Insignificant. A thing to be tossed away. Left to rot. She's struck by the thought that for whoever did this, it wasn't personal, hadn't been passionate.

She takes in the finer details. The plastic coat. It'd clearly been cold when she died, most likely wet too. It was the type of coat you wore when you were torn between keeping warm and dry and looking decent. It wasn't the clothing for here, Grinton, a small hamlet in the midst of one of the most isolated Dales. No, this was winter, but a night out, a night out in town. Wanting to be noticed. The realisation that for someone she had been.

She scoots back a little, finding space to turn without the necessity of breathing in Crawley's liberally applied aftershave or yet another close encounter with his knees and thighs. She checks the space. The table and chair, the torn poster on the wall. The yellow carpet, a touch of homeliness along with the white Formica cupboards where rations would have been stored. 'No backpack,' she notes. 'And her shoes. Hardly the footwear of choice for anyone living up here, let alone a serious walker or hiker don't you think?'

'Fashion of the female variety is outside my domain, Fisher. Removed from my purview as it were. *Cherchez la femme* as they say.'

They didn't. Not in Fisher's presence, but such things were better left for another time, a different debate.

She peruses the group. Three men. No wonder they don't see it. The obvious.

'She's no walker or hiker,' she says. 'Not even a little bit of one. She liked to get dressed up. Took care in what she wore. She's most likely from town, at least a town.'

'Our Beckie's like that,' Ramsay observes, pausing in the collection of fibres from the floor. 'Wondering what to wear. But aren't all you women? You know, whatever else you do, your lot take ages getting ready.' He waves his tweezers in the air, evidence bag in the other, puffing out his chest to make clear which side he's on here in the whole *your lot* selection. With the

TWO

hood of the Tyvek over-suit, it gives him the appearance of a badly-judged garden gnome. 'Beckie changes her dress five times before we go out. Coat at least twice. Isn't that just, you know…women?'

The three men turn to Fisher, the unelected, *de facto* expert on all matters feminine. 'For fuck's sake,' she mutters.

ALSO BY BARRY N RAINSFORD

All the Dead Men Lie

Hollow - Who Put Bella in the Wych-Elm?

Printed in Dunstable, United Kingdom